Praise for

The

Last Equation

of

Isaac Severy

"Full of delight. Though Ms. Jacobs's writing has echoes of Thomas Pynchon, Nathanael West, and J.D. Salinger, her terrific book displays in abundance a magic all its own."

—*The Wall Street Journal*

"Engaging, clever . . . A sharp puzzle mystery, full of stimulating questions that make it impossible to stop turning the pages. . . . Isaac Severy left me with the lasting realization that mathematics is a love language. Well done, professor."

—Sophia Bush

"The Severy family would fit right into one of Wes Anderson's eccentric comedies . . . Nova Jacobs gives us a portrait of family function and dysfunction that will be familiar even to those of us without fatal genius in our genes."

—*Raleigh News & Observer*

"In lovely, inventive prose, Jacobs reengineers the tropes of family drama to explore age-old conundrums of destiny versus self-determination . . . [A] remarkable debut."

—*Kirkus Reviews*

"This captivating story about a struggling bookseller whose recently deceased grandfather, a famed mathematician, sends her on a quest for an elusive and a potentially dangerous mathematical formula is cerebral, eccentric, and endearing."

—*Chicago Review of Books*

"A page-turner that will leave you hunting for the clues alongside the main characters."

—*The Daily Beast*

The

Last Equation

of

Isaac Severy

– A Novel in Clues –

NOVA JACOBS

TOUCHSTONE

New York   London   Toronto   Sydney   New Delhi

An Imprint of Simon & Schuster, Inc.
1230 Avenue of the Americas
New York, NY 10020

First Touchstone trade paperback edition December 2018

TOUCHSTONE and colophon are registered trademarks of Simon & Schuster, Inc.

For information about special discounts for bulk purchases, please contact Simon & Schuster Special Sales at 1-866-506-1949 or business@simonandschuster.com.

The Simon & Schuster Speakers Bureau can bring authors to your live event. For more information or to book an event, contact the Simon & Schuster Speakers Bureau at 1-866-248-3049 or visit our website at www.simonspeakers.com.

Interior design by Jill Putorti

Manufactured in the United States of America

10 9 8 7 6 5 4 3 2 1

The Library of Congress has cataloged the hardcover edition as follows:

Names: Jacobs, Nova, author.
Title: The last equation of Isaac Severy : a novel in clues / Nova Jacobs.
Description: First Touchstone hardcover edition. | New York : Touchstone, 2018.
Identifiers: LCCN 2017032828 (print) | LCCN 2017041863 (ebook) | ISBN 9781501175145 (eBook) | ISBN 9781501175121 (softcover)
Subjects: LCSH: Secret societies—Fiction. | Mathematicians—Fiction. | BISAC: FICTION / Mystery & Detective / General. | FICTION / Family Life. | FICTION / Literary. | GSAFD: Mystery fiction.
Classification: LCC PS3610.A356483 (ebook) | LCC PS3610.A356483 L37 2018 (print) | DDC 813/.6—dc23
LC record available at https://lccn.loc.gov/2017032828

ISBN 978-1-5011-7512-1
ISBN 978-1-5011-7513-8 (pbk)
ISBN 978-1-5011-7514-5 (ebook)

For Jeremy

An intelligence that, at a given instant, could comprehend all the forces by which nature is animated and the respective situation of the beings that make it up, if moreover it were vast enough to submit these data to analysis . . . For such an intelligence, nothing would be uncertain, and the future, like the past, would be open to its eyes.

—PIERRE-SIMON LAPLACE,
A PHILOSOPHICAL ESSAY ON PROBABILITIES, 1814

SEVERY FAMILY TREE

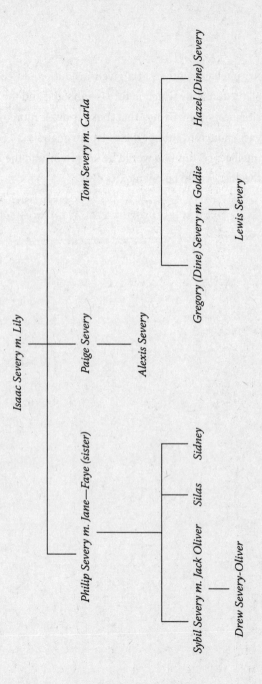

Prologue

On the morning he was to die, the old man woke early and set about making breakfast. He put eggs to boil, bread to toast, tea to steep, and as he did so, felt he understood why prisoners on death row request such commonplace meals on the eves of their executions. They didn't crave elaborate spreads of coq au vin, foie gras, octopus salad, oysters on ice. These poor souls longed for burgers, fried chicken, pizza, ice cream. Whenever he would come across reports of these ill-fated last suppers, it was the childlike ones that got to him most: the strawberry shortcake eaten by Chicago serial killer John Wayne Gacy before his lethal injection; or that kid in Texas, Jeffrey Allen Barney, who said he was very sorry for what he had done to that woman, and asked only for a carton of milk and two boxes of Frosted Flakes.

The old man, too, had simple tastes. Though he was by nearly all standards a man of culture, his culinary preferences were aggressively ordinary. He had enjoyed a variation on the same breakfast for as long as he could remember. Why stop now that someone was coming for him?

He did, however, prepare two of everything, arranging twin cups and saucers, and two egg spoons on the breakfast tray. *Animals escaping the flood*, he thought, as he placed two brown, soft-boiled eggs side by side. He had always been a generous host, and he would be one to the last. Besides, it was early, and his visitor would no doubt be hungry. And how about some music to make the proceedings more pleasant? He selected a well-loved classical CD and pressed play on the living room stereo.

Sunrise was still an hour away when, with only ambient light from the kitchen to guide him, he carried the tray to his usual spot at the far end of the yard. A café table sat ready with two chairs beside a Jacuzzi platform. He arranged the sets of plates, napkins, and cutlery, and took a seat on the side of the table facing the yard, his back to the fence. He poured Earl Grey from a pot into one of the teacups and glanced at his watch. The phosphorescent face read 5:35. He still had time to escape, to get in his old Cadillac and drive somewhere far from here, but he was done being afraid. He was ready to die. All he had to do now was wait.

PART 1

The Merchant

The Resurrection Cemetery sounded to Hazel Severy more like a threat than a place of peace and final repose, but as far as she could tell, it was shaping up to be a lovely service. Her grandfather's casket, draped in white roses and gold embroidery, positively glowed in the Southern California sun. If there had been any doubts that Isaac Severy, a Catholic suicide, would receive a proper send-off with the full regalia, those doubts were now dispelled.

From her seat among the chairs arranged on the vast mortuary lawn, Hazel glanced around at mourners' faces both familiar and strange. Her hand went to the pocket of her dress trousers, into which she had slipped an unopened envelope not an hour before. It had arrived that morning inside an overnight FedEx packet mailed from her store. Assuming it was a bill or some other piece of bad news, Hazel had groaned when she saw the package with her name sitting on her brother's breakfast table. But when she tore open the sleeve, she found a small blue envelope with a sticky note from her sole employee:

This came for you the day you left.—Chet

It wasn't a bill or an eviction notice. It was a letter from her grandfather; more precisely, her adoptive grandfather, the man whose body now lay in that attractive walnut box. The envelope

3

was one of those candy-striped airmail types, a nostalgic indulgence of his. Isaac's name appeared nowhere on the envelope, but the address of her Seattle bookstore was written in his shaky hand. The postmark read October 16. On October 17, he would be dead.

She stared at the winged "*Par Avion*," at a stamp featuring a sunflower, and felt increasingly light-headed. It was too much to take in, this unexpected missive from the dead, so she slipped it into her pocket unopened. In fact, she thought she might let the reading of it forever remain a future possibility. As long as the envelope was sealed, she would have one last communication waiting from Isaac.

She had brought the letter with her to the funeral as an odd sort of comfort, but as she sat in the unusually blistering October sun, watching her grandfather's casket warp and buckle behind her own tears, she pushed a corner of the envelope deep under a fingernail until it stung.

The call had come a week ago. She had been pacing her Pioneer Square bookstore, hatching a desperate scheme to abandon her life, one that involved either disappearing into a country of exotic coordinates or landing in debtor's prison. She loved Seattle, and she loved her store—in a mostly unstable life, books had been the only reliable refuge she had known—but she now owed a figure so large she was certain there must be a corresponding digital ticker somewhere, climbing upward daily like the national debt.

The bleat of her store phone had interrupted her thoughts. She picked up the receiver, mustering her usual bright greeting, "The Guttersnipe, can I help you find a book?" After a pause, the halting voice of her brother, Gregory, told her that their beloved Isaac had been found dead in his backyard. By his own hand. The housekeeper had chanced upon him that morning in his Jacuzzi, a set of live Christmas lights coiled in the water with him, one of its bulbs crushed.

Hazel couldn't have said how long the conversation lasted—or, in her deep disbelief, how many times she had made her brother repeat himself—she knew only that when she closed up her store immediately afterward, the sun had set, and she was exhausted from crying.

But she wouldn't be going home. Having lost her apartment in Belltown weeks before, she was now living in the narrow space behind her shop. The back room was cramped and airless, with barely enough space for her mattress. She had moved most of her things into storage, bought a mini fridge, and begun sponge bathing at the bathroom sink. She had told no one of her indignity, not even Bennet, her boyfriend of almost two years. Every night, she exited her shop for the benefit of whoever might be watching, maintaining the ritual of locking up and walking to the bus stop before doubling back to reenter her store from the alley. Better confined to the back than spotted through the shop's windows at odd hours by her landlord. This wasn't the first time she had been homeless. She supposed it was in her DNA. And what is DNA, Isaac had once asked, but an invisible road map of how our lives will play out? If that were true, Isaac's own genetic GPS had sent him careening off course.

That night, as she sat cross-legged on the mattress, eyes parched from evaporated tears, she recalled a curious detail from her conversation with Gregory: Isaac had prepared two breakfasts for himself that morning, one half eaten, the other untouched. She had heard vague reports of his absentmindedness, but in her weekly phone calls to him, he had sounded as quick as ever, always armed with amusing stories, and never repeating the ones she'd already heard. At seventy-nine years old, Isaac had been remarkably healthy. He had looked no older than sixty-five, and the only ailment she had known him to have was his lifelong struggle with migraines. Migraines ran in the family, but mental illness? Depression? Had she been so consumed with her own daily battles that she had missed something obvious? Now, as she stared at his casket, she felt a fresh stab of shame.

She removed her hand from her pocket and returned it to her lap. What if she had been the only one to receive anything that might be defined as a suicide note? As the priest appeared and began to speak, Hazel couldn't help but study those family members around her for hints that they, too, had received a surprise delivery.

Most of the fair-skinned, light-eyed Severy clan had chosen seats shaded by the surrounding sycamores. Strange, though, how this Nordic-blooded family thrived in—even seemed to prefer—the merciless Southwest sun. It was rare for a Severy to permanently stray east of the Rockies or north of Napa Valley. Few had ever moved outside a twenty-five-mile radius of Pasadena's Caltech. It was she alone, with the dark eyes and hair, who had succumbed to gloomier regions.

If any of the family had received a letter from the dead, their expressions betrayed nothing but ordinary grief. Only Gregory, seated across the aisle, his two-year-old son passed out on his chest, noticed her studying the crowd. She wondered why they weren't sitting together, considering they'd arrived in the same car. Their separation across the aisle suddenly seemed significant to her, emblematic of a gap that had been widening between them the past couple of years. Having a child did that to a person, certainly, but with Gregory, it sometimes felt as if he were being steadily pulled away from her by a source of gravity she couldn't identify. Her brother gave her a sad smile and returned his attention to the homily.

"Who died?" Hazel's grandmother, seated beside her, asked no one in particular.

"Isaac Severy," Hazel whispered, as if he were a mutual acquaintance.

"Everyone's going these days," Lily mused. "That's what happens when you reach a certain age. It's one long ghoulish parade."

Hazel gave her grandmother's hand a squeeze. She was struck by how pretty she looked, even though she was wearing what appeared to be every necklace she had ever owned, and her eyes had been emptied of their former intelligence. Lily Severy had once been a celebrated translator of Spanish literature, but her mind had faltered in recent years, and for the past few days, she had alternated between anguish over a loss she couldn't quite place and a dreamy fascination at all the activity around her. In her more lucid moments, Lily did appear to be aware that she'd been married to a mathematician, though the details were muddled. At the elderly care facility where she now lived, she liked to educate her nurses on her husband's invention of calculus. "You know, it wasn't that German fellow, like they all say."

The next two hours were a warm broth of tears and praise served up for one of the most beloved academics in Southern California. What seemed an endless procession of Caltech colleagues and students took the microphone and spoke of Isaac's unearthly level of brilliance, not only in the mathematics department but also in diverse disciplines touched by his acrobatic mind. They spoke of the equations he had created for Caltech's Environmental Sciences, such as the ones that could anticipate the complex movement of oil spills, the ever-changing paths of migratory birds, and the erratic pattern of melting ice in the Arctic. They spoke of his ferocious curiosity and of his heart. "He wasn't just my hero, he was my friend." There were allusions to Sir Isaac Newton, for whom he had been named. A fitting kinship, joked one of his Jewish colleagues, for here were two Isaacs who despite all evidence to the contrary simply *must* have been Jews.

Just as Hazel was growing restless, her uncle Philip, Isaac's eldest child, stepped behind the microphone. Philip was a lean, delicate man with hair so light his eyebrows were nearly invisible. As a result, he had a perpetually afflicted look, as if he were under constant assault from light and dust. Today his eyes were hidden behind a pair of dark glasses, but that didn't stop him from squinting every time the sun struck him at a certain angle.

He unfolded a piece of paper with his long fingers before peering up at the gathering. "As many of you know," his fragile voice began, "my father had passions that went beyond mathematics. There was almost nothing that did not interest him. He was a devout scientist, but he was also a religious man who grappled with the entire idea of faith."

He then read Emily Dickinson's "This World Is Not Conclusion," a poem Hazel remembered well from college, and one that was now making her feel some real affection for this uncle whom she had seen often while growing up but still barely knew.

After struggling through the final stanza, Philip withdrew quickly, leaving behind a restlessness that lasted several minutes. Hazel shifted in her chair, inadvertently catching the eye of Philip's younger sister, Paige, seated half a row down, her stout body swathed in black silk. In her prime, Aunt Paige had been a brilliant political statistician, but she'd apparently done little with her talent in recent years, and her standing in the family was now one of a recluse and grump. She had never married, but there was a grown daughter somewhere—Alexis, was it?—whom no one ever saw. Whether Alexis resided north of Napa or east of the Rockies was anyone's guess, and Hazel didn't spy any likely candidates here today.

At last, the queue behind the microphone shrank to zero, and a few people stood. But the sound system gave a startling buzz, calling attention to a young man who appeared before them as if by conjuring trick. He didn't speak right away, taking his time sifting through bits of fuchsia-colored paper. Hazel found something about the man instantly arresting. He sported the beard of a woodsman but was otherwise dressed in the shabby welfare-academic vein. He cleared his throat and spoke in a vaguely British accent.

"Good mathematics is generally impossible to read aloud," he began, "but why should that stop us?" He laughed nervously, and when no one joined him, he resumed. "A *proof*, as many of you know, is a number of true statements leading to a logical conclusion. Proofs are the cornerstone of mathematics and are really meant to be seen, not heard. If, for example, I were to read aloud Andrew Wiles's famous proof of Fermat's Last Theorem, which is a hundred fifty pages, by the way"—another laugh—"we'd be here for days."

"Who is this guy?" a woman in Hazel's row asked.

"However," the man continued, "what I have here is not a real proof—only fragments scribbled on these cocktail napkins—but what if, as a kind of tribute, I read just a scrap of his work? An everyday bit of fluff floating around his head, so that we might have some idea of what it was like to be Isaac Severy? So I hope you'll indulge me while I read this bit of 'ordinary' mathematics: Let dx over dt equal A times x plus f of x plus *epsilon* times g of x . . ."

Hazel had a strange urge to laugh. Yet there was something soothing about the cadence of his voice as he delivered this long chain of letters, numbers, and symbols. Isaac would have liked the absurdity of this moment, and she suddenly missed him terribly.

"Is he reading an equation?" someone behind her whispered. "You've got to be *fucking* kidding me."

Hazel didn't take her eyes from the man as he continued his recitation, but her hand had wandered to her right pocket. She slid her fingers inside, over the crispness of the envelope, and before she knew it, she was running a fingernail along the lip until she could feel a thin sheet of paper within. Almost without thinking, she had broken the seal, and now there seemed to be no retreating from Isaac's letter.

2

The Theorist

Philip Severy had no one left to impress. The full weight of this fact descended upon him as he stood in front of family and strangers, blinking away the lighthouse glare of his father's coffin. His sister, Paige, had ordered the thing outfitted with white roses and metallic vestments. Had she meant it as some kind of joke? Because if she had intended their father's death box to be both heinous and comically reflective, well, bang-up job. Philip pushed his sunglasses flat against his face and struggled through some words he had prepared.

When he returned to his seat, his twin sons were wiggling a few chairs down. Their teenage bodies were present, but their minds were no doubt reliving their last tennis match. Silas and Sidney worshipped tennis, lived for it—would probably even die for it in some offshoot universe where one was forced to choose between such things. *Death or a world without tennis?* "Death!" they would chime in unison, before linking arms and marching off the nearest cliff together. They loved the sport in the purest way that one can love a thing, with the whole of their selves. Philip was not like his sons in this way, not anymore, and it was only now that he knew this with terrible certainty.

As another Isaac Severy fan took the podium, Philip's attention wandered to a translucent spider making its way over the charcoal dunes of his slacks. At that moment, the dark folds of cotton twill were this tiny spider's entire known universe—and the sudden intrusion of Philip's forefinger to flick it into the air must have been an extraordinary phenomenon that the spider would never be able to explain. *I was there, and then I wasn't.*

His wife touched his arm. "You were great up there. You all right?"

Philip nodded. Why shouldn't he be all right? His father had killed himself a week ago. No reason, no warning. *Killed himself.* It sounded absurd and wrong. Like vicious gossip. Just two weeks ago, they had been sitting together at his sons' final set in the Junior Tennis Open quarterfinals. His father, relaxed that day, had taken a break from questioning Philip on a recent journal article he'd coauthored and from wondering aloud if the work was up to Philip's usual standards.

Watching his twin sons face off against each other, Philip had said, "I forget which one I'm rooting for."

His father had smiled. "Whichever is your favorite."

As the ball went into the net, Philip let out an ambiguous holler directed at neither son in particular. He didn't have a favorite son because he harbored identical feelings toward all three of his children: profound dismay at having fathered such unremarkable offspring. He loved them—of course he *loved* them. Silas, Sidney, and their much older sister, Sybil, were beautiful, glowing things who laughed and smiled like he did, and whose eyes were their mother's startling green. But how he—a Stanford-MIT-educated particle physicist and professor of theoretical physics at Caltech—and Jane—a Stanford-Harvard molecular biologist by training, if not by profession—had produced three academic mediocrities never ceased to be a source of bewildering disbelief and low-grade depression.

He would periodically unfold the genealogical map in his mind and try to isolate the genetic offender. His own parents certainly weren't to blame. His father, a distinguished professor at Caltech for forty years, had devoted most of his life to the study of chaos theory and nonlinear dynamics, while his mother had translated Spanish Baroque literature to great acclaim. Jane's mother and father, both doctors, of course, boasted equally impressive levels of accomplishment. But there were suspect siblings on both sides who pointed to genetic weakness. Jane's sister, Faye, for one, was clever only when it came to marrying rich men and living off the alimony. His own sister, too, had abundant faults. She had been working on a book on probability for decades, a book some were beginning to suspect didn't exist: "What's the 'probability' you'll ever finish that thing, eh, Paige?" But Paige had proven her cleverness in other ways, and her shortcomings were entirely social in nature.

And then there was Tom, the youngest of his siblings, a troubling specter who still hovered over them. He had left behind two now-grown foster children, who'd long ago been adopted into the family. Philip had seen them earlier, hadn't he? Yes, there were Hazel and Gregory, seated near the front, their dark, angular faces looking nothing like their adoptive clan.

Aside from these two reminders, the family had mostly forgotten how Tom had once moved among them, following his own pained choreography. He had been something to love once—magnetic, even—and at one point could easily have been Philip's intellectual rival. Philip wanted to remember that Tom, and not the Tom he had last seen in an orange jumpsuit trying to contain his hatred for his older brother from behind bulletproof glass. Yes, Thomas Severy was proof positive that there was decay lurking in the family's genetic code.

Philip's daughter, hair spilling down her shoulders like a draft of sunlight, turned in her seat and whispered something to her own daughter, Drew.

"Pa-Pop's definitely in heaven, sweetie," Sybil assured her.

"How do you know?" Drew asked. "If you can't see him, how do you know?"

"Because sometimes you just know," Sybil explained. "Just like you know my arm is in my sleeve even if you can't see it."

The little girl frowned. "But—"

"Shh, it's quiet time."

As Philip watched a patch of sun play on Sybil's beautiful head, he marveled at how nature had not made at least one of his three children dutifully bright. But then, that wasn't how the coin toss of heredity necessarily worked. "Good things come in threes," wasn't it? Of course, it could go the other way, and for Philip and Jane Severy, it had come up three, indeed: *dumb, dumb, dumb*.

Jane always protested when Philip expressed disappointment in their children. "Sybil has more social intelligence than the both of us. Have you seen her work a crowd? She's not the twit you imagine."

In Philip's view, the extent of their daughter's effort to prove she wasn't a twit was getting into Stanford eleven years ago—not without some parental legacy points, naturally—but Sybil had done nothing spectacular during her six listless years there except meet her husband, Jack, get pregnant, and embrace a particularly Jesus-y brand of Christianity. Upon graduation, she had transformed herself into a Sunnyvale wife, mother, and artist—artist *of sorts*, for her work, which involved slapping a found object to a canvas, was ghastly, and Philip couldn't see how pieces like *Shopping List #15*, *Pine Cone #2*, and *Some Garbage I Found #236* were worth getting excited about.

He tried his best to focus on the mourners who were lining up to enumerate his father's many qualities. Philip would need to recall these sentiments later at the reception. "So kind of you to mention . . ." "So thoughtful of you to say . . ." Etcetera.

Philip wished he could get out of having to talk to the people who would soon invade the family home. In fact, he wished someone had spared him news of his father's death entirely. He wanted to be told twenty years from now, because without his father, the very important role he had been playing for his entire career—Professor Philip Severy in *The Hunt for the Unified Field Theory*—now quite suddenly lacked an audience. In the movie house of his life, had there really been only one person sitting out there all this time? It was now apparent to him that he didn't love his work with the whole of his heart and mind, as he had once believed, but he had loved it for another's sake. And he needed to find a way to restart the show or be forever regarded as just another annotation in the history of theoretical physics. Forget about Stockholm calling; his days of reliable brain activity were numbered. He was fifty-seven, and in these Wild West days of particle collisions, he was feeling increasingly isolated and immaterial. He was running out of time to wrap up the secrets of the universe in one big elegant bow.

Forcing his attention back to his surroundings, Philip noticed that the twins were gone from their seats. He looked to Jane for explanation, but she was focused on yet another STEMy dweeb addressing the crowd. These were his people, of course, but for some reason, Philip could no longer stand it. He stood up and started walking, with no particular destination, just away over the gently rolling grounds.

He spotted his sons in an open expanse of grass, hitting a make-believe ball with make-believe racquets. From this distance, he couldn't tell which son was which. That was, of course, what made their matches so captivating: the two were so similar that it was either boy's victory. His father had tried to impart to the twins the roles of probability and statistics in their game. Tennis, after all, was so temptingly mathematical.

tennis match – c + ! = tennis math!

Because they were physically identical, his father would say, in the heat of a game, it probably came down to the angle of the sun, an eddy of air, the tensility of a racquet string, or whether the memory of a girl's smile skipped across one of their minds. "We don't think of girls while we're playing, Grandpa," they would groan. (Or at all?)

It occurred to Philip that tennis and theoretical physics had at least one thing in common: both favored the young. As he sat down in a cool spot of grass, taking in their imaginary game, he wished desperately to be his sons' age again. *Oh, to have a teenage brain—hell, a twenty-five-year-old brain—neurons igniting like rods in a lightning field!* Philip leaned back against a headstone and wondered if, in those final minutes before the power from a tiny seven-watt bulb shot through the saltwater to stop his heart, his father had wished for the same thing.

3

The Mathematician

The man with the beard was still at the podium when Hazel extracted the letter from her pocket and unfolded it. She glanced around quickly for fear of being observed, but the people near her were either focused on the speaker or involved in their own thoughts. The letter was typewritten, which wasn't exactly surprising—Isaac had often saved his penmanship for his math—but he had used his IBM Selectric, an ancient typewriter that duplicated letters and punctuation arbitrarily if one didn't hit the keys in just the right way. He clearly had never bothered to get the machine fixed or to use correction tape.

```
My Dear Haze,,,

   My time is over. This fact has become as clear to
me as theeee crescent moon setting outside my study
window as I write this. I wish I could dodge my as-
sassin, I wish I could flee to the Cottte d'Azurrr or
somewhere equally beautiful. But our killers find us
all, so why flail so desperately?

   Hazel, I am counting onn you to carry out an un
pleassantt request. I would do it myself were I not
being followed. Know that I am offf sound mind when
```

```
I ask that you destroy my work in Room 137. Burn.
Smash. Reformat the hard drives. I cannot get into
why, only that you must do this quickly. Before
others find it.
  The equation itself you must keep. (I leave it with
the family member they would least suspect.) Deliver
the equation to one man only: John Raspanti. His fa-
vorite pattern is herringbone.
  Important:


1. Do not stay in or visit the house past ttthe end
   of October. Three will die. I am the first.
2. Do not share this with anyone. Do not contact
   police, even those related to you. Nothing can
   be done about the above.
3. Once you have committed this letter to memory,
   destroy it.


SSShore up your courage, my dear.

                                      Eternally,
                                        Isaac
```

Hazel's neck grew warm, and her hands began to tremble. She shut her eyes, and as the words *assassin, destroy, equation, Do not share this with anyone* impressed upon her mind, a swarm of dread invaded her chest. But the dread was followed by something else: something subtler, an almost hideous thrill. She drew in a sharp breath, tucked the paper back in her pocket, and tried to return her attention to the service, but fragments of the letter scrolled across her mind. Was her grandfather really suggesting that he had been murdered? Who the hell was John Raspanti? And what did herringbone have to do with anything?

Mathematics continued to pour from the bearded man's mouth, accompanied by sharp hand gestures to emphasize certain symbols. Hazel scanned the crowd, which looked increasingly agitated. She had completely lost track of time but guessed that the speaker had kept them captive for at least a quarter of an hour.

When the man finished and stepped back from the mic, the entire gathering stood at once. Even Lily sprang to her feet. Only Hazel was slow to stand. Her insides had tightened, and her grandmother's earlier words, *ghoulish parade*, echoed in her ears.

For the mourners who managed the twenty-mile drive to the Severy home in the Hollywood Hills of Beachwood Canyon, up switchbacks to the house on the bluff, lunch awaited. Hazel again caught a ride with her brother and his wife. As she stepped from the back seat, she opened her eyes wide and inhaled deeply, hoping to ground herself in sense memory. The two-story Victorian, distinctly out of character in a canyon of Spanish and Normandy Revival, had always carried a whiff of bygone imperialism. Its aerie perch looked out on Hollywood and the Deco domes of the Griffith Observatory, but Hazel thought the decaying clapboard, combined with a healthy population of tropical flora, gave the house an almost colonial feel, like some faded British outpost.

Inside, she surveyed the now fatherless objects littering the house: broken conch shells, moldy campaign buttons, a cast-iron apple corer, a carved piece of bone. A dinner guest had once likened the house to a Joseph Cornell box, each room with its own codified charm, subdivided again by a recessed nook or secret cabinet. And within those niches were still more chambers of discovery, if one knew where to look. Now, as Hazel examined Isaac's curios, they seemed laden with hidden meaning, each one a potential hazard or clue.

She stepped into a book-lined alcove not only to evade the rapidly filling living room but also to consult with herself as to *what the hell* she was going to do with the contents of her pocket. From a bookshelf flagged with family snapshots in lieu of bookmarks (her grandparents had been sentimental that way), she pulled down Newton's *Principia Mathematica* and plucked from its pages an old photograph of Isaac standing amid roses in LA's Exposition Park. As she directed her growing anxiety at his image, Hazel became aware of a clutch of guests huddled in the next room, none of whom she recognized. Their words were indistinct, yet she sensed they were gossiping about her grandfather.

". . . a bit unhinged, maybe . . ."

She didn't like their tone, and, as sometimes happened with her—had been happening as far back as she could remember—Hazel conjured up a scene of comic violence, in which she burst into the room and pelted the group with smoked salmon from the buffet table, before jamming a broken schmear knife into a few necks. Then, amid screams and sprays of blood, she fled the house, triumphant. The idiotic image evaporated, and she returned her attention to the photo where her then-middle-aged grandfather was looking overheated in a corduroy jacket. She had seen the snapshot countless times and had no need to study it now so thoroughly. She was merely delaying the moment when she would have to make herself visible to the mourners roaming the house. *Go be with your family.* Yes, these people were technically her family, but she had never entirely felt comfortable among them. She could fake it, of course—*had* faked it for much of her life—but with Isaac gone, her feelings of "other" were rapidly intensifying.

Nearly half the place was filled with mathematicians of one type or another. Growing up, she had thought little about the mental caliber of the guests who filtered through the house. But now, as an adult, Hazel could grasp the critical difference between mathematics and mere arithmetic, and she quickly discovered that there was nothing like a talent for the former to separate pure, distilled intelligence from the affected kind one picks up at college.

In the numbers arena, Hazel had always been lacking. She had barely gotten through precalculus in high school, and, after moving to Seattle for college, she had dived into the arts and humanities with scattershot enthusiasm—drama, dance, literature, history—sidestepping the hard and fast in favor of the slippery and indefinite. If she had been a member of any other family, she might have been confident in her choices. But with the Severys, Hazel often felt that whenever one of them looked at her—even Lily, who had double-majored in comparative literature and mathematics at Berkeley—they weren't really seeing her but were scanning a set of data points visible only to them, like insects in ultraviolet. She could practically hear them whispering, "Why entrust this one with the letter?" Hazel had been asking herself this very question. As if her grief wasn't enough to bear, she'd now been given this cryptic assignment?

She returned Isaac and the rosebushes to the *Principia* and nervously checked her phone, which set off another sort of anxiety: Why hadn't Bennet's name appeared in the call log? Why couldn't she rely on him to support her today of all days? First, he had begged off joining her on the trip because of a work emergency, and second, after offering her a ride to the airport, he had diminished the favor by greeting her with a Nikon camera to the face. Though Bennet worked for an artsy furniture design company that promised to "blur the line between form and function, between our furniture and ourselves," he nursed loftier creative ambitions outside of work. To that end, he insisted that his "emotions project," or whatever he was calling his next art installation, demanded constant photographic vigilance. *Click.*

After examining the shot, he'd said, "I can never capture your sad face. Why is that? Cheerful, stunned, irritated—never sad."

"Can you exploit my grief later?"

She could, of course, snap a photo of herself now so that her boyfriend might complete his collection. *This is funereal me—sad enough?* Though at that moment, her face more likely betrayed rising panic. Hazel slid her phone back in her pocket, at the same time checking the opposite hip. Her pockets weren't terribly deep. What if the envelope fell out as she sat down?

With a mind to concealing the thing safely somewhere, she left the alcove and made straight for the hall, avoiding the populated end of the house. As she turned a corner, she halted at the sight of a middle-aged man in a light herringbone jacket chatting up a female guest, but it was only Isaac's accountant, Fritz Dornbach. There was comfort in seeing this man whom her grandfather had always liked, and it occurred to her that if she were to confide in anyone, she could do worse than the family's attorney-bookkeeper. But then, Isaac couldn't have been more clear: *Do not share this with anyone.*

She stole behind Fritz toward the staircase, which someone had roped off with some tasselled curtain ties, presumably to discourage wandering guests. Hazel ducked under the barrier. The second-floor landing was dim, its windows curtained shut. As her pupils adjusted, she made her way past Isaac's study door, where her step triggered a groaning floorboard—the same loose board under which she and her brother had once kept treasures and left each other secret notes. A loose nail pressed up through her shoe, as if a kind of prompt, but she discarded this as a potential hiding place; it was too easy for Gregory to get nostalgic and stumble upon it.

Turning to the study door, she imagined herself twisting the glass knob to reveal Isaac on the other side, hunched in a chair, looking up with a patient smile. For a second, she even thought she could hear his rhythmic murmuring coming from within, the sound of a mathematician thinking out loud. *A murmur of mathematicians.*

She continued down the hall to her old bedroom, where she was considering staying the next night or two. She had thrown her luggage in her brother's car just in case. Besides, with the house likely going on the market, this could be her last chance to stay in her old room. Whatever dangers Isaac imagined the house posed, he needn't have warned her about not staying past October: she planned to be back in Seattle well before Halloween.

The bedroom hadn't changed much over the years. It still contained her adolescent belongings: stuffed animals, ceramic figurines, a bookshelf filled with childhood reading. At another time, these keepsakes might have brought her comfort, but as her eyes scanned the books' spines—Madeleine L'Engle, Ellen Raskin, C. S. Lewis, E. L. Konigsburg—Hazel felt bewildered and alone. Had this house ever really felt like home? Or had it always been just another way station in a transient childhood? She and her brother had loved Isaac and Lily deeply, but had never entirely rid themselves of the feeling that they were long-term charity cases, forever crashing on the couch of an intimidatingly distinguished family. For a time, at least, she had successfully smothered this feeling of inexpressible exile.

As she pulled the envelope from her pocket and contemplated a hiding place among her Hercule Poirot novels, she took one last look at the contents of the letter, wondering if the desire not to disappoint Isaac over the years had turned into a more general habit of avoidance. What if she chose to do nothing with the letter? She was flying back home in two days and was hardly in the position to be tracking down a room number she'd never heard of, let alone obliterating her grandfather's legacy. And then to be chasing down some guy named Raspanti? A man apparently fond of only the most popular men's suiting pattern there is?

Turning to the window, Hazel thought back to the innocent hours before she'd opened the letter. What had she been expecting? Not this sober directive from the grave, but maybe: *"Lily no longer recognizes me"* . . . *"My ability to do math is deteriorating"* . . . *"No shame in bowing out gracefully, you understand."* But with all his talk of being followed and wishing he could flee—what was she supposed to do with that when he'd forbidden her from going to the police? Could it be that Isaac had lost his foothold on reality and that these were mad ramblings?

Just as she was slipping the letter into Agatha Christie's *The Mysterious Affair at Styles*, Hazel heard the loose floorboard outside creak. She shelved the book and stepped into the darkened hall just in time to see someone—a man, she couldn't see his face—leaving her grandfather's study. He shut the door and seemed to waver for a moment before disappearing down the stairs.

She became aware of a prickling sensation, as if charged particles were scaling her spine. Being alone on the second floor suddenly felt like a bad idea, so she shut the bedroom door and made her way to the social level of the house.

Downstairs, she fell into some hugs and nice-to-see-yous before going to the buffet table for something to settle her stomach. When she had filled her plate, she nearly stumbled over little Drew

Severy-Oliver, who was sitting in the middle of the floor, an Audubon guide open in her lap. Hazel was often blind to the allure of small children, but with Drew, she couldn't help but melt a little.

The five-year-old looked up. "Did you know that the albatross has the widest wingspan of any bird there is?"

"Really? I had no idea."

"Yeah. No one does."

While Drew flipped through her book for more bird facts, Sybil appeared and gave Hazel a sideways embrace. "My little bug isn't bothering you, is she?"

"Oh, no. I'm getting a much-needed ornithology lesson."

"Birds are her big thing right now, and plants. She's already identified all the plants in our backyard. She's bored with them now, of course."

Drew peered up at her mother. "Did she say ornithology?"

"No, honey. She didn't."

Drew bounced toward Hazel. "But you did, didn't you?"

Hazel looked to Sybil, who grimaced.

"Ornithology is the study of birds!" Drew announced.

"Drew, please. Not now—" pleaded her mother.

"Orology is the study of mountains. Orthopterology is the study of crickets and grasshoppers!"

"Oh, God," Sybil said, running a hand through her hair. "She's memorized all of the 'ologies' in alphabetical order. When she reaches *zoology*, she starts all over again. There are hundreds of them. Hundreds . . ." She broke off, exasperated.

"Well, I'm feeling very inadequate," Hazel said.

"Osteology!" Drew sang. "The study of bones."

"She's going to be very smart. Everyone says so," Sybil said in unmasked dismay. "We have to go find Daddy, Drew. Say bye to Haze."

"Bye."

Sybil lifted her daughter from the floor and floated away, but not before Hazel heard: "*Ov*ology, the study of eggs . . ."

Nothing like a know-it-all child to make you feel completely worthless. Hazel looked down at her food, realizing she wasn't at all hungry. A drink, that's what she needed. A strong drink would put the letter out of her mind.

She headed for the kitchen, first having to circumnavigate the depressed geeks who were closing in on Philip and Paige, the new default celebrities of the family. Without meaning to, Hazel met Paige's eyes again. Her aunt had always been an intimidating figure. Hazel's early memories of her usually involved some odd comment thrown her way that she had been too young or too nervous to comprehend. Only later did she register it as a steady stream of disdain and sarcasm. Hazel mustered a cursory smile at Paige and moved on.

Her search of the kitchen cupboards turned up a precious half bottle of Isaac's rye, perhaps the last of his stores. She took a quick swallow from the bottle before pouring herself a proper glass.

In the living room, she noticed a young foursome gathered in a recess, a bronze bust of Copernicus peering out from their animated orbit. From the unconcealed arrogance in their voices she guessed they were grad students, and from the volume of their conversation, that they were happily intoxicated. The bearded man who'd spoken at the funeral stood among them. She saw up close that his hair was a bit of a nest and that his suit—not herringbone, she noted, but a faint checked pattern—was probably a size too big. His anxious look from that morning had gone and he was now engaged in confident conversation with a cute brunette. But Hazel sensed his eyes following her, and as she took a seat in a nearby club chair, she could feel a lingering heat from his gaze.

The four had moved on from reminiscing about Isaac to complaining about relationships. The brunette grumbled about her computer-scientist ex, who was a dead ringer for Albert Camus but whose broodingly handsome braincase had been empty.

"No joke," she said. "I had to explain Riemann's zeta to him, like, *zeta* of *s* times." Laughs all around.

"I bet he was fun, at least," a redhead broke in. "Try dating a number theorist who thinks it's the height of hilarity to celebrate only prime-numbered birthdays. Oh, *ha*-ha!"

The beard was still focused on the brunette. "So you dumped him."

"Afraid so."

"Hey, I hear you," said the fourth member of the group, a man with unfortunate acne scars. "People who don't get mathematics can be shockingly dull—"

"Now, wait a second," Beard interrupted. "Take this book on the shelf here: *Numbers: How the History of Mathematics Is the History of Civilization.* I mean, sure, the history of math is tied to human progress and all that, but the title is meaningless. There are other things to life."

"Like what?" demanded the brunette.

"Oh, I don't know, nature, long naps, a dog chasing a ball, food—"

"You don't think nature is packed with mathematics? Or that the advent of agriculture was totally dependent on rudimentary geometry?"

"Sure, but it was also dependent on people being hungry."

The brunette tutted. Hazel couldn't see her face, but she imagined it sucking a cigarette.

"Look," continued Beard. "You can plug in anything—*Architecture: How the History of Building Shit Is the History of Civilization*—literally anything."

"Booze?"

"How the History of Fermentation—"

"Mustard."

"How the History of the Spice Trade—"

"What's your point?"

"My point is that I'm sick to death of all the pretension, of insisting that the abstract science we call mathematics is more vital than anything else, because if God forbid someone doesn't memorize the zeta function for his girlfriend, he's some straw-munching rube."

This wasn't the first time Hazel had heard a heated discussion like this in the Severy house, but it suddenly struck her as hilarious that people actually talked like this.

"You know," the brunette broke in, "speaking of pretentious mathematicians, I wasn't the one who got up at a funeral and made a hundred people listen to number garbage for twenty minutes."

"Number garbage?"

"That's right."

"Whatever you say," said Beard, but the brunette was already stalking off to the kitchen, her friends right behind her.

Beard glowered at his drink as if rebuking his own reflection. When he reoriented himself, his eyes alighted on Hazel.

She shifted uncomfortably on her cushion and cleared her throat. *"Big Comfy Chair: How the History of Sitting Down . . ."*

He laughed. It was a boozy cackle that lasted several seconds and brought an involuntary smile to Hazel's face for the first time in days.

"You heard all that?" he asked.

Feeling self-conscious, she cracked open a book sitting on an end table. "Oh, no. I was just reading up on"—she flipped back the cover—*"An Extended Treatise on Mathematical Modeling,* by Hermann Henck . . . ?"

He tried not to smile.

"I actually know him. The man is deadly." Beard suddenly frowned in the direction of the kitchen. "Christ, I seriously don't know what's wrong with me lately. I've been such a prick."

"You mean to that girl? I wouldn't worry about it."

He planted a hand on Copernicus's bronze face.

"Yeah, I don't really know them, anyway. And I'm not apologizing to a mathematician who can't recognize decent math when she hears it."

"It's funny," Hazel said. "I don't think I've ever heard an equation read out loud like that. Definitely not at a funeral." At this, she was surprised to see him glance away, the skin above his beard reddening.

"I guess it was a bit much."

"Not that I would've understood it had it been written out."

He smiled. "If you had an hour or two, and a basic understanding of differential equations, I could—"

"Oh, don't waste your time."

He took a swallow from his glass. "I'm probably not that far behind you. My number talents are pretty unspectacular nowadays. Ordinary, even."

Hazel half stood so that she was leaning on the chair's arm.

"I'm Hazel, by the way. Isaac was my grandfather."

He gave her an odd, searching look.

"I don't believe you."

"Oh, it's not biological," she said quickly. "I don't have a brain that anyone would want to cut open." When he didn't respond, she kept talking. "He told me once I had a mind for logic, but turns out he was just being nice."

"Now that I think of it, maybe I have heard him mention you." He held up his last bit of whiskey: "To Isaac."

After tossing it back, he set the glass next to the heliocentrist's shoulder and glanced around the room. "Do you know any of these people?"

Hazel followed his gaze.

"A few. But honestly, without Isaac, I'm a bit lost in crowds like this."

He nodded. "This is supposed to be my tribe, but all I can say is, I know exactly what you mean." He suddenly pulled out his phone and frowned. "I'm very sorry, Hazel. I'd like to stay, but I have to be somewhere. I'll see you around?"

"I don't actually live here."

"Neither do I."

She was about to ask his name, but he made a sudden awkward move toward the kitchen, pausing to examine a piece of artwork on the adjoining wall. It was a large red canvas with a snarl of string fixed to the center. He stared at the identifying tag: *Found Twine #126*.

"Sybil made that," she explained.

"I wonder what the odds are."

"Odds?"

"Of stumbling upon twine one hundred and twenty-six times in your life."

He turned away again, but thought better of it.

"Sorry, I'm Alex," he said, producing a hand. "I should have mentioned that Isaac was also my grandfather, which if I'm not mistaken makes us related. Don't mean to rush off, it's just that I'm late. Good-bye, Hazel."

She stood stunned at the front window, watching his rumpled figure move away from the house. Did she really have a cousin she didn't know about? She didn't expect his journey across the vast lawn to clear up her confusion, but she studied his slightly uneven stride as if he were stomping out clues to his identity. She felt her brother step up beside her.

"So you met Paige's spawn."

She turned, eyes wide, and laughed. "Alex is *Alexis?* Of course."

"Insane, right?"

"Why didn't you tell me?"

Gregory shook his head. "Just found out from Aunt Jane. What a surprise to discover that our mysterious cousin isn't the pretty girl I imagined, but a wannabe Englishman."

"Why would Paige lie like that? Or at least not bother to correct anyone?"

"I guess it's not a proper joke unless it runs on for thirty years."

They watched Alex's figure grow small and vanish down the flight of canyonside steps. "He does have a weird accent."

"Jane says he picked it up while in school overseas. Couldn't possibly have been intentional."

"I don't know. He seems nice, in a neurotic sort of way."

She expected her brother to say something about all his years as a detective for the Los Angeles Police Department and his preternatural ability to know people at a glance, but instead he put an arm around her.

"How'd you turn out to be so generous?" he asked, leaning his head on hers. What once would have been an effortless gesture now felt stilted, as if he were trying to make up for something. Still, she returned his half embrace, and for that moment she felt close to him again.

"It's just terrible you all couldn't have grown up together," their aunt Jane told them long after the house had emptied. "Alex should have been part of the family, but Paige does what she wants, I suppose.

Whether it was her insecurity over his not having a proper father or what, that's no reason to go on this long—though the father isn't exactly some delinquent. Out of the picture, sure, but he's paid for Alex's entire education. I mean, Philip and I knew that *she* was a *he*—Isaac let it slip about a year ago, said he was bored with Paige's insistence on 'privacy'—but even so, we just met the boy on Friday. Though he's hardly a boy anymore."

Jane poured iced teas and set out a plate of leftovers from the reception. "When I confronted Paige yesterday, she grudgingly admitted that her son has great mathematical potential, or did once."

"He told me that he was ordinary," Hazel said, staring through a window at Isaac's hot tub. Why had Isaac confided to Jane about Alex but not to her and Gregory? Then she remembered the letter and the fact that much of her grandfather's life had clearly been kept from her. What was one more secret?

"Ordinary?" Her aunt laughed. "Alex was a prodigy like his mother—won a fellowship to study at the Max Planck Institute in Bonn, but dropped out after an autobahn accident. There was some cerebral cortex damage, but Paige wasn't all that sympathetic; claims he used the accident as an excuse to give up on mathematics entirely. Maybe it broke Paige's heart—what little she has."

"So what's he doing now?" Gregory asked.

"Freelance photographer out of Europe, apparently. For travel magazines and the AP. He was living in Paris for a while. Paige doesn't think he's making much of a living, though I'm not sure how she'd know. Did you notice they weren't even sitting together this morning? I haven't seen them interact once."

"Where's he staying?"

Jane shrugged. "I told him he could stay with us, but he says he has a friend in town. A girlfriend maybe, who knows."

Gregory must have made a face because Jane said, "Oh, don't

look so surprised. I've seen pictures of him, and he really is a good-looking man underneath all that hair. Wouldn't you say so, Hazel?"

Hazel nodded an agreement as she continued to stare at Isaac's hot tub, dark and covered, dusted with droppings from a pepper tree. Beyond it, a gibbous moon was rising from the leaves of a date palm. As her aunt chattered on, Hazel rinsed out her glass at the sink and stared out at the pale blue satellite. It had never seemed so frightening and beautiful as it did to her now, knowing that only several nights before, Isaac had looked out his study window at a sliver of this same moon, as he composed the last words anyone would ever receive from him.

4

The Policeman

An accident on the shoulder of the freeway made Gregory think of Isaac. He might have pulled his Honda Civic over to see if his assistance was needed, but the strobes told him that plenty of police had already arrived, so he continued on, preserving the sensitive momentum of the interstate. Isaac would have approved. At one time, it had been his grandfather's quest to return Southern California to its streetcar paradise. Isaac hadn't necessarily wanted to rid the road of cars—"Let's be sensible"—he had simply wanted to make car culture more efficient. He had even wrangled some public funding before the city council decided that drought and the homeless were more pressing issues. But during that brief window, when he and the city had held hands and gazed into a bottleneck-free future, Isaac was quoted in the *Los Angeles Times* as saying, "What's the use of mathematicians if we can't solve the gigantic math problem staring us in the face every time we drive to work? Traffic is a car dilemma, yes, but it is also a mathematical one."

With the accident receding in his rearview mirror, Gregory looked to his left across the median. If he had kept his original engagement tonight instead of going home, he would be shuttling along the opposite side of the freeway about now. But he had reluctantly cancelled. It was with a woman he very much wanted to see, but there were limits to his duplicity.

Besides, his sister was coming over for dinner. He felt compelled to make up for his bad brothering of late, as in his complete inability to return a simple phone call or text. Just because he could barely manage his own life, that was no excuse for neglecting his only real blood connection. Maybe they could take this opportunity to become close again, as they had been when they were young. Hazel and Gregory together again—or Hansel and Gretel, as they'd been called in their schooldays, a taunt that had mysteriously followed them no matter how many times they changed homes or schools. They could have a laugh about that tonight.

He wasn't looking forward to the news he had to give Hazel. He had considered not telling her at all and sparing her the anxiety, but one of the family was bound to let it slip—assuming they, too, had gotten their notices from the California Department of Corrections and Rehabilitation.

Gregory's attention was diverted by the sight of a girl, seven years old maybe, seated in a sedan one lane over. She had clearly been crying, which triggered in him an involuntary mix of compassion and fury. He couldn't stand the sight of a sad child, so much so that he had turned his entire career at the LAPD into rescuing them. Now that he was a father, the intensity of his reaction to seeing unhappy children was almost unbearable. While most new parents became myopic in their fixation with their own offspring, for Gregory, it was as if every child was his own.

He looked back at the girl, whose resemblance to his sister at that age—unbrushed hair, wide-set eyes—was startling. Something about the way she stared, toy gripped to chest . . . Gregory would tell his sister the news tonight. He would wait until his wife had gone to bed, then put on a pot for tea.

Haze?

"Yeah?"

She would look up from her mug, a flicker of concern passing over her face.

I have something to tell you.

There were so many things he could tell her, but for tonight, he would stick to just one.

He's out of prison.

"What?"

He's out.

"I don't believe you."

Yes, well . . .

After a lengthy explanation, he would try to persuade her not to worry, but Gregory himself was having a difficult time ignoring the secret dread that had been compressing his insides like a C-clamp. Aside from Hazel, Isaac was the only one who would have understood his current apprehension. But now he was gone. No matter how much Gregory tried to tell himself it would all be fine, he didn't quite believe it. And he wanted to, if only for this evening.

About a mile from home, Gregory realized he was being followed. But when he identified the car's retro headlights as those of a 2005 Ford Thunderbird convertible, he relaxed. There was only one person he knew who drove that car: Fritz Dornbach, Isaac's accountant of nearly fifteen years. Because of Fritz's additional law degree, he also did some legal work for the family. But his main purpose had been to shield Isaac from having anything to do with bookkeeping, banks, or money, a role in which Fritz seemed to take particular pride. One could almost see him boasting at the annual CPA conference about his genius client: "Sure, he may be close to solving Goldbach's conjecture or whatever, but swear to God, so much as show him his own checkbook, and he's out in the barn frantically petting rabbits." But Isaac's distaste for money management had nothing to do with ineptitude. "Finance isn't math," Gregory's grandfather liked to say, "it's number enslavement."

The convertible overtook him, and by the time Gregory pulled into his driveway, his diminutive pursuer was standing in front of the house, his peppery hair comically windblown. Fritz had on his optical-illusion shoes, the ones designed to boost height while obscuring where his actual feet were resting. It wasn't much of an illusion.

"I called," Fritz said. "Maybe you couldn't hear the ringing coming from your purse."

Gregory wasn't in the mood for banter. "What's up, Fritz?"

From behind his back, Fritz produced a folder, decorated with an illustration of a monarch butterfly. "My assistant picked out the folder," he mumbled.

"Am I supposed to know what this is?"

But Gregory had some idea. Just days after Isaac's death, Fritz had left a lengthy message on his voice mail: "Why is everyone, including your friends at the LAPD, acting as if a perfectly happy guy electrocuting himself is normal? I mean, before he's even finished breakfast? A breakfast with two place settings, I might add." But had his grandfather really been happy? With his work stalled (he hadn't published anything serious in years) and the love of his life in a home for the senile, that was debatable. As for the extra place setting, this had been explained away by the housekeeper, who said that Isaac often made an extra breakfast for her on the mornings she stopped by.

Fritz held out the folder. "It's the bank records I was telling you about. Steady cash withdrawals at the end of each month for the last five and a half years. Not a ton, but not exactly pocket money."

"I don't see how it's my business."

"You're the detective—at least have a look. I drove all the way over here."

Gregory relented and took the folder. "You never asked him about it?"

"Once or twice, but all he said was that he liked cash. I teased him about slowly stashing a fortune away in that rat's nest house of his, but then I forgot about it." Fritz turned in the direction of Pico Boulevard, where a car horn had started wailing. "He never did fix that gridlock thing, did he?"

"Gridlock isn't real mathematics. Or that's what he said when he lost his funding."

Fritz moved to his car. "You know what he told me once? That the whole universe is one giant computer, and every second it's calculating its own future down to the last detail—right down to some guy getting angry on the road."

Gregory nodded. "He did like a good metaphor. Join us for dinner?" Fritz had become something of a family friend over the years, but this was less an invite than an end to the conversation.

"Can't, I've got a date. But I'm having a little masquerade in Hollywood this weekend, if you and Goldie are up for it."

"Not sure I can handle one of your parties, Fritz. We're taking Lewis trick-or-treating."

"Right. Another time, then?"

Gregory watched the accountant maneuver himself back into the driver's seat of his Thunderbird. It wasn't unlike watching a child clamber onto a chair, and for some reason the image made him sad, and he turned away.

*   *   *

After putting his son to bed, Gregory sat down to a late dinner with his wife and sister. Though he had seen Hazel the previous Christmas, it felt as if it had been much longer. She looked healthy but older: cheeks not quite as round, eyes not quite as hope filled. But then again, he knew his own face was looking increasingly excavated.

On account of their guest, Goldie had made a dinner featuring several complicated courses. In addition to putting in extra time in the kitchen, she had also put some effort into her appearance: her brassy curls were pulled up from her neck, her lips painted coral, and her cheeks dusted with bronzer. His wife wasn't pretty exactly, but she did her best to highlight her assets.

"Such a beautiful service," Goldie said halfway through dinner, a phrase she had uttered at least ten times since yesterday. "Wasn't it beautiful?"

Hazel, who had stayed mostly quiet since her arrival, mumbled in agreement. She seemed unusually distant, though Gregory knew the same could be said of him.

As his wife chattered on about the funeral, he imagined letting the news fall right there at the table, followed by Hazel's disbelief.

"But it was a life sentence."

He was well behaved.

A pause as she considered recent events.

"The timing is weird, isn't it?"

Maybe, but you know what Isaac would say: 'concurrence of events,' and all that. It doesn't mean—

"Did Isaac know he was out?"

We didn't have much of a chance to talk about it—

"Daddy!"

Gregory's interior stage play was interrupted by his two-year-old

40

son, who had tottered into the room grasping a rubber fish Hazel had brought as a present. As Lewis began to explore the tail with his mouth, Gregory made a mental note to check the toxicity of the material.

He pushed back his chair. "I'll put him down." He took up Lewis in one affectionate swoop and, planting kisses all the way down the hall, went to deliver the second bedtime story of the night.

When the dishes were cleared and his wife had turned in, Gregory put a kettle on and sat Hazel down in the kitchen. In the event she didn't believe him, he was ready to produce his letters from the Department of Corrections. But Hazel looked tired and distracted, and was rapidly losing her ability to engage as the evening wore on. She would be calling it a night soon, going back to the house to enjoy the comforts of her old bedroom. He was certain that plying her with hot chocolate would do the trick, but when he handed her a mug with the name of her store, The Guttersnipe, printed along the rim, she seemed to crumple.

"What?"

"Nothing."

She got up, surprising him by grabbing some Captain Morgan from a shelf. She wasn't a big drinker, but gave both their mugs a liberal splash. As Gregory looked down and watched the cool rum disrupt the harmony of milk and chocolate, he imagined the liquor, milk, and cocoa particles following a dispersion equation of their own making. It had been years since he'd studied fluid dynamics in school, but moving gas and liquid still had the power to command his attention. To this day, he stared entirely too long at the whorls escaping a smoker's lips or a stray seed pod gliding along the surface of a pool.

He took a sip of the spiked chocolate and waited for Hazel to look up. Although he'd long ago lost the ability to read her moods, he could see that something was wrong, beyond the loss of their grandfather.

"You all right?"

She shrugged. "Just the usual self-evaluation that happens when one of the few people you care about dies. And the other one has lost her mind."

Tell her now. But before he could form the words, she was wiping away tears with the back of her hand.

"Did I tell you I lost my apartment last month?" she said.

"You didn't mention that, no." He tried to maintain a calm expression.

"Did I mention that I'm so embarrassed about it that I haven't even told my boyfriend? My very successful boyfriend, who wouldn't at all secretly judge me?"

"Jesus, Haze. Where are you living?"

"In a charming cupboard in the back of my store."

At the thought of his sister trapped in a tiny, dark space, Gregory felt a dizzy spell coming on. Or maybe he was just tired. He put both palms flat on the table and took a deep breath—a grounding technique he had used when they were young, whenever it felt like their wobbly little world might spin off its axis. Hazel reached over and touched his arm.

He forced a smile. "Well, it all sounds *very* cozy, Haze."

"Oh, it is. So cozy it's slowly killing me." She took a hard swallow from her mug. "I guess I could close the shop. Get a job, like you hear about. But the thought of spending the rest of my life being harassed by some boss, and surrounded by those fluorescent lights and awful ceiling tiles, you know the ones—" She caught herself. "Sorry."

"No, no, I like depressing lighting and bad ceilings. I actually prefer it."

She started to laugh, but her eyes didn't follow, and soon she was crying harder than before.

He wished he could say something to make her smile, as he'd been able to do when they were small. She would have been curled up on a twin mattress, sad face pressed to her teddy bear Cedric—an oddly posh name, given their surroundings. Though Gregory, now thirty-three, was barely two years older, he had once taken on his role as big brother with gravity, always hunting for new ways to protect and comfort her.

In the absence of Kleenex, he offered her a stack of napkins. "You know you can come live with us. I mean it."

"I appreciate it, but"—she took a napkin and pressed it to her eyes—"what the hell am I going to do?"

"Have you thought of going back to school?"

She groaned. "Why does everyone ask me that like I'm some illiterate dropout?"

"What did Isaac say about all this?"

Hazel looked away. "He only would have tried to give me money, and I know he didn't have any. All of it went into the house and taking care of Lily." Talk of Isaac's money made Gregory think of Fritz's butterfly folder.

By the time they reached the silt at the bottom of their mugs, he knew he wasn't going to be telling his sister about Tom. Because if he told her that on top of everything else, their former foster father was out of prison, she might have a mental collapse right there at the table. The news would have to wait until he could do something about Tom. Something concrete. Or at least until Hazel was back in Seattle, far from the man who could once again infect both of their lives.

5

The Letter

At almost two in the morning, back in Beachwood Canyon, Hazel awoke from a nightmare—something about the bay engulfing Pioneer Square and her shop floating out to Puget Sound. As she lay in the dark of her old room, with the lingering image of herself marooned on a slab of shelving, she wondered why her dream symbology had always been so irritatingly obvious. Yes, her store was "underwater"—got it. Why couldn't she have coded, indecipherable dreams like most people? Yet behind all the unambiguous imagery, there had been something lurking: Isaac's letter.

Hazel had read the letter countless times that day and felt just as helpless and confused as the first time. She had almost told Gregory about it after dinner, tempted by what felt like a precious, fleeting moment of brother-sister camaraderie. Instead, she'd offered up a list of substitute miseries—all completely valid, and certainly responsible for her stress levels, but not the real reason she had totally lost it at her brother's kitchen table.

It was an unusually blustery night. The house creaked and moaned under the strain of the wind. A stiff palm frond fingernailed its way back and forth across a window. She'd forgotten how spooky the house could be after dark, but felt comforted at least that Sybil, Jack, and their daughter were sleeping downstairs. They had intended to stay with Philip and Jane in Pasadena before flying back home to the Bay Area, but had returned to the canyon after Sybil quarreled with her parents. Hazel had gathered little about it other than what Jack had whispered to her: "Not easy being the offspring of a genius, you know . . ."

Hazel let her gaze fall across the room, where a shaft of moonlight illuminated the spines of her mystery novels—one of which concealed Isaac's letter. Agatha Christie, Dorothy Sayers, Gladys Mitchell, to name a few: they were all books she had read greedily as a child, but whose plots later congealed into a single generic mass. Once in a while, a certain character or revelatory moment would float back to her, but she could rarely remember which book or author. Now a fragment of something seemed to be calling to Hazel from the shelf—something to do with the murder of a paperback writer.

She got out of bed and threw on a pilled robe. She remembered the story now, or at least the end; the entire solution hinged on a single clue left on the ribbon of a typewriter. When the hero-detective unwound the spool, he found the final thoughts of the victim, including the identity of his killer, left in the negative imprint of inked ribbon: *Mykilleris* . . . The story, though not terribly sophisticated, had ignited her young imagination, and now—thinking of Isaac's typewriter—she couldn't get to his study fast enough.

She slipped out of the bedroom and made her way down the hall, careful to avoid the rickety floorboard. The house was still, and the only sound came from a chronically leaky bathtub faucet. Tat-a-tat-*tat* . . . The drips pounded the porcelain with the discipline of a drum machine, and it seemed that even in this tedious sound, her grandfather was present. Many years ago, Isaac had sat in the kitchen with her and Gregory, lip-syncing to the rhythm of an intensely weepy kitchen faucet with uncanny precision—tat-a-tat-tat-o-*tat*-a-tat-o-*tat-tat!*—while she and her brother giggled uncontrollably, delighted by his ability to inhabit the spirit of the tap.

"See, the drips only appear random," he told them after their laughter subsided, "but if you listen carefully, you can pick out the pattern." And with a pen, as if jotting off Morse code, Isaac marked out the dots and dashes of the "chaotic" system, which, he explained, was not chaotic at all—for chaos theory had been clumsily named. Short drip, long, short, silence. One could alter the system, making it more or less complex by loosening or tightening the handle. "And you know," he continued, "bad plumbing isn't the only thing that drips. The entire world drips, too, and if you pay very close attention, you can anticipate the next drop."

Everything, of course, had been a game to her grandfather, and Hazel had to ask herself: Was he playing a game with her now?

The study was as she'd last seen it: all dark wood and heavy books, an egghead's sanctum. She rolled aside his chair, ducked beneath the massive desk, and lifted Isaac's ancient IBM from its home on the floor. A gentle tug of the cord revealed that it hadn't been unplugged since its last use. She lifted the case and took out the ink cartridge, holding it to the desk lamp. She slowly pulled the ribbon loose like dental floss, but there were no fossilized letters in the ink, only shiny new ribbon. The cartridge had been replaced. She tipped the garbage can with her foot. Empty. So that was that.

As Hazel attempted to respool the ribbon, she heard a noise. After a pause, she heard it again. The floorboard outside. On instinct, she stood up and yanked the typewriter onto the chair, letting the ribbon fall to the floor. She rolled the chair under the desk and turned to the nearest bookshelf, pretending to examine the titles. The door opened, and Sybil, in a girlish nightgown that just brushed her knees, stepped into the dim light.

"Oh," Hazel said, trying to appear cool, "did I wake you?"

Her cousin said nothing, just gazed sleepily in her direction.

She noticed, not without passing envy, that Sybil was just as radiant at two o'clock in the morning as she had been earlier that day. Hazel also gathered that she was, in fact, asleep. She had never witnessed one of her cousin's sleepwalking episodes, though she had heard all the stories—the most repeated one involving Sybil's wandering out of a Park Avenue hotel on her honeymoon, hailing a taxi, and a frantic Jack having to flag down his own cab and chase his silk-pajamaed wife all the way to LaGuardia Airport. There was an undeniable levelheadedness to Sybil's nighttime adventures. She always put on shoes before stepping outside, and she had the uncanny ability to sleep-navigate.

Just as Hazel considered waking her cousin, Sybil fell against the door frame and muttered, "No, no, no. I told you already—" She let out a long whine and slid to the floor, where she began to quietly cry.

Hazel was about to prod her awake when the hall light came on, and Jack shuffled into view. He had a dark, brooding face, superficially similar to the men Hazel tended to like, Bennet included.

"There you are," he said, sliding an arm around the weeping Sybil. "Sorry about this, Hazel."

"Should we wake her?"

"Better not." He pulled Sybil to her feet. Hazel thought he looked remarkably unrattled given his wife's distress. Nor did he appear in the least bit curious about what Hazel was doing up this time of night. "Back to bed, darling."

As Hazel watched the pair move toward the stairs, she wondered if her cousin was really the upbeat wife and mother she appeared to be in her waking hours.

When she could no longer hear the creaking stairs or the sobs, she closed the door and set the typewriter back on the desk. After respooling the ribbon and clicking it back into place, she was overcome with the need to write something. She rolled a piece of paper into the drum and began to peck at the keys, as if searching for a new form of communication with the dead.

```
Dear Isaac,

  Are you sure you are of sound mind? (Have to ask.)
How am I supposed to help you when you haven't told
me where to look? Room 137? Not helpful. This isn't
exactly a "By the way, can you water my plants now
that I'm dead?" type of favor. I am broke and have a
business that is failing. Tomorrow, I'm going to have
lunch with my brother and then I'm going to get on a
plane and resume my life. What else can I do? I hope
you'll forgive me.

                                    Miss you awfully,
                                    Haze


PS: You can't expect me to destroy the letter. It
is the last thing I have from you, and I just can't
do it.
```

As she was typing this appeal, Hazel noticed something—or rather, she noticed the absence of something. The keys weren't sticking; the metallic ball stamped away without stutters. How, then, had Isaac's letter been riddled with the typewriter's habitual tics? She inspected the casing and found his initials—I.D.S.—scratched into the blue plastic. It certainly was his machine. Had he gotten the thing repaired after he'd typed the letter? She slid open his desk drawers one by one, hoping to find she didn't know what. A receipt for typewriter repair? She found only mechanical pencils, notebooks of equations, and folders filled with clippings from the obituary pages—a lifelong obsession of his.

Finally, giving up, she pulled her impromptu letter from the roller. She was not a detective, she told herself, and this was not a whodunit. Yet in a final move of genre-inspired panic, Hazel dropped the page and—*snip snip*—its corresponding piece of ribbon into the trash bin and set a match to it. After the flame swelled and died, she doused the ashes with water from a spider plant and tossed the mess out the window. It was the same window, she noted, that Isaac had mentioned in his letter. Seeing her sleuthing to the end, she pulled out her phone and after a few clicks, pulled up a lunar calendar. Yes, it had indeed been a setting crescent moon the evening of October 15, the night before he posted his letter—two days before his death. As she looked up at the now-dark patch of sky, a string of words began to gather in her mind, where they arranged themselves into yet another puzzling question: *Why go twentysome years without fixing your typewriter, only to get it repaired the day before you die?*

6

The University

On the Monday morning following his father's burial, Philip arrived at his office in the Charles C. Lauritsen Laboratory of High Energy Physics to find two things attached to his door. The first was a stiff envelope sticking out of the jamb at neck level, as if poised for a tracheal paper cut. In neat pen it said: "Please read. Re: Your Father." Philip pulled it from its crevice. There was no return address, only a strange design in the corner: a tiny spiral with a tail extending downward, like a disembodied brain. He folded the envelope and slipped it into his jacket pocket in exchange for his keys.

The second item was a flyer taped to the door's frosted glass, featuring a photo of himself staring into the camera with a look of mild digestive discomfort. Right below, a bouncy font announced the talk he would be giving later that week, entitled: "New Non-Perturbative Results for Non-BPS Black Hole M-Brane Constructions in M-Theory." The lecture was part of a series of dry-run talks to be given in preparation for the International Conference on Particle Physics at the CERN laboratory in Switzerland in the new year. While standing above the world's largest particle accelerator, men and women like Philip could reveal the brilliant math they had been forging behind closed doors—mathematical physics attempting to answer the only question he and his colleagues found worth asking, the question that had eluded even Einstein: How do we unify the four forces of the universe into one law?

But at that moment, standing in front of his Caltech office of twenty-five years, looking at a photo of his visibly younger self, Philip didn't feel in a position to be answering questions about anything, let alone the nature of the universe. He squinted to read the small print at the bottom of the flyer, which told him that his lecture was that Wednesday at five fifteen. *Yes, right.* He would have to scramble to prepare something now, something that didn't make his research sound as if it had completely stalled. A conversation with his father would have helped spur him on, and the realization that he would never discuss anything with him again—would never pop into his father's old office in the Sloan Laboratory of Mathematics and Physics, just two buildings over—made him feel unbearably old.

Philip unlocked the door and, avoiding a pile of sympathy letters at his feet, stepped to the window for some air. He cranked open the fourth-story casement to reveal yet another cloudless day in paradise, the sun doggedly illuminating every speck of campus, every leaf on every olive tree. Philip had never quit marveling at how much intellectual power inhabited this 124-acre patch of Southern California. How anyone managed to ignore the swaying palms and raging light outside their windows long enough to have a single intelligent thought still mystified him. Give him a gloomy country—England, Sweden, Russia—and he'd show you a nation of busy scientists. Give him a balmy paradise, and he'd point to people finding every reason not to do theoretical physics. Caltech seemed to be the exception.

Rescuing the envelopes from the floor, he tore into each with a letter opener Jane had given him many years ago as a tenure gift. Ever the sentimentalist, she had had the knife inscribed with a small heart close to the blade, and Philip now found his thumb exploring the heart's delicate ridges and the sweet, if obvious, inscription: *You are my constant.*

He paused for a moment to take in a pair of official-looking goldenrod envelopes. Their strident color and government seals insisted that they be opened immediately, but there was a limit to the information he could take in right now. Philip opened a side drawer and dropped them inside.

Sifting through the sympathy cards, his eyes passed over the words *irreplaceable* and *adored*, and over names he knew well and those he recognized only dimly. But the words and phrases were just vacant syllables, incapable of conveying the true nature of any person, let alone his father. "He has left a great *blah blah*" . . . "If there's anything I can *blah*" . . . "He will be truly *shut the hell up*". . . "Never have I met a more *seriously, fuck off* . . ." Philip was trying to decide what to do with the letters when he remembered the envelope in his pocket. He pulled it out and stared at the spiraled brain again. The symbol suddenly seemed familiar. But from where?

He was about to pick up the knife again when Anitka Durov, a fourth-year grad student from Ukraine, appeared at his door. He didn't have to turn to know she was standing there; her voice was unmistakable. After however many years of living in the United States, she showed no signs of giving up her thick accent.

"Professor Severy, I wanted to say I'm very sorry for your loss," she said with a peculiar flatness, as if she were holding a tourist's phrase book just out of sight.

"Thank you," he managed.

"I was sorry we didn't get to talk at the service."

"I didn't realize you were there," he said, glancing up.

She smiled. "I met your father once. He was an incredible man."

"That he was."

"His exploratory work on highway systems was quite brilliant."

He started to clear a space in his desk for the letters as she continued. "This idea that traffic is a single, predictable organism rather than a bunch of separate objects?"

He threw her an impatient look. "If you'll excuse me, Anitka—"

"It's a bad time?"

"They do make me teach once in a while."

"Sure, I get it." She pivoted theatrically out of the room.

But as he gathered his material for the lecture, Philip could sense her lingering outside the door, waiting to ensnare him the instant he crossed the threshold. Anitka Durov was the last person he wanted to see at the moment, and not just because she had the strange power to unnerve him. She had become a departmental pest, an unpopular doctoral candidate who, after having completely rejected her original course of study, was now desperately hunting for a dissertation advisor. Her original advisor, Kimiko Kato, one of the top string theorists in the world, had emphatically refused to work with her, female solidarity aside. And now Philip had become Anitka's prime target, despite the fact that her intended thesis was in polar opposition to everything he stood for. She had formed a deep attachment to him after he had come to her rescue the previous spring in what became known across campus and the physics blogosphere as "the Durov Affair." Anitka Durov had, against all odds, pulled off one of the most improbable hoaxes in the history of scientific journals when she submitted a phony, pseudonymous paper on an underexplored question in string theory to the *European Review of Theoretical Physics*.

When the prank was discovered, as she had taken no real pains to hide its true authorship (apart from a fake author website easily traceable to her IP address), Anitka was promptly suspended. She fought the suspension aggressively, arguing that there had been a noble, twofold purpose to her hoax: first, to expose the flaws in the editorial review process of physics journals, and second, to humorously demonstrate (though none found it funny) the lack of scientific rigor in the string theory community at large. How was it, she asked, that after two weeks, only one reader had noticed anything wrong with her half-nonsensical paper?

It would have been one thing, the department felt, if she had simply submitted her paper to the online *arXiv*, where it could have been deleted or ignored, but to commit fraud to actual paper, in a real archival journal, was inexcusable. Yet Philip knew that the faculty's indignation had little to do with "serious scientific fraud," as the members so condemned it. The truth was far more personal. In nearly any other circumstance, they would have applauded the entire confidence trick, smugly congratulating themselves for being in on the joke. Anitka's name would have been bandied about at parties, praised at the blackboard, and waggishly cited in academic papers, but because she had lampooned the work of many distinguished theorists—going so far as to copy and paste verbatim from their papers to create a kind of humiliating pastiche—the targeted faculty were less inclined to find her stunt cute or admirable.

Philip was the only professor to come to Anitka's defense, calling her demonstration "reckless and stupid" but "ultimately carried out in the spirit of academic risk taking." After a few months of suspension and a warning from the department, Ms. Durov was permitted to continue her studies. But Anitka's reputation had been blighted by the whole episode, and now, as she was homing in on Philip as an advisor, he was regretting his former heroics.

He stepped into the hallway.

"Maybe we could talk later," Anitka suggested as he headed off to class.

"Why don't we catch up over email?"

"Or over a drink?"

"Uh . . ."

"Look, I don't mean to be pushy," she said, "but I need your thoughts on my dissertation."

"You've changed topics, then?"

"You know I haven't."

His chest rose and fell. "As I've said before, you'd be better served finding someone else—at this point, someone outside the school who might be of actual help to you."

"I'd like your opinion on some new ideas is all. No strings—" She swallowed the pun.

He was only half listening as he locked up his office. "Well, I can't talk before Friday."

After a small nod, he retreated down the hallway, expecting her to call after him, as was her habit. When she didn't, Philip turned around and was surprised to see her marching in the opposite direction. He watched her for a moment, his eyes involuntarily straying to the curve of a hip as she turned into the stairwell. He looked away, feeling a stitch of guilt as he realized how brusque he'd been with her. But how else to rid himself of a pest?

He checked his watch. In his rush to flee Anitka, he had given himself excess time to make it to class, which didn't start for another ten minutes. Philip ducked into the faculty lounge. Not being in the mood for departmental chitchat, he was pleased to find the kitchen deserted, but as he crossed the room, he noticed a colleague seated at a corner table, nose to the woodgrain, pencil scribbling. It was only Andrei Kuchek, and chitchat-wise he was harmless.

For as long as Philip had known Kuchek—as many papers as

they had coauthored as members of the department's string theory group—Philip was still made to feel like a stranger whenever he walked into a room where his friend was working. Kuchek was the classic specimen of a nearsighted, socially challenged academic: a man who devoured his work whole and avoided speaking to anyone unless absolutely necessary. For this, he was mercilessly, though affectionately, teased. Kuchek's own students routinely called him the Asp or Professor Aspy, which Philip had initially assumed was some unkind allusion to Kuchek's lean, snakelike appearance. Only later did someone inform him that *Asp* was short for *Asperger's*, a syndrome for which Kuchek seemed a strong candidate.

"Morning, Andrei."

No reply. Typical. It was the little game the two of them played, though Philip could never be sure that it wasn't entirely one-sided.

"Good to see you at the service, Andrei. Really, it meant a lot."

Nothing.

"How's the coffee this morning? . . . What's that, you say? Extraordinary?"

He was filling his mug with steamless coffee when he realized he was still holding the brain-spiral envelope in his other hand. He set down the coffeepot and, with a butter knife from the rack, slit open the envelope. On a single rectangle of white cardstock, in tidy penmanship, it read:

So sorry to hear of your father's passing. A truly monumental loss. I had been in touch with him regarding his recent research.

Please call. Whenever is convenient for you, naturally.

P. Booth Lyons
Government-Scholar Relations (GSR)

There was a phone number at the bottom, 703 area code. Wasn't that Virginia? *P. Booth Lyons.* Philip stared at the card for a long minute before he realized he had been holding his breath. Why the hell was P. Booth Lyons contacting him? His father had playfully referred to him as either "Phone Booth" or "that spook," because Lyons had been borderline harassing Isaac for years, dating back to his retirement. But it was all through letters, emails, and persistent voice messages from his secretary, which led Philip to believe that he was probably harmless. Though there had been one night, after Isaac found a note on his front door (that's why the brain-spiral seemed familiar), that Philip had briefly considered getting a restraining order so that his father might live out his emeritus years in peace.

The last time the subject had come up had been over a father-son lunch at the faculty dining hall, during which Philip had started to wonder about his father's mental stability. "Mr. Phone Booth is starting up again," his father had said over a chicken salad. "If I want to start my career as a mathematical spy, I guess now's my chance."

"Right."

"I'd kind of like to know what this Government-Scholar business is while I'm still alive. Should we go meet him?"

"I don't know, Dad. What happened the last time a bunch of mathematicians and physicists got together to help the government? Oh, right: somewhere in Asia, a quarter million people died because their skin melted off."

"Yes, yes, but how do we know that the 'Government' in 'Government-Scholar' is the US? He's never actually specified which government we're talking about."

"A con man hazy on specifics, huh? The man is harassing you. Let's not indulge him."

A frown from his father. "Have you always been this way? So staid and unadventurous?" Isaac was not generally a vicious man, but he continued, "I think this tranquilized attitude of yours is enfeebling your mind and your work. I keep up with everything you're doing, Philip, and frankly . . ."

In that second, he wished his father really were battling senility, because that would hurt less than the alternative.

"Dad, stop with the dramatics, please. We're allowed to have fallow periods. As you well know."

Isaac Severy famously didn't have fallow periods, yet Philip watched his face for a sign that he had hit the mark. It had been years since his father shared what he was working on. Philip had stolen early glances at his father's traffic equation, but when pressed on it, Isaac would evade all inquiry, saying only that the mathematics wasn't ready.

This time, Isaac had looked away, avoiding his son's eyes for the rest of the meal.

"If you're not careful, Philip, you'll have brain rot. Just like your brother."

It was then that Philip had started to suspect that his father's latest work, whatever it was, was only a mirage.

He abandoned the unpleasant memory and took one more gulp of coffee before leaving the faculty lounge.

"Yeah, see you round," he told Kuchek.

Philip took a final glance at the note. *I had been in touch with him regarding his recent research.* Oh, really? And what research would that be? The topology of the geriatric brain? The calculus of killing yourself in a whirlpool bath? Philip flirted with the idea of calling the 703 number. "Hello, Mr. Lyons? Yes, I'm familiar with my father's work, and I find it unlikely that it would be of use to anyone, let alone government scholars and their relations. Good-bye." Still, a worm of curiosity had worked its way into his brain, and Philip wondered if his father had really been serious about contacting this man. And if so, why. He made a mental note to check his father's study for anything unusual, and his old campus office while he was at it. Then he slipped the card in his pocket, put on his best Advanced-Topics-in-Supersymmetry face, and made his way to the lecture hall.

7

Headquarters

Hazel had been sitting on the steps outside LAPD headquarters for twenty minutes when she heard someone laughing. She turned to find Detective E. J. Kenley standing behind her, the woman's trim figure framed in the entryway.

"You homeless now, or did your brother stand you up?"

Hazel smiled, stood to greet the towering detective, and was pulled into a vigorous embrace.

"We're supposed to be getting lunch at Langer's," Hazel said. "It's the only place that doesn't make him gag."

"Right. What's that thing he likes to say?"

"I'll eat when I'm dead?"

"Dumbest thing I've ever heard," E. J. said, laughing again. "He's out on a case, but you're welcome to loiter upstairs."

Hazel followed the detective through security, where she flashed a badge that read MYP in large letters. Minority Youth in Peril was E. J.'s pet project. Years ago, she had gotten fed up seeing her "little brothers and sisters" disappear quietly into the shadows while the clockwork of the media snapped into atomic precision any time a blond girl from the suburbs vanished. "Want to get away with kidnapping?" E. J. had once asked in a letter to the *Los Angeles Times*. "Snatch up a black kid from the Jordan Downs projects and watch the ice-floe reflexes of the press. But so much as touch a towheaded girl in Utah, and the entire world yanks out its hair in collective anguish."

The elevator opened onto the third floor, and they started down a modernist corridor flooded with natural light. When Hazel had last visited her brother at work, the building had still been relatively new, smelling of paint and freshly rolled carpet. Now the carpet shone with the steps of countless heels, and the pumpkin-colored walls seemed to belong to another era.

"I was sorry to hear about Isaac," E. J. said as the spacious hall gave way to the hive of the main office. "I know he was like a father to you both. You want some coffee? Let's get some coffee."

Hazel trailed her through the belly of the Juvenile Protection Unit, catching glimpses of what her brother had to face every day. What appeared at first to be your average corporate office—everything Hazel had tried to escape in life: grids of fluorescents, watercoolers, inspirational posters—had, upon closer inspection, a more chilling quality. A desk detective scrubbed through digital footage of a teenage girl curled on a couch sobbing, while an adjacent screen featured a toddler's legs blighted with hash marks.

"Waffle iron," E. J. whispered.

"God, you're kidding," Hazel said, her hand instinctively moving to an old scar on the side of her neck. She fingered its long, petal-shaped groove, hardly aware she was doing it.

As E. J. continued down the hall, Hazel paused at a strip of corkboard lined with pictures of men, young and old. Their eyes all held the same exhaustion, the same depleted look of lives spent by turns fighting and giving in to dark impulse. A few of the photographs had a red masking-taped *K* covering the face.

"That's how we mark the dead ones," E. J. explained. "For karma."

"Karma?"

"Late last year, this scumbag's working on his truck, gets gasoline on his clothes. Later, he starts fiddling with the gas water heater and—*whoosh!*—the pilot light turns him into a human torch. A neighbor saw everything, but by the time she got her bony ass to the phone, it was all over. Some people here like to call that karma, or the universe having its way. I call it plain spooky."

Hazel didn't want to think about the universe having its way with people, scumbag or not. She didn't want to think of Isaac in that tub with those string lights.

E. J. ushered her into a break room and poured two mugs of coffee.

Hazel took one. "I don't get how you can, you know—"

"Come to work every day?"

"Yeah."

"You disconnect a little, make it a scavenger hunt. You go crazy otherwise."

"And my brother?"

E. J. laughed for no apparent reason. "You'll have to ask him."

After a few polite questions about Hazel's life, E. J. pointed her toward Gregory's cubicle by the far windows. She then excused herself to resume her search for the missing Jasmines and Jamals of Los Angeles.

From her brother's desk, Hazel could see the gleaming spire of city hall across the street. Mercifully, there was no evidence of distressed children in the immediate area, just nostalgic prints of LA architecture along one wall—including Union Station, its Art Deco interior overlaid with the image of a sleek train. Her brother's desk was austere, save for a small photo of Lewis and a coffee mug featuring a math geek's coy declaration of love: $\sqrt{-1}$ <3 μ. It had been Isaac's gift to Gregory at an age when a boy can still be anything, when his brain has not yet run up against its own border checkpoints.

Before Hazel knew what she was doing, she began opening his desk drawers. She was snooping, of course, yet her body seemed to know this before she did. It felt like she'd been craving this the entire trip: a moment that might illuminate her brother's increasingly detached behavior, because God forbid she confront him herself. Most of the desk was locked, except for the center-left drawer, which opened to reveal a stack of folders. The folder on top, with its illustration of a butterfly, seemed out of place, like something you'd see in a girl's backpack.

When Hazel flipped back the cover, the contents looked deadly boring: financial printouts of some kind. She shifted her attention to the blue folder below it. Inside was a small stack of long-lens photographs, all of a man with close-cropped white hair and sunglasses. Most of the images showed him walking, waiting at bus stops, or reaching into trash cans. Someone, presumably Gregory, had jotted times and cross streets in the margins. The man seemed familiar, but maybe it was because he reminded her of the men she'd just seen on the wall. How strange her brother's life was, creeping after creeps, stalking the stalkers. She wasn't sure what made her more uncomfortable: the man himself or Gregory's surveillance of him. She closed the folder quickly and slipped it back into place.

She was about to do the same with the butterfly folder, when she spotted Isaac's name in the corner of a page. On closer inspection, she realized the printouts were her grandfather's bank statements. Highlighted in yellow, at one-month intervals, were withdrawals of $2,700 in cash. The statements went on for pages and pages, years back, and every month the same withdrawal. A sticky note on the second page read: *Let's talk?—Fritz.*

Hazel noticed a Xerox machine a few desks away. But just as she had the thought to dash off some copies, Gregory's voice drifted from down the corridor. She put back the folder and struck a pose at the window, as if she were having one last look at the city before returning home.

Her brother seemed annoyed as they headed outside to the parking lot. She made a few comments about E. J., how nice it was to see her again, but he only grunted. "Must be fun being a detective," she almost added, but reminded herself that policing the wheel of abuse that trundled eternally through the generations could hardly be a good time. Then again, from her perspective, sleuthing around LA seemed preferable to returning to a demeaning existence up north.

And there it was again, the feeling that had been sneaking up on her all day: she didn't want to go home. Or was afraid to. The sense of something left dangerously unfinished nagged at her, as if Isaac's letter might haunt her like a paper ghost. But she had a life to get back to. Bennet had been a bit aloof lately, sure, but if she took a frank look at her own behavior, *she* was the one putting up emotional blockades. She hadn't even told him she was living in her store, so how could she rely on him if she couldn't even manage a basic level of honesty? They were supposed to be each other's safe house, but she wondered if, in their twenty-two months together, that had ever materialized in any real way. Even her bookstore wasn't the sanctuary it had once been. So if not her store or her boyfriend, then what was she going back for? *Stop it*, she told herself. *You can't abandon your life because it's hard. Make it work, love your boyfriend, save your business. Buck the hell up.*

As they climbed into Gregory's Honda, Hazel idly wondered if she should install a camping shower in the bookstore bathroom. She'd be digging through trash cans next, like that sad man. And those bank statements—she could certainly use $2,700 a month herself. She felt slightly guilty for having snooped, but if the statements were important enough for Fritz to make copies, why hadn't Gregory let her in on it?

When they were turning onto the freeway for the airport, Gregory cleared his throat. "I guess I screwed up lunch, huh?"

She nodded. "Say good-bye to cream sodas and hot pastrami on rye."

The invocation of a Langer's deli sandwich—the best in the city—did nothing for her food-indifferent brother. She changed the subject and asked him about work, but all she got out of him was "There's a lot of field stuff lately. It's good to get out of the office."

She gave him a sideways glance, wanting more than ever to tell him about the letter, to bring him into the fold.

"Remember Isaac's typewriter?" she blurted.

Gregory was focused on making the next exit. "Of course."

"The one with the sticky keys?"

"Sure, not that it ever stopped him from using it."

"Isaac had it fixed."

"I know."

Hazel turned. "You know?"

"I fixed it."

"When?"

"A couple years ago. I tried to fix it long before that, actually, when I was at Claremont. An engineering professor asked us to repair a broken machine for our final exam. The math thing wasn't working out, and I wanted to impress Isaac, I guess." Her brother's expression soured, as it often did when he hit on the topic of mathematics. "I took the whole thing apart but only made it worse and almost failed the class. So about two years ago, I thought I'd redeem myself."

After a pause, he asked, "Why?"

"No, it's just . . . nothing." An idea was forming in her mind.

"I guess I've never really lived down those four years," he continued. "It only made things worse that my name was Severy. May as well have been Hawking or Kepler."

"Please, Eggs," she said, invoking her old nickname for him, chosen for the bratty reason that her brother disliked eggs, and it vaguely rhymed with his name. "You have to be a genetic freak to be a Severy. A person has the same chances of being born a Bolshoi ballerina or an albino—"

"Not all mathematicians are freaks," he interrupted. This was an old argument of his. "Some just have a head start in life."

"Well, you've turned into a fine detective," she said, changing the subject. "Not to mention an excellent typewriter repairman—it works perfectly now."

He frowned. "So you were using it?"

"Oh," she said, stalling. "I was poking around his office and took it out to play with. Nostalgia, I guess."

"Anything else of interest?"

But his question seemed far away, muffled, because a more compelling question now demanded her attention: If Gregory fixed the typewriter years ago, why were there mistakes in Isaac's letter? The answer came to her in an instant, as if Isaac had whispered it into her ear. *"Because the mistakes were intentional, my dear."*

Hazel tapped at her window urgently. "Can you pull over here? Bathroom break."

"We're blocks from the airport."

"I really have to go."

Gregory sighed and cut across a lane. He pulled into a McDonald's parking lot while Hazel searched for Isaac's letter through the pockets of a ridiculous rolling bag that Bennet had given her, her initials stamped conspicuously across the front. Tucking the letter in her purse, she made her way to the overcooled McDonald's bathroom. She unfolded the note on top of a hand dryer and, with a pen, examined the lines carefully, underlining all words with redundant letters, including the stuttering comma:

```
, , ,
theeee
Cottte d'Azurrr
onn
pleassantt
offf (of)
ttthe
SSShore
```

"The Côte d'Azur on pleasant of the shore," she muttered. It was almost a sentence, but it didn't sound like much of a clue or directive. Côte d'Azur—"coast of blue"—the French Riviera. She hoped he wasn't sending her on a European treasure hunt. He couldn't expect her to go jetting around, digging holes along the Mediterranean. She tried rearranging the words: "On the shore of the pleasant Côte d'Azur . . ."

Hazel startled herself by setting off the hand dryer, and it was at that moment that something about the words clicked. A smile spread across her face, and she laughed out loud. She refolded the paper, slid it into her purse, and practically ran back to the car.

"Everything all right?" Gregory asked. But she could see that his concern was forced, the muscles of his jaw working to contain his irritation. "It's been, like, fifteen minutes."

"I know. Sorry."

She climbed in, rapidly thinking of an excuse not to get on that plane. She apologized again and found herself saying that she'd left her wallet at the house. She would have to reschedule her flight.

"Brilliant. You have a ride tomorrow?"

"I'll figure something out. I'm really sorry."

Gregory made several sharp turns until they were headed back north on La Cienega Boulevard. Hazel adopted the frustrated expression of a traveler who's just left her ID at home, but to herself, she silently recited the first line to one of her favorite books, F. Scott Fitzgerald's *Tender Is the Night*—the first eight words of which Isaac had planted in his note expressly for her to find:

On the pleasant shore of the French Riviera, about half way between Marseilles and the Italian border, stands a large, proud, rose-colored hotel.

Almost immediately, her shiver of delight at having cracked her grandfather's puzzle turned to a small, quaking fear. Now that she could see Isaac was leading her somewhere, how could she let go of his hand?

As they eased their way up the switchbacks of the canyon, their cousin Alex came into view, striding long-legged down the hill, cuffs in the dust, camera slung across his chest.

"Is he looking to get hit?" Gregory asked.

As if taking the hint, Alex turned toward a clearing between houses, where a set of communal steps led to the bottom of the hill.

Hazel rolled down her window. "Shouldn't we stop?"

Gregory hit the brakes just as Alex's head was about to vanish below the staircase. Hazel called out to him, her voice tremulous and strange in her own ears.

He spun around, and when he saw her, he smiled. "Hello, Hazel." But as he approached the car and saw who was driving, his smile retreated. "Oh, hey, Greg . . . ory."

"We thought you'd left," Gregory said. "Where is it you live again? France?"

Alex didn't answer but said, "Did you hear what happened? Drew became very sick this afternoon."

Gregory pulled the parking brake. "Is she all right?"

"Yes, but Sybil was in hysterics. I don't know the details, actually. I'm sure you'll hear all about it."

"So you're leaving?" Hazel asked.

Alex shifted his weight. "About that. I'd prefer you didn't mention that you saw me on the road. I sort of slipped away after my mother arrived. Kind of horrible, I know, but we're not exactly close. It looks a bit weird, you understand, my abandoning the family in a time of crisis and all that. Anyway, I'd appreciate it."

"We didn't see you," Hazel agreed.

Alex looked at her for a steady moment, and she looked back. She had never liked beards on men, but Alex's didn't bother her. Maybe it was because he wasn't trying to make a statement but looked as if he genuinely couldn't be bothered to shave. Gregory put the car into gear, signaling an end to the conversation, and before she had a chance to say good-bye, they were pulling away. Alex looked after them for a few seconds before spinning around and resuming his descent. As she watched him disappear in the side-view mirror, she had the feeling that if she were to see him again, it would be from this same angle, as if he were never in the process of arriving but always heading off to somewhere far more important.

"Doesn't he have a job?" asked Gregory.

"He's a photographer, remember?"

"That's not a job. Maybe it used to be back when it was a real skill."

Her brother's sulkiness had clearly curdled into a bad mood. She wondered what he would make of Bennet's latest photo installation.

"What's he doing at the house, anyway?" Gregory added.

A squad car passed them on its way down the hill, and as they pulled up to the house, they found an ambulance in the drive.

"Jesus," he said. "Paramedics?"

Words came back to Hazel from the letter: *Three will die. I am the first.* She felt shaky as she stepped from the car.

In cool defiance of the crisis, the Severy twins stood on the grass with their racquets, attacking a fusillade of balls erupting from a mechanical nozzle. The machine had been a present from Isaac. "If you want to win at any one thing," Hazel remembered him saying, "you must do that thing more times than anyone else. Winning is aggregation." Had she also heard him say "Death comes in threes"? Or was she making that up? She and her brother stepped over the grass, ducking to avoid a stray ball. Their uncle was on the porch, leaning against a column and smoking a cigarette.

"I didn't know Philip smoked," Hazel whispered.

Philip frowned deeply, regarding them with only a flicker of interest. It was a look Hazel had seen directed at her many times, as if his mind were in a place she couldn't possibly grasp. Still, she couldn't help being fond of him, even if it was in a distant, admiring sort of way.

Ignoring their cousin's request, Gregory announced immediately, "We saw Alex on the road. He says Drew's sick?"

Philip crushed out his cigarette on the railing and lit another.

"She ate a poisonous seed, but not nearly enough of it. She threw it up and seems to be fine now. We're not thrilled the paramedics called the police. It only upset Sybil."

"Procedure, I'm afraid, to protect the child," Gregory said.

"I'm sure, but when they realized that a curious kid had merely taken plant identification a little too far, they left."

Hazel cast a glance at a nearby bush. "It wasn't the castor bean, was it? Lily warned us about those."

"No, thank God." Philip's eyes widened for a second. "It was the *Mirabilis californica*, also known as the four o'clock plant. Which, it seems"—he looked at his watch—"is the time now."

They followed their uncle to the living room, where Drew, looking flushed as if with fever, sat at a window seat bundled in blankets. A stuffed toy unicorn, its fur still factory white, was propped on the sill. Sybil, Jack, and Jane sat around her, while two paramedics conferred nearby. Though Alex had mentioned his mother was here, Hazel was still surprised to see Paige—who rarely made family appearances unless forced—on an ottoman in the corner, looking like she might bolt at any moment.

"It was a speck, Gramma," Drew was saying. "A speck of a speck of a speck—"

"I know," interrupted Jane, "but a speck of a speck of poison is still poison, and you can't do that ever again."

"Oh, don't let us all pretend she didn't know what she was doing," Paige muttered. "She eats up the attention." Either no one heard Hazel's aunt, or they chose to ignore her.

"Well," Sybil said, "Drew won't be reading any more Audubon guides until she's much older."

"But I still have the bird book," the girl said.

"There might be poisonous birds, how should I know?"

"Poisonous birds." Drew snorted. "With fangs!"

"Well, she seems to be in good spirits," Philip said, crossing the room to tousle his granddaughter's hair. "Although maybe if you gave her something to engage her mind instead of toy unicorns, she wouldn't go experimenting in the garden."

"Please, Dad, not now," Sybil said.

Hazel stood mutely at the edge of the group. She was relieved Drew was all right but mostly glad she had missed the worst of it. There was only so much Severy drama she could take in one trip. Besides, something about having all the family in one room—minus Isaac—made her feel decisively locked out, like a perpetual interloper. She was wondering if her brother felt the same when she turned to find him gone from the room. Her need to flee back to Seattle returned, but it was immediately followed by the invisible tug of Isaac asking her to stay—or, rather, her grandfather pulling her toward a particular spot in the room.

As the family continued to chatter among themselves, Hazel slipped to the opposite end of the living room where a large imitation Honoré Daumier painting of Don Quixote hung. It had been a present from Isaac to his wife many years ago, on the day her *Don Quixote* translation had been published. He had chosen the famous vertical of the knight riding his bony white nag, his lance held skyward at a slight angle. Isaac had hung it in such a way so that the weapon pointed to a shelf of Lily's translations.

It was the same bookshelf that held the vast majority of her grandparents' fiction library. Hazel climbed the stepladder, grateful that they had taken the trouble to alphabetize, and ran her finger along the spines. From a spot where a Fitzgerald volume should have been, she pulled a placeholder photo of teenage Philip and Tom: shaggy hair, short shorts, both standing obediently at the edge of the Grand Canyon. The photo was most certainly an oversight on Isaac's part, as nearly all reminders of his younger son had been relegated to a box somewhere. She could hardly bear to look at Tom's face, and after reading the back—"*This Side of Paradise* borrowed by ??"—she returned the brothers to their place. She was heartened to find *Tender Is the Night* a couple of spaces down. Tugging it from its spot, she noted that it was Scribner's facsimile of the original 1934 hardcover, in good shape, too, despite the fact it was missing its original clamshell box. She had sold one just like it in her own store for a handsome price after buying it for pennies at an estate sale. Part of the charm of this printing was its slew of minor errors, most notably the extra z in *schizzoid* on page 199. (Had Fitzgerald been similarly cursed with a disobedient typewriter?)

She flipped past the front matter to the first line of the first chapter: *On the pleasant shore of the French Riviera . . .* But there was nothing there to find. No scribble from her grandfather, no applause for her cleverness or hint of what she was supposed to do next. Hazel fought back disappointment as she searched through the rest of the book and found only a couple of impromptu bookmarks—one a scuffed gift card for the store Book Circus, the other a Polaroid of Isaac listing all the prime numbers, 2 through 47, on a bathroom mirror in red marker. His head was turned from the camera, his reflected eyes smeared behind 29 and 31, yet she could still sense his playful smile. As she stared at the image, she realized that what she really wanted to discover was not another clue, but a more personal message. She wanted him to reassure her, not just in this specific quest but in her life. *"Don't worry, you are in the right place, doing the right thing."*

After taking one last look at the photo, she deferred to tradition and slipped it into the now-empty space on the shelf. She was stepping down the ladder, book in hand, when Paige shouted, "Looting his shelves already? How much do you think you'll fetch for that one?" She laughed to let everyone know it was a joke, but it didn't sound like one to Hazel, who imagined throwing the volume at her aunt's head with such force that the woman would topple backward off her seat, eyes wide, limbs clutching the air.

"Hundred bucks. Maybe more," Hazel shot back.

"That's where your Audubon book belongs: on a top shelf where your paws can't reach it," Jack told his daughter.

Drew sat up suddenly. "Has anyone seen my new cousin, Alex?"

A few eyes turned to Paige, but her mouth was drawn tight.

"I heard he left," Philip said.

"No!" Drew shouted, transforming quickly into the five-year-old she was. "Alex? Are you here?"

Drew's sudden enthusiasm for a relative whom she hadn't known existed three days ago incited a round of laughter.

Hazel started to back out of the room when her brother reappeared. "Did you find your wallet?"

"Yeah. I mean, I know where I left it."

Slipping into the kitchen before he could question her further, she stood at the counter, staring at the book in her hands, suddenly fearing a reversion to her former state of purposelessness. Could there, in fact, be a message from Isaac hidden somewhere in the novel as there had been in the letter? Then again, weren't people always finding secret messages in the Bible, the Constitution, Shakespeare? Look hard enough for ciphered meaning, and you'll find it?

Hazel closed her eyes and riffled the pages with her thumb, as if the book were a deck of cards. It was an old trick of hers; whenever she felt stuck, she would use any available book as a kind of oracle. It was a game, but one she played with a straight face. She stopped her thumb and let the volume fall open. She slid her finger down the left page, stopped, and opened her eyes, ready to take the given words as prophecy. But there were no words under her finger, only one of the many crosshatched pencil illustrations scattered throughout the book. The image was so dramatic, she almost laughed. A man lay dead on a train platform, his luggage piled around him. At the edge of the frame, an anonymous gloved hand gripped a still-smoking revolver.

8

The Other Severy

The next day, the sun shone garish and bright in a cloudless sky. From his car parked down the street, Gregory monitored the guests trickling out the front door of Hollywood's Harvard Hotel. As he watched dreary faces pass under a faded letter *H*, he thought back to Hazel's strange behavior the previous day. There had always been something slightly impulsive about his sister, as if she were obeying a set of irrational edicts given only to her. He wasn't entirely surprised, for instance, that she couldn't keep a business afloat. But yesterday she'd seemed particularly off, almost as if she sensed something was bothering him, and that the something was Tom. But even if she had somehow guessed—she could be alarmingly perceptive, it was true—she could never envision what Gregory might be planning.

He returned his attention to the hotel, remembering something Fritz had said about one of Isaac's metaphors: the universe as massive computer, continuously determining its next moves. It had been Isaac's life ambition to tap into this computer, and Gregory imagined his grandfather's mathematics now calculating the entire rhythm of Los Angeles—who would live, who would fall ill, and who would step out the front door of a hotel and meet his demise. What if Isaac's universe-sized analogy was, in fact, a true description of how the world worked? Didn't this giant mainframe relieve the burden of calculation from the individual? If so, would Gregory ever be responsible for what he did next?

The double doors of the hotel opened again, and two men emerged. The first was of no interest to him: Hispanic, inked barbwire curling up his limbs. The second man was the object of Gregory's surveillance: tidy in a white T-shirt and jeans, cloaked behind dark wayfarer sunglasses. He gripped a small duffel, which Gregory knew held gym clothes, a thermos, a water-logged notebook, and a blue Bic pen. There would also be a plastic lunch sack and a migraine medication of fickle efficacy.

The Harvard Hotel on Harvard Boulevard was not a hotel, of course, but a halfway house for former inmates. Like most residences of its kind, it maintained a low profile in order to keep families in the neighborhood from coalescing into pesky committees bent on their banishment. Criminals have to live somewhere, but why did Tom Severy have to live within five miles of Gregory's house?

As he had done on the previous five days, he held his breath when Tom came into view. His former foster dad was pale and light-eyed like Philip and Paige, and when blasted with the autumn sun, he squinted in the familiar way. He was remarkably toned—by Severy standards, anyway—and his once emaciated body had a wiry compactness. The stress of a twenty-year prison term, however, was apparent. His hair had gone white, and his skin clung red and tired to his face. His entire body pitched forward, with a slight hitch to his stride. It wasn't quite a limp, but it was on its way.

Gregory stepped from his car and into the shade of a ficus tree, though he needn't have worried about being seen. Tom's eyesight was terrible. Yet he couldn't rid himself of the idea that the man he had once called his father somehow detected his presence, was expecting him even. Tom had been wise enough not to make an appearance at his own father's funeral—Gregory had dutifully monitored the crowd that day, prepared for such an occurrence—and as far as he could figure, Tom had no way of knowing what he and Hazel currently looked like. Gregory was vigilant about keeping images of himself and his family off the internet. Even if Tom did notice that he was being watched or got close enough to make out his face, he would hardly recognize his onetime foster son. The last time they had seen each other had been in a courtroom. Gregory had just turned twelve.

Tom made his way east to the Metro station at Hollywood and Western. Gregory tailed him into the tunnel below, and when Tom boarded the Red Line for downtown, Gregory chose a seat one car over. Given the immediate surroundings, he might have been in New York or London, except that the LA Metro felt oddly sanitary; there simply weren't enough freaks and foul smells to put it at the level of a thoroughly used rail system. At Pershing Square Station, Tom exited the train and emerged into the sun.

His first stop was a nonprofit health club a few blocks from the station, where he would spend an hour on the second floor while Gregory waited at a deli across the street. Under his watch, Tom hadn't missed a day at this miserable little gym. Gregory supposed that aerobic and weight-bearing exercise was a carryover from prison—a healthy alternative, perhaps, to Tom's self-medicating of years past.

After his workout, hair slick from the shower, Tom would walk a block to the Central Library. There, he would make his way through the grand rotunda to the reference section, where he would pore over medical textbooks, face inches from the page, scribbling notes until closing. The two times Gregory had managed to walk behind Tom unnoticed, he caught sight of bizarre photographs: all varieties of screwdrivers and chopsticks being thrust into patients' eye sockets. Gregory wondered if it was the lobotomy's potential for pain alleviation that interested Tom. Had the pain really gotten to the point where an ice pick through the head was the only option left? But then if Gregory had found himself in the tiny minority of migraine sufferers for whom medication was useless, wouldn't he, too, fantasize about extreme prefrontal surgery?

At the end of his studies, Tom would take the train back north, sometimes stopping off at a Ralphs grocery before returning to his room by curfew. As far as Gregory could make out, Tom was not looking for a job, and he didn't imagine that the gate check issued to him at Lancaster State Prison would last him very long. Would Tom eventually contact his brother or sister for money? Or would his pride win out?

The only indication that Tom was conscious of money was his habit of peeking into trash bins along his route and tossing soda cans into a plastic sack. To keep the sack from filling up too quickly, he sometimes lined up the empties in front of the back wheels of an idling city bus. When the bus pulled away, he would crouch at the curb to collect his neatly flattened disks. Gregory often imagined, instead of crushed aluminum, Tom's flattened skull on the blacktop—or Tom caught under a bus and dragged for miles, the asphalt flaying the skin from his body.

Sometimes Gregory would wince at the brutality of his own imaginings. He would picture Isaac looking down on him, seeing in his omniscience the violent imagery in his grandson's head. But then Isaac would have to appreciate that these images were out of his control, that they possessed a weight and momentum all their own, like a steel ball gathering speed on a sharp grade. All Gregory could do was stand back and watch the physics in his head play out.

It was already past noon when Gregory settled into a library carrel to keep an eye on Tom. He had just opened a coffee table book on lost LA landmarks when a text came through from the woman who was not his wife:

I need to see you.

His glad heart thumped as he quickly replied:

When.

After he had stared at his phone for several minutes, waiting for her response, he looked back down at a double-page photo spread of the original Brown Derby on Wilshire Boulevard. The now-demolished restaurant had been built in the shape of a colossal bowler hat, and he wondered if he would forever associate this ridiculous building with the joyous anticipation he now felt.

A second text came through, but this one spoiled his mood: it was from E. J., asking where he'd been all morning. She was entering her mother-hen mode at the office, monitoring detectives' comings and goings, and generally making herself a nuisance—as if she had already promoted herself to captain. He would have to continue his vigil another day. But just as Gregory stood up, he saw Tom close the book he was reading and stride in his direction. Panic coursed through him.

He knows.

There was a dormant need in him to meet Tom halfway, to wrest the Bic from his hand and jam it into an eye cavity, and deeper into the tissue of his brain, until Tom screamed and stopped screaming. Because the man didn't deserve this untroubled postprison retirement; he deserved upper-limit pain. He deserved to have cheap blue ink bleeding from his awful rabbit eyes. But Gregory remained in his seat and watched Tom head to a neighboring shelf. He let his body relax, and before Tom had a chance to turn around again and possibly get a good look at the person who had been following him for a solid week, Gregory collapsed the image of the Brown Derby and left the library.

9

The Secretary

On the morning of his advertised lecture, Philip woke with the image of a spiraled brain tumbling through his mind. He sat up, and when he was lucid enough to recall what the image signified, he remembered that he still needed to search his father's study. The drama yesterday with Drew had prevented him from conducting a thorough search, but now he had a more pressing worry: his lecture. The lecture in which he would reveal to his entire department his profound lack of new ideas. Perhaps he could dislodge some paltry insights from his mind before breakfast. But as he switched on a lamp and reached for a notebook from the night table, he felt a sudden pressure behind his left eye. It was a sensation that would start to unfurl and pulse, and within twenty minutes, if he didn't take his meds, it would feel as if his brain were being pushed through a juicer. He stood up, the resulting pain forcing him to grab hold of the headboard.

"Jane?"

But he knew Jane was gone. Having dropped the twins at school, she was likely on her morning run, a brutal course of murderous inclines that she enjoyed enough to repeat in the evenings.

Philip sat for a moment and closed his eyes. His migraines were mostly on the livable end of the spectrum—essentially, fierce headaches with the occasional flash of light that presaged the pain. Or like today, the creeping sensation of a phantom hemorrhage. At least his brain responded to the triptans his doctor prescribed. He didn't suffer as his father had—or, worse, his brother. Poor Tom, afflicted with the kind of pain that made you wish you were dead: the hallucinatory, vomiting, nail-gun-to-the-cortex kind, with medicine offering so little relief. A migraine specialist had once confided to Philip, "When it's really bad, and the treatments don't take, I've had patients try to kill themselves." It hadn't come to that for Tom, but it might as well have.

Smoking yesterday had been a mistake. Philip had fallen back on his old ritual of purchasing a shiny red pack of Dunhills. It wasn't just the Drew episode that had rattled him but the hostility coming from his daughter. His unfortunate comment about Drew's toy unicorn had later ruptured into a full-blown argument, though it was really a rerun of a quarrel they'd had before. Philip had tried to apologize, but Sybil made clear that she'd had enough of his and the entire family's superiority. "So it's a cute little unicorn and not a chemistry set, so what? Not everything has to be supersmart all the time!" she had cried, threatening to stay in Beachwood Canyon for the rest of their trip. Philip sighed. He would have to make things right with her before they left town.

He needed his pills, but the only movement he could manage was to turn off the bedside lamp and lean back against the headboard. He would just rest a minute. In the dark, he could see one of Sybil's creations on the wall above the bureau: *Broken Shoe #1*. However much he disliked the piece, however much it conjured up the creaking meat rotisserie of his daughter's mind, for some reason he couldn't look away. Philip had little sense of how much time had passed when Jane appeared in the room. He could just make out her disciplined runner's figure against the light from the hall. She held out a single pill and a glass of water. "How long have you been sitting here?"

He gulped it down. "No idea."

He put down the glass and pushed his face into her stomach. The thought of pulling down her spandex was less a solid desire than the memory of desire. He was still able to enjoy her beauty and admire her graceful shape, but lately he found it difficult to locate his own lust. He wondered if anything was capable of inspiring strong feelings in him ever again. It was as if his work and sex drive were in collusion.

"Oh, I can't make your lecture today," she said, as she moved to the closet. "I promised I'd take Drew to the zoo."

"You don't have to come to my lectures, you know."

"I do like to keep up with what you're doing," she said faintly. Philip knew that his wife's interest in his work had become generalized long ago. She still enjoyed the idea of it, still took pride in informing strangers that her husband was a hotshot string theorist, but she no longer cared about the details. Maybe she sensed there was very little to know these days, because all his work worth knowing about had been completed more than a decade ago. He was now an aging professor whose best ideas were behind him, whose office was being eyed daily by younger and younger theorists.

Intelligence fades. Sex fades. The thrill fades. Where is all the wisdom that is supposed to compensate for the loss? But if his father's death had taught him anything, it was that there was no real wisdom with age, only forced compliance.

As Philip strode to the overhead projector to begin his talk on "New Non-Perturbative Results for Non-BPS Black Hole M-Brane Constructions in M-Theory," he took in the practically empty room.

Putting on his best arch smile, he quipped, "I hear John Britton is giving a lecture next door."

The small audience erupted in laughter, knowing full well that Britton—the closest the world currently had to an Albert Einstein—was ensconced in his turret office somewhere in Princeton. Whenever Philip heard the man's name (or uttered it himself), he would sink a little. It was hard enough to have an actual father you could let down without also having a string theory father to remind you that you weren't nearly as brilliant as you thought you were. In addition to Britton, there seemed to be a growing file of these monster minds, all shaking their heads in Philip's direction. *You vere such a clever boy. You vere going to solve the mysteries of the universe, remember?*—Was that a German accent? Was his imagination really falling back on Einstein as a taunt? Though it could just as easily have been Erwin Schrödinger or Werner Heisenberg. Maybe this is where he would have his meltdown, at last. Right here at this decrepit overhead projector. *You should have seen it! Professor Severy just sort of disintegrated in 151 Sloan.*

With the apparition of dead geniuses hovering, he took a deep breath and focused on the black-hole mathematics scribbled in front of him. There was comfort in his black holes. These sinkholes in space-time were plentiful in the observable universe, commonplace even to astronomers. But for string theorists like him, they were precious hives of higher-dimensional objects—branes—that could help solve the quantum mysteries of the cosmos. After ten minutes, he found a comfortable rhythm, glancing up once in a while between equations to catch his colleagues Kuchek and Kato scrunching their brows and taking spasmodic notes. The only person without a pen in hand was Anitka. She wore a tight, fuzzy peach sweater and watched him with a small smile that seemed to say, "Your determination is adorable, but you're making fatal assumptions. There's going to be a revolution, you'll see, and I'll be leading it." Maybe she was right, and this was just some giddy mathematical game they'd all agreed to play. Beautiful math signifying nothing.

There were no follow-up questions, and after an uneven round of applause, the hall emptied. Philip left the room, expecting Anitka to jump him when he reached the door, but when he stepped into the hallway, he was greeted instead by a woman balancing on a towering pair of heels and gripping a shiny black case. Clearly not a student, though not faculty, either. She crinkled her eyes in an attempt at a smile.

"I apologize for barging in late like that."

"Quite all right. I didn't notice."

The woman's dark red hair spiraled to her shoulders, and she wore a slightly militaristic navy suit, the kind that made Philip imagine she had a dozen more like it in her closet at home. He saw that she was attractive in a pointy, secretarial sort of way, but she had blunted any middle-aged prettiness with a large pair of harlequin glasses.

"It's fascinating, this idea that everything is made up of tiny vibrating strings of energy," she said, head pitched slightly to one side.

"Well, yes, that's what we're hoping to prove."

"Funny, I didn't hear you say the word *string* once in there—just a lot about branes, branes, branes."

"I'll try better next time."

Philip was wondering if he was about to be suckered into explaining his work to an inquisitive dilettante, when she stuck out her hand. "Nellie Stone. I work for Mr. Lyons."

"Lyons." Caught off guard, he took her hand. "You work for P. Booth Lyons?"

"That's right. He sent me to make sure you received his note."

"Maybe he should have come himself."

She turned her head so that she eyed him through a single tear-drop lens. "Mr. Lyons is very busy."

"Naturally."

"And he hates telephones. He prefers in-person introductions."

"Phone Booth hates phones, huh?" he said, but added quickly, "I didn't realize I had so little time to respond before he released the hounds."

"Just one hound." She attempted a smile again, but it looked like a grimace.

"It's just that Lyons was very aggressive in trying to get ahold of my father. And now that my father's gone, I'm not looking to inherit your employer's enthusiastic attentions."

She produced a card from her case. "We're based back east, but we have feelers out here. I've written our California contact on the back—my direct line. Mr. Lyons would like you to join him for lunch on Sunday."

Philip looked at the card, which featured their logo, the familiar brain-spiral.

"I'm afraid I'm busy."

"I understand you don't work Sundays."

"I'm not a schoolteacher, Ms. Stone."

"I was only suggesting—"

"—and I don't plan on meeting your boss for lunch," he said, handing back the card. "If I did, it would be at my convenience."

"Keep it," she insisted. "Do what you like with it."

Philip slipped the card into his pocket. "Look, I know you're doing your job, but I'm not all that eager to meet someone who's looking to profit from my father's death."

"So you're saying there might be something to profit from?"

"That's not what I'm saying."

Her face relaxed for a moment, losing some of its sharpness. "I realize your father only just passed away, Mr. Severy, and I apologize for the graceless sense of urgency here, but—"

"*Graceless* is a good word."

"—but Mr. Lyons would like to meet you for lunch all the same, after which you may cut off all contact. I should add that he has excellent taste in food. You won't be disappointed."

"And can I ask what it is Mr. Lyons does?"

"Government-scholar relations. It's on the card."

Philip tried to keep a straight face. "Sounds a bit vague, doesn't it? Like the Institute for Progress or something."

"I'm not familiar with that organization, but I'm sure Mr. Lyons can address all your concerns."

Still wanting a straight answer, Philip said, "He's a kind of intermediary, then?"

"That's right." She gave him a wink and neatly swiveled on one heel. "Hope to hear from you soon, Mr. Severy. Have a good night."

Philip was too annoyed to respond. It seemed yet another small humiliation that someone had come to his lecture only to seek out some phantom project from his departed father. As he watched her tip-tapping to the exit, he felt an intense craving for a cigarette and a martini. He was just thinking he might indulge in the latter without any serious repercussions, when he turned around and saw Anitka standing there.

The Hayman Lounge was Philip's go-to watering hole, which, aside from the game room in the basement, was the only place on campus to get a real drink. The lounge occupied a single room on the Athenaeum Club's main floor, and was tastefully decorated with framed portraits of Caltech's Nobel laureates. Philip had long ago picked out the spot on the wall where he decided his own picture would appear—between physicist Richard Feynman and quark pioneer Murray Gell-Mann—and he habitually glanced at the space every time he entered the lounge. But one wins a Nobel Prize for measurable results, not pretty math, and it was going to be some years before a string theorist was invited to dine with the king of Sweden.

The lounge was empty when Philip and Anitka sat down at the bar at six thirty, but within an hour, the surrounding tables had filled with club members and a group of employees from the Jet Propulsion Laboratory, who were loudly discussing a NASA budget crunch. The more Philip drank, the louder the JPL people became.

Anitka suggested they move to the quieter end of the bar. Philip agreed, though he tried not to look too disturbed with the intimacy of their new spot. He had spent the last hour trying to talk Anitka out of her anti-string crusade, warning her that she was on her way to career suicide with zero hope of a postdoc if she insisted on following her own underdeveloped theories instead of the one she had been trained to explore.

"Keats was not a physicist, Philip," she responded, using Philip's given name for the first time since he'd known her. "Beauty does not equal truth. And if we continue to operate in this mystical fairyland, we might as well jump right into bed with those intelligent-design crazies, where they'll turn to us with their idiot grins and say, 'See, told you it was magic.'"

Philip smiled, marveling at her certainty. "If you don't look at subatomic particles and see at least *some* magic—at least a sense of wonder—then what are you doing here?"

"Magic? Next, you'll be using the term *God particle*. How many years have passed now with no real results? Just a bunch of nerds going on about elegance? If string theorists continue to fail at producing experimentally measurable results, while at the same time discouraging rival theories, they'll soon be unworthy of the name *scientist*."

Philip had heard all this before, of course. He didn't tell her that he'd been following an online forum devoted to discussion of her phony paper. "Where are your predictions? Where are your verifiable results?" she had asked in one of the forum's threads. The replies were sneering:

"For a start, Ms. Durov, string theorists have already predicted something called *gravity*. So, um, there you go."

To which she responded: "Oh, really, and what are you going to predict next? Heliocentrism? That the sun will rise at dawn? Next time, you might try predicting something we haven't all agreed upon in advance."

By his second martini, Anitka was still ranting. "Sometimes I think high-energy physics exists only to provide artists with existential metaphors, as if we're all here just to make a few shitty playwrights feel smart."

Philip wondered if she really was as reactionary and unromantic as she wanted everyone to believe. "You know what your thing is, Anitka?"

She was leaning forward in such a way that told him they were both well on their way to getting drunk.

"You lack the imagination for this stuff."

"Oh, is that what I'm lacking?"

"Okay, so your snow job with that journal showed a hell of a lot of imagination, but the hours you put into that silly paper could have been channeled into real mathematics."

Her face seemed to be getting closer by the minute.

He looked down at his near-empty glass and signaled the bartender for another. "I'll say one last thing. You could be a great scientist if you would stop throwing rotten fruit at the rest of us and take an honest look at your own work."

His third martini appeared, and after a couple of swallows,

something very strange happened, something he instantly wished hadn't: Anitka blossomed right in front of him. It wasn't that he hadn't noticed her beauty before—Anitka's good looks were not purely a result of gin and vermouth—it was just that he had never bothered to look at her long enough to take her in. *She's a departmental irritant, remember? A pest!* She also tended to downplay her appearance by dressing in accordance with the sartorial rule of academia: the more subjective the discipline, the better the fashion sense; or to put it another way, the more poorly one dressed, the closer one was to the Mathematics Department.

But tonight, with the peach sweater against her skin and her hair pulled from her face, she was indisputably radiant. Those smooth Slavic cheeks and large, languid eyes—and that Russian accent. A flower in the Siberian tundra. *Seriously, Philip, what is wrong with you?*

As he strived to keep his eyes from straying below her neck, he had a sudden insane thought, one that hadn't crossed his mind in thirty years of marriage: *I could start a love affair right here and now. I could reignite my passion for life and beauty and science. And why not? Because something has to change. Something has to restart this broken-down machine.*

He longed to ask her, "How does someone so beautiful get into theoretical physics?" But Philip wasn't impaired enough to start asking such clumsy questions, and besides, he could guess the answer. Anitka had grown up in the Ukrainian countryside, where beautiful girls were everywhere, six-foot goddesses hatching out of the ground like white turnips. And they weren't suffocated with praise as they are in the States; they weren't told from the age of five how lovely they were, because beauty had little value in a country where one was just trying to survive to the next week.

"Isn't your wife expecting you for dinner?"

He cleared his throat. "She doesn't really wait anymore." He didn't mean for it to sound so pathetic.

"I would wait."

Philip responded by folding a napkin into increasingly small triangles. Anitka alleviated the silence by opening the cocktail menu. "I want my next drink to be exotic. Should I get a Heisenberg Highball?"

"Hmm. *Uncertain.*"

She hid her smile in the menu. "That is terrible. How about an Oppenheimer's Manhattan?"

"I've had that one. It's quite good."

"No way! They make an *Einstein on the Beach!*"

As she rattled off a few more punny cocktails, Philip started to build a case in his mind for infidelity. There was, after all, a long history of scientific breakthroughs fueled by the intense combustion of this or that love affair. There was Robert Oppenheimer stealing away to see his lover Jean Tatlock one last time before leaving with his family for New Mexico to begin work on the atomic bomb, and Soviet physicist Lev Landau's steady extramarital activity as he labored on his theory of quantum liquids. Einstein's infidelities, of course, were lifelong and thoroughly documented, boring even in their transparency.

Perhaps most spectacularly, there was Erwin Schrödinger, who, while married to his wife, Annemarie, had one affair after another, each romantic intrigue corresponding to a vigorous period of output and discovery. Schrödinger had done his best work on his quantum wave equation in December 1925 during an extended stay in an Alpine cabin with one mistress whose identity still remains a mystery. The equation he had produced so feverishly between their lovemaking sessions would later win him the Nobel in physics. Schrödinger's good friend the mathematician Hermann

Weyl—who, incidentally, was back home fucking Schrödinger's wife during said stay in the mountain cabin—said of Schrödinger, "He did his great work during a late erotic outburst in his life."

A late erotic outburst. That's what he needed.

Philip's gaze settled for a moment on Dick Feynman's jaunty portrait across the room—a man who was remembered as much for his naughty, winking personality as for his physics. "Even I," he seemed to be saying from his eight-by-ten-inch prison, "had a lifelong weakness for topless bars and Vegas showgirls. You think I moved to California for the academic prestige? Nah. It was the girls, Philip, the girls!"

"Do you want to share a Three Mile Island Iced Tea?" Anitka asked innocently.

"I think I'm set."

"How about a Bloody Marie Curie?"

He stood abruptly. "I have to go."

"But we haven't gotten to my dissertation."

"Yeah, well—"

"How will you get home?"

"I have a rocket ship outside."

Anitka burst out laughing, nearly falling off her chair. "Oh God, how did we get so smashed?" She steadied herself by grabbing his arm.

He looked at her hand. "I have a daughter your age, you know."

She slapped the top of the bar. "That's so funny, because I have a second cousin who's your age."

And with that, he grabbed his jacket and lurched out of the Hayman.

On the considerable walk home, Philip would have heaps of time to think over all the stupid things he had said that evening. *I have a daughter your age?* You can't say things like that to a woman you were going to have to see later in sober daylight. And why was he practically fleeing?

He wondered what Jane would think of his current three-martini state. (Or had it been four?) Just as he was calculating how much drunkenness he could walk off before he reached home, he noticed a car trailing him through the Athenaeum parking lot. This feeling of being followed so disturbed him that he flattened himself against a hedge to wait for the car to pass. When the dark sedan pulled alongside him and stopped, an irrational shudder of fear moved through him. The passenger-side window slid down.

"May I offer you a ride, Professor Severy?" a man asked from the driver's seat.

The interior of the car was half in shadow, and Philip couldn't make out the driver's face. "Do I know you?"

"Ms. Stone thought you'd like to be seen home."

"Ms. Stone?" The man wore a suit, maybe a chauffeur's getup. "I don't under—"

The driver started to explain, but as he spoke, his Spanish accent seemed to thicken, and Philip was having a hard time making any sense of it. He was also feeling alarmingly pinned between car and shrub.

"Sorry," he said, holding up a hand. "I really don't know what you're saying. You'll excuse me—"

He stepped through a serendipitous gap in the hedges, leapt onto the sidewalk, and headed swiftly in the general direction of his house. But the encounter—the whole night, really—unsettled Philip deeply, and in the forty-five minutes it took to walk home, he glanced behind him nearly a dozen times.

10

The Hotel

After the drama of Drew's encounter with the four o'clock plant had run its course, Hazel returned to her dubious scavenger hunt. She explained to the family that she wasn't quite ready to return to Seattle and the hassles of running her store, which was partly true. She tried to imagine walking into her shop the next morning, struggling to banter with customers while overdue notices collected daily on her counter. She imagined turning the store over to her employee, Chet, for the afternoon, asking him to tidy the displays or spruce up the store signage, knowing full well he'd just use her absence as an excuse to catch up on his reading. (And why not? Wasn't that the whole point of working in a bookstore?) She knew that Chet's reading wasn't just reading, but research for an unnameable book he'd been working on for ages, one she pretended not to notice he was writing.

She'd then take a crisp walk to Bennet's design studio. But she could only envision unhappy scenarios: Bennet so absorbed in the lines of a swivel chair that he barely registered her arrival. Or, worse, her boyfriend testing out a rocking-chair love seat with that cute assistant designer—the one with the bangs and sparkly tights—each pretending to evaluate the chair's merits but secretly relishing their forced proximity to each other. And Hazel standing there, stupidly gripping a bag of Bennet's favorite pastries.

She didn't know why her mind insisted on imagining the worst, but the truth wasn't so much that she was afraid to go home; it was that she couldn't rid herself of the idea that she now had a purpose in Los Angeles. She finally had a function among the Severys, and an obligation to the man who had rescued her and her brother so many years ago.

Hazel spent much of the next two days holed up in Isaac's study, poring over his letter, certain that the text was key to revealing the place where he'd hidden his work, perhaps somewhere in the house. Just in case, she called the Caltech math department to ask if there was a room 137 in their building. There wasn't. Maybe 137 wasn't an actual room but a code pointing to the text of the letter. But any permutations she tried—anagrams, wordplay, both vertical and diagonal acrostics—evaporated into nonsense. Not for the first time, she searched the internet for a John Raspanti but came up with the same results. There were several people with that name, none of them in the Los Angeles area, none of them with academic jobs or even a tenuous connection to her grandfather, and certainly none wearing herringbone.

After many hours of groping down blind alleys, Hazel returned to *Tender Is the Night*, refusing to believe that her grandfather had been out of his mind. She had to keep looking. The gift card for the now-defunct Book Circus seemed to her irritatingly unhelpful. The Hollywood bookstore had gone bankrupt years ago, and its multistoried complex now housed a combination gym and health food store. She quickly discarded the thought of haunting racquetball courts and bulk food aisles in search of camouflaged mathematics, and instead looked back through the novel. She scanned it several times but didn't notice anything unusual, other than an underlined word on the second page, *littoral*, next to which was scribbled a definition in Isaac's hand: "of or pertaining to the seashore." Hazel had probably looked up that very word when she'd first read the book back in college, though she hadn't retained its meaning. She scrambled the word for anagrams but could produce only *tortilla* and *R. T. Lolita*. She did the same for Raspanti's name, but after a few *hop ninja rats* and *no Japan shirt*s, she gave up.

A less nonsensical discovery came to her the second night as she lay in bed, weaving the gift card between her fingers and trying to recall Book Circus's motto: "Run away with the Circus"? "Send in the Books"? As the lamplight caught the store's clownish logo, she noticed that an edge was pulling away slightly from the black plastic. She went to her desk for a better look and realized that it was just a cheap sticker. She peeled it off to find a gold embossed script underneath: "Hotel d'Antibes, 5819 Foothill Drive, Los Angeles." It wasn't a gift card at all but a hotel key card. *A large, proud, rose-colored hotel . . .* Perhaps Isaac's allusion to Fitzgerald's first line was no literary coincidence. Is this where she would find room 137?

Hazel would have shouted an exclamation had it not been for Sybil, Jack, and Drew sleeping downstairs. She considered throwing a coat over her pajamas and borrowing Isaac's Cadillac, but she knew the sputtering engine would wake them. Instead, she called Bennet, suddenly craving the sound of his voice. She wanted to hear him say that he missed her, that his dog missed her, that he'd discovered this new restaurant with devastating crab cakes, and when was she coming home already? But his voice mail answered. Hazel listened to his deep, unhurried greeting asking her to leave a message, and hung up.

She couldn't sleep, and for the next hour, she stared at the ceiling, pushing a swirl of negative thoughts about Seattle out of her mind. Instead, she tried to summon the constellations she and her brother had tried to create on their bedroom ceilings using strings of white Christmas lights and a box of pins, an ambitious compensation for their city's lack of actual star cover. They had painted some of the bulbs black in order to get the intensity of each star just right, but succeeded only in making a mess. As her eyes eventually closed and she drifted toward sleep, Hazel imagined a reality in which their star project had been a success instead of a childish tangle, in which those white string lights were still suspended from their bedroom ceilings instead of having ended up in that bubbling water with Isaac.

At nine the next morning, after devouring a few pancakes left behind by Sybil and Jack, Hazel made the five-minute drive from the canyon to a hotel just up the hill from Hollywood's Franklin Village. As she stepped from the Cadillac and squinted up at an imitation French chateâu that was neither proud nor rose-colored, she tried to imagine what Isaac could possibly have been doing here, so close to his own house. With its blue mansard roof and multiple stories of louvered shutters, the Hotel d'Antibes really must have been something in its day, but now it was merely clinging to old triumphs, waiting for an imaginative investor to come along. A few feeble rosebushes and bougainvillea adhered to its facade, a surface that must have once been creamy like cake icing but was now cracked and gray. The anemic lawn was flanked by a pair of shaggy fan palms, and enclosed on three sides by a malformed hedge.

A green information box on the sidewalk informed her that this was a "building of note," which was, presumably, a notch or two below historical landmark.

Erected in the 1920s as a set of apartments, the property was transformed into a hotel during the Depression after tenants could no longer afford the rents. The new hotel quickly became a playground for the elite, and over the next two decades was the setting of myriad Hollywood legends—ruinous romances, overdoses, questionable accidents, and career sabotage—a place where those with means could check in for a few months and fashionably let themselves go.

At the bottom was a quote from a movie mogul:

If one is contemplating a mental breakdown in style, one need look no further than Hotel d'Antibes. Just don't make a mess of the damask.

She started up the walk, already anticipating the dull stench of the lobby. As Hazel entered the reception area, passing beneath a low-hanging chandelier, the burgundy carpet sent its catalog of memories wafting up her nose. A family of four gathered at the concierge desk, the father in the process of interrogating a clerk about which sightseeing bus they should take.

As Hazel stepped across the lobby, taking in the balding furniture and old lamps recently invaded by compact fluorescents, she noticed a particularly tragic paw-footed sofa. She couldn't help but think of Bennet and his hatred for all things antique and decomposing, even the stodgy charm of her bookstore. She pulled out her phone and sent him a text—*I'm in a hotel you would loathe*—along with a snap of the sofa.

The vacationing family didn't appear to be coming to any decisions, and seeing no reason to announce her presence, Hazel headed straight down the first-floor hallway. Aside from the distant buzz of a vacuum, the building was silent, leaving her to wonder if anyone other than the family was staying here. The hotel had retained the snug feel of an apartment complex, and though it had been retrofitted with electronic locks, all the rooms had their original wood-paneled doors. She turned a corner, nearly bumping into a tiny Hispanic woman pushing a cart of linens, and watched the room numbers climb. The hallway came to an abrupt end at 129.

She retraced her steps, searching for a missed turn, but there was none. She could play dumb at the front desk, but remaining anonymous for as long as possible seemed the wiser move.

"One three seven," she whispered aloud, mentally flipping the digits to form all six possible combinations. She called the elevator from the lobby. When the doors jerked open, she stepped into the mirrored car and found buttons for seven floors. She pressed 3, and the elevator began its whining climb. The mirrors around her were dark and spotted with age, but there was enough reflected light to make out an infinite chain of Hazels queued up within the car's walls.

The doors opened onto the housekeeper she'd seen earlier, now polishing the plate for the call button.

"Can I help you?" she asked.

"I'm fine, thanks," Hazel said, stepping down the hall.

The woman stared after her. It occurred to Hazel that there was likely no one staying on this floor.

She found room 317 and waved the key card in front of the lock pad, but the light blinked red. For the benefit of her audience, Hazel threw up her hands in mock frustration.

"Wrong floor," she muttered, returning to the elevator.

The tiny woman was already pushing her cart through the doors. "Up?"

"Yes, please."

The maid, however, had not selected a floor—maybe she planned to polish the mirrors next—so Hazel pressed the top floor.

For the next several seconds, the woman attacked the surrounding brass trim.

Hazel exited onto the seventh floor. After the elevator shut behind her, she started toward room 713, but a noise made her stop. It was the faint mechanical jerk of the elevator doors opening again, not below, *but above.* The sound was followed by the rattle of the cleaning cart. There was an eighth floor.

Hazel hit the only call button, and when the doors opened, she inspected the elevator's panel. There were in fact eight buttons, four on each side, but the one next to 7 was blank. She pressed it. The button glowed, and the car ascended. When it stopped abruptly, and the doors creaked open, she found the surprised maid standing on the other side, still gripping her rag. The woman said nothing, just waited to see what Hazel would do.

This floor was not like the others. The carpet was the same, but the hall stopped short, with only a single unnumbered door at one end. She hesitated, staring back and forth between the maid and the door. Finally, the woman made a comic sweep of her rag for Hazel to pass.

"Thanks," Hazel said, moving past her down the carpet. It was only when she was a few feet away from the door that she saw something was attached to it: a small, white tag taped below the peephole, like a label on an old library card catalog. In pencil, someone had written: *137.*

The housekeeper cleared her throat. "Excuse me, Miss."

Hazel turned.

"Are you with Mr. Diver?"

"Diver?"

Diver! Of course. Keeping with the theme, Isaac had taken his alias from *Tender Is the Night*'s charming but ill-fated main character.

"Yes, yes. Dick Diver," Hazel said. "He's my grandfather."

"Then you probably know that Mr. Diver requested complete privacy and no maid service." The woman said this in clear, unbroken English, as if she had been waiting to spring her fluency on Hazel. "But I imagine we're overdue for some freshening and clean towels. You'll let us know, won't you, please?"

"Of course."

"I'm Flor. Just ask for me at the desk."

Flor turned back to her cart.

"Flor? Do you know how long Mr. Diver's had this room?"

The woman frowned. "He didn't tell you?"

"He's not well."

"Oh, I'm sorry. He's been here many years. Five maybe?"

"Five years? Are you sure?"

Flor nodded. "It's a special room, you know. We rent it only by word of mouth—for people who wish a certain *isolation*. The story is that the original owner wanted a secret apartment where his wife couldn't find him."

Hazel looked back at the number on this secret door, imagining that it had been taped there quite recently for her benefit; the curl of the 3 seemed distinctly Isaac's. She thought of asking Flor what she made of the improvised room number, but the housekeeper had already disappeared into the elevator, taking her cart with her.

Hazel waved the key card in front of the lock, and when the light blinked green, she swung the door wide and flipped on the light. A small chandelier came on, revealing a carpeted entry with a hallway breaking off to the right, a bedroom to her left, and a living room ahead. The hotel's distinct odor had evaporated and was replaced with a stuffy though not unpleasant bouquet of leather, wood, dust, and card games, the smell of an extinct sort of bachelorhood. Clearly, someone hadn't opened a window in a while.

Given Flor's concern about the condition of the room, the place was, except for the dust, exceedingly tidy. She pushed open the hallway doors to find a king-sized bed under a creaseless quilt and a bathroom and second bedroom in the same unspoiled condition. If Isaac had slept here, he was careful to erase all evidence.

Hazel passed a kitchenette and entered a spacious living room decorated in a clubby bohemian fashion set off with modern Danish pieces. A shelf set into one wall held a collection of vintage liquor bottles. In front of it, a pair of leather-upholstered chairs confronted a baize-topped card table, where a suspended game of checkers awaited its next move.

At the far end of the living room, a computer monitor dominated a small wooden desk. Tacked to an adjoining wall hung an oversized map pocked with red adhesive dots. Hazel stepped closer and saw that it was a street map of LA and the surrounding area. The dots had chains of incomprehensible numbers written on them.

The map immediately made her think of Isaac's traffic project. A similar map had hung for years in his study at home, though with flags instead of dots. Had he returned to the project? Hiding his obsession from his family? She scanned the dots, but they didn't appear to correspond to the map's roads or freeways. The points were scattered across the city, gathered here and there in dense pockets, and thinning out as they neared the map's edges. Was this the work she was supposed to destroy?

Hazel turned to the computer and hit the power button. A minute later, a prompt appeared on-screen: Password Required.

"Are you kidding me?" she said, wondering how long whatever she was supposed to be looking for would be dangled beyond reach. But Hazel reminded herself that Isaac had given her everything she needed to know up to that point. If he wanted her to access his computer, surely he had provided the password.

She pulled her grandfather's letter from her purse and read it again, even though she practically had the words memorized. But she couldn't see any more meaning to be extracted. Hazel surveyed the contents of the room, hoping to spot a clue in the decor. There were several board games stacked on a shelf, many of them old or obscure, including the unpopular geography game Ubi, and Letter Jungle, a disastrous cross between Scrabble and Hungry Hungry Hippos. The wall map seemed her most likely ally, but she couldn't begin to know how to make sense of it. On the opposite wall, a large sunburst mirror reflected her frowning forehead.

Reminded of the photograph of Isaac covering a bathroom mirror in prime numbers, Hazel took the Fitzgerald novel from her purse. She flipped through it again and found something she had disregarded before. Inside the cover, written in light pencil, was a short string of numbers. This being a used book, she had initially assumed this was an old Dewey decimal or inventory number, as she used for her own store; but when she looked at it properly, she saw that it didn't resemble either one: 137.13.9. There was that number again, 137, and there was that same 3 of Isaac's. When Hazel pulled up the password prompt again, she typed in the digits, both with and without decimals, backward and forward and in various combinations. But she got only *Sorry, password incorrect.* She even tried typing the primes she remembered from the Polaroid in one solid block.

Sorry, password incorrect.

Finally, *littoral.*

Sorry, password incorrect.

Hazel pushed the chair back from the desk and flung open the drapes. As her eyes adjusted to the sun, she saw that the full-length window let out onto a rooftop patio. She slid it open and climbed out into an enclosure of succulents, prickly pear, and agave, wondering how anyone was able to tend the garden if the maids weren't allowed through Isaac's room. Could there be direct access to the patio? She stepped to the railing but didn't see one. As she looked out over Hollywood and the 101 Freeway, a profound sense of unease came over her. There were no more messages to follow, no more codes to decipher. If his work was important enough to require all this secrecy, why leave it to her? Why not to Philip or Paige, or even Gregory, someone who might have an idea what to do next?

She imagined her grandfather's response traveling to her from some distant, unspecified place: *"I leave it to the one they will—"*

—least suspect? But am I really to destroy this? How can I do anything when I can't access your computer?

"After I mailed you that letter, there wasn't much time before—"
Before what? What happened that morning?

Hazel went back inside to call her brother. She thought of asking him to meet her at the hotel, where she would show him everything. He'd know what to do. But when the line rang and his voice mail kicked in, Isaac's warning, *Do not contact police, even those related to you,* came back to her with full force. She hung up. But a question lingered. Why shouldn't she trust her own brother?

In frustration, she fell back onto a damask sofa and covered her face with a pillow.

Hazel opened her eyes to the drapes billowing in the breeze. She sat up, head aching. She held her grandfather's letter crumpled in one hand. Her phone had woken her. Fishing it from the sofa, she saw she had a voice mail from Bennet. The ache in her head was now overtaken by a constriction in her chest, and the instant she heard his cool, detached voice—"Listen, we should probably talk . . . "—she knew what was happening. *It's the girl with the tights, isn't it?* He went on: "I hate to do this over the phone, and with everything that's going on, but I thought you'd be back by now. Please call me."

But she couldn't bring herself to call. Instead she held the phone out in front of her and snapped a photo. She sent the image to Bennet with the words: *This is my sad face.*

11

The Appointment

Philip sat down at his desk and examined the card Nellie Stone had given him. The name *P. Booth Lyons* looked up at him in a neat serif—and now something that had been lunacy to him last week seemed perfectly sensible. His father would want him to resolve this, to find out who this Phone Booth was and what he wanted. *"Aren't you curious?"* he could hear his father asking. *"Don't the riddles of the world interest you at all?"*

But Philip wasn't kidding himself. He knew exactly what he was doing when he picked up the phone, dialed, and waited for Ms. Stone's schoolmistressy voice to answer. Yes, he was calling to demand what it was about his father's work that was worth his being stalked through the Athenaeum parking lot the other night. But he was also running away from a student who was making him perspire at the mere idea of seeing her shadow on the milky glass of his door.

He had known Anitka Durov for years without ever having been affected by her charms, but now the creeping symptoms of something—*something not allowed*—had quite suddenly revealed themselves in his body, like a covert disease. What had been shaping up to be a mere "late erotic outburst" had transformed over the past few days into a kind of madness. He hadn't felt this way in ages (not since Jane) and had forgotten over his many years of arcane concerns and hunched inquiry just how involuntary this sort of attraction was, how completely out of one's control or reason. He could almost hear his father chiding: "*Oh, but you can't, Philip. You may not be the towering physicist you had hoped—heir apparent to Newton and Einstein—but you'd never betray the ones dearest to you. Do people even have affairs anymore? Isn't that some clichéd activity from decades past?*"

But any kind of sermonizing was useless, because that's not where passion lived—it wasn't anyplace in the brain where one could go in and futz with the wires. The entire stupid, blushing, infatuated area was, by its very nature, blocked off and totally indifferent to your long list of arguments against its existence: *You're married! Happily!* Happily? *She's not even that beautiful!* Oh, but she is. *Jane would find out! What the hell are you thinking!* And so went the lone voice of principle in his head, bellowing at a locked gate.

He thought of his parents' apparently successful marriage. Had his father ever been afflicted by this nonsense? Or his mother, for that matter? At the thought of Lily, he knew he was overdue for a visit. That's what he should be doing this afternoon, making a leisurely drive to Santa Monica with Jane and the kids, taking in the ocean air with Mom. But the idea of having to keep up with her batty cognitive processes depressed him. Or, more accurately, the fact that his father had practically discarded his mother, sent her away to an assisted living facility—and Philip had done nothing to stop it—depressed him. But then, once the mind was shattered, whether it be from senescence, illness, or drug abuse, it was as if the person were already dead. That's how it was with his family.

The phone picked up after a single ring, and Ms. Stone's unceremonious voice greeted him. "Good afternoon, Mr. Severy. So happy to hear from you."

Philip cleared his throat. Caller ID was forever taking him by surprise. "Hello, Nellie. Can I call you Nellie?"

"Of course." He could hear her smile traveling down the line. "You can call me Lennie if you'll agree to that lunch."

"All right, but it'll have to be today."

A pause. "Could you hold for a moment?"

The line went silent for what seemed like several minutes. Philip was considering hanging up when her voice returned. "Can you come out to Malibu? I'll send a car."

Twenty minutes later Philip found a town car idling on California Boulevard. It might have been the same car that had followed him through the parking lot that night, but when he questioned the driver about it, the man shrugged and said he only worked days.

Once inside the humming cocoon of the back seat, Philip's tension fell away, and for the next hour, through traffic on the Santa Monica Freeway and all the way up the breezy Pacific coast, he was able to put the haunting image of Anitka aside and focus on some notebook mathematics. One of the advantages of his chosen profession was that he could work anywhere with nothing but pencil and paper. Whenever a stranger asked Philip to describe what he was scribbling, if he was feeling generous, he might use a metaphor he had borrowed from a colleague at Princeton: his brand of mathematics was like stepping into a mansion where all the lights had been turned off, the curtains drawn, and the light switches strategically hidden. The mansion was infinitely large, with an endless number of rooms and doors, and with various physicists working at opposite ends of the estate. The hope was that someday they would all meet up in the murky middle.

But for now, Philip was on his own. His task was to map his particular wing, one room at a time, without breaking or knocking anything over. It was only when he had mapped out one area of the house that he could properly move to the next. When entering a darkened room, he would stumble around for a while, arms chopping the air, bumping into this or that. Each identifiable object gave him clues to the surrounding objects. *Where there is a dressing table, there must be a chair. Where there is a brass poker, there is a fireplace.* As was the nature of this madly designed manor, the light switch was never near the door but always in the last place he looked. Not until he turned it on could he fully appreciate the strange elegance of his surroundings.

Philip had been stuck in the same room for years now, with no apparent solution within reach. He had often considered abandoning the room altogether, but in the end he knew that this room belonged to him, dark as it may be. He would keep returning to it, an hour at a time, until he knew its contents, until he found the light switch at last. He would die here if necessary.

Rolling down his window, Philip let the Pacific air hit his face. Yes, he would be just fine. *She is a passing psychosis.* He wasn't going to give in to some insane impulse simply because his father had died and left his life's purpose in chaos—chaos with a small *c*, the messy kind.

An hour and fifteen minutes had gone by when the car halted in front of a stark house, all light and modern angles. It sat near the edge of a bluff, like a pile of blocks waiting to be knocked into the sea. Nellie stood at the threshold, wearing a linen pantsuit in the same off-white hue as the building. There was something about the way she was looking out that struck him as odd, as if she were hiding something, concealing her own anticipation. Could it be that there was really something to his father's recent mathematics? Might she and P. Booth Lyons know something he didn't?

As he stepped from the car, Nellie extended an arm, as if guiding a dear friend in from a blizzard. "He hasn't arrived yet. But let's enjoy the rest of the afternoon, shall we?" She led Philip through a glass-covered atrium, down a naked hallway, and into a large room bathed in natural light. Everything was spare and white and glass.

"Is he off relating with scholars?" he asked.

She didn't even pretend to laugh. "You're the only scholar he's interested in at the moment."

"You mean my father is."

She didn't answer, only motioned him to some molded modern furniture along one wall. "We'll wait here."

Philip took a seat. "Is it your practice to have people followed?"

"Excuse me?"

"The Athenaeum parking lot."

"Oh, that." She smiled. "I'm sorry you didn't take advantage, frankly. It happened that I didn't need the car that night, and I noticed you'd ducked into the club. It was impulsive of me."

Before he could respond to this, the doors swung open and an efficient-looking man in white appeared. He set a bottle of spring water and a platter of painstakingly constructed delicacies in front of Philip.

"Thank you, Sasha," Nellie said. "I just hope it won't spoil our guest's lunch."

Philip popped several caviar-topped morsels into his mouth, taking it on faith that he wasn't going to wake up later in a posh torture chamber in Mr. Lyons's basement. He mumbled approvingly. It was the best food he had tasted in months, and it instantly lightened his mood.

"Told you," she said from across the room.

The server hurried away, and Philip turned in the direction of a large picture window. He couldn't see the water below, but the vacant sky told him it was there. The clouds were turning pink in the diminishing light. "Nice life you lead here."

From her place behind a glass desk, she answered without a trace of enthusiasm, "He makes sure my life stays interesting."

Philip scanned the periodicals filed in a nearby rack as he plucked another morsel from the platter. "So are you a Helen or an Eleanor?"

When there was no response, he turned and saw that she had opened her laptop and was studying the screen intently.

"Sorry?" she said, looking up. "Is there something else you need?"

He decided on a different question. "What does the *P* in P. Booth stand for?"

"Phone, isn't it?" she answered dryly. "Actually, I don't know that I've ever asked. Even close friends call him Lyons or Ly."

Nellie returned to her laptop and began clicking away. Philip studied her.

"So you're not an inquisitive person."

Her fingers paused above the keyboard. "You know, Mr. Severy, until you came along, I always thought of myself as inquisitive, but you're throwing my entire sense of self into doubt." She resumed her task, her words per minute noticeably increasing.

He watched her impassive expression and wondered if Nellie was really the shrewd professional that she projected and not some smartly dressed dunderhead who had been trained in the art of phony smiles and musty diplomacy.

His phone buzzed. When he saw his daughter's name on the display, he remembered that it was Halloween. After taking Drew trick-or-treating, Sybil and Jack were coming over for dinner and staying the night. Jane had even reminded him of it that morning. At least Sybil wasn't angry with him anymore. But Philip let the call go to voice mail and instead texted his wife: *Might be a little late.*

He stood up, irritated by the delay. He examined a collection of framed photographs on a mantel near Nellie's desk, images of her standing next to or shaking hands with significant-looking men and women in suits. Philip recognized one of them as a former Pentagon chief.

Her desk phone rang, and she picked up. "Yes . . . yes," she murmured. "Of course."

She replaced the receiver. "He's very sorry. Why don't we wait in his study?"

Somewhat curious to see more of the building, Philip followed Nellie through a set of double doors and into a room that was smaller and darker than the first, but similarly arranged. He was suddenly struck by the notion that in ten minutes Nellie would receive another call from her boss, instructing her to put him in yet a smaller study. They would keep moving from study to study, each one progressively shrinking, until at last a small door would open and a doll-sized P. Booth Lyons would arrive, sweaty and apologetic.

At Philip's feet was a large, yellowing fur rug and above him a collection of what appeared to be fiberglass animal heads, all of them white, affixed above the desk and along the walls. The heads, which glowed softly like Japanese lanterns, stared down from their wooden plaques: lion, zebra, rhinoceros, buffalo, antelope.

Nellie noticed him peering up at an unfazed lioness. "Aren't they beautiful?"

"I haven't decided." In truth, he found them unnerving.

"They're trophies from Humane Hunt," she said, taking a seat in Mr. Lyons's leather chair.

"Never heard of it."

"That's because Mr. Lyons invented it. Club members can hunt down real Kenyan or Tanzanian game without killing them." She gestured to a glass case in the corner near the door. Inside were a pair of what looked like futuristic hunting rifles. "It's similar to a taser, though it works at greater distances, delivering a jolt of electricity that temporarily stuns the prey. The hunter then uses a special camera to capture the 3-D contours of the animal, which—"

"I get it. You create a mold of the head and throw it up on your wall like a real trophy. I'm sure the animal experiences no stress or upset whatsoever."

"Exactly," she said, oblivious to the sarcasm. "As long as the hunter is careful, his prey wakes up within twenty minutes unharmed."

Philip looked down at the fur beneath his feet. "What about the rug?"

"Oh, a casualty, I'm afraid." She blinked at it with what looked to be genuine sorrow. "The method isn't flawless."

Philip took a seat at the immense desk opposite her. "So while I'm kept waiting, how about fielding a few of my questions? No bullshit answers this time."

"I'm sure Mr. Lyons would be happy to—"

"I'd like to hear from Ms. Stone."

She leaned back. "What would you like to know?"

"How he makes his money, what this Government-Scholar business is, and why Lyons has been after my father all these years."

Nellie laughed. "But you and he will have nothing left to say to each other."

"You can start with the money," he said coolly, trying to project a sense of control he didn't feel.

Nellie took a sip of water before answering. "Some of it's family money; he makes no secret of that. But Mr. Lyons has also made a very successful business by tapping into the intellectual wealth of our country, acting as a kind of matchmaker between government and academia—scientists in particular: mathematicians, physicists, geneticists, neuroscientists. The US government, even its military contractors, are woefully ill-equipped to digest all the strategic promise coming out of the academic community. There would be countless missed opportunities if it weren't for his keeping up on not just scholarly developments but also emerging talent. It's because of Lyons that nanotechnology has already found its way into the military, not to mention several technologies we now take for granted. I can't disclose specifics, of course, but he likes to find talent early, before research is published, which involves a bit of creative persistence."

"Creative persistence, is that what you call it?"

"He can be aggressive when going after someone he admires, yes."

Philip was rethinking his earlier summation of Nellie as a dunderhead. The way she spoke of her boss's business seemed to go beyond rote memorization and into deep admiration.

Philip pressed her. "My father found his aggression to be borderline stalking."

"There is a private detective aspect to his work, sure," she replied. "You won't find him popping up in the news or on any search engines, because GSR is operating, quite necessarily, under the radar. If he wants the government to benefit from these connections, he has to make sure that others can't benefit—particularly the governments of rival countries. And that involves discretion."

"If everyone is enlightened, no one is."

"That's the general idea."

"Why not broker between science and business? Surely there's more money in it."

"Mr. Lyons is a patriot. He does have clients in the business world, but Uncle Sam comes first."

She smiled proudly.

"You're being strangely forthcoming for having told my father nothing for so long."

"Well, we can't have you bolting for the door before our host arrives." Nellie pulled out a cigarette case and extended it to him. They were Dunhills.

"How'd you know I smoke?"

"I didn't."

He longed to pluck just one cigarette from its silver bed, but declined. "Better not. They're migraine fuel."

Nellie lit one for herself. The linen of her suit quivered as she stepped to the window.

"I should correct you," she said, sliding the window open. "Your father wasn't unaware of all I just told you. He came here several times in the months before he died."

"He met with Lyons? That's not possible."

Nellie sent a lungful of smoke slinking outside. "I should know. I was here."

Philip stiffened in his seat, digesting the idea that his father had deliberately kept this from him, had hidden something that had become a private punch line between father and son.

"Let me ask you this: How much did you know about your father's work?"

He let the question hang there for several seconds. Apart from the fact that Isaac had been cagey in the final years of his life, he and Philip had been very different scientists. They were both fluent in the same mathematical language, could understand what the other was doing, but the nature of particle physics—string theory in particular—was so at odds with Isaac's very solid, quantifiable world. In the murky depths of chaos theory, his father had found regularity, uniformity, pattern. If Isaac Severy had a motto, it would have been "The universe is knowable." Philip's motto, and that of everyone who dealt in the quantum, was "The universe is knowable, up to a point." In Philip's view, not everything had been predetermined from the moment the universe sprang into being. In fact, his father's world and the horrors of determinism were partly why Philip had become a particle physicist. There was safety in a universe underpinned by uncertainty, where not everything could be predicted precisely, where particles were moody, erratic, and strange. Because in that reality, at least, there was room for surprise, room to decide, room to correct error.

Nellie rephrased the question: "Did your father share his latest project with you?"

"Listen, I find it hard to believe—"

"Thank you. You've answered my question."

"If you've already met with him," Philip said, angry now, his voice rising, "and several times—if you're to be believed—then why are you bothering me about it? You know far more than I do."

"Because, Mr. Severy, he died before things were finished, before we were able to come to an agreement."

Philip leaned across the desk and said evenly, "You mean he left your employer empty-handed."

"Your father divulged just enough to leave us wanting the rest."

Philip sensed a desperation in her statement that quickened his pulse. It had been a mistake to come here. He stood up. "I'll be going."

"I know this must be upsetting for you, but please, if you'll just wait—"

"Enough." Philip drew himself up tall to disguise his unease. "If you think you can waste my time here on some power trip while you peddle this garbage about my father's cooperation, just so that I'll hand over his supposed research to you and your very weird boss, then you are both out of your deranged"—he gestured at the walls for emphasis—"animal-electrocuting minds."

Nellie stepped toward him. "So you really have no idea what he was working on?"

Philip thought again of his father's peculiar reticence about his work. Could it be that Isaac Severy had shown these people what he had refused to share with his own son? He pushed the thought away. It was just too sad.

"I know what he was working on," he said finally. "He was working on mathematics, and in my world, that doesn't turn much of a profit." He walked to the door. "You needn't bother contacting me again."

Seconds later he was in the hall searching for the front door. Nellie didn't pursue him, but he imagined her tracking him via a mesh of lenses and fiber optics. He found what looked to be the same glass-covered entryway, but when he opened it and stepped out, he found himself on the side of the house surrounded by hedges. It was already dark, and the house was encircled in flood lamps. Heading up a stone path in the direction of what he hoped was the street, he found himself looking through a massive, single-pane window at a ground-level office. A young Indian woman sat at a desk near the window, poring over a stack of books. After a few more steps, there was a partition and another desk. Behind it, a silver-haired man in delicate glasses scowled at a tablet computer, but when he noticed Philip walking past, he quickly smiled. It was an easy smile, patient and friendly, but Philip didn't like it and hurried away.

When he reached the sidewalk, he walked swiftly from the house in the direction from which he had come. *What the hell is this place? What else did my father keep from me?* He'd walked a couple of blocks when a dark town car turned onto the street and made its way toward him. On instinct, Philip stepped into the nearest driveway and pressed himself along a border fence. When the car had passed, he took out his phone and dialed for a cab.

12

The Party

To keep herself from spending the entire evening in bed or on the floor, Hazel forced herself to attend Fritz Dornbach's Halloween party. She needed something to distract herself from the fact that Bennet had broken up with her over the phone for no good reason other than "We've always been different—you know that, Hazel." And although she hadn't dared confirm it in their very short conversation, she was certain he was already spending long, feverish nights with that assistant designer.

In an attempt to minimize the pain, she asked herself if she loved Bennet as much as she had imagined. She wanted the answer to be no, but aside from her grandfather, he'd been the closest person in her life, and his frank rejection felt like the onset of a terrible illness. It also felt like further proof that she belonged nowhere and with no one, and that she had somehow done this to herself. This idea of self-sabotage had come up in therapy years ago (back when she'd been able to afford it), but it was one thing to acknowledge it in the room and quite another to alter her behavior. Whatever the root cause of their breakup, Hazel was willing to bet that Bennet's designer friend was a more confident, emotionally grounded version of herself—one of those embrace-life, consequences-be-damned kind of girls who'd been given a steady IV drip of self-worth since infancy. Well, let him have her. *Hazel* was going to a party. Maybe in loud music and idiotic conversation, she could forget Bennet and Isaac and the intolerable heaviness of recent days.

Wearing a gray wool suit and a champagne wig that she'd unearthed from the attic, she took a city bus to the crush of trendy nightspots near Hollywood Boulevard. In Fritz's spare-no-expense hunt for a wife, he had rented out a two-story club for the evening, stocked with doormen and red carpets. To those who assumed Fritz to be nothing more than a dull middle-aged lawyer-accountant, it was on such evenings that the ribald man beneath the suit emerged. Even if Fritz didn't find the love of his life that night, the party was a timely move because on Halloween, despite the weather's slide into autumn, the women of Los Angeles shrugged off their cardigans to reveal vast expanses of skin and a limitless capacity for affection.

Hazel gave her name at the door and ten minutes later was seated on a second-floor banquette, eagerly downing a stiff cocktail that had been handed to her by Fritz before he'd left to pursue a leggy pair of dragonfly wings. Hazel watched the undersized attorney trudging off in his King Louis XIV getup, which ostensibly allowed him to wear heels without being called out on it. The comedy of this image had no effect on her sullen mood.

As she waited for the cocktail to do its work, she made conversation with a tuxedoed realtor named Jim. He gulped a martini from an oversized glass and every now and then, in case anyone doubted his identity, he would call up the James Bond theme from a chip on his bowtie. But mostly Jim talked about how people he didn't know should behave and about how lucky he had been in life. "It's true," he said, "I pull nice things toward me, like a magnet." Hazel nodded along but wondered how these promotional sorts always seemed to find her.

"So, who are you shupposed to be, anyway?" he asked in a splintered Sean Connery lisp.

"Oh, a vague Hitchcock blonde. I was going for Kim Novak, but the suit isn't quite—"

"So what are you doing later, Mish Hitchcock?"

Suddenly, the drink hit her, and she didn't know whether Jim was really asking what she was doing later or they were merely role-playing. The alcohol was, in fact, magnifying her misery, and as a wave of tears pressed at the back of her eyes, she found herself telling Jim about her broken heart. It all came out in a clump of disconnected thoughts and run-on grammar, and at the end of it, she took a long drink.

"That's tough," he said, rattling the ice in his glass. "Another cocktail?"

"I really shouldn't. But don't you think there's this idea out there in the world," she rambled on, "that men are always the obsessive ones pining away, as if women aren't just as consumed and humiliated by the whole thing? I don't know, am I making any sense?"

Jim nodded emphatically, then turned his response into an opportunity to describe a lucrative land deal he had recently brokered. He was still talking when Hazel spied someone vaguely familiar entering the club in a turbulent white wig, floppy suit, and fake mustache. She squinted, trying to place the man behind the costume. He crossed the room, and as he drew nearer, she craned her neck to keep him in view. It was the way he moved, the long-legged stride, that tipped her off. It was Alex.

He glanced over at her briefly, but his face showed no sign of recognition. He walked past her to the bar, where a blonde in a tiny bee costume wriggled for the bartender's attention.

"You know that guy?" Jim asked.

"Sort of." She looked back at the bar. Alex was frowning at the bee, who had turned to show off her wings.

Jim took a water gun from his pocket. "Bond can kick Einstein's assh any day."

"Twain."

"What?"

"I think he's supposed to be Mark Twain. It's the linen suit."

Though Hazel was annoyed that Alex hadn't recognized her—after all, she had identified him, and his costume was arguably more ridiculous—she was also surprised at the intensity of her own annoyance. Her cousin was still frowning at the bee, though his frown was now of the attentive, interested kind. Hazel knocked back a piece of ice and stood up. She wasn't in the mood to have the spectacle of romance played out in front of her. "It was nice chatting with you, Mr. Bond, but I have to go adjust my wig."

"No. Please. Don't," he said while simultaneously turning to a woman behind him.

As Hazel walked away, she heard the Bond theme erupt, followed by high-pitched laughter. Both were quickly drowned out by a DJ who had begun spinning a deafening beat from a nearby booth. Hazel plugged her ears and, halfway to the bathroom, ran into Fritz. She was suddenly very glad to see him and wondered if he might not be able to help her in some way, though she was feeling too buzzed to pinpoint how.

"Fritz!" she shouted. "Do you think we could talk?"

He smiled, but was clearly distracted by something behind her.

"I need to ask you something important." *What was Isaac working on when he died?*

"Does it have to be now, hmm?" He twitched in the direction of his pretty dragonfly.

"No, no. I'll find you later."

"Please do, my dear." Fritz adjusted a curl and stomped off, leaving Hazel to assume it would be the last she'd see of him that night.

After a slight tilt of her wig in a gilded mirror, she found an empty couch in a dark corner, far from her former location. The idea of lazy conversation with strangers had struck her as appealing earlier, but now all she wanted to do was sit and watch pretty people grasp for one another and let her recent troubles dilute with drink. She waved down one of the darkly feathered blackbird waitresses and pointed to a random cocktail on a menu tent. She then sank into the sofa to watch a gathering at a table several feet away, where a man in a tuxedo was conducting a shell game with three overturned bowler hats and a foam ball. A female Sherlock Holmes edged her way to the table—houndstooth dress, haughty air—and began pointing to the hats. When the bowler came up empty every time, she stamped her stilettoed foot and demanded another turn.

Hazel couldn't help but smile at the scene. Why was it that the entire world now seemed reflected through Isaac? He had loved shell games, specifically the kind that forced a player to consider the probability of a ball being under this or that cup. The Monty Hall problem had been a favorite, named after the famous game-show host who made contestants pick prizes from behind one of three doors on *Let's Make a Deal*. One evening in the kitchen, while helping to crack nuts for one of Lily's pies, Isaac had posed a variation of this problem to eleven-year-old Hazel. He hid a bean under one of three walnut shells and asked her to locate it, and when she took a guess—"the middle one?"—he told her she wasn't necessarily wrong, but that he'd give her one more chance to change her answer if she wished. He then revealed the last walnut to be empty, leaving two nuts still overturned.

"Would you like to change your answer or keep it?" he asked. She thought about it for a long moment and said, "Keep my answer," because why should it matter? She still had a fifty-fifty chance, regardless. But after playing the game twentysome times in a row, she noticed that she'd lost roughly two out of every three games. At last, she said, "I want to change my answer." When her grandfather asked her why, Hazel looked down at the shells and said, "Because, Grandpa Isaac, when you lift one of the empty shells, you change the game."

He looked at her, startled. "Do you know how many very smart people can't grasp this concept?" he said. "And you, eleven years old, figured it out in ten minutes. Math may be your least favorite subject, but you have a logician's mind, kiddo."

She hadn't believed him, of course, not really. He was just being supportive, trying to boost her interest in algebra or whatever irritating subject she happened to be studying in math class. It had been kind of him then, but it was one thing to play shell games with her in the kitchen and another to construct some kind of mad, life-sized version of the game.

Suddenly someone shouted very close to Hazel's ear, "Look, Sherlock Holmes!"

Hazel turned and, seeing the source of the shouting, groaned. The blonde bee had materialized one couch over, Alex at her side. A wall sconce cast an orb of light on the pair, lending the scene a sickeningly romantic quality, one that Hazel promptly sabotaged with images of exploded glass, screams, and blood. But the usual comic absurdity she gave to such fantasies was absent. There was a weight in her chest that felt uncomfortably close to jealousy. Alex murmured something in the bee's ear, which made the bee laugh hard and loud. When her laughter subsided, she announced, "I have to go to the little girls' room," and skipped away.

The instant his companion was gone, Alex set down a hardcover book he had been carrying, the title of which Hazel couldn't make out, and pulled from his floppy suit a notebook. He flipped through it methodically and, every now and then, made a notation in pen. Hazel just sat there with a drink to her lips, thinking she should probably reveal herself but not wanting to spoil her one chance at invisibility.

Just as she tried to see what Alex was writing, he slipped the notebook into his jacket, grabbed his book, and hurried off.

Hazel looked hard in the direction he had fled. Following some strange instinct, she stood up and pushed her way through warm bodies until she spotted Alex's furry white head descending the staircase. When she reached the bottom of the stairs, she caught sight of him striding toward the exit. *There he goes, the White Rabbit, always running off.* Hazel imagined a poor, distressed bee upstairs, returning from the little girls' room, searching the couches for a man who had made her laugh.

Out on the street, past the stanchions and red carpet, Hazel looked for a blaze of white, though she didn't exactly know what she'd do once she caught up with him. She moved closer to the curb and, on tiptoe, scanned the horde of gruesome characters lining the sidewalk. These were the drunk agitators, their costumes graphic and bloody. She was already unsteady on her heels, and after getting jostled by a pack of Salem witches—faces white, stiff nooses leading to imaginary gibbets—Hazel shoved back but was immediately knocked into a lamppost. Regaining her balance, she spied Alex halfway down the block, pant cuffs trailing along the Walk of Fame. Where could he be rushing off to? He didn't even live here.

Hazel realized now that a different impulse had overtaken her completely. She no longer desired to be seen by him but instead only wanted to understand this odd relative. She was still slightly drunk and not entirely confident in her abilities to tail somebody. But the streets that night were abundant with distractions, so she stepped out of her heels and started down the pavement, remembering something her brother had once said about following people: "Stay on the opposite side of the street. Try not to cross when your target does. Don't get cocky." Hazel ignored these rules, though she tried to keep a good half block behind Alex.

As she approached the corner of Hollywood and Vine, she was forced to negotiate an unruly group of revelers. It took her a few seconds to figure out that they were a collective silent movie: a ghostly Harold Lloyd and Mary Pickford, a dancing title card warning "Look out!" and a long-limbed piano slapping out a tune on himself. Had she paused to acknowledge Harold Lloyd turning to her with a mute scream, she might have missed seeing Alex disappear into the historic Taft Building.

She hurried through the crosswalk and up to the Taft entrance. The lobby looked empty, and as she tugged open the heavy door, she could just make out the sound of an elevator door closing. Before a security guard could stop her, she bolted across the lobby. She might at least catch the floor number.

"Excuse me, you can't just—"

"Hold on a second."

"You'll have to sign in—"

Hazel watched the brass-plated elevator dial move—something she'd always wanted to do—and when it swung from M to 1 and stopped, she walked back across the lobby, proud of herself, though now really feeling that last drink. A female security guard in animal ears called to her from the front desk.

"Who you here to see?"

"Um, would it be possible to see the first floor? If I wanted to rent a space?"

The guard sighed and slid a card across the desk. "Call this number during the week."

Hazel pocketed the card and looked around, wondering if there was a way to give the guard the slip, make a dash for the elevators.

"Anything else, ma'am?"

Hazel snatched a mini Reese's from a pumpkin-shaped bowl. "No, thanks."

Outside, she rounded the corner of the building and scanned the floor above the street for any lighted windows. Finding none, she sat down on a bus bench and slipped on her heels. What was she doing? Was she really going to stake out this guy? She felt the first spits of rain, and just as she was thinking of calling an Uber, a strange thing happened: a small fleet of Checker cabs appeared in the intersection. She wondered if she would see such a thing ever again, let alone in Los Angeles. Ever a sucker for the increasingly obsolete, she hailed one and asked the driver to take her back to Beachwood Canyon.

"Actually," she said, shutting the door, "could you make it the Hotel d'Antibes on Foothill Drive?"

By the time they pulled up to the hotel, rain was lashing at the cab's windows. Peering through the weeping glass, Hazel saw that the place had acquired a certain charm in the hours since she'd left it. The rooms glowed red from behind gossamer curtains, and the grounds were sculpted in arabesque shadow. She imagined that she saw a warm light coming from the direction of Isaac's room, but she knew this was an illusion, as the eighth floor was set back from the street. She paid the driver and made a run for the entrance.

The lobby was empty and the concierge desk abandoned. She

stepped across the acrid carpet and called the elevator, which took an entire minute to arrive. When the doors opened, she stepped in the car and felt inside a pocket of her purse to make sure the key card was still there. Then she hit the blank button.

"Hold the elevator, please," a voice called from the lobby.

No, don't think I will. She jabbed at Close Door, that placebo of buttons. Finally, the doors started to move, but it was too late because a man slipped through the narrowing gap—all soggy hair and sloppy Southern gentleman. Alex.

"Is there a room 137, by chance?" he asked breathlessly.

Hazel stepped back into a corner of the elevator, her neck growing prickly hot. Alex was trying his best not to smile, but the effort only made him look more satisfied with himself.

"Oh, and I've been wondering all night," he said, leaning back against a mirrored wall. "Are you Tippi Hedren from *The Birds* or Kim Novak from *Vertigo*?"

"Why are you following me?"

"Well, Hazel," he said, as the elevator began to move, "usually it's the person behind the other person who's doing the following."

She started to respond but realized she had nothing to say.

"It's fine, actually," he continued. "I was hoping to draw somebody out. Tired of searching alone."

Tired of searching alone? She wasn't sure what he meant by this, but it did make her consider for a second that he, too, had received a message from Isaac. She wanted to ask him, but that would require a level of trust in Alex she wasn't sure she had. Instead, her neck and ears still burning, she looked down at the book he had been carrying all night: *A Connecticut Yankee in King Arthur's Court.*

Eager to deflect some of her discomfort, she said, "Do you really think Twain would be caught dead carrying around his own book?"

Hazel detected a smile growing from behind his woolly mustache.

"Good point."

It was at that moment she knew what was different about him. His beard was gone. His structured jaw, shiny with rain, was completely clean-shaven. She wondered how she had been able to recognize him at all.

"You'd make a disastrous detective," he said, producing a miniature KitKat bar from his pocket. "I tailed you pretty easily after you left the Taft."

"I thought you'd gotten in the elevator."

"What, to room 137?" He shook his head. "I hid behind a planter after asking to use the bathroom. Anyway, I don't think the Taft room numbers go up that high. I should know because for the past week, I've been scouring the entire city for that bleeding number." He flashed the notebook tucked inside his jacket, as if this were ample evidence.

"Can I ask how you even knew to look for room 137?"

He waved his hand vaguely, as if the question were unimportant. "Isaac mentioned it once. He said it was his unofficial office or something."

So Alex hadn't gotten a letter. Or was he merely covering? The elevator stopped and opened onto the eighth floor.

"But I'm hoping that tonight," he said, stepping out and registering the hall's single door, "my search is done."

Alex fed the KitKat into his mustache and munched his way down the hall, stopping several paces before the door to stare at the number scribbled there. "This was one of the first hotels I tried. Never thought to look above the first floor."

Hazel struggled to think clearly, but that last cocktail was still impairing her brain.

He turned and examined her face. "I should have known Isaac would entrust his work to someone like you."

Hazel wasn't sure how to respond to this, but she tried her best to adopt a poker face. "Is that what you think? That he left his work to someone ludicrous like me?"

"Yes, not a number person. Makes sense, actually."

"What's the big attraction to his work, anyway?" she asked.

He crumpled the candy wrapper. "Why do you buy a new album from your favorite band? Or book by your favorite author? I'm a fan, and I can't just leave it sitting in a room."

"I can't let you in there. I sort of promised."

"Do you even know what's in there, Hazel?"

"Do you?"

"I know the language."

"Well, I may be a not-number person," she said icily, "but I'll figure it out."

Alex looked back at the penciled numerals and closed his eyes for several seconds, as if 137 were the solution for which he was inventing an equation. When he opened his eyes again, he said, "I'll leave, if that's what you want. Last wishes of my grandfather and all. Sorry, *our* grandfather—almost forgot." His cheeks colored, which on someone so outwardly proud struck Hazel as poignant. Was there ever a truer sign of emotion than blood hurrying to the surface of the skin?

She pushed her hand into her suit pocket, where the uneaten Reese's was becoming pliant. "It's probably best you go," she forced herself to say. "You can't tell anyone about this, either."

"Of course." He nodded gravely and backed away. "So what'll you do with it? Oh, never mind. Tell me years from now, when I no longer care." He turned and headed toward the elevator. "I'll see you around, then."

Doubtful. Didn't he live in Europe?

As the distance between them grew, Hazel realized she didn't want him to go; she was, in fact, desperate for an ally. She'd never crack that password alone. But it wasn't just that she needed help—there was something about Alex that felt safe, like having a part of Isaac with her again. Hazel turned and touched the card to the reader until it blinked green. When she stepped inside, she didn't close the door. Instead, she threw it wide open and looked back into the hall.

Alex spun around and smiled. She wondered how many things he got people to do for him because of that smile.

"You're brilliant, Hazel. Truly." He walked back down the carpet and stopped just short of the threshold. He held her gaze for a second. Then, eyes moving past her into the dark beyond, he stepped trancelike into the room.

13

The Old Spot

Gregory had abandoned his surveillance of Tom early that night so that he and Goldie could take their son trick-or-treating. But as much as he adored his time with Lewis—and nearly cried when he saw the little bear suit Goldie had sewn for him, complete with furry brown ears and a tail—he struggled to be present with his family. Whenever Gregory's mind wandered to Tom or to his other preoccupation (the woman he very much wanted to see), he would bring his focus back to his son, who shyly held out a plastic pumpkin at every door, accepting with renewed surprise the treats that were dropped into it. Hazel's rubber fish had turned out to be a fitting present, and Lewis would growl like a grizzly and tear into it every time a door opened.

Goldie had wanted Hazel to join the festive chaos of the evening, but when she didn't answer her phone, Gregory suggested that she'd likely gone to Fritz's party and to leave her be. But privately he wondered why his sister was still in town. Her lingering presence made him nervous, and he couldn't be entirely confident in his plans for Tom until she was safely away. He would call her tomorrow, he decided. He would escort her to the airport again if he had to.

When it began to drizzle, he and Goldie took their son home.

Lewis's sugar high kept him up way past his bedtime, but when he was finally asleep, Gregory began to plot the rest of his evening. He took one last look at his sleeping son, who still clutched the hide of his bear costume, and felt a stab of self-hatred at the idea of what he was about to do. As he shut the bedroom door, the feeling diminished. It was lucky that his wife was turning in early—she had run around most of the day making last-minute adjustments to Lewis's costume, and was now complaining how exhausted she was. He wouldn't have to make some stock excuse about a work emergency; he could slip quietly out of the house and be back before morning.

As he lingered in the hallway, waiting for Goldie to switch off their bedroom light, his phone vibrated with a text:

Can we do another night?

Gregory closed his eyes, fighting back the urge to call her right then. Instead, he replied that he needed to see her now, that this was not negotiable, that they had waited long enough. Wasn't she the one who had said "I need to see you," not three days before? He'd come to her if necessary, disrupt her entire evening. But as soon as he resorted to this threat, he regretted it: *I'm sorry, my love. I'm just desperate to see you. Can you get away for an hour?*

After an agonizing eight minutes, she responded, *Our old spot. 45 min.*

Gregory immediately erased the conversation (one couldn't get nostalgic with digital exchanges) and began to gather items for a romantic evening. He bagged a bottle of wine, two glasses, some crackers and cheese, an old blanket from the linen closet, and—in case the rain returned—two umbrellas. He stole out of the house, buoyed by desire. Her reference to their old spot made him smile, and he felt that familiar surge of momentum, not like the rolling steel ball but like an unstoppable wave moving farther and farther from land. As with his stakeouts of Tom, he could feel an inevitability about their meetings—a force that had been set in motion long ago, and there was a thrill in letting it take him over.

He might have suggested a hotel that night, but meeting out of doors carried an undeniable charm. It was also cleaner, with less risk of a data trail. But soon they wouldn't have to worry about any of that. She had made him a promise last week, a promise he held folded in his pocket. He would have hardly believed it had she not written it down. But as he parked his car on the hill he knew so well, high above Los Angeles, and made his way to a secluded spot beneath a sprawling sycamore tree, surrounded by a carpet of grass and city lights, he knew that he needed her to say it. He needed to hear the promise from her own lips tonight.

After fifteen minutes, he saw her approaching, winding her way toward him across the moonlit grass as if it were a stage. When she was a few yards away, he couldn't stand it anymore. He rushed to meet her, drawing her graceful body to his, slipping his hands under her coat to feel the satiny fabric beneath. He kissed her face, but she looked around suddenly, as if fearing discovery, and moved to the tree.

She laughed at her own paranoia and tried to smile, but he could see that she was more nervous than usual. He pulled her to the blanket, and they fell onto the soft wool, where they would soon play out a familiar scene under the branches. Still, Gregory couldn't dismiss the sadness and fear he had just seen in her face. So he told her that he agreed with her, that they should leave their spouses, that they should start the process now so that in the new year they could finally be together. When he had finished, she nodded slowly and sat up. But what she said next, he could hardly believe. As she turned her eyes to the ground and said what she had to say, he shut his eyes tight, as if to block out the words. He tried instead to focus on the crickets, listening for the beat of insect wings in the background. He wanted to isolate everything that was not her voice and turn up its volume, so that he didn't have to listen to the thing he feared more than anything in the world.

14

The Map

For the past hour, Alex's password attempts had come in rhythmic bursts, as if he were composing music instead of trying to hack into a computer. From her place in the kitchenette, where she was preparing a pot of coffee, Hazel could almost imagine the modulations of the keyboard as a sonata for the tone deaf, with Alex's singsongy muttering as harmonic counterpoint.

As she returned to the living room and set a cup of coffee next to him on the desk, she thought of how Alex's fingertips had grazed hers briefly after they'd entered the room. But when he spied the computer, he had pulled away and rushed to the desk. Now, shirtsleeves stuffed up past his elbows and his Twain wig and mustache discarded, he hummed and muttered to himself, oblivious to her presence.

She took a seat on the couch behind him and stared at the back of his head, wanting him to crack the password, yet fearing he would—fearing she had made a serious mistake letting him in.

Then, loud enough for her to hear, he said, "It has to be numeric."

"How do you know?"

"It just has to be."

"You're forgetting. He left this to me."

He frowned at her, as if entertaining this. "We do have one thing going for us," he said. "The computer doesn't lock us out after too many failed attempts, which means he wanted someone to crack it."

"Can you tell me at least what your strategy is?"

"No strategy, just every number combination I can summon." He began to list aloud the mathematical series and constants he was trying, most named after people Hazel had never heard of.

Euler's constant (.57721 . . .)
Planck's constant (6.626 x 10^{-34})
Fermat numbers (3, 5, 17, 257, 65537 . . .)
Ramanujan's number (1729)
Mersenne primes (2, 3, 5, 7, 13, 17, 19, 31 . . .)
The largest prime known to man ($2^{57,885,161}-1$)
Natural base of logarithms: e (2.71828 . . .)
The golden ratio (1.61803398 . . .)

As midnight approached, Hazel had a second cup of coffee and scrutinized the giant map of LA. She peered at the cryptically numbered dots, sitting in fertile clumps in various neighborhoods—Atwater Village, Lincoln Heights, Inglewood—in plots of irregularly shaped land defined by this or that freeway. Hazel didn't find maps of Los Angeles particularly compelling, because a map of LA wasn't really about place. When Angelenos looked at a rendering of their city, it wasn't to trace the shape of the land or to locate one's favorite park or body of water. Seattleites did that. San Franciscans and New Yorkers did that. Hazel would bet that if you picked a random woman living in Manhattan and handed her a sketch pad, she could draw her little island by heart, affectionately dropping in Central Park, the Met, the West Village, that fountain she likes.

But Los Angeles residents didn't care where the Getty Museum was in relation to Grauman's Chinese Theatre, Dodger Stadium, or their apartment. A Los Angeles map wasn't there to reveal how the places you loved were arranged in two-dimensional space. It was there to tell you which one-dimensional arteries you were going to take to get there.

This map, however, she was starting to like. Her grandfather had been consumed with eliminating the city's gridlock, but these dots showed no apparent relation to streets or freeways. Isaac had created a map that was about something else. But what?

"What about one of these numbers on the map?" she asked Alex.

He shook his head. "Wouldn't make sense."

"Why not?"

"It's not impossible, but it would be . . . inelegant. These things usually have a certain something, an *aha!*"

Hazel thought about their room number. "What about 137? Is that *aha!* enough?"

Alex smiled. "It's the first number I tried."

"Strange thing to call an eighth-floor room, isn't it?"

"You know Isaac was fascinated with that number, don't you?"

She didn't answer right away. Instead, she found a piece of hotel stationery and jotted down for him the numbers Isaac had left inside the book cover—137.13.9. "Not until I saw this."

He stared at the numbers for a long moment. "Where did you find these?"

"It doesn't matter," she said. "What do they mean?" When Alex started to enter it as a password, she stopped him. "I tried that."

He tried various combinations of the numbers anyway and then sighed. "One thirty-seven is a spooky integer that shows up all over the place in math and physics. Most famously, it appears in a constant governing the interaction between charged particles, like electrons."

Feeling her vision blur slightly with fatigue, Hazel took a position on the couch closest to Alex as he went on to explain how the Austrian physicist Wolfgang Pauli had been so obsessed with the number 137, it nearly drove him mad. As an old man, when his nurses were wheeling him into a room at the Rotkreuzspital in Zurich, the physicist looked up at the number on the door: 137. He reportedly groaned, "I'm never making it out of here."

"And did he?"

"Pauli died in that room. Pancreatic cancer."

Hazel frowned. "You don't think Isaac meant to die in here, do you?"

He shook his head. "He's got more subtlety than that. I think it was his idea of a joke. But these numbers, I have no idea."

Maybe it was the way Alex spoke or maybe it was her increasing exhaustion, but any suspicions she may have had about him seemed to fall away.

"Why did Isaac never talk about you?" she asked.

He looked up, startled by the question.

"If Gregory or I ever asked about our cousin Alexis," she continued, "Isaac and Lily were always cagey."

He gave her a mischievous smile. "Are you doubting my identity, Hazel?"

"Well," she said, a smile breaking on her own face, "I am taking your word for it that you are who you say you are. You could have the real Alexis bound and gagged somewhere, for all I know."

Silently he reached inside his jacket, produced an EU passport, and handed it to her. Hazel flipped past a collage of stamps to his bearded image, casually confronting the camera. She read the name: Severy, Alexis James.

"You didn't take your father's name?"

"I changed it, first year at university." He took back the passport. "Though it wasn't to flatter my mother, believe me. I suspect the reason Isaac never talked about me is because he was deferring to his daughter, who preferred to leave my existence vague."

"That doesn't surprise me," Hazel said. "I've never been a big Paige Severy fan. Sorry."

"Don't be. My French financier father is even less enthusiastic about parenting, if you can imagine. Sent me off to boarding schools all over Europe, making sure to ship me far from where he was living at the time. I had to seek out what information I could about both sides of the family—the Severys being the far more interesting of the two. But my mother made it very clear that she found having a child inconvenient, and I think she did her best to bury my existence. She gave birth to me in relative secret and didn't bother telling anyone until years later, even when I started to show real academic promise. Even then, she didn't bother to correct anyone's confusion over my androgynous name."

He laughed softly. "It's funny, but I knew Isaac mostly as a fan of his work, not as a relative. I can count my actual visits with him on two hands. When we finally met for the first time on one of his trips to England—I was in middle school—I felt as if I'd known him forever. It was this moment of 'Oh, there he is. There's my family—'"

He stopped short, and Hazel thought she detected a glisten in his eyes, but Alex quickly blinked it away.

When he fell silent, she leaned in closer. "We may have had *slightly* different childhoods, but actually, I had a very similar experience with him." She looked down, aware of how close their knees were to touching. "Isaac had a way of making you feel immediately . . ."

He looked up. "Like a part of something great?"

"Yeah," she said, with an intensity that surprised even her. "It was like he had chosen you to join some thrilling spy ring."

He smiled. "I wouldn't have put it like that, but yes—as if all that stood between the world and an Axis victory was you."

After another silence, Hazel ventured, "Did he really mention me?"

"Yes." Alex frowned, as if trying to recall a precise moment. "He said he and Lily had adopted two kids, though he preferred to think of you as grandchildren. It was only much later that I heard about Tom—the rough plot points, anyway."

Now it was Hazel's turn to fall silent, and in that moment, she felt an intense desire to tell Alex about her own tangled past. In fact, she marveled at how natural it would have felt to tell him everything. Yet at the same time, a familiar something was holding her back—and in this small hesitation, Alex gave an unintended meaning to her silence.

"God," he said, rolling his eyes. "I've really been prattling on, haven't I? How *can* you be so fascinating, Alex?"

"No, not at all. Really, it's just—" She broke off, unable to explain how she wanted to keep talking but didn't know quite what to say.

"You're absolutely right. We should get back to it." Alex spun around to resume attacking the keyboard.

So they were both orphans in their own way, both estranged from their birth parents, with Isaac as their true guardian. As Hazel savored this fact, Alex fell back on increasingly mundane number combinations, all of which he listed aloud for her:

The births and deaths of famous mathematicians.

The births and deaths of famous scientists.

Historic dates and anniversaries.

At one point of extreme hopelessness, he resorted to the Fibonacci series, each number the sum of the previous two: *0, 1, 1, 2, 3, 5, 8*... And then, truly desperate, he tried various approximations of pi.

Into her third cup of coffee, Hazel was wide awake again. She pulled a woolen throw around her and propped herself on a pillow to watch Alex work. She listened to him rattle off numbers and the related anecdotes about them.

"Are we absolutely sure the password isn't a *word*?"

"His language was numbers," he said, pausing to run a weary hand down the length of his face. "But no, I'm not sure."

"Once you're in, what exactly do you expect to find?"

He stopped typing and looked up. "Something brilliant, of course."

When Alex began to rub his eyes with increasing frequency, Hazel convinced him to take a break in the kitchen, where they raided the minibar for snacks and drinks. They opened two sleeves of Fig Newtons and made awful cocktails with whiskey and several flavors of Kern's nectar.

"I meant to ask you," she said. "If you knew I was at the party, why let me spy on you like a creep?"

He paused, as if weighing his response. "I thought you didn't recognize me, and then I realized that *you* thought I didn't recognize *you*, and outside of Shakespearean comedies, when does that ever happen? You know, what do you call it?"

"Stupid misunderstandings while in costume?"

He smiled. "Exactly. I was curious where it would lead."

Hazel couldn't argue with this. He had basically articulated her own reason for following him from the club.

Back at the desk, Alex munched on fig bars washed down with Kern's as he listed aloud more number combinations. Some compulsive need arose in Hazel to make him laugh again, as she had the first time they'd met. To that end, she offered up her own mathematical series:

The dumb integers (1, 2, 3, 4, 5, 6 . . .)

Professor Snobitorium's pompous constant (Oh, you don't know it?)

Hazel Severy's "Some Numbers That Come to Mind" (5, 187, 12, a million . . .)

Alex acknowledged her attempts at levity with patience, but he called her a pest and returned to his task. The sound of him talking to himself was soothing, pushing her toward sleep, but she forced herself to stay alert, keeping Alex's hunched form as a point of focus. She finally stood up, bleary-eyed, and took the remains from the snack tray back to the kitchen. When she returned to the living room, she was surprised to find the blue light of morning already filtering through the curtains. Her itchy wig lay huddled against a leg of the card table, where she had tossed it hours earlier. Her real hair probably looked appalling. She searched the couch cushions for her purse and phone. It was 6:19, almost eight hours since they'd arrived.

With Alex still at the desk, she slipped down the hall to the bathroom. Looting a vanity kit, she brushed her teeth and flossed. Then, pulling this or that trick out of her purse, she tried her best to minimize the appearance of having stayed awake all night. At least the smell of her suit had dissipated. But then why should she care? Alex wasn't a rebound possibility; he was a relative, if not a strictly biological one.

Alex's muttering grew louder for a moment, penetrating the thin walls, before subsiding again. And in a sudden burst of clarity, she realized what she had known to some extent all night: *that singsongy voice.* Okay, murmuring wasn't a fingerprint. It certainly wasn't scientific. Yet in her gut, she knew it had been Alex in Isaac's study the day of the funeral. Alex going through Isaac's things. Alex stealing down the stairs afterward.

She confronted herself in the mirror. *So?* She still needed help getting into the computer in order to deal with its contents. Then she could get back on a plane to Seattle knowing that she had made Isaac happy—wherever he was, whatever that meant. That was the goal, wasn't it?

She took a deep breath, and when she left the bathroom, she was startled to find Alex standing at the end of the hall looking at her.

"I was afraid you'd left," he said.

"Did you crack it?" she asked breezily, as if she wasn't at all surprised to see him standing there.

"Goose eggs, I'm afraid." Leaning against the wall, he tripped the light switch, flooding the hall in warm light. He made no move to turn it off. She couldn't help but notice how nice his face was, minus the beard and phony mustache, and she thought it a shame that such a face should go unremarked upon.

As his eyes settled on her for a moment, his hand rose to his neck, to the corresponding place, she realized, where her scar was. The upturned collar of her jacket had concealed it last night, but this morning she had failed to properly cover it.

"What's this?"

"Oh." She hesitated. "Childhood accident."

"You don't have to tell me."

"No, it's fine. It's a burn, actually." This wasn't entirely a lie, but it wasn't the truth, either.

His eyes went a bit wide.

Knowing that she wasn't ready to tell the story, not here in the hall, anyway, she said only, "It looks way worse than it felt."

He let his hand fall from his neck. "That's what memory does, I guess. Deletes the pain."

Hazel was suddenly aware of the diminished space between them, as if they had been involuntarily inching toward each other for the past minute. Or was she imagining it? *One of us should say something.*

Alex seemed aware of their increasing closeness, too, because he very abruptly turned and pitched himself into the living room. She followed.

"Listen," he said, assuming a casual position on an arm of the couch. "If I knew more about what he told you before he died, it might give me a better idea how to get in."

"But he didn't tell me anything." Again, this was not strictly a lie.

"Then what does he expect you to do with all this?"

How could she tell Alex, who clearly worshipped Isaac's work, what she had been asked to do with his mathematical legacy? How could she tell him about the command to destroy everything (except some equation)? How could she reveal Isaac's vague warning—*Three will die. I am the first*—or details about a man she was supposed to contact? Hadn't she spilled enough already? Yes, she was using Alex to get inside the computer, but wasn't he using her?

She moved to the wall. "You haven't said much about the map."

"Until I see the math, Hazel, it could be anything."

On impulse, she took out her phone and snapped four shots of the map, each image a separate quadrant of the city.

"Is that a good idea?"

She didn't answer because she had just noticed a pair of red dots that had previously escaped her attention. They were positioned directly on Beachwood Canyon. She motioned Alex over. "It's not easy to tell, but these two dots could be on Isaac's street. It could be the house."

"Maybe. The stickers are too big to say for certain." He moved in closer. "Actually, there are three."

She squinted.

"One's partially hidden behind the other, see?"

"You're right." She read one of the visible dots aloud: "1-0-1-7-1-5-0-5-5-5-3-1." She started to read the other "1-1-0-1-1-5 . . ." before turning to him. "Do these mean anything to you? Is it a code, maybe?"

At that moment, a loud and efficient rap came at the door.

"You should get it," Alex said, his voice oddly urgent.

The rap came again, and she left the room. Through the warped peephole, she spied an Eschered image of Flor, bearing a steeple of towels. She relaxed and opened the door.

"Good morning," the housekeeper said. "I know it's early, but I heard you up. Fresh towels?"

Thinking it best to appear normal, Hazel accepted them. "Thank you."

"I should tidy for you, yes?" Before Hazel could protest, Flor had moved past her down the hall.

"Actually—" Hazel started to say, but the woman was already in the bathroom, unnecessarily wiping up.

Hazel returned to the living room where Alex sat staring at the suspended checkers game.

"We have maid service," she announced helplessly.

He didn't appear to hear her. "Did Isaac like checkers?" he asked.

"Why?"

"Because either he was playing a game with himself or . . . he had a visitor."

Hazel tried to picture her grandfather allowing someone into his hideout, the one he took such pains to conceal.

"Do you really think he'd bring someone up here?"

Before Alex could answer, Flor appeared, a cell phone to her ear. "Excuse me. The front desk is asking if anyone called for an Uber."

"Oh, right," Alex said, jumping up and checking his phone. "I have an appointment to get to. Thought we could share a ride."

Hazel smiled, though she was disappointed their time together had come to an end. "Of course."

When they stepped outside, she was glad to find the cloud cover still lingering, making the early hour more tolerable. As they climbed into the back of an awaiting SUV, she reflected on how quickly Bennet seemed to be receding from her mind. Or was this an illusion brought on by the strange excitement of the past ten hours? She worried that once she was alone again, the double pang of heartbreak and anxiety would return.

Alex suggested that they drop her off at the house first and that he continue to his destination from there. She thought of asking where he was going, but that old reflex of not wanting to appear like she cared too much kicked in. As she gave in to the SUV's lurching movements, she thought back to the map and wondered aloud, "What did you know about Isaac's traffic project?"

Alex began to idly spin his wig on one finger like a plate. "How much do you know about chaos theory?"

"Some." Hazel thought of the *drip-drip* of the kitchen faucet, and of how her brother had used the theory as a very cute excuse not to clean his room: "My room isn't messy, it's an intelligent system hiding in apparent disorder."

"There was that book everyone was reading in the nineties," she offered. "And I know Isaac used chaos in his work."

"Then you know he was trying to create a mathematical model of traffic using chaotic math."

"Right, his project with the city."

"We talked by phone quite a bit during that time," Alex said, smiling sadly at the memory. "That project was supposed to be his way of helping drivers better navigate the roads, but it quickly turned into this obsession—this need to forecast specific events. Some might argue that Los Angeles traffic is already fairly predictable: just avoid the morning and evening commutes. But that's an oversimplification of motorist behavior—it doesn't take the 'noise' into account. It doesn't consider everything we can't foresee: a driver's mood, the weather, debris in the road, rubbernecking, a flat tire, a stray dog, a fly buzzing in a driver's ear. Isaac knew that if he was going to truly predict the patterns of traffic, he would have to know absolutely everything. *He would have to deal with the noise.* Of course, there's no way to predict each of those tiny chance occurrences—it would be insane to try. But with mathematics, if he could somehow boil all this arbitrary activity down to a single mathematical constant, he might predict congestion, even accidents, right down to the precise minute and location."

"It's funny," Hazel said. "I never thought to ask him, why cars? I mean, no one likes traffic, but if that kind of prediction is actually possible—and not just sci-fi nuttiness—why not predict the next meteor impact or terrorist attack? At least something more dangerous than whether someone's going to have a fender bender on the 405."

Alex gave her a knowing look, one that a teacher might give a clever student. "Yes, but for Isaac, there was safety in studying something as mundane as vehicle gridlock. It's ongoing, it's local, it was a starting point." Alex fell back against the seat. "But then he gave up."

"I thought the city yanked his funding."

Alex looked out the window as they left the traffic of Franklin Avenue and turned onto Beachwood Drive. "You're right. He never entirely gave up on things."

Hazel thought of the map, of all the dots that seemed to ignore the freeways. "What if his traffic project just evolved into something else?"

He turned to her. "You know, of course, that even if we crack this, we might find nothing but demented grandpa mathematics. Good-natured numerical oatmeal."

Good, she thought. *If his work is oatmeal, I can destroy it without guilt.*

As the SUV wound up the canyon, Hazel realized these were their last few moments together. "So what's our next move?" she asked in an oddly spunky tone, as if she were the sidekick in a teen mystery. But Alex didn't have a chance to respond, because at that moment, as they turned a corner on Durand Drive, the driver shouted something that made his passengers lean forward. Through the windshield, they could see three police cars and an ambulance filed along the shoulder. At the bottom of the steps leading up the hill to the Severy house stood a small crowd.

The first person Hazel noticed was a neighbor from down the road, sitting on the ground in his gray jogging suit. He was bent over, the hood of his sweatshirt twisted around and held to his face. She knew it was illogical, but her first panicked thought was of Gregory.

"Stop the car," she said.

As the driver hit the brakes, she was already climbing out. A group of Beachwood residents and police were blocking her view of the hillside. As she moved toward them, she was vaguely aware of her costume, a visible morning-after aura clinging to it. But no one seemed to notice or care.

"Poor thing," someone said.

"It was *far* too dangerous. I don't know how many times I said so."

Hazel nearly cried out with relief when she spotted her brother. She headed through the crowd and threw her arms around him.

He turned to embrace her without taking his eyes from the hill. He looked exhausted, his expression one of restrained misery.

"A neighbor found her on his run," he said.

Hazel pulled away and pushed herself toward the scene. Near the bottom of the concrete steps leading up the bluff to the house lay a woman's body, turned upward, head pointed downhill. Her arms and legs were bent in a gruesome imitation of the cardinal directions, her neck twisted in such a way that her face was hidden from the crowd. But the hair was unmistakable: the pre-Raphaelite locks of Sybil Severy-Oliver. Instead of her hair tumbling down her shoulders, it was spilling away down the slope. She wore some kind of robe or coat, which was only half on, and her silk nightgown rode up her thighs, exposing the elastic of her underwear. One foot wore a satiny bedroom slipper. The slipper's mate, in the echo of a fairy tale, sat several steps up the hillside.

Police suspended yellow tape between the trees. A detective snapped pictures. The paramedics took their time readying a stretcher. Hazel found everyone strangely calm, except for Jack. He was a few yards off, weaving back and forth through a cluster of oaks, motioning with his hands and shouting unintelligible insults at the greenery. Without warning, he turned and screamed at the crowd, "Would somebody cover up my wife? For fuck's sake, *somebody* cover her!"

Hazel returned to her brother's side and pushed her face into his shoulder.

"They're saying she was asleep," he muttered.

"I don't understand," she said, glancing toward the hill, where the sight of Sybil collided with a night of junk food and no sleep to form a wave of nausea. "I thought she was in Pasadena with her parents."

He nodded. "Apparently she had another fight, with Jack this time. So she packed up and left."

Hazel forced herself to step away from Gregory and look for Alex, but he was suddenly standing right beside her, his hand encircling her wrist. The thrill of his closeness was hard to ignore. "Stay at your brother's tonight and don't come back here. I'd get as far away from this place as possible."

In that instant, with Alex's breath warm in her ear, something occurred to her. *Don't stay in or visit the house past the end of October.* She pulled her hand free and checked her phone, as if needing outside confirmation of the date. It was, of course, one day after Halloween. November 1, 2015, or *110115*.

She opened her mouth to tell Alex what the numbers on the map meant, that they were, in fact, painfully commonplace. Month, day, year—then what—hour, minute? But he'd already figured that out, hadn't he? She was about to ask him, but when she turned around, both he and the SUV were gone.

PART 2

What a to-do to die today, at a minute or two to two!
A thing distinctly hard to say, but harder still to do.
We'll beat a tattoo, at twenty to two
a rat-a-tat-tat-a-tat tat-a-tattoo
and the dragon will come when he hears the drum
at a minute or two to two today, at a minute or two to two.

—EDWARD GERMAN & BASIL HOOD,
MERRIE ENGLAND, 1902

15

The Professor

Twelve days after Isaac's funeral and five days after Sybil's death, Hazel found herself again at the Resurrection Cemetery surrounded by family. She had never been particularly close to her cousin, yet she felt sucked down by a swift undertow of misery along with the rest of the Severys. The final image of Sybil sat hard in her gut, and thinking back to that morning in the canyon, she was struck by how brutally emptied of life a corpse really was—as if Sybil's tumble down those steps had transformed her into a discarded object or a sack of garbage for all that her body resembled a moving, breathing person.

Sybil had been cremated (no stately coffin draped in roses for her), and the mourners numbered far fewer than at Isaac's burial, yet the whole day felt like a hideous rerun of grief. A stubborn marine layer sapped the morning of light, and a silence pervaded that seemed unsettling even for a funeral. Philip and Jane, standing above their daughter's breadbox plot, appeared blank, as if they had resolved never to open their mouths or express another emotion again. Jack looked catatonic. His eyes were dry, but his face had puffed and reddened to an alarming degree. Drew was nowhere to be seen. When Hazel mentioned this to her sister-in-law, Goldie whispered that Drew was in the care of Jane's sister until

Jack was "in the right place" to explain where Mommy went. Hazel didn't think Jack was in the right place to be doing anything outside of assuming a fetal position on the grass.

Apart from Drew (and Lily, whom the family wished to spare from unnecessary confusion), there were two family members conspicuously absent from Sybil's burial. Gregory had left the house at six that morning claiming there was an emergency at work. Though he apologized to all for having to bow out, Hazel worried that he might be hiding something, if only his feelings. She wondered if her brother's absence wasn't a kind of avoidance or denial. He had always been intensely attached to Sybil, despite adulthood having pushed the cousins apart.

The second absence was less surprising. Since that morning in the canyon, after Alex had vanished, she kept hearing his hushed words to her: "Stay at your brother's tonight and don't come back here." Now she wondered if he hadn't followed his own advice and left the city entirely. She had considered tracking him down to tell him she knew what the numbers meant, as he had no doubt already figured out, but Sybil's death seemed to trivialize her every thought about finding Alex. Still, the idea that he was gone for good, back to whatever mathematicians do in Paris, made recent events more awful. When she had doubled back to the room at the Hotel d'Antibes the night after Sybil was found, it was as much to see if Alex would show up as it was to confront the now terrifying map on the wall.

Alex did not show up at the hotel, nor did he leave any messages at the front desk. She was left to reexamine the contents of the room alone, now with the certainty that the map held a cache of terrible predictions—or at least the knowledge that something would happen Halloween night in Beachwood Canyon. Isaac, the map seemed to say, had not left behind numerical oatmeal but portentous mathematics. Her eyes zeroed in on the twisted veins of Beachwood Canyon and on the three dots pasted there. She could now see from their numbers—date, hour, minute—that not only was Sybil's death represented but also Isaac's: 101715055531. If these numbers were accurate, Sybil had died at eleven minutes past midnight; Isaac, at precisely 5:55 a.m. and 31 seconds.

Three will die.

So what about the third dot? Isaac had suggested in his letter that there was nothing to be done about it, that fate could not be stopped. Still, Hazel desperately needed to see the date and time on that final sticker. But when she tried to peel off Sybil's dot to reveal the one beneath, she couldn't pull them apart. She would end up tearing them both, so on instinct, she took both dots from the wall for safekeeping until a solution presented itself.

She turned back to the computer, the events of the previous night drifting back to her like some distant historical event, as if Sybil's fall had opened up a rip in time and separated Hazel forever from that night with Alex. Yet it seemed more urgent than ever that she get into her grandfather's computer. But if Alex couldn't crack it in the course of an entire night, how could she? She took one last look at the map. There were, of course, other dots scattered around the city, scribbled with future dates and times, but what could she do? The knowledge of other deaths would only distract her from her task of protecting the family, of making sure no one stayed in Beachwood Canyon.

That same night, the shock of Sybil's death and the grim revelation of the map were complicated by another, lesser disaster: a water main had ruptured that day in Pioneer Square directly beneath her store. Chet called to inform her that although her merchandise was still dry, her store had gotten the worst of it. They would need to shut the doors indefinitely.

"Seriously, this may be one of the worst Pioneer Square floods since the eighteen hundreds," he told her. "Do you want me to wait for you?"

"No, just shut it down. Put a fun sign in the window."

"When are you back?"

"Way things are going, maybe never."

After a delicate pause, he informed her that he was writing a piece about the flood for *Seattle Weekly*, for which he was a stringer.

"I hate to ask, but do you have a quote for me?"

She had, in fact, hired Chet after he'd interviewed her for a somewhat embarrassing portrait in the weekly, titled "Amazon Warrior: Young Book Dealer Defends Lost Art of Reading," though the more accurate title would have been: "Impulsive Woman Defends Own Laziness, Amasses Staggering Debt, Repeatedly Drowns in Water-Themed Nightmares."

At last, she said, "Just because you love books doesn't mean you should sell them," and hung up.

There were mounting bills she couldn't pay. On the morning of the service, Hazel received a package from Chet stuffed with them. He also enclosed a list of particularly impatient callers, one of whom he dubbed "Mr. Persistent." The man had called several times in her absence but refused to leave his name or the company he represented. There was also a note:

Dear Ms. Hazel Severy,

I wish to connect with you on an important matter. Since you have not yet contacted me, I leave you my temporary stateside number. I look forward to speaking very soon.

Regards,

L. F. Richardson

626-344-9592

These bill collectors were certainly getting clever. There was that initialed name evoking someone of refinement, plus an attempt at the offhand, as if he were dashing off a message to a friend of a friend. As Hazel folded up the note, she refused to entertain the idea of Isaac's estate coming to her rescue, and besides, despite Fritz's best efforts, her grandfather's wealth was tied up entirely in the house. After everything was sold off, paid off, and distributed, she sort of doubted there would be much left. Hazel took the note to Goldie's office, fed it into the shredder, and hurried to iron her funeral outfit, which had been sitting crumpled at the bottom of her suitcase.

Toward the end of the service, as Jane, Philip, and Jack were kneeling down to scoop up handfuls of dirt, Hazel glanced up the hill in the direction of Isaac's headstone. The unusually heavy marine layer gave one the impression of peering through gauze, but through the gray, she spied a tall man in a dark coat standing above Isaac's plot. Only his back was visible, his legs shrouded in mist and his bowed head concealed behind an up-turned collar. She knew it was Isaac's grave because of a curious topiary that stood a few feet to the left of his headstone: a shrub that had reminded her of a mushroom cloud. Seconds later, the man turned, revealing an almost regal, aquiline profile, and stared in the direction of their gathering. He stood motionless for some time, though whether he was studying them or merely taking in the atmosphere, she couldn't tell.

At the sound of dirt hitting metal, Hazel turned back to the service in time to see Sybil's parents letting handfuls of earth fall dully over the box containing their daughter's remains. When Hazel looked back toward the man a second later, she could just make out his hunched form as he walked off swiftly into the haze.

*　　*　　*

The reception at Philip and Jane's Pasadena home was quiet and small. Hazel spent much of the time loitering near the piano in the front room, examining framed photographs of Sybil that had been arranged in a formation of unbroken loveliness. As she took in the pictorial record of Sybil's youth and adulthood—both remarkably absent of any awkwardness or skin disturbances—Hazel's mind persisted in re-creating her cousin's fatal fall. Poor Sybil, murdered by gravity. The weakest of all universal forces, wasn't it? She imagined Sybil moving across the lawn, eyes half closed, stepping to the edge of the concrete flight, reaching out for a nonexistent handrail, encountering only air. She loses her balance, topples . . . Hazel replayed the scene several times, with minor variations. But there was a second scenario, still lacking in definition, now asserting itself: a scene connected to the dots on Isaac's map. How the map knew that tragedy would strike in the middle of the night at the exact latitude and longitude of Beachwood Canyon's Durand Drive, she could only guess, but the third dot on the map was inserting itself into Hazel's mind with increasing menace.

Three will die. I am the first.

She had followed both Isaac's and Alex's advice to stay away from the house, immediately moving her things to her brother's place in Mid-City. This was not before verifying that none of the family would be staying in the canyon, either. No one, it turned out, wanted to be near the place, but Hazel received several puzzled looks for her sudden fixation on family members' immediate accommodations.

As she continued to examine the photos that populated the living room, she discovered a five-by-seven that made her instantly light-headed. It was of Alex and, judging from the brand-new frame and lack of dust, had only just been placed among the others. He stood at the black mouth of an anonymous cathedral, tanned and darkly handsome, very un-Severy-like, probably looking much like his negligent father. Hazel certainly didn't need any more prompts to remind herself that Alex existed. Over the past several days, under a mantle of gloom, she had sketched out a vivid picture of him in her mind: the way he spoke, how he could switch from frothy conversation to scholarly clarification and back again with ease, and how his troubled brow could transform into a smile in an instant.

She had no idea how she could get in touch with him. Alex's mother had been at the funeral, hovering at the periphery, but when Hazel approached her afterward, Paige scuttled off to her car, pretending not to see her. Paige did not appear at the reception, leaving Hazel to assume she had retreated back to her hovel in Venice Beach. Alternatively, the thought of asking her aunt Jane for anything other than how she might help in this emotionally eviscerating time struck Hazel as monumentally rude; she may as well ask her if she could borrow twenty bucks to go stock up on some Boone's Farm. If Alex couldn't be found or relied upon to help her, she would have to dismantle the computer herself, check out of room 137, and ship everything up to Seattle. But for what? A giant bonfire of melting plastic and hard drives?

The sane thing to do, of course, was to hand off the responsibility to someone Isaac would have trusted, despite his warning that no such person existed in the family. Just as she entertained this thought, she looked up and saw her uncle Philip standing at the window, staring out into the side yard. Hazel realized that she had not spoken to him in any meaningful way since Sybil's death. As she took a few steps closer, she saw that he was watching the child of one of his and Jane's friends play on a small slide. The slide had presumably been set up for Drew, though Hazel couldn't imagine it holding the girl's interest for long.

Hazel approached cautiously, her voice coming out in a croak. "Uncle Philip?"

He turned, eyes crimson, and blinked at her. His earlier blank expression was gone, and Hazel found herself shocked by the raw feeling on his typically composed face. He pulled her into a warm embrace. "You stayed," he said, his voice raspy in her ear. "Jane and I know you didn't have to."

As he pulled away, Hazel quickly stuttered something about how sorry she was, what a shock, what a lovely, lovely person Sybil had been. She was barely aware of what she was saying but wondered at the same time if she might segue into inquiring about his father's work, find out if he knew what Isaac had been working on before he died. Ridiculous, of course. *Listen, I know your daughter's dead and all, but I could use your help destroying your father's mathematics.*

Philip thanked her for her kind words and turned back to the window. The child was now struggling up the slide's wooden ladder. After several seconds, Philip said, "Do you know how many steps run down that canyonside, Hazel?"

It was an odd question, but she knew the answer. "Two hundred fifty-seven, isn't it?" There were multiple sets of staircases tucked between property lines that allowed for shortcuts up the west end of Beachwood Canyon. Isaac had liked to notify the guests who took these stairs not only of the number of steps they had just climbed but also that 257 is a prime number—one of the so-called Fermat primes, exceedingly rare.

Philip nodded. "I have yet to find someone who can't answer that question. My father apparently drilled it into all of us. And do you know the number of steps on the hillside, leading from the road to the house?"

He was referring to the steps down which his daughter had tumbled.

"No, I don't."

"Twenty-nine."

Hazel combed her memory for the significance of that number but could find nothing.

"Sybil was twenty-nine," he said. "The age she'll be forever now, I suppose."

Hazel searched for something comforting to say, but he continued: "This knee-jerk mathematization of the world, of course, when applied to everything, is deeply stupid. Isn't it funny that I seem to be realizing this only now? You know, when I was young and bruised quite easily—*actual* bruises, I mean, purple and green—I can remember being forced to play this or that sport in school, and for days afterward I would count up the accumulated spots on my arms and legs. At the time, it seemed a way of turning something unpleasant into a useful activity. You know, sort of tricking oneself out of feeling awful? I think I was even proud of this impulse, but now . . ." He laughed. "It's merely a not-so-subtle illustration of a terrible family pastime. Let's all ignore the blatant fact staring at us down the gun barrel of being alive—I mean pain, because it's *all* pain—and just break it down into its component parts, shall we? We may as well be practicing numerology."

Philip turned and smiled down on her, his eyes even redder than before. He blinked rapidly, as if trying to loosen something from his eyes. "Sorry, don't mean to speechify, it's just—" Before she could tell her uncle it was all right, that she was, in fact, glad they were talking (flattered, really, that he would reveal such thoughts to her), his gaze darted past her to the other end of the living room, where the twins had begun a ragtime duet on the piano. They had clearly taken lessons, but they had no sense of rhythm, and the resulting commotion was jarring. "Excuse me, will you?" With a quick squeeze of her shoulder, Philip left to ask his sons to select a piece more appropriate for the occasion.

A second later, Fritz Dornbach was standing in Philip's place. He looked tired and bloated, possibly fending off a hangover. "Unspeakable thing, isn't it?" He looked out the window at the same child, who was now battling an exasperating amount of friction on her way down the slide.

Hazel nodded. "Terrible."

Silas and Sidney began to pick their way through Chopin's funeral dirge.

"I have this vague recollection," Fritz said, "that you wanted to talk to me about something on Halloween."

"Oh, did I?" Hazel was starting to feel embarrassed at all her clumsy attempts to gather information. "I don't remember. I was drinking quite a bit."

"I know the feeling," he said, suddenly patting his jacket pockets. "I have something for you, you know." He located a folded piece of paper, one of those old-fashioned slips for jotting down messages. "Frankly, I'm a little tired of this guy tying up the phone lines."

Hazel unfolded the note.

Urgent
For: Hazel Severy
From: Prof. L. F. Richardson
Message: George C. Page Museum Theater @ 3 p.m. Saturday, Nov. 14. Please come alone.

"*Professor* Richardson?"

"You know him?"

Hazel now wished she hadn't shredded that earlier note. "Did he leave his number?"

"No, he was way more interested in getting your cell number, which we didn't give him."

Hazel's head began to ache.

"Fritz?"

"Hmm?"

"How did Richardson know I'd be in town?"

"Oh, well, he was very persuasive, and he did say he was a good friend of Isaac's. Did I forget to mention that? He also had some kind of accent, in case that's relevant." Fritz coughed. "Page Museum . . . Isn't that the tar pits?"

"Yeah."

"Maybe I should go with you, in case he tries to push you into a bog."

Hazel frowned and dropped her voice to a near whisper. "I maybe remember what I wanted to ask you on Halloween." The truth was that she didn't know until it came out of her mouth: "How do you think Isaac died?"

Fritz's expression changed to one of surprise. He let a few seconds go by before answering, "Maybe he was very sad, and none of us could see it. That can happen, but . . ." He frowned. "There was always more going on with Isaac than he let on. Don't you agree, Hazel?"

That night, back at her brother's house, after a quick search on his computer, she found the only professor by the name of Richardson with whom her grandfather might have been acquainted: Lewis Fry Richardson. From what Hazel could gather, he was quite famous and had several fan pages of the nerdy, poorly designed variety.

He was an English mathematician-meteorologist and a pioneer of mathematical weather prediction, an ambitious field with as-yet-lackluster results. Richardson was also an early pioneer of chaos theory, along with meteorologist Edward Lorenz, the latter of whom coined the ubiquitous term *butterfly effect* to refer to minuscule events having far-flung consequences. (An insect twitches in China; weeks later, a man's hat blows off in Bermuda.) Yes, this was exactly the kind of person her grandfather would have befriended, and exactly the kind of man who would be interested in Isaac's most recent work, save for one detail: Lewis Fry Richardson had been dead for sixty years.

16

The Leave

Dear Professor Severy,

Please accept my sincerest condolences on the loss of your daughter. Though I never had the pleasure of meeting Sybil, I have no doubt that she was as remarkable a person as her father and grandfather. True brilliance, after all, is a hereditary monarchy—as I think someone brilliant once said.

I cannot imagine the extent of your pain, but please know that you and your family are in my thoughts. Perhaps you find my concern somewhat odd considering that we have not, in fact, properly met, and that our most recent meeting was suspended. But I had a great fondness for your father, and that fondness extends to the entire Severy family.

Do not hesitate to let my office know if there is anything I can do to be of service to you during this very sad time. I say this without any hope of gain, but simply as an unlikely friend.

Sympathies,
P. Booth Lyons

The note irritated Philip more each time he read it. It had been written on fine letterhead, with the precision of one clearly devoted to the art of cursive. As his eyes passed over the lines, he could almost picture Nellie taking dictation at her desk, her boss pacing in front of her with all the self-importance of a big-game hunter, the dough of his neck rising over his oxford collar. "I had great affection for your father—no, strike that—*fondness* for your father. Did you get that, Ms. Stone?"

"You know nothing about my family," Philip muttered, crushing the paper and tossing it onto a growing pile of cardstock on the far end of the dining room table. It was obvious that Lyons wouldn't stop until he got whatever he was after, but Philip no longer cared. On the near end of the table, among languishing flowers, sat a growing heap of envelopes. Most remained, and would remain, unopened. Sympathy cards were all necessarily alike, a form letter in which modifications were allowed only for proper names and flattering adjectives. And while Isaac's condolence cards had been filled with an assortment of descriptors—*brilliant, towering, generous, funny, kind*—it seemed that Sybil's were all variations on a theme: *lovely, luminous, glowing, exquisite, enchanting.* P. Booth Lyons had been the only one to suggest that Philip's daughter had been anything other than an ordinary girl in an extraordinary body; that she had been, in fact, remarkable.

Since Sybil's death a week before, Philip and Jane had scanned their mental horizons for someone to blame. But the only candidate they could come up with was Philip's paternal grandfather for having bought the Hollywoodland plot back in the 1950s and then installing a precipitous flight of concrete steps down which a parasomniac could fall and break her neck. Philip decided not to dwell on the irony of his grandfather having been a successful structural engineer at JPL.

The police, of course, had thoroughly interrogated Jack, more out of routine than any serious suspicion, but the investigative follow-up stalled when Jack had a psychotic break after Sybil's funeral and had to be hospitalized.

Drew, who had yet to be told of her mother's death, had been transferred to Philip and Jane's care until her father could be released from Cedars-Sinai Medical Center. But because neither of them was in any kind of emotional place to take care of a small child, Jane's sister, Faye, was flown in from Phoenix to live with them indefinitely. She immediately transformed herself into a substitute housewife and therapist, alternating her time looking after Drew and comforting her grieving sister, all the while making endless pots of tea and trays of baked goods. Faye repeatedly soothed the little girl with the fib "Mommy and Daddy needed to go home for a little while, but they'll be back for you." If Jack wasn't better soon, Philip and Jane would have to correct this lie themselves. They would also have to look into enrolling Drew in a local kindergarten or, more suitably, the first grade.

But Drew being Drew, she besieged everyone around her with questions. "Am I being punished?" "Was it because I ate the poisonous plant?" "Was I very bad?" she asked repeatedly. Faye assured her that it wasn't her fault and that her parents loved her, but Drew remained unconvinced. Yesterday, the day of the funeral, she had stopped asking questions altogether, and now sat mutely on the couch with her Audubon guide open in her lap. That morning, Philip had caught her whispering an alphabetized list of birds—cattle egret, cave swallow, cedar waxwing, cerulean warbler, chestnut-backed chickadee—but mostly she was silent and still, leaving the couch only when it was time to eat or go to bed. Philip understood, of course. He and his wife had been operating on a variation of this same routine all week.

Silas and Sidney were taking a brief hiatus from their practice for the SoCal Junior Tennis Open. (Even though only Sidney had qualified for the finals, the twins practiced as an inseparable unit.) Being the teenagers they were, they moped around the house for days, supremely confused about their feelings. The two had wept openly upon hearing that their grandfather had died, but their older sister's death had thrown them into a dumbfounded silence. They went to school as usual and in the evenings quietly eyed their racquets, wondering when propriety would allow them to snatch them up again and flee to the nearest court.

Jane had gone into the blackest of depressions, the kind from which she could send back only the crudest messages—"My girl . . . my little girl"—and allude to wanting her own life to end. Not in a serious way, she insisted, but in the way a mother who loses a child will entertain. Faye responded by forcing her sister out of the house for a daily run in Eaton Canyon, leaving Drew with the twins. "One has to keep up one's interests," Faye told her, "even if the interest is gone." Philip had to admit that for all his sister-in-law's general obtuseness and materialism, she was a godsend, and he didn't know how he'd cope without her. His wife had completely shut down, and his ability to communicate with her had gone with it.

Philip was pushing a pile of cards into a wastepaper basket when he let the can fall to the floor. He couldn't stand the sight of another flower or card. He needed to get out of the house. Now. They both did. He abandoned the mess, grabbed his car keys, and headed to the garden to find Jane. Maybe without her sister circling, he could get her to talk to him. Maybe they could find a way at last to be of some small comfort to each other.

An hour later, they were cresting a ridge overlooking the heart of Eaton Canyon when Jane turned to him: "If she were our only child, I think that would be it for me." They stopped just feet away from a sheer drop of eighty feet. Philip slid his arms around his wife and held her, though not tightly enough to betray his alarm at the proximity of the edge.

"Do you think people know how they're going to die?" she asked.

Not being in the mood for morose speculation, he hesitated.

"I mean we're all going to die," she continued. "It's already predetermined; we just don't know how it's going to happen. But maybe our subconscious is able to catch a glimpse of it somehow. Like that mathematician, the code breaker for the Allies, what's-his-name—"

"Turing."

"Right. Do you think every time Alan Turing looked at an apple, there was a shiver of recognition?"

Turing, after breaking Nazi Germany's Enigma code during the war, had been harassed by the British government for being gay—or at least for not bothering to hide it. When given the choice of a prison sentence or chemical castration, he chose the latter, presumably because prison would have hampered the possibility of yet a third option, one he chose to exercise in his home laboratory one day with only his appetite and a cyanide-laced apple. In this case, Jane was likely right. Philip could imagine Turing having watched the poisoned-apple scene from Disney's *Snow White*— the mathematician's favorite movie—and experiencing a moment of intense recognition, as if remembering an event that had already happened.

"Isn't it amazing," she continued, "how he could be so unhappy, yet considerate enough to make it look like an accident? So he could spare his poor mother the heartache? I would do the same for you and the twins: give you the gift of plausible deniability."

"Can we not do this, please?"

"For Godsake, allow me my morbid fantasy, would you?"

Philip was quiet for a moment. He stared out at the canyon,

where the late-afternoon sun turned the rock a fierce orange. "Well, we're not recreational chemists, for one thing," he said finally. "The poisoned apple worked only because it was semicredible that he spilled cyanide on his lunch."

"All right, so where's our semicredible accident?"

"I don't know. I think I feel a shiver of recognition every time I look at your sister's lasagna."

In his desperation for levity, Philip had wanted to make her laugh, but the attempt misfired. She pulled away, wicking the moisture from her eyes with the ends of her sleeves.

"I don't understand," she choked. "How can you be so cool? Where's *your* breakdown?"

"I have to stay sane for you. You want me to go to pieces like Jack? End up in the psych ward at Cedars?"

"At least I'd have company."

"What do you want me to say, Jane? Our child is dead, and I'm heartbroken. I cry every day. I've taken leave from work."

"I guess the meaning of the universe is just going to have to take a back seat to the death of your daughter—your very unremarkable daughter."

Philip didn't know how to respond to this. Where had she gotten that word, *unremarkable*? It had been confined to his head, yet somehow Jane had intuited it.

She turned back to the precipice. The sun hit the side of her face, throwing it into a frightening motif of shadow and fire-orange. It was at that moment that he saw his wife's grief turn to rage, toward the world and toward him.

It was true that Philip had taken an immediate leave from Caltech for the rest of the term; his colleagues had insisted. Professor Kato agreed to take on Philip's graduate seminar and supersymmetry class, while Kuchek temporarily absorbed Philip's graduate advisees. Still, the next morning, Philip got up and went to school, if only to sit in his office and stare at neglected equations on his blackboard, or walk a purposeless route through campus, even at the risk of running into people who would wonder why he wasn't at home. But he could feel Jane's anger becoming dark and heavy, and being of no use or solace to her, he didn't know what else to do with himself.

Late fall was Philip's favorite time of year on campus, and despite his misery, he could still appreciate the season. People back east liked to insist that Southern California didn't really have seasons and that autumn in particular failed to have any real meaning. There was some truth in this, but Philip enjoyed the subtle indicators that the Northern Hemisphere was tipping away from the sun. Besides the sweaters and light jackets that appeared in November, the olive trees slowly surrendered their crop to the pavement, and the few campus oaks changed color in revolt against the prevailing evergreenery.

That morning, as he passed the Sloan Laboratory of Mathematics and Physics, Enid Elderberg—spiky grapefruit-colored hair, stud in her nose—waved to him from the steps, a pair of file boxes balanced in one arm. Philip found Elderberg's fashion sense a transparent stab at making pure mathematics look hip, but then he'd heard she was quite brilliant, so why the hell not.

"Philip, hi." She fumbled with her boxes before setting them on the pavement. "We were all very sorry to hear about your daughter. If there's anything—"

"Thank you, I'm fine. Really." He didn't think he could handle any more pity.

He was about to move on, when she said, "You heard about our break-in?"

"Break-in?"

"Someone forced open several offices on the top floor last week, including mine."

Philip only now remembered that Elderberg had been the one to move into his father's old office. His father had rarely used the space since his retirement, but he had never entirely moved out of it, either.

"These boxes belonged to Isaac," she continued. "I had them locked away in a cabinet, so I doubt anything was taken."

Philip peered up at his father's old window. "Student mischief?"

Elderberg shrugged. "Who knows? Unsettling all the same. I was about to drop these at your office, actually."

"I can take them now, thanks. Sorry, with everything going on, I'd completely forgotten about clearing out his stuff."

"Please," she said, helping him gather the boxes. "I was happy to have the great Isaac Severy occupy my workspace for a time."

The boxes were heavy; Philip's muscles ached just from the short walk to the parking lot. He loaded them into the trunk of his car and tried to tell himself that the forced entry was a coincidence. Nothing had been taken, after all. But then, how would anyone know? He lifted the lid of the top box to reveal a collection of discolored newspaper clippings.

The articles were all from Southern California papers, mostly the *LA Times*, their dates spanning decades. "Film Producer Dies in Freak Yard Accident." "Man Electrocuted in Pool, Faulty Wiring Blamed." "Man Drowns off El Segundo Beach." "Static Electricity Turns Man into Human Torch." "Father Dies Locked in Own Refrigerator." "Family Car Rolls Backward onto Mother." Some of the articles were flagged with a red Sharpie.

Isaac had been a nut for these sorts of gruesome incidents. As Philip recalled the similarly grim clippings that littered his father's house, he felt an urgent pulse travel up the back of his neck, followed by a phantom strobe of light. These auras happened more frequently now, which led him to suspect his migraines were evolving in some way, finding means to outwit his medication.

He shut the trunk and ferreted his pill bottle out of the glove compartment. Philip had managed to convince his doctor to up his prescription significantly, allowing him to accumulate a decent stockpile, but his Subaru reserve would need replenishing. There was a single pill left, and as he tipped the bottle over like a liquor shot, he felt the very image of an upmarket junkie. A highbrow, tweedy version of Tom.

Glancing up briefly to make sure no one had seen this undignified move, he noticed a black town car with opaque windows parked in a corner of the lot, facing out. As he felt the pill slide down his throat, he was overwhelmed by the suspicion that he was being watched, and had been for days.

A second later, he saw Nellie Stone in a black brim hat and sunglasses cutting across the parking lot toward the town car. Philip quickly ducked behind the wheel to avoid detection, but something made him look back in the direction from which she had come. In the shadow of the physics building, he could make out Andrei Kuchek standing there. His colleague wore an irritated expression and clutched a pile of books to his chest, as if it were armor. Kuchek took one last look in Nellie's direction, mumbled something to himself, and hurried back inside.

Philip felt his anger returning. Letters from Lyons he could ignore, but these repeated intrusions into his life? Nellie had left several messages on his phone the past week, all of which he had deleted without listening to.

When the town car had pulled out of the lot and was gone, Philip locked up his car and tracked Kuchek to the faculty lounge, where he poured his colleague a cup of coffee and asked him about the encounter.

"What did she say, Andrei? Was this the first time she's approached you?"

Kuchek was typically unresponsive.

"Did you hear what I said, Andrei? Andrei."

Kuchek dropped his pencil and answered in his strong Czech accent, "I told her you were on leave. Pushy woman. Why don't you ask her what she wants yourself? I haven't the time."

"I know, Andrei. Don't worry, I'll see that she doesn't bother you again."

Kuchek picked up his pencil and, in a rare moment of curiosity about someone not connected to his work, asked, "Who is she?"

"Someone who knew my father," Philip said. "If you see her again, please don't speak to her."

On his circuitous way back to the parking lot, Philip found himself standing on the modernist footbridge of the Millikan Reflecting Pool in the fading sunlight. He wasn't sure why he'd come this way; he felt ridiculous on this tiny bridge, like a character in a storybook. He knew he should go home to Jane. He knew he should make time to have a closer look at his father's boxes. But he felt so inert, as if he were waiting for something to happen—and then it did.

Philip jumped slightly at the sound of her voice.

"I wanted to say how sorry I was about your daughter. I hope you got my card."

He turned. Anitka stood at one end of the bridge, wearing a saffron-yellow cardigan and striped scarf, a look more New Haven than Pasadena, and her face was strangely blank—no, unhappy. He had never seen her look sad before, and it stirred something protective in him.

"I was on my way to the library. Good to see you."

"Anitka—"

She stopped.

"Your dissertation. How's it coming?"

"Still looking for an advisor," she said with forced cheer. "I have feelers out to John Britton."

Philip felt the familiar twinge of professional envy. "And how is Great Britton taking your attack on his work?"

"He hasn't responded, exactly." She began to step away. "Walk me to the library?"

They started down the tree-lined path in the direction of the Athenaeum, and in a rising sensation of déjà vu, Philip realized this was the second time they had walked this way together. His preoccupation with Anitka had dimmed dramatically since Sybil's death, to the point where he was sure he had conquered his mania entirely. But he now knew that whatever Anitka had injected into his bloodstream, his recent grief was not an inoculation, just an aggravating course of antibiotics. They overshot the library. Neither of them mentioned it, and they soon found themselves in the quiet of the adjoining neighborhood.

"You're lucky to live and work here, with your family so close," Anitka said.

"Yours is in Ukraine?"

She nodded. "I haven't seen my parents and brothers in two years. I tell myself I can't afford the travel, but the truth is, I can't stand the look on their faces when they see me—sort of this desperate pride. I'm the only one who really aspired to anything, and now they expect me to be this sensation, to get rich off science." She laughed. "It's idiotic fantasy."

"You're in the right place for what you're doing."

"But what percentage of PhDs go on to make any kind of living? There are a few slots at Caltech for tenured string theorists and, what, a handful at a few other schools?"

He gave her a sidelong smile. "Remember, those positions are for people who don't despise the reigning theory."

She waved her hand with an annoyed flourish. "That's exactly my point. Think of the few people, like you, who are able to make their livelihood from it. How can I possibly make a life out of introducing a rival to the dominant ideology? And even if I do finish my thesis and graduate, what then? Maybe I get a job teaching $F = ma$ to morons? Or I can hope for an ad: 'Wanted. Unemployed Theoretical Physicist with No Marketable Skills Outside Pondering the Nature of the Universe.'"

He had never heard her talk with such self-effacement.

"You were right, what you said that night," she continued.

"I'm just one person," he protested. "Don't go—"

"Please. I realized last week, you've been right this entire time." She came to an abrupt stop in front of a ranch-style house. "This is me."

She turned and stepped up the drive, slipping through a wooden gate to the backyard. He didn't move. *How about leaving right now, Philip?*

"Are you coming?" she called over the fence.

He briefly closed his eyes, and followed. *Just visiting is all.* He walked alongside the house to the back, where a small guest cottage dominated the yard. Anitka stood facing him, her figure framed by a charming ivied trestle. She turned up the stone path to her door and unlocked it.

Inside, she pulled off her scarf and left him alone to survey the place. There were a few sparkly cushions on the couch to indicate that a woman lived here, but little else. The chipboard shelving along one wall bowed under the weight of books and academic papers. Next to it was a dry-erase board, doodled with the mathematical objects that populated the landscape of their discipline. In the center hovered a playful verse from a dead physicist:

Age is of course a fever chill
That every physicist must fear
He's better dead than living still
When he's past his thirtieth year
–Paul Dirac, 1926, age 23

"I've always hated this rhyme."

She laughed from the kitchenette. "I guess I like to live my life in a state of perpetual horror."

Shifting his attention back to the books, Philip noticed an entire section of shelving devoted to chaos theory and nonlinear dynamics—not her area of study—including a collection of his father's bound papers, flagged with sticky notes. He pulled one off the shelf and looked through its curled and dog-eared pages.

"You're a fan of my father's."

"What did I tell you?"

"Everyone says that, but this is serious."

She returned with two mugs of tea and handed him one.

"I find his mathematics enjoyable. Don't you?"

"Sure, but he's my father."

"It's like reading music."

Philip smiled.

"I once found a mistake," she said.

"You're kidding."

"Oh, a small thing. Nothing, really. I thought of telling him, but then he died."

But then he died. She had a talent for being blunt while just skirting offense.

Philip wandered to the far side of the room, where an oval table was covered in academic papers and journals. He looked through the titles and saw all the familiar authors: Veneziano, Schwarz and Green, Nambu, Witten, Maldacena, Britton—all the monster minds who had contributed to two string theory revolutions.

"You've been reading."

"Yes, and I wanted to tell you something," she said with unusual calm. "I had this moment the other night where I felt like the most intractable problem would have been obvious to me had I cared to solve it." She walked to a window and pulled open the blind, revealing a view of the grass. "I was in the yard, right here, and I heard whistling from a teapot inside the main house—they always make tea and forget the pot is on the stove—and at that exact moment, it was like someone had just walked up and handed me a telegram." She turned back to the table. "I was aware right then of bumping my head against my own ceiling. I knew with certainty that I am not a physicist, or at least not an academic. I have never been so certain of anything."

He had followed her to the window. It occurred to him that for once she did not seem to be putting on an act. The bluster she had been walking around with for as long as he had known her fell away. And that made her even more attractive, nearly irresistible, and he marveled at how she had once meant so little to him.

"It's best that I figure this out now, right?"

"I think you're being hard on yourself."

He realized he was standing very close to her, and he forced himself to return to the bookshelf and the doodles. It had taken immense effort to pull away from her, and he knew it was time to leave. That's when he noticed something. On the whiteboard, in the middle of all the multicolored donuts and other manifolds, was an alien object: a brain. More accurately, the spiraled brain with the little tail he'd come to know so well. The ink didn't look quite as faded as the other figures, as if it had been drawn more recently.

"Anitka. What's this?"

She stepped up beside him, her face achingly close. "I'm not sure what you're pointing at."

He turned to face her. "This symbol. Where did you get it?"

She smiled. "Don't you recognize a Fibonacci spiral when you see one?"

He looked back at the drawing and saw that it was, in fact, the famous spiral based on the Fibonacci sequence—at least, an untidy version of one. His own brain was clearly playing tricks.

"It's not my best work, I grant you," she said, blinking up at him with her large, sleepy eyes.

"I should go," he said.

Without warning, she took a gasp of air and threw her hand up to her face. Philip's chest tightened, his standard response to watching someone about to cry—his wife, his children—but this time it was a strange, unbearable constriction.

She let her hand fall and looked down at her tea. "Oh God, I'm really sorry. I don't want to keep you." She was trying to sound casual, but he saw that her lashes were damp. He didn't know if he could stand seeing one more sad person in his life right now. He was sick to death of sadness, of responsibility, of the weight of everything, and he longed for just one moment of contentment, if not outright pleasure.

He stepped toward her and, setting her mug aside, put a hand on her waist. He leaned his entire body into her and kissed her. They stumbled sightless to a wall, and he pressed her against it, inhaling the perfume of her: the various lotions and hair products, the faint trace of saline, the stale wool of her cardigan. As he moved his lips over her skin, he began to subtract all the superficial smells in his mind until he was left with the muted fragrance of the skin itself. He thought he had never experienced anything more delicious, this small sensory detail that was Anitka Durov's scent, and he gave in to it entirely.

17

The House

On a nearly treeless street in South Los Angeles, Gregory pulled up in front of a sun-blanched Craftsman house. He was supposed to be driving to Culver City, where he had an appointment with one of the victims in a recent sex abuse suit leveled at the LA Unified School District. But afternoon traffic had been surprisingly thin, and he was running early. So when his car had reached the nodding pumpjacks of the Inglewood oil field, he'd veered east. As he made the left turn onto Stocker Street, he could feel the hand of Isaac's universal computer making the calculations to guide his car past Baldwin Hills, Crenshaw Boulevard, and Arlington Avenue.

It had been almost twenty years since he'd seen the house—that is, up until a few days ago, when he'd followed his onetime foster father here. Tom had gotten off a bus and shuffled several blocks to this spot, where he stared through the fence at his old home before the sun became too much for him. Hands clutching the back of his head, Tom quickly returned to the bus stop to curl up in a tormented ball. Though he still visited the gym and library on most days, Tom's schedule was becoming increasingly erratic, and Gregory had lost track of him several times. Gregory knew, of course, that this moonlighting of his couldn't go on indefinitely. He needed to make his presence known to Tom, to push his face into Tom's and say, "Do you know me?" He should have done it when he had him here at the house. But it was too late for that.

The place was now abandoned and had for some time been tanking the surrounding property values. Garbage ringed the yard, and the grass had turned the color of a soiled mattress. A high chain-link fence discouraged trespassing, but it hadn't stopped Krylon vandals from leaving their mark. Why Tom had felt the need to drag himself to this place—to the scene of his past crimes—Gregory could only guess. Perhaps it was the same reason that Gregory was here now. Maybe they both needed to remind themselves of how and why they'd become the men they were.

After pulling a pair of bolt cutters from the trunk of his car, Gregory paused on the sidewalk, recalling the moment when he and Hazel—ages nine and seven—had first emerged from the caseworker's van and stepped onto the curb. They had been so happy to have a new home (a house!) that they hadn't bothered to take in a full 360 of the neighborhood. But then, anything had been better than the endless carousel of foster homes or, worse, "the Hall": a county holding pen where abused and neglected children went to receive additional helpings of abuse and neglect.

Gregory and his sister had endured the caprices of the foster care system for five years, ever since their mother had gotten sick ("cancer" was all they were told) and died alone and penniless. Their father had given them the surname Dine not long before abandoning the family. And since there were no living relatives—or at least none willing to take them in—Hazel and Gregory Dine became orphans. Having been barely four years old during the transition, Gregory could hardly recall the "before" time, the fuzzy memories soon indistinguishable from the vague motherly images he invented in his head. Only one thing seemed certain as they entered the public school system and began to compare themselves with other children: Hansel and Gretel, as their peers dubbed them, were genetic trash.

Gregory and Hazel's new foster parents had seemed nice at first. Tom Severy, they were told, was the son of a famous professor and was himself a teacher at a local grade school, while Carla, his wife, was a bartender and freelance decorator. The home showed little evidence of Carla's latter occupation, but she could certainly make a mean G&T for her guests.

They weren't rich, but they seemed like decent enough people. They were also, as Gregory came to discover, self-medicating people, jotting off imaginary prescriptions in their heads that would end in evenings of needles, pills, and lots of lying around. For Carla, it was for some kind of undiagnosed mental imbalance—bipolar disorder, probably. With Tom, it was his terrible headaches that would overtake him suddenly, and if he didn't take the correct combination of drugs, he would be left immobile for days. Though truthfully, Tom was pretty immobile whether he had a migraine or not. Once, Hazel—who couldn't have been more than eight—had naively tried to present Tom with an aspirin she had managed to swipe from the school nurse, sending Tom into peals of fun-house laughter.

It didn't take Gregory long to realize that he and his sister had been taken in by full-blown junkies. Apparently the social workers assigned to their case had been blind to all the clues, so taken were they by Tom Severy's impressive academic bloodline. They had been equally ignorant of the couple's "friends" who hung around the house at odd hours, or that the front door was left unlocked day and night. But then, with an excess of orphans in the system, perhaps the state hadn't bothered to look too closely at the couple who were oh so eager to take a pair of older, unadoptable children off its hands. *You want the kids long-term, and you won't separate them? They're yours.*

And then the foster care checks began to arrive in the mail, and Tom never did go to that teaching job they'd heard about. Turned out he was only an occasional substitute anyway. And that professor so lauded by their caseworkers? He never appeared. Neither did the rest of Tom's family. But Gregory and Hazel didn't know what normal was supposed to look like. Their foster parents were careless, sure—they didn't always feed them on time, or buy them clothes, or give them anything other than a couple of twin mattresses on the floor to sleep on—but they weren't intentionally cruel. Not at first.

Near the back of the house, Gregory used the bolt cutters to penetrate the fence and slip through. The backyard was in a similar state of neglect, but a large, healthy fig tree, at least, still presided over the scene. Gregory had loved the tree. It had been the pride of the house, bearing summer fruit that he and his sister would devour. They would scoop out the figs' soft bellies and chew on the peels. Now the tree gave him the creeps. *Should have brought an axe.* But then, who can blame a tree for the sins of the house?

Gregory circled the trunk until he found a hefty branch on which a rope swing had once hung. The swing had long since been cut down, but two pieces of frayed rope still choked the bark. His sister had never used the rope swing properly. Hazel would always stand on the seat and, pushing against the trunk, rotate the swing until the old, knotted rope twisted around her little body. Then she would let go—sending the swing, and herself, twirling in the air. But one day, there had been a sharp *snap!*, and the seat had fallen out from beneath her. The tangled cords had held fast to her body—and neck—leaving her dangling above the ground gasping for air, as if she had clumsily tried to hang herself. God knows how long she'd been there, but when Gregory found her, she was unconscious.

Now he lifted himself into the tree and, with the bolt cutters, worked at both knots until they fell. Back on the ground, he picked up the pieces and studied them. To this day, if he looked closely enough at the scar on his sister's neck, he could pick out the telltale helix of this same rope.

He walked to the edge of the yard, where squatters had evidently set up camp at the barbecue pit. There were empty cans, bottles, plastic plates, and a lighter scattered nearby. Gregory started a fire with some twigs and dropped the pieces of rope into it. As the flame grew, he pulled a note, hastily scribbled in pencil, from his shirt pocket.

I'm leaving Jack.

Gregory's heart had somersaulted in his chest when he'd first read these words at Isaac's funeral reception. There had been the excitement of being so near to her in front of so many people, touching the tips of her fingers as she passed him the message. He'd had to wait to touch her for real, a desperate fumble in the garage two hours later. It wasn't an ideal affair; he knew that. Apart from the fact that they both had small children, there was the distance. They hadn't been able to see each other more than a dozen-odd times since the thing began three years ago, the months in between supplemented with texts and phone calls. Two years ago, when Sybil had been creating art for an upcoming show in San Francisco, she hadn't been able to see Gregory for four months, despite the fact that Drew was in day care. So early one morning, on impulse, he drove six hours north to Sunnyvale, spending the entire afternoon in Sybil's bed and returning that night to his oblivious wife. A few times, the lovers arranged to meet halfway between their cities at some arbitrary motel along Interstate 5. Once, with the necessary cover stories in place, they splurged on a romantic night in Big Sur. Gregory had gotten used to the infrequency of their trysts, but for some reason on this last visit, the thought of not being with her for good had become unendurable.

He looked back at the note, which now made him ill. Gregory had been in love with Sybil for as long as he'd known her, since they were children. He had been in immediate awe of this fairy-tale girl, who looked as if she'd just emerged from a haunted wood yet walked around Los Angeles as if she were just another person. It was only after she'd gone away, gotten pregnant, and married Jack—"a massive mistake," she confided to him—that she realized she loved Gregory, too. She was supposed to have left her husband, just as he was to have left Goldie. That was the plan. She had concerns, naturally, about breaking up their families and about Gregory's short temper, but for that brief moment in time, she had wanted to be with him.

She had been right, of course. He was an angry man. When exactly had he become this way? When had he become the person who held rage so perilously close to the surface? Gregory looked back at the house, his eyes singling out a window near the ground. It was a small, miserly pane of glass that allowed only a spear of light to pierce the darkness below. He wished he could set fire to that space, with Tom locked inside. He could imagine the resident cockroaches skittering across Tom's skin to escape the flames. Yes, Gregory's life would have looked very different if it hadn't been for the germ planted so early, a seed nurtured with a steady compost of maltreatment and indifference. It was Tom, not Sybil, who de-served to die.

Gregory held the lighter to the note until it caught fire. He dropped it into the pit and watched spirals of smoke pull themselves up and up, turning paper and rope into anonymous airborne particles. When the flame died and the smoke straightened, he stirred the ashes with the bolt cutter until there was no evidence that these objects had existed at all.

18

The Dead Man

On the Saturday she was to meet the man with the dead professor's name, Hazel could hardly sit still or hold a conversation. This was a problem, as in the days since Sybil's funeral, Goldie had become increasingly attached to her. Wherever Hazel was in the house, her sister-in-law sought out her company, desperate for dialogue with someone other than a two-year-old.

Gregory was gone every day, slipping out for work before Hazel got up and returning home close to midnight. This was just the way of things, Goldie explained over daily cocktail-hour therapy. "He's *so* overworked." Her sister-in-law's frustration at having married someone who couldn't talk about his job came out in ever-increasing doses. "And who could expect him to after what he does all day?" Goldie asked. "But where does that leave me and Lew? This is the life I chose, I guess." Hazel listened and tried to appear sympathetic, not letting on that the deep furrow between her brows was for her brother, not Goldie.

What surprised Hazel most was just how much she enjoyed spending time with her nephew. With each passing day, as she learned to play Lewis's games and decode his peculiar chatter, her protective feelings toward him magnified. But she suspected these were less maternal instincts and more a creeping fear connected to that fatal dot on the map.

During the first week of her stay, Hazel had woken up in the middle of the night with a deep anxiety about that third dot. She hadn't remembered dreaming about it, but she had the sudden need to see it. Slipping into the laundry room, she found the iron and began to gently steam the two stubborn paper dots apart. When they started to loosen, she pulled up an edge with a pair of tweezers. Slowly, the figures beneath revealed themselves through bits of adhesive: 110115001146. Though the ink was a bit smudged, these numbers were clearly identical to the first dot: November 1, just after midnight, the time of Sybil's death. At first Hazel felt relief, taking comfort in the idea that Isaac had simply pasted over the smeared digits with a more legible version—in which case, there was no danger of another Beachwood Canyon death. But if this dot was redundant, where was the third death promised by her grandfather?

Hazel wasn't about to monitor the entire family's movements, but she felt a supreme unease stalking up on her, like the growing momentum of a sinister machine. Besides this, she felt completely snared by indecision. She knew that if she didn't get back to Seattle soon to pick up the sodden pieces of her business, the Guttersnipe was done. But what about this invitation from a self-described friend of Isaac's? What about the hotel room? Having already visited room 137 again, there seemed nothing left for her to do there, though the front desk called her daily. Having given the hotel her phone number, she received multiple voice messages inquiring how they might contact Mr. Diver now that his phone had been disconnected. A clerk claimed there was new demand for the space and requested an early deposit for December of $2,700. Well, that certainly explained Isaac's bank statements. "Will he be paying in cash as usual?" the clerk asked. She didn't know what else to do but stall with false promises to pay.

At two o'clock on Saturday, an hour before Professor L. F. Richardson would be waiting for Hazel at the La Brea Tar Pits, Goldie suggested they take Lewis to the beach. Hazel begged off the trip, making a lame excuse about having to meet an old friend.

"Oh," Goldie said, visibly disappointed. "Can I drop you somewhere?"

"No, no. I'll drive," Hazel said, grateful that she'd had the foresight to take Isaac's Cadillac on the day she fled the Beachwood house.

When Goldie's Prius was gone, Hazel locked up and started in the direction of the Cadillac. Competition for street parking had been fierce, and she'd had to leave it under the shade of a magnolia two blocks from the house. As she was about to cross the street, she stopped short. A man sat in the driver's seat, his face obscured by the reflection of trees and sky. She stepped behind a streetlamp, her heartbeat increasing. Had this L. F. Richardson found her? But when she took a second look, she recognized the hands tightly gripping the steering wheel. It was her brother.

She crossed the street and rapped on the passenger-side window, but Gregory looked up with such fright that she was immediately sorry. He rolled down the window, his alarm turning to irritation.

"You know I hate being snuck up on. Why are you smiling?"

"I'm really sorry," she said. "It's just weird finding you here."

"This isn't your car," he said coldly. "You can't just take things."

Hazel was so puzzled by his anger that she didn't respond. She climbed into the car, not daring to ask what the hell he was doing there in the middle of the day. She suddenly remembered a French film she had seen years ago about a guy who just stops going to work—he would make a show each morning of putting on a suit and eating breakfast with his family, but then just wandered the city all day, having a slow and spectacular breakdown. She noticed a half-empty liquor bottle at her feet.

"You never drink," she said, picking up the bottle. Cutty Sark.

"Yes, well." He gestured in a vague way, his mood suddenly leveling. "I thought I'd try letting myself go, see if it's as relaxing as it looks in the movies."

"You could go back to the house," she suggested gently. "Goldie took Lewis to the beach."

He let a few seconds tick by. "I know how it looks, Haze."

"Tell me. Because I really don't know."

"Everyone's been out of it since the accident."

Why did the word *accident* suddenly sound like a euphemism?

"So this is because of Sybil?" she asked softly.

He didn't answer, just took the bottle from her hand. She thought of the expression she had seen on her brother's face the morning Sybil was found, a look of smothered pain. How odd that Gregory knew about Sybil's fight with Jack, as if he'd made it a point to know such things. Hazel always suspected that her brother had a thing for Sybil, but after he got married, she'd put the idea out of her mind. When they were young, of course, it had been Gregory who had sought out Sybil's company, despite the fact she was a few years younger. It was Gregory who had always managed to find an excuse to be where she was.

Hazel thought he might take another swig of whiskey, but instead he set the bottle in his lap, reached across the seat, and took firm hold of her hand.

"You know you can talk to me, Eggs."

He gave a barely perceptible nod and continued to look straight ahead.

They hadn't held hands like this since they were children, since that one night long ago, when sister and brother—ages nine and eleven—had sat outside their home watching a pair of LAPD officers carry off their foster father. Hazel had been half reclined on a stretcher, a bandage around her neck wrapped by paramedics after they'd brought her back to consciousness. Gregory sat beside her on the ambulance bumper. In the confusion before Hazel was taken to the hospital, no one had thought to shield the children from the spectacle of Tom's arrest.

As Tom was led across the lawn, Hazel gripped her brother's damp hand and watched Tom scream and spit in their direction. "Carla and I took you in, you little shits! Saved you from that county hellhole and this is what you do? You have no clue what it's like to live in my head! No fucking *clue!*" After being pushed into a squad car, he stared out at them with frenzied, questioning eyes, as if suddenly trying to puzzle through why he was there. Tom was there, of course, because the police had just discovered an arsenal of drugs in his basement and the body of his opiate-addicted wife in a basement tub. The autopsy would reveal that Carla had not in fact died of an overdose, but of dehydration. Her blissed-out body, planted beneath a working faucet, had given out for lack of water. In Tom's narcotized daze, he had either not noticed his wife's body or decided he wasn't in any hurry to report it. It was Gregory who had coolly dialed the paramedics from a neighbor's house, but only because he'd found his sister suspended in a tree that afternoon, her neck in the serpent's grip of a rope. The paramedics in turn called the police. Child abuse. Drug possession. Foster care fraud. Failure to report a body. Manslaughter, if not murder.

Hazel touched her neck, but she wasn't thinking of her scar or of the stories she sometimes invented about it to shut down questions; she was thinking of Gregory's twin horror story, far worse. On summer break, less than a year after they'd come to live with Tom and Carla, he was locked away in a dark basement closet without water or food. What had begun as punishment for some forgotten offense turned into the trauma of his life after their foster parents either forgot he was in there or pretended to forget—it was never clear which. Did they know that he would lie there for days without sleep, his voice hoarse from screaming through concrete? Did they consider the roaches that would come out at night to crawl across his huddled body?

At seven years old, Hazel had been too young to grasp the quiet horror that was unfolding belowground, but kept asking, "Where's my brother? Is he hiding?" Beyond searching every room, closet, and cupboard of the house, save the perpetually locked basement, she had felt completely helpless. When Gregory was finally let out, to what seemed like feigned surprise from his jailers, he gulped a soda he was given and promptly threw it up. After that, he was in bed for a week, his body covered in bruises from having thrown himself against the closet door. The human body can survive for five days without water; Gregory had been in that closet for four. He eventually regained his strength, but his mood turned solemn and black. He hadn't been raped, sexually abused, or subjected to direct physical pain, but Hazel wondered later if her brother's confinement to that hole of deprivation had not, in fact, been worse.

They both had endured daily miseries that, in their frequency, were arguably more corrosive than any one event—overhearing classmates whisper that they smelled bad, stealing food to avoid the mockery of free lunch, piling on towels at night in want of warm blankets—but it was Gregory's nightmare alone that had come to stand for those two and a half years in that house.

Why hadn't they left? Run away? Why hadn't she or Gregory told somebody? The person who asks these questions has never been an orphan. Because for orphans, all options appear equally hopeless, equally menacing.

No, the monster was not coming back. Ever.

They had been sitting in the Cadillac for close to twenty minutes.

"I have to go," Hazel said, squeezing his hand.

Gregory didn't ask why, just took a deep breath and nodded. Bottle in hand, he pulled himself from the car, slammed the door tight, and with a forced jaunty wave started down the block.

As she slid across the cracked vinyl, watching her brother disappear around the corner, Hazel understood why he had chosen to hide out here. Whatever else was going on in his life, whatever he couldn't say, there was something about the old car that was comforting. It wasn't the most beautiful model of Cadillac, boxy and cumbersome as it was, but if nothing else, it was a time capsule, bearing with it memories of rescue and safety. When Isaac and Lily had stepped in to claim Hazel and Gregory as their own, whisking them away in this very car, how surprised she and her brother had been to discover that Tom's extended family was normal. There was the beautiful house on the hill, with plush beds and fresh linens waiting. How marvelous to find food in their refrigerator instead of shriveled vegetables and expired condiments. (Although after his closet confinement, her brother's relationship with food had, paradoxically, become one of strange indifference.)

When enveloped by such unflagging attention—love, really—it had been easy to get over her hurt, or at least to mostly forget. Had Gregory done the same? Or is that why he had joined the LAPD? Perhaps it had been on that night, as she and her brother witnessed Tom's arrest, that Gregory had resolved to become a police officer. Though he had tried in college to push his brain through the latticework of mathematics, maybe he had always known he was meant for another line of work.

Hazel pulled out Isaac's keys and turned the ignition. It was ten before the hour. She would have to hurry if she was to keep her appointment with the dead man.

The thick odor of tar rose from the ground as Hazel hurried across the park to the museum. Here and there, patches of crude oozed to the surface of the grass, betraying the vast stew of petroleum and animal bones that lay beneath. She stepped in an inky puddle and had to drag her shoe along the grass for several yards. It was ten past the hour. She was late.

After paying admission, and passing a sign whose sole purpose, it seemed, was to disappoint children—No Dinosaurs Were Found in the Tar Pits—Hazel grabbed a map. There were, in fact, two theaters in the building. Richardson's message had not specified which. The first was screening a documentary with slick production values, while the second featured an educational film that looked to have been produced during the Carter administration. Hazel chose the latter, taking a seat near the door. Her heart was still beating fast from her dash across the park. Or maybe it was anticipation.

On-screen, a panicked cartoon horse fought back against the tar's vacuum grip while a pack of wolves watched from nearby. The narrator was unmoved: *"Tar deaths often occurred in clusters . . . A single animal's cries might attract predators, such as these dire wolves."* She remembered the film from early trips to the museum. It had been a heady time for her and her brother, when the dream of stable childhoods had, at last, come true. In fact, wasn't it here, at this very museum, that their new parents had asked Hazel and Gregory to think of them as grandparents, even though they were officially adopting them as their own? Isaac had said, "We're too old to be new parents. 'Grandma and Grandpa,' it just feels right." Later, Hazel wondered if this decision hadn't been a kind of nod to Tom as their onetime father of sorts. Whatever his misdeeds, Isaac and Lily's addict son had brought the four of them together.

The wolves on-screen were in trouble. *"These predators are walking into the same trap that befell the horse . . ."* Despite the relative happiness of those museum outings with Isaac and Lily, the idea that these prehistoric animals just sat in a pool of tar waiting to die had always terrified her. She'd become familiar on those trips with the phrase "dying of exposure," which sounded to her like the worst fate imaginable. It had also brought to mind her brother in that closet and the sickening question: Can one die of exposure, trapped not in tar but inside a house?

The drama on-screen was doing nothing to quell her anxiety. She turned and studied the room. In the glow of the projection, Hazel could see a group of well-behaved schoolchildren seated in the back, an alert teacher posted beside them. A young couple in the row behind her couldn't contain their giggling, presumably at the film's mossy animation. A family of five was seated in her own row, all looking unimpressed. She didn't spot anyone who looked like an enigmatic professor with an appointment.

The soundtrack swelled to distortion: *"And this process, over thousands of years, preserved the bones in excellent condition, allowing visitors of the George C. Page Museum to marvel at these fascinating creatures. Enjoy your visit."*

As the house lights came up and the theater emptied, Hazel remained in her seat. She studied the museum map, keeping her body angled toward the entrance. When the last of the children had filed out, she heard a voice behind her. His accent was thick, Spanish or Italian.

"May I compliment you on your scarf?"

She glanced over to find a spectacled man of late middle age seated in her row—the father of that family. Or had he only been sitting next to them? In his brown windbreaker and leather sandals, he looked like a European on vacation.

Hazel looked around to see if the man wasn't addressing someone else, but they were alone.

"It really is a nice scarf," he tried again.

"I'm not wearing a scarf." Her hand went to her neck for confirmation.

"Herringbone, isn't it? My favorite."

Herringbone.

She looked at him sharply. "Mr. Richardson?"

"Ms. Severy?"

The lights cut out, and his face vanished. Music swelled as the opening credits for the next show began.

"Or is it Raspanti?" she asked over the soundtrack.

"Yes, I hope the late Mr. Richardson doesn't mind my borrowing his name. I'm trying to keep a low profile while I'm in the States."

"Are you even a professor?"

"I prefer mathematician. But, yes, I teach at the Polytechnic University in Milan."

"So why are you here?"

The screen cut to black, and the film's narration started: *"Imagine Los Angeles thousands of years ago . . ."*

His voice called from the dark. "Meet me near the sloths."

When the screen lit up again, the doors were gently swinging, and Raspanti was gone.

Hazel left the theater and walked deeper into the museum. She hesitated in front of the long-limbed skeleton of *Nothrotheriops shastensis*: the giant prehistoric sloth. There was a large illustration of the beast on the wall, its lummox face staring out in a plea for its own extinction.

Just as Hazel was wondering if all this subterfuge was necessary, she turned to find Raspanti standing on the other side of the skeleton, peering into the blind cavities of its skull. He was quite tall, with a sharp Roman profile, like something straight off an ancient bas-relief. She understood at once that this was the man she had seen lurking that day at Isaac's gravesite.

"Unfortunate-looking animal," he said, pulling up the collar of his jacket, as if he believed himself to be wearing a trench coat and not a windbreaker.

In sympathy of the chill, she wrapped her cardigan more snugly around her, unsure where to begin with her line of questioning.

Raspanti leaned in a little, smelling faintly of tobacco and foreign hygiene products. "Isaac said you would make contact, but I was becoming impatient. He also said you would have something for me."

Hazel hesitated. "An equation, you mean?"

He smiled tightly and glanced over one shoulder. "Quiet, please, Ms. Severy."

"Even if I did have it," she said, dropping her voice, "how do I know you're the one I'm supposed to give it to?"

"You think I'm an impostor?" He let the accusation hang in the air for a moment. "If the watchword isn't enough for you, it shouldn't be too difficult for you to confirm who I am."

As he started to turn away, she stopped him. "I searched John Raspanti. No mathematics professors came up."

He nodded in understanding. "Your grandfather doesn't like to make things easy, does he? He liked to call me John, but it's Gian with a *G*. Giancarlo."

Raspanti walked off, stopping a few yards away at the diorama of a Columbian mammoth, one of Hazel's favorite exhibits. The animatronics beneath its matted fur would jerk to attention every few minutes, accompanied by a faraway roar.

She pulled out her phone and entered his full Italian name into a search engine. Up popped a portrait of Raspanti on the Milan Polytechnic site. There was also a group photo from a mathematics summit—men and women arranged Solvay Conference–style—with Raspanti towering next to her grandfather, an arm thrown around his shoulders. These were younger Raspantis, but clearly the same man who stood in front of her now.

She stepped over to the diorama.

"Why didn't Isaac just give you the equation himself?"

Raspanti blinked rapidly. "You think I don't ask this same question? You think I had any idea he was going to do that to himself? What I know is I get a letter in the mail one day telling me he is leaving his life's work to me, so that 'they' won't get their hands on it. He told me you would be the courier."

"Well, he could have sent you an email attachment and saved me the trouble."

The man frowned. "They would be looking for that. Phones are equally unsecure."

"Who's they?"

The mammoth rattled to life. "*They* are always the same: one of two groups who enjoy exploiting science for their own ends. The first group uses scientific advancement as a tool for war. The other wants to make more money than they already have. One kills, the other steals. If either group gets ahold of Isaac's work, it would be, well, regrettable." Raspanti dropped his voice to a near whisper. "The equation is just the beginning—a seed—for chaotic prediction. Can you imagine if the government had a formula to predict anything it wanted? Or Wall Street? You think *they* are going to share this formula with people like you and me?"

"So it *is* a predictor."

"Of a very specific kind."

"Then why not destroy the whole thing and be done with it?"

"Should we scrap particle physics because it produced the H-bomb?" His voice dropped again. "There is value in the equation, even if we don't use it to forecast the future. All brilliant math has jewels locked inside that can be harnessed. When Andrew Wiles proved Fermat's Last Theorem in 1994, he did so on the backs of other great theorems. I have a German colleague who coined a term for the phenomenon—*genieschultern*—'on the shoulders of genius.' And so it goes, on and on."

"That's fine, Mr. Raspanti. But it doesn't really matter because I don't have the equation."

"Or you have it and don't know where to look."

She wondered if she should just hand over the contents of the hotel room to him—*Here, you figure it out*—even though Isaac had expressly asked her to destroy everything. But then, where was this alleged equation if not on the computer or the map?

The map. She pulled out her phone and swiped through the images she had snapped on her trip: a wide shot of the Beachwood house, her old bedroom, Drew smelling a flower, Gregory frowning at her. But the photos she was looking for were not there. She searched the trash. Gone. Feeling suddenly unsteady, she leaned on a nearby panel display for support.

"Is something wrong?" Raspanti asked.

"I took photos of his map—four of them—but they're gone."

"A map!" Raspanti said in a loud whisper. "With specific points, predicting events down to the day and minute?"

She looked up. "How did you know?"

"He showed me a similar map for Milan, a kind of test run. He was anticipating events there like a seismologist predicts earthquakes." Raspanti shook his head. "No, like a seismologist *wishes* he could predict earthquakes."

"And by *events*, you mean . . . ?"

Raspanti didn't answer. He was staring at the mammoth again.

"Isaac's own death was on the map," she continued. "And my cousin's, who died in a recent accident."

He turned sharply. "Isaac's death was on the map?"

"Yes. It is a *death* map, isn't it?"

Raspanti grabbed his head, as if reevaluating everything. "No, no. Your grandfather wasn't predicting just any kind of death. That would have been too broad. Pointless, even. People die every day in the most unremarkable ways."

"Then what?"

"Can't you guess?"

She could, but she didn't want to say it out loud because it was too heavy, too terrifying. She wanted this all to be over so she could go home.

The joints of the ancient elephant began to grind and shift, and when the animal thundered to life again, she said, "I have something to show you."

Thirty minutes later, with Raspanti right behind her, Hazel unlocked room 137. As she pushed open the door and led him down the hall, she knew something was off. She took one step into the living room and stopped. The computer was gone, the map was gone. Otherwise the room appeared untouched. There were no overturned tables or tossed sofa cushions, just the quiet absence of her grandfather's work. Raspanti glanced around, unsure of what he was supposed to be looking for.

Hazel stared at the now-blank wall and swallowed hard, not wanting to see what she was seeing. "It was all here," she said finally. "No one else had the key."

The Italian ran a hand through his hair, suddenly understanding. He moved to the window leading to the roof. "How difficult would it be to break in?"

Hazel flushed. There was only one other person who knew about the room. She couldn't bring herself to admit what a moron she'd been that night. Drunk, giddy, and foolish.

Raspanti instinctively moved to the spot where the computer had been. "What's this?"

She joined him at the desk and looked down. In the center of the glass-topped oak sat a shaggy white wig and mustache. They appeared not to have been carelessly left behind, but to have been placed there deliberately. The mustache was turned upside down in the shape of a smile.

"Looks like Einstein left his calling card," Raspanti said sourly.

"Twain," she corrected him. "Mark Twain."

19

The Offer

On Saturday morning, Philip drove Silas and Sidney to their tennis lesson and forced himself to sit courtside through the entire instruction. Though he had found excuses to slip away to Anitka's cottage every day for the past week, he had recently made a point to be more present for his sons.

Philip tried to concentrate on the boys' practice, but he had taken two of his emergency Vicodin at breakfast, on top of his migraine medication, and was now feeling a bit high. So while he appeared to be studying the twins and their sylphlike instructor, he was really seeing Anitka's figure spring about the court, dark hair catching auburn highlights in the sun. Anitka didn't even play tennis, but he actually clapped after watching his lovely phantom slice a drop shot that Silas couldn't return.

He stopped clapping when he looked across the court and swore he saw Nellie Stone in the bleachers. She was sitting next to a large man whose face, masked in shadow, Philip couldn't quite make out. When he blinked and they both disappeared, he promised himself he'd cut back on the pills.

Afterward, Philip treated his sons to their favorite ice cream parlor. Between bites of banana split, Philip realized Silas and Sidney were staring at him.

"What?"

"You're being kind of weird, Dad."

"Just tired," he said, trying his best not to sound drug addled. "How do you like your new instructor?"

"She's fine," they replied together.

Philip almost said, "Well, she's certainly fit," but realized that this would sound creepy. Besides, his sons didn't appear to notice female beauty, and Philip was imagining the day when they would announce in unison that they preferred men. He had already prepared himself for the expression of unfaltering acceptance he would wear on his face. And at that moment, watching them scoop mint-chip ice cream into their mouths, he felt that he wanted nothing more than their happiness, whatever their preferences—academic or otherwise. He wondered if this feeling would last.

The family reconvened for a late lunch at home, where Philip's medicated high turned to anxiety. Anitka texted him several times that afternoon, and he had to repeatedly excuse himself in order to peck out a reply. After Jane commented on his multiple trips to the bathroom, he mumbled something about indigestion and retreated upstairs to delete both ends of the exchange.

Around four thirty, the house phone rang. It was Kimiko Kato calling with an arcane question about a certain five-dimensional manifold Philip used in his work. Her query didn't have an easy answer, thereby giving him the perfect cover to step out for a couple of hours. After he hung up, he had to suppress a smile as he told his family that he needed to catch up with "the group."

Faye, detecting his eagerness to leave, questioned him.

"The group, huh?"

"Yeah."

"All men?"

"One woman. Japanese. One of the best physicists in the world."

She sniffed. "You're not just saying that, in the way men like to pat women on the back?"

"We do allow women to be great scientists now and then."

Faye asked if he could drop her off at the grocery store on the way. Philip agreed, though had some difficulty concealing his irritation. As they headed out the door, he cast a final glance back into the house and saw Jane watching him from the staircase, a thin smile on her face. He tossed her a mock salute before pulling the door shut, and for the next fifteen minutes, her smile seemed tethered to him. He was so distracted by it, and by the idea that the smile had meant something, that he could barely maintain his end of the conversation with Faye in the car.

"So where is this group going?"

"Just a lounge on campus."

"So you're like beer buddies, but instead of sports and girls, you talk about the meaning of the universe?"

"Well, I don't know about *meaning*." He turned into the Ralphs grocery store parking lot. "If you were to eavesdrop, it wouldn't sound as important as all that."

"Please, it's called the theory of everything, isn't it?"

"A slight exaggeration."

A self-satisfied smile spread across her face. "You know what I think?"

He was so unnerved by how much she looked like Jane in that moment that he found himself unable to respond.

"I think you're one of those men who's important enough to be able to downplay the value of his own work, but you know full well how valuable it is. I bet you think there's no work in the world more important than yours."

He wasn't prepared for this level of psychological dissection coming from his sister-in-law.

"I'm onto you." She gathered up her shopping bags. "You should let me join your group sometime. I might have a thing or two to say about the universe myself." She cackled, as if she had said something very clever.

"Hey, thanks for doing all this," he called to her as she was getting out. "It's because of you that Jane's getting better."

She stuck her head back in the car. "You really think she is?"

"Don't you?"

She shrugged. "You're not around her like I am. I don't blame you for not picking up on the subtleties."

"You should have seen her before you arrived."

Faye sighed. "My sister's not like me. She doesn't always let you know what's going on with her. Thanks for the ride." She slammed the door and strode with purpose toward the white-hot blaze of the supermarket.

As Ralphs receded in his rearview mirror, the image of Jane's smile from the stairs returned, sliding from an innocent expression of trust into an unspoken plea. And as he turned into Anitka's neighborhood, his wife's small mouth transformed into a gaping hollow of despair, and just when it had reached terrifying proportions, the cottage door opened and the nightmare vanished.

He spent the next two hours on Anitka's full-sized mattress, the two of them blissfully negotiating its meager expanse. But for Philip, the hours weren't entirely free from worry. His sister-in-law's prying had made him nervous. If he didn't get back in time for dinner, he wouldn't put it past her to check his cover story. Philip quickly showered, dressed, and returned to bed to kiss Anitka good-bye.

"Don't go, please." She pulled him back onto the pillow and pretended to tackle him. "Besides, you never showed me your father's boxes."

He blinked at her in surprise. "Jesus. You really are a fangirl."

"You promised."

"Did I?" He took her hand and kissed it. "There's nothing to look at, just some books and newspaper clippings."

She propped herself up on one elbow. "Is my interest irritating?"

"Mildly." He smiled. "But it'll have to be next time."

She gave him a mock frown and rolled out of bed. As he watched her head to the bathroom, he wondered if anyone would be picking over the remains of his own office when he died, or stalking his family for unpublished gems.

Over the aggressive pulse of the showerhead, Philip shouted his good-bye. It was better to make a quick exit. No protracted farewells. But he found it difficult to leave and lingered in the living room. He had not yet spent an entire night at the cottage, though he could have easily come up with a pretext to spend several nights with her: an out-of-town lecture, a last-minute symposium somewhere, a weekend retreat at the Aspen Center. Yet for all his romantic desperation and the many avenues of deceit open to him, Philip lacked the stomach for such an elaborate lie.

He paused at Anitka's bookshelf, running a finger over his father's old publications. Remembering that Anitka had said she'd corrected a mistake somewhere, he pulled the papers one by one from the shelf, and, finding one title significantly vandalized with her scrawl, he rolled it up and stuck it in his coat pocket.

A second later, the bedroom door opened and she sauntered over, tying on a loose robe.

He thought of telling her about the paper, but he was sure she would protest, insisting it was nothing. Instead, he kissed her forehead and said, "I'll see you tomorrow."

As he turned to the front door, he noticed that her whiteboard was now blank. No more doodles. No more Fibonacci spiral. Just the faint afterimage of marker.

"I decided you were right about that Dirac poem, after all," she said, following his gaze. "It really is depressing."

Outside, the Santa Ana winds were coming in cold and strong, and the palm leaves above Philip's head rustled like butcher paper. Something was nagging at him. Was it Anitka's enthusiasm for his father's work? Or was it that he was deceiving his wife in these small, wretched doses? He had parked two blocks away this time in an effort to evade the phantom private eyes his guilty mind imagined were following him, though a block could hardly have made a difference. He followed the *chirp-chirp* to his Subaru and was just reaching for the door handle when the headlights of a car came on behind him. Philip froze—*Ah, it's over now*—and as he turned toward the lights, he tried to invent a reason for his being in this neighborhood.

A woman called from the car. "I'm sorry to alarm you, Mr. Severy."

He peered past the light and saw a black sedan sitting there. The slim shadow of Nellie Stone emerged from the back seat.

"Ah," Philip said, relaxing only slightly, "the unrelenting secretary."

"Whenever my phone rings," she said, "I'm always hoping it will be you. It never is."

"Flat-out stalking, is that what we've come to?"

"You do make me feel like the unhinged girlfriend."

"What do you want, Nellie?"

"The car was just cleaned. We could lean against it and chat." She called to the driver, "Arturo, would you kill the lights?"

The headlights promptly dimmed, yielding to the sodium glow of a streetlamp. Nellie was wearing a charcoal overcoat and scarf. She was without her glasses, which made her look strangely defenseless, like a nocturnal creature tossed outside at midday. Perhaps the lenses had been masking the hollows of her eyes, for Philip could now see she was not younger than him, but a peer.

She reached into her coat for cigarettes and a lighter, extending the pack to Philip as an offering. As he came close, she gracefully hipped the back door shut and Philip thought he saw movement behind the tinted window. Was it just a play of the light? Photons were certainly crafty things, especially when confronted with glass. One never knew what a particle of light might do to fool the eye. As Philip looked at the dark window, his unease increased.

"Someone with you?" he asked, selecting a Dunhill.

She didn't answer. Instead, she set the end of her cigarette ablaze and did the same for him. The wind picked up, and he inverted the collar of his coat. He wondered if she might suggest the car as shelter from the weather, but she didn't show any signs of discomfort.

"I was very sorry to hear about your daughter."

He chose to ignore this. "Did you know there was a recent break-in at my father's old office?"

"Really?"

"And for some reason, Government-Scholar Relations came to mind."

She shook her head. "It's unrelated, I'm afraid. Besides, a burglary would have been unnecessary."

"Why's that?"

"GSR is no longer searching for Isaac's work."

"Giving up, then?"

She smiled. "You can't look for what you've already found."

As she studied his face for a reaction, an alarm sounded deep within Philip, accompanied by the sudden need to protect his father's work—work he still wasn't sure existed.

"I'd be happy to explain," she continued, "if you would only consider—"

"Meeting with Mr. Lyons?"

"Actually, that's not why I'm here."

He checked his watch. "Then you should get to it."

"I'm here to recruit you. We'd like you to work for us."

He laughed. "You really are deranged."

"Give it some thought. We pay well. Extremely well, in fact—"

"So you're asking me to leave my position at the university to work for an organization I know nothing about, one that appears to have questionable hiring practices, and has quite possibly stolen from my dead father—all for the paycheck? You think that's what motivates me?"

"For the intellectual satisfaction, then."

"You know my answer."

"But you haven't heard the entire question." She sent a puff of smoke downwind. "I wonder what Anitka Durov would think."

He frowned. "What has she got to do with this?"

"I thought she might have an opinion."

"So this is blackmail now?"

"Please, we're not so classless as that. I'm only trying to get your attention. How about lunch tomorrow, take two?"

He turned to walk back to his car.

"So you have no interest in seeing your father's work?" she shouted above the wind.

He stopped and turned back. "I have no interest in being shadowed or contacted repeatedly, or having you know more about my life than my family does. I'd like to be left alone."

"What, so you can slip back into academic obscurity? Let your brain decay while you bed the latest grad student?" She allowed her Dunhill to drop, smashing the butt with her shoe. "Or is it that you'd rather not be reminded of your father's legacy when you're struggling so valiantly for a shot at your own?"

Philip froze. He felt his anger rising but could not deny the painful truth of this statement.

She went on. "Could it be that you're not—an inquisitive person?" Nellie lit another cigarette, the flame of her lighter twitching in the wind. "What about all those questions you had for me that day in Malibu?"

"You mean the day Lyons stood me up?" Philip shouted.

Nellie paused for a reflective moment. "We've been unfair to you, Mr. Severy. *I've* been unfair to you, and I'd like to make it up if you'll let me."

A staccato buzzing came from her pocket, and her slender hand dove in to silence it. "But looks like it'll have to be another time."

"Short leash?"

She gave him a knowing look and pivoted to the car's back door. When she opened it, Philip moved forward to get a better view of the back seat. But he saw that it was empty—just black padded leather and a snakeskin handbag. The only other person in the car was the driver, who made a move for the ignition.

"Just a second, Arturo." Nellie rested her arm on the door and turned to Philip.

"Do you remember the one question you asked me that I couldn't answer?"

"Which one was that?"

"You wanted to know what the *P* in P. Booth Lyons stood for."

"You said you didn't know."

"It was probably wrong of me to keep it from you, given how important your father was to us." She snuffed her cigarette in the door's ashtray, and when her hand returned, it was holding a business card, like magic. He would have been no more surprised to see the queen of diamonds.

"I have one, thanks."

"You don't have this one. It's the only one like it in the world."

He took the card from her. There was no number or contact information, just a serifed name floating in cream:

Penelope Booth Lyons.

He frowned, struggling to interpret what he was seeing. "Penelope."

"But I prefer Nellie," she said. "Fewer syllables."

She climbed into the car and pulled the door shut behind her. A second later, the window slid halfway down.

"So, I'll see you tomorrow? No more secrets, I promise."

Philip didn't respond. It was as if two incompatible ideas had suddenly catapulted into his brain and were now forced at gunpoint to reconcile.

The engine of the town car hummed into action, and the headlights returned.

"You'll let me know about tomorrow, then? I'm not going to chase you anymore, Philip. When you're ready to see your father's work, you'll tell me."

The dark glass of the window gradually eclipsed her assured smile. And when her face had disappeared from view, the car slipped into gear, and the woman who called herself P. Booth Lyons drove away.

20

The List

It was dusk, and the offices of the Juvenile Protection Unit were nearly empty. From his spot at a window overlooking downtown Los Angeles, Gregory tried to appreciate the twinkling cityscape, how the honeyed glow of sunset could give way so rapidly to night. But he felt uneasy, as if something were about to happen that he couldn't control. Maybe if he looked hard enough, he'd be able to pick out Tom's figure below, making its wretched way back to the subway. At some point, he feared, Tom was going to abandon his routine altogether. He might even pick up and move, far from where he could be surveilled. Gregory couldn't allow that to happen.

He returned to his desk to gather his things and lock up the cabinets. The coffee he'd poured earlier was now cold. Even so, he picked up a spoon and stirred it absently, imagining that if he moved the spoon counterclockwise for long enough, he might be able to suck the heat back into the mug. Longer still, and the cream would unmix itself and swirl back into the hypnotic pattern it had once made. But there was no fighting the laws of thermodynamics. One couldn't uncool coffee, just as one couldn't unkill a person.

E. J. paced nearby, wobbling slightly on her heels. Must be date night with her husband. For nineteen years, E. J. had thrown her life into saving the city's imperiled children, yet despite everything she'd seen in those years, she managed to conduct herself with extraordinary lightness. He had the sense that the second E. J. got home to her husband, she could kick off her shoes, let her job roll off her back, and enter into the ease of spousal banter. That's the kind of detective she was. She didn't need to use rage as a release; she didn't need to meet violence with violence, as he did. She could just switch it all off.

But these past weeks, E. J. had been acting strange: first mothering everyone in the office, and then retreating. Now this emphatic pacing. Her behavior worried him, and he might have asked her about it had he not wanted to invite similar questions about himself. For instance, he'd hardly shown his face at work for the past two weeks. If it hadn't been for Hazel catching him in the Cadillac that morning, he'd likely still be sitting there now.

E. J. caught him looking in her direction. She scratched her scalp with the corner of a lime green folder.

"You have a second, Greg?"

He hesitated. Curious though he was, he didn't really have time for a chat. It was his fourth wedding anniversary, and Goldie was preparing a fussy meal that had taken days of planning. She wanted him to be excited about the dinner, though she knew full well that whether it was steak flambé or a ham sandwich, it was all the same to him. Whatever reaction Goldie was looking for, he usually managed to simulate the appropriate response. He was lucky she was rotten at detecting emotional mimicry.

"What's on your mind, E. J.?"

She zigzagged to his desk and placed in front of him a mug shot of a hollow-cheeked, dead-eyed woman whose gray hair was pulled back from a face that showed no emotion except for the beginnings of a smile. E. J. tapped the photo with a lacquered nail.

"Recognize this harpy?"

He did: that rubber-band crease of a mouth that wanted to stretch into a full smile but settled instead on a smirk. It nauseated him how little shame these criminals displayed on camera. It was the rare mug shot that showed honest disgrace or regret. Most of these people—child molesters, abusers, rapists—held their chins high, as if they had made the decision before the photo was snapped that they were going to retain some *motherfucking dignity*. Some even smiled, as if looking cheerful were somehow an imaginative response to having been caught doing something deeply horrible. It was the smile of guilt that Gregory had come to know well, the one that said, "Funny how life has led me to this moment, isn't it?"

He shrugged. "They all start to look the same."

She slapped the back of his head. It was supposed to be playful, but it hurt. "You think I'm an idiot? I know you don't forget."

"The Burgess case," he said at last. "Rita? Rhonda?"

"*Rhoda*. Rhoda Burgess, wife of that sadistic fuck who kept those kids chained up in his basement?"

His gorge rose. "Sure. He didn't even touch them, as I recall, just recorded their gradual starvation for some internet racket. Ran the whole thing out of his house in Castle Heights, until someone from the gas company came to check the meter and found a skeleton trying to break out of a basement window."

"Mr. Burgess got life," E. J. said, jabbing the photo again. "While the missus here—"

"Skipped away scot-free."

"Not a day in prison. Claimed she didn't know what hubby was doing down there all those years. Cried and carried on in front of the judge."

"So, what do we have on her?"

"She's dead."

"Even better."

"Died back in August. Took a dive off a downtown overpass. Her head was promptly flattened by a bagel truck."

"Great. Tape a *K* on her face and put her on the wall with the rest. We owe the driver a drink."

"Don't be patronizing."

"Well, sorry if I don't get all misty over the suicide of a woman too stupid to realize there was a miniature concentration camp in her basement."

"She didn't kill herself."

"No?"

"A witness came forward. Homeless guy who lives under the overpass says he saw the whole thing. Says the woman was pushed. There's more."

E. J. lined up the green folder beside Rhoda's photograph and flipped back the cover to reveal at least ten more mug shots.

Gregory sifted through the pile. They were mostly men, a few women—cases that had appeared on his desk at some point. He knew their faces well: the bad skin, the vacant eyes. "Looks like our typical deck of cards," he observed.

"Really?" She pointed across the office to the karma board. "Half of them have been staring at us for years."

"What are you saying?" he asked.

"All of them are closed cases, some going back six years. The thing they all have in common? They all got off easy: light sentences, acquittals, community service, finger wagging."

"Uh-huh."

"The other thing is that they're all dead."

"Well, some of these guys are pretty old."

"Then I guess 'old' makes you clumsy. This guy drowned in his bathtub; this woman took an accidental overdose of insulin; this one fell off his roof while doing some home improvement."

"So, accidents." He locked up his desk and stepped toward the window. "Could it be that you're looking for a pattern where there isn't one? What is coincidence but the concurrence of events?"

"The *concurrence of events*? You're really going to give me a lecture on probability? I get it, Greg, you come from math people."

"So, out with it. What's your theory?"

She joined him at the window. They were silent for a moment as they looked out toward Parker Center, the old LAPD headquarters. The Glass House, as it had been known, was either destined for historical landmark status or demolition—depending whom you asked—and from time to time, you could find wistful detectives gazing in the direction of their old, possibly doomed home.

"This is serial," she said at last, turning to face him. "The deaths will continue unless we stop it."

Her stare was so intense, he had to turn away. "How long have you been looking into this?"

"Since the witness showed up back in September. I wanted to be sure."

"You report this to anyone?"

"Just you." She clicked her tongue against the roof of her mouth the way she sometimes did when she was thinking. "Even if I don't, someone else will make the same connection. Eventually."

Gregory ran a hand through his hair. "Listen, my wife is going to have my head if I don't get home for dinner."

"Go. And keep this between us?"

He smiled. "Of course."

"Love to Goldie."

"Same to Cal."

Gregory grabbed his jacket and headed to the elevator.

A sign informed him that the elevators were being serviced, so he continued down the hall to the stairwell. As he pushed through the door and rounded the first corner, the image of her came to him, as he knew it would. For the rest of his life, whenever he climbed or descended a set of stairs, he would think of her—it was his punishment, he supposed. Had they stuck to their original plan, to their promise to be together, she wouldn't have fallen down those steps.

I'm leaving Jack. Just days after having written those words, Sybil changed her mind quite suddenly. She had "consulted God, prayed a lot, you know?" And instead of leaving Jack, they were going to try for another child. "We can't do this anymore. You have to stop contacting me, Gregory."

This is what she said as they sat together on that blanket in the moonlight. Sybil had agreed to meet him only because it would be their last time together. If they saw each other again, it would have to be as cousins. At first he didn't respond, as if he hadn't heard her properly. But when he finally spoke, his voice frightened her so much that she flinched. She stood up and went to the edge of the yard overlooking Hollywood, shivering in her thin coat. He followed, unfolding the note she had written him, and held it to her face. "Remember what you said? Why say it if you didn't mean it?" She shook her head, lashes clotted with tears. She had a daughter to worry about, a daughter who could have died because her mother had been distracted. Too preoccupied with her own selfish emotions to notice that her child was shoving poisonous flowers into her mouth. "What kind of example is that, Gregory?" When he told Sybil he wasn't going to give her up just like that, she called him angry and obsessive. She thumped a fist on his chest, and that's when he realized how tightly he was gripping her. "Just let me go, let me go," she protested. Instead, he pulled her to him with even more desperation.

But when his sweet Sybil said with uncharacteristic bile, "I'm sick to death of your anger, Gregory, and sick to death of you," he suddenly let go. He knew the force with which she was pulling away would send her reeling backward, but as he played the scene over in his mind, the difference between letting go and pushing blurred. Had he really meant for her to tumble backward down those steps? Had he really intended for the person he loved so much to die almost instantly? Yes, perhaps in that moment, that was exactly what he had wanted.

As Gregory continued down the stairwell, he felt his stomach lurch at the memory. He slowed and grabbed the banister for fear of falling himself. At the ground floor, he threw open the door and let the cool air hit his face. It was then that he felt tears pooling in his eyes. When he reached the plaza, he blinked back at the building and saw that E. J. hadn't moved from the window. She didn't see Gregory pass below. She was still looking in the direction of the Glass House, no doubt planning her next move.

He would have to act soon with Tom. The days when he might have managed situations like this at his leisure were coming to an end. It was all coming to an end, and the end point was out of his control. All he could do was let the universal computer lead him to it.

21

The Recluse

Hazel woke the next day with what felt like a hangover, except she was sure that she hadn't drunk anything the night before. She squinted at her surroundings, struggling against an acute sense of disorientation. She was in a tidy, unfamiliar bedroom, but it wasn't her brother's guest room. As her eyes fell on a Deco chest of drawers and an Art Nouveau print framed above it, it suddenly hit her. She had spent the night at the hotel. She vaguely remembered having texted Goldie that she was staying out so that she and Gregory could enjoy their anniversary together; at least she'd remembered to do that much. But she couldn't remember having felt this terrible ever, including the time she'd gotten food poisoning in college. Then again, she knew this wasn't physical; this was an emotional illness, which is always worse.

She didn't have to look at the clock to know that she'd slept most of the day. Still, when she propped herself up and grabbed her phone from the bedside table, she blinked at it in disbelief. It was four fifteen in the afternoon. Hazel fell back on the pillow and draped an arm across her face to block the light edging in around the blinds. As the events of the previous day came back to her in shaming detail, she groaned aloud and turned into the fetal position. *Christ. You idiot.* She could feel the entire weight of her stupidity in her stomach, tightening into a nauseating ball.

Hazel shut her eyes tight, and in the darkness behind her lids, Alex's charming smile played for her on repeat—a smile that seemed to say, "You, my friend, have been played." Alex had most certainly exploited her attraction to him, and by getting caught in his snare, she had failed one of the only people she had loved. What a fool Isaac had been to trust her. Hazel really hoped there was no afterlife because she didn't want her grandfather to see the magnitude of his error.

She made a feeble effort to sit up, but the pain of Alex's deceit seemed to be pinning her down. As did Raspanti's admonitions from yesterday. Once he had realized that Isaac's work was missing and that the owner of the wig was responsible, he had said darkly, "You let a man into the room, let him snoop into your grandfather's math? Isaac should never have left it to you, that much is clear."

"Look, I needed help—"

"And did you seek this man's help, or did he charm his way into the room?" When she didn't answer, he said, "I see."

"Alex isn't some random stranger. He's my cousin. Isaac's grandson."

"One with a strong mathematical background, I'm guessing, and oh so very curious about Isaac's work?"

"That about describes my entire family."

Raspanti had calmly picked up the phone, dialed the front desk, and requested that a cab take him to the airport. Hazel then followed him downstairs to the lobby, where she watched him pour himself some drip coffee. She did the same and trailed Raspanti outside.

He sat hunched on the front steps, blowing at steam from his cup. She knew he was making a point of not looking at her, which only made her more angry with herself.

She sat down and took a sip of coffee. It burned her tongue, and she winced. "I screwed up. I know that."

Still not looking at her, Raspanti said, "It wouldn't surprise me if these people recruited a Severy mole to poke around Isaac's things, to wait for the equation to show itself. I suppose you didn't have a chance."

"You don't need to make me feel any worse. I already hate myself for failing him."

"You think this is a simple failure? A case of family disloyalty?" He turned, staring her straight in the face. "It's a disaster on a scale you can't know now, but one day you will. It sounds cruel, but you will read the paper one morning, years from now, and you will know what you have done."

Hazel set down her cup and covered her face with her hands. That familiar pressure was building behind her eyes, but she refused to cry. How could it be that Isaac had made her a custodian of such consequence?

"We could find him," she said finally, lifting her head. "We could get the equation back."

Raspanti removed his glasses and pushed at his eyes, as if staving off a headache. "The equation is gone. Now that they have it, it's theirs forever."

"So you're just going to give up? Go back to Italy?"

"If what you say about the map is true, Isaac was killed for his mathematics. If you think they're just going to hand it back to you, you're delusional."

Hazel's stomach seized. She realized that this was the first time someone had said out loud what she'd been fearing since the moment she'd read the word *assassin* in Isaac's letter. *Isaac was killed for his mathematics.* There it was, stated as fact.

The taxi arrived. Raspanti stood and went to meet it.

Hazel felt desperate to stop him. She felt desperate about a lot of things: about the burden she'd been carrying around for weeks, about the implied murder of her grandfather, and about the fact that she had completely and totally failed him. At that moment, she felt she would do anything to get rid of this awful feeling in her gut.

"What if you're wrong?" she called out just as Raspanti was climbing into the cab. "What if I can get it back?"

He paused. "If you can get it back," he shouted, "I will personally fly you and the equation to Milan, first class, and I will teach you the meaning of great mathematics!"

"Is that a promise?"

Raspanti laughed bitterly. "Ciao, Ms. Severy." He shut the door, and the taxi pulled away.

Hazel watched until it was out of sight, and when she stood, her legs were shaking. She took a moment to steady herself before returning to the eighth-floor room to stare at the now-empty wall. She paced the carpet, ears alert, hoping wildly that she would hear the elevator open and Alex's footsteps in the hall. She imagined opening the door to find him standing there, shaking his head and explaining that this had all been a hilarious misunderstanding. But no one came.

When she realized she hadn't eaten since breakfast and was starving, Hazel ordered Thai food from down the street. Gobbling it on the patio, she looked out at the lights of Hollywood and wondered how the hell she was going to right her mistake. But the more she reviewed her options, the more her situation seemed maddeningly beyond repair. Even if she wanted to run away from her problems—just get on a plane back to Seattle—there was hardly anything to go back to. She had no store, no boyfriend, no life.

Now, at nearly four thirty in the afternoon the next day—practically sunset—Hazel kicked off the covers and forced herself out of bed. Still fighting queasiness, she stumbled to the bathroom and turned on the shower full blast. She shivered as she undressed and climbed in. The cool spray felt remarkably good, and she let it beat down on her while she waited for the hot water to kick in.

What if Raspanti *was* wrong? What if she could find Alex? What if she could exploit *his* weakness and snatch the equation right back? But then, what was Alex's weakness? She thought back to the stories he had told her that night, of his past, of his uprooted life, of his father and mother. She wondered how much of it was accurate and how much had been a ploy to get her to feel safe with him. The part about his mother, anyway, she knew was true. You couldn't make that woman up. *Wait: his mother.* Even if Alex was estranged from Paige—and even if the mere thought of seeing her made Hazel sick all over again—the woman was still a possible lead.

After toweling off, she felt steady enough to dress, make a cup of tea, and eat a few bites of last night's leftovers. She took it on faith that the Thai wasn't at least partly to blame for her indisposition, but putting noodles in her stomach seemed to lift her nausea. Feeling well enough to venture outside, Hazel took one last look at the empty wall, grabbed her things, and headed to the door. As she made her way down the narrow hall to the elevator, Raspanti's fatalism was still loud in her ears: "*If you think they're just going to hand it back to you, you're delusional. The equation is gone.*"

The elevator doors opened. *We'll see.*

It was dark by the time Hazel left the hotel and drove to Venice Beach. No one was rushing to get to the ocean on a Sunday evening, and the Santa Monica Freeway was wide open.

Paige Severy lived in a bungalow a block from the Venice board-walk, an odd location for a cloistered intellectual who probably hadn't owned a swimsuit in years. Yet there she was, stuck in the middle of this vibey surf community, reportedly working on a book of infinite length. Hazel found her way through an overgrown yard to the front door. The porch light was out, but she could detect an incandescent glow from somewhere within. Finding the bell painted over, she rapped on the lopsided door. Within seconds, there was the scrabbling of paws on hardwood and the barking of two dogs of very different sizes. Mild scolding followed, the sound of which set Hazel immediately on edge.

"Come now, Hodge. Let's see who it is. Podge, dial it back."

The door cracked open, revealing half of Paige's face as she eyed the shadowy stoop. Hazel tried to inject some confidence into her voice: "Aunt Paige, it's me. Hazel."

Paige pulled the door wider and peered out, her fuzzy head crowned with bejeweled reading glasses. She looked down at her niece and smiled blandly. "So it is, an orphan on my doorstep."

Hazel wondered how many more reasons she needed to dislike this woman.

"Is it a bad time?"

"A bad time for what? Roses? Dysentery? I guess I'll have to let you in. *Hodge, Podge—hush.*"

Hazel entered the house, where the cool, salted air gave way to the warm smell of wood and paper. She was greeted by a large Weimaraner of an intense gray-blue.

"That's Hodge. The mutant is Podge."

Yapping at the Weimaraner's paws was a delicate thing with scant hair and confused breeding. Hazel feared it would bite, but she bent down anyway to pat its tiny deer skull.

"I found this guy outside, just before a storm hit. *Yes, you'd have*

blown to Catalina if it weren't for me, isn't that so? I hope you're a
tea person."

"Oh, don't bother. Really."

"You're already a bother," Paige snapped. "My work was interrupted the moment you put your knuckles to my door, so I may as
well share my hot water."

Hazel didn't argue. A tea kettle was beginning to whistle, and
the dogs followed their waddling mistress into the kitchen.

"You can have a seat in the back room," Paige called above the
sounds of china.

Hazel moved down the dim hallway, discerning that the living
room to her left was indeed inhospitable. She couldn't see much,
but the strong whiff of boxes and mildewed paper told her that this
was a repository for books. The smell instantly reminded Hazel
of the Guttersnipe. It was a dark, pulpy scent she had loved for so
long, but for the first time, she wanted to run from it. It seemed to
hold all that had betrayed or hurt her: her store and the grueling
business of peddling unwanted objects to unwilling people; and
Bennet, a man she realized only now approached the world with
a kind of stylish indifference. Was it any wonder she didn't fit into
the chic lines and curves of his existence? Someday she hoped to
no longer associate this smell with the ruination of her life in Seattle, and that once again the aroma of slowly rotting paper might
be irresistible.

She followed the source of the lamplight to the rear of the house,
where what had once been a back porch was now a den. A desk
stood at one end of the room, piled high with papers and books,
and a sofa at the other. The sofa looked as if it had been hollowed
out at the center, no doubt from having been used as a bed. Her
suspicions were confirmed by an alarm clock sitting on the floor.

"Sit there," Paige ordered from behind her.

Hazel took a seat on one end of the sofa, careful to avoid the sinkhole. She straightened her spine a little: she was no longer going to be intimidated by this woman.

The dogs collapsed onto a rug in the center of the room, little Podge curled inside Hodge's legs.

"So you're here about my son." Paige poured dark tea into both cups.

"Yes, actually," Hazel said, a little thrown. "How did you know?"

Her aunt handed her the sugar bowl, pouring some milk for herself. "For most of my professional life, I was paid to know all the potential answers to subjective questions outside the normal bounds of statistics: Will candidate A's smart wardrobe alienate working-class voters? Is candidate B's corny sense of humor endearing or off-putting? Will revelations of mental illness in candidate C's family garner sympathy or scare people off? The question here being: Why is Hazel, who has never particularly liked her aunt, paying said aunt a surprise visit on a Sunday evening? Only one answer makes sense."

"Impressive," Hazel said, stifling her annoyance. "Do you know how I can reach Alex?"

Paige took a seat at her desk, swiveling to face her niece. "Alex has a habit of slipping off the grid—gets that from me. You must want to find him somewhat urgently, otherwise you would've simply called. Have the two of you become entangled somehow? Perhaps you've developed some confused feelings for him. He's not a *blood* cousin, after all, and you didn't grow up together. It wouldn't be the first time that's happened in this family, but I suppose I'm straying into speculation."

She glanced at Hazel and took a satisfied sip of tea.

Hazel tried to ignore the burning sensation at the tips of her ears and a sudden desire to upend the tea table and kick her aunt's chair out from under her. There was also a brief clip of Hazel emptying the contents of the teapot onto Paige's head. "You've really thought it through, haven't you?"

"Please, this isn't a Poe mystery; it hardly requires a C. Auguste Dupin level of detection. It took me a few seconds. Most people go around thinking that life is magical and mysterious, filled with all kinds of unknowns. Bullshit. Once you decide the universe is knowable, all kinds of answers become available to you."

"I guess I don't go around thinking that way."

"Of course you don't. Very few people are blessed with a methodical brain. Like everyone else, you probably stumble through life getting into trouble, debt, and heartbreak."

Hazel had no intention of betraying the accuracy of this statement. Instead, she looked around, taking in the study as a depiction of her aunt's blessed brain and lonely life. She wondered if there might be some visible clue as to Alex's whereabouts, but on the shelves lining the room, there was no evidence of family at all. No photographs, no mementos. There were only three-ring binders—hundreds of them—all grimy white, each labeled alphabetically, *A* through *J*, in colored marker. Was this the never-ending book project?

Aware that she looked to be snooping, Hazel forced her eyes back to Paige. "I really don't want to waste your time. Do you have any idea where Alex might be staying?"

"He and I don't speak."

"Do you at least know if he's still in the country? If you had to find him—"

"Have you heard a thing I've said?" Paige snapped.

In response, Hazel stood abruptly, not caring to hide her frustration. "Thank you for the tea." But after returning her cup to the tray, curiosity won over, and she glanced back at the binders. "Where are *K* through *Z*?"

Paige tapped her forehead. "Up here. When it's complete, *The Book of Probabilities* will clock in at around five hundred sixty-five volumes."

"You have a ways to go, then."

Her aunt smiled, almost sadly. "I have a secret for you. It will never be finished. I will die before I ever get near *Z*."

"If you can't finish it, why write it?"

Paige readjusted her toadstool mass. "Because what else is there to do but work on what one is good at?"

Hazel wondered how her aunt was making any money on this, but wasn't about to ask. Besides, Hazel knew something about living your life with complete disregard for profits. At least her aunt had something to show for it.

"You know"—Paige wagged an arthritic finger at Hazel—"your generation could stand to live in the pursuit a bit more. You're all rushed to get to the end. To *succeed*. Alex is the same. He can see only the end result and is totally incapable of appreciating mathematics for its own sake. If there is no tangible reward at the end, he sees the work as pointless. It's an empty way to live, in constant pursuit of the trophy. It's the reason he has failed."

"Well, he's still young," Hazel said lamely, more in defense of herself than of Alex.

"His probability of succeeding as a pure mathematician drops precipitously with each passing year, and his chances of succeeding at applied mathematics aren't much better. Plus, he has a lazy brain."

"I thought he had an accident."

"Right, his so-called brain damage from that autobahn incident. Horseshit. The real story of his failure is far more spectacular."

When Hazel didn't respond, Paige said, "Don't pretend like you don't want to know."

Hazel sat down again while her aunt dumped more sugar in her tea.

"There is a group of twenty-three problems in mathematics, called Hilbert's problems—intellectual puzzles more than anything, though mathematicians take them very seriously. Most have been solved, but there are a few remaining. One particularly stubborn problem was solved by my son many years ago while he was at the Max Planck Institute." Paige looked up to measure her guest's reaction. "Wondering why you haven't heard about such a triumph? Why Isaac never mentioned it?"

Hazel nodded.

"You've never heard about it because someone else beat my son to the proof. By a couple of weeks." Paige appeared amused by this. "An unassuming Russian, who'd been working in his mother's basement for years, quietly published his proof. No fanfare, just mailed it off. And in our world, publishing is everything."

Hazel assigned this new information to her previous image of Alex. Now that she thought about it, beneath all the bluster, there had been an air of defeat about him.

"But that's not his fault," she said. "It's just bad luck."

Paige smiled. "Maybe. But it's what he did afterward that revealed his true character. He did nothing. Zero. Completely gave up mathematics. He blamed it all on this supposed car wreck, of course. But I knew."

"Is that why you don't speak to him?"

She shrugged. "He doesn't speak to me because he knows I disapprove of his vagrant lifestyle. Bumming around Paris, going to parties, sleeping around, God knows what else. How he affords all this laziness, don't ask me."

"Maybe he has another source of income," Hazel suggested pointedly.

"Well, obviously. Though I don't buy this AP photographer nonsense." Paige snorted and swiveled back to her desk. "Now you'll really have to excuse me. I'm attacking a particularly difficult section on the odds of succeeding as a jazz musician."

Hazel stood up, unsure how to transition out of the room. "I'll find my own way out."

"Wait!" Paige practically shouted.

Hazel paused at the door.

"I made an agreement with myself long ago that I would leave the warmth to warm people. But tell them that I let you in, won't you? That I didn't turn a relative away? No one in this family gives me any credit."

"I will," Hazel said, suddenly overcome with sadness for this aunt she had never liked.

She started down the hall, glancing back just as Paige splashed something from a bottle into her teacup. When she reached the front door, she could hear her aunt muttering something to her dogs.

Outside, Hazel closed the gate to the yard and, for lack of a better idea, turned in the direction of the beach, guided by the light of the surrounding bungalows. After removing her shoes and socks at the edge of the concrete, she stepped onto the cool sand and kept walking.

When she reached the shoreline, she let the incoming tide engulf her feet. How long had it been since she'd touched the Pacific? Living on Puget Sound for so many years, surrounded by water on all sides, it was easy to lose track of the last time you set eyes on the actual ocean. It was easy to forget how this boundless expanse seemed to exist for moments like this, when you are rigidly stuck, with nowhere left to go.

Hazel closed her eyes. In a very literal interpretation of Raspanti's doomsday prediction, she imagined herself opening her laptop one morning, clicking through her usual news sites, and finding variations on the same headline, her mistake writ large: *"Powerful People Do Irretrievably Terrible Thing."* Had she really inflicted such a grave injury onto the future? Was her mistake irreversible?

She stepped backward and collapsed onto dry sand. Below the crash of the surf, she could just make out an alien sound, a pinging coming from her purse. She fished out her phone and discovered she had a text from Bennet. She considered deleting it but didn't have the willpower not to read it first:

H, Hope you can make the opening. xB

She clicked on the attached link, and up popped a website for a Seattle art gallery. Bennet's show, the one he had been working on for years, had arrived:

New Exhibition—Bennet Hewes

This Is My Sad Face: The Shock of Human Emotion

Below it, a mixed-media likeness of her own face stared out at the viewer with a flash of irritation. The photo underlying the image had been taken near the beginning of her relationship with Bennet, the light of a setting sun glancing off one cheek. But the details of her skin were gone, smeared over with paint, wax, and paper. It wasn't a bad piece, and she knew this exhibition was a big deal for him, but she could only bring herself to reply, *Nice title.*

He must have taken some perverse pleasure in naming his show after her last message to him. Hazel scrolled up until her previous text and accompanying selfie filled the screen: *This is my sad face.* She could hardly stand to look at it and was about to tuck away her phone when she noticed something about the image: behind her unhappy head was a fragment of Isaac's map—evidently, the single shot of the map that had escaped erasure. She zoomed in on it, and to her astonishment, the resolution was sharp all the way in. Having spent little time exploring her own phone, she was still mystified by its capabilities. Hazel pulled in close enough to make out the names of downtown streets and to read the dots Isaac had placed there. There were a few dots sitting in a cluster, one reading 101515013122—or October 15, 2015, 1:31 a.m. and 22 seconds. If the dot was accurate, just a month ago, near the corner of Maple Avenue and East Sixth Street, some poor soul had breathed his or her last. But then, that was to be expected on Skid Row. A couple of blocks away were two more dots, near the historic district, where two people had apparently died in August within minutes of each other. "*Your grandfather wasn't predicting just any kind of death,*" she remembered Raspanti saying. Okay, if not just death, then what?

You know what.

She shut her eyes tight. When she opened them again, they settled on a single red circle, near the intersection of Alameda Street and the 101 Freeway, the location of Union Station. She read the numbers: 111515. November 15. Today. The rest of the string read: 212506. That was tonight.

Hazel couldn't know where Alex would be or what he would do next, but if *she* had been the one to steal Isaac's equation, she would certainly want to see if the thing worked. Tonight, at 9:25 and 6 seconds, something was going to happen at Union Station. That gave her less than two hours.

22

The Equation

As Philip headed up the coast toward Malibu, he realized he would have to navigate from the unreliable memory of having been driven there weeks before. He wondered if he should have called ahead to warn Nellie or had her send the car, but he was done with formalities. Besides, if he had to flee from her a second time, he wanted a getaway vehicle.

Philip had left the house in a gust of unspecified urgency and with a quick kiss to Jane, who had been keeping herself busy in the kitchen with clippers and an ailing plant. She hadn't even looked up, tending to the leaves with obsessive focus. He found himself disappointed that she hadn't asked where he was going. A simple "Where you off to?" and he pictured himself falling to the floor at Jane's garden-clogged feet and unloading it all. Not just about GSR and Nellie but also about his inability to work, about how he missed his father horribly—as much as he missed their daughter, in fact. He would have even confessed his betrayal of their marriage, and how this young oddball physicist at the dawn of her career made him feel confused. It would have been an ugly confession, and he would have deserved a prompt clog to the face.

It was well into the afternoon when he parked. The house stood boxy and graphic against the sky, looking more unreal than it had the first time. Philip headed up the walk and rang the bell. A man with a trim beard, around his own age, answered. He was tall, spectacled, and indifferently dressed, wearing untucked shirtsleeves and dress socks minus the shoes. It was the same man he had seen through the ground-floor window on his first visit.

"How can I help you?" the man asked in a watery English accent.

"I'm Philip Severy, here to see . . . your boss."

The man opened the door wide. "The magic word."

"What's that?"

"Severy, of course," he said, looking his visitor over with intense curiosity. "The name gets batted around here a fair amount. I'm Cavet, by the way."

Philip followed Cavet as he turned down a familiar hallway leading to the back of the house.

"It's all last names here. Lyons likes it that way. Sorry about my appearance, but it's the weekend, and I don't normally answer the door. You can wait here."

They entered the expansive anteroom where Philip had waited during his previous visit. He frowned as he recalled how Nellie had sat there at the desk, no doubt pretending to work as she sized him up and tamed him with good food, all the while having him wait for a man she knew would never arrive.

"If I know Lyons," Cavet continued, "she won't keep you waiting long. Not this time."

Philip drifted toward the desk, inspecting with renewed eyes the framed photographs on the mantel shelf: not of Nellie posing with her boss's clients, but of Nellie posing with her own.

Cavet hesitated at the door. "I hope you make the right choice, Severy." Then he winked and withdrew.

Philip walked the length of the room, stopping at the glass wall that framed ocean and sky. It looked as if it might rain, which added to the strange sinking feeling in his chest. As he watched the cloud cover descend on a colorless Pacific, the misery of the previous night came back to him. The twins having gone to a friend's house, he and Jane had endured a silent dinner together, with both of them drinking more than usual. But when little Drew emerged from her room in her PJs and asked—for the first time in a while—if Mommy and Daddy would be back for her soon, Jane had to flee the room for fear of breaking down. Philip had wrestled back his own torment until Faye swooped in to take Drew back to bed.

He followed his wife outside, where she had fallen onto the grass. "I can't stand it, Philip," she choked. "Where am I supposed to put all this?" She thumped at her chest as if trying to dislodge something from her rib cage. He took her fist in his hand and whispered, "One day at a time, darling. We'll go on our hikes again like we used to." Jane took back her fist and began to tug nervously at the lawn. The tugging became strangely methodical as she put her face to the ground to seek out anything that wasn't grass. "Maybe there's a better time for weeding," he gently suggested. But she didn't appear to hear him. So Philip just sat there and kept his wife company as she crawled along, sending fistfuls of weeds flying. He didn't dare turn to the house, where he sensed her sister watching from the doorway, as if to say, "See?"

He thought again of this morning, of how Jane hadn't looked at him once, of how she was looking thinner and thinner every day. Of course she hadn't asked where he was going; she had completely lost interest in the world around her. The question was: How long was he going to watch her waste away?

A thin mist accumulated on the window. Philip's mind was growing weary of all the gloom and began to seek out a reliable pleasure source: Anitka. *Anya*. He liked repeating her Russian diminutive over and over in his mind. *Anya*. But just when he had isolated the perfect image of her standing at the foot of her bed, dairy smooth skin, untying a black robe, an unwelcome voice invaded his fantasy.

"You think yourself clever showing up in your own car?"

He turned, searching for her, but the room was empty. Her voice issued from a hidden speaker somewhere: "You think this gives you some control over the situation, Mr. Severy?" There was the usual smile in her voice, betraying some secret delight.

"No, no," he answered. "You have all the control, Nellie. You've made that very clear."

The speaker sighed. "Why don't you come to me?"

"And where's that?"

"Go into my study."

He crossed the room and pushed open the double doors onto the faint smell of cigarette smoke. All the animal trophies were dim, except for the lioness, which cast a glow on the case containing the taser rifles. Nellie's voice leapt to a speaker at the desk: "The door in the corner, walk through it. Turn right."

He was soon in a bright, functional hallway with a door at the far end. Her voice floated above him: "The door leads to a stairwell. Wait at the bottom."

He descended two flights of stairs—*How deep does this place go?*—until he was confronted with a pair of earmuffs and goggles hanging beside a metal door.

"You'll want to put those on," she instructed.

He did as he was told, and on the other side of the door was a second door. He pushed it open and found Nellie standing with her back to him, head-to-foot in khaki, staring down the scope of a hunting rifle. She took aim at a rapidly moving target: a black cutout of an antelope. She fired into the antelope's flank—with what looked to be real bullets—and removed her earmuffs. He did the same.

"Good of you to come," she said. Her secretarial glasses had returned.

"I'm guessing you're zoned for this."

"Of course. I do have *some* influence."

"Influence or money?"

"So I'm just some rich eccentric, is that it? Throwing money around on private firing ranges?"

"It's what I thought when I assumed you were a man. Is there any reason to change my mind now?"

She smiled, so wide that her irises nearly disappeared. Then she clicked on the rifle's safety and held out the gun to him. "Care to perforate some cardboard?"

He shook his head. "What happened to your taser rifle?"

"It doesn't give the same kick. Heads up."

They shielded their ears, and she fired at the leaping silhouette, creating a blossom-shaped wound in its side. When it was gone, she tore off her muffs and dismantled the rifle. As she removed the magazine, she exhaled heavily, clearing the air for a new topic.

"I won't make you guess my age," she began, opening a gun cabinet behind her, "but my company has been an unofficial contractor of the US government for nearly thirty years."

"Christ, you really are off the radar."

"Some may question the legality of it, but no one ever questions the great deal of good we've done for this country. GSR makes a profit, of course—the Lyons estate could afford to subsidize this operation for only so long. But considering the enormous benefit we're offering our customers, the US government being one, well, you can't put a proper price on that. Besides, Lyons is an American above all. Even his cars, as you may have noticed, are domestic."

She caught herself and laughed. "Listen to me, boasting about myself in the third-person-male again."

"Must get awfully confusing for you."

"You can't imagine." She locked the cabinet and led him farther down the hall. "It took years of work to get to the point where I could even think about recruiting someone like you. You can guess how, as a twentysomething—a girl, really—having just come into my inheritance and trying to build my own business, how few would look at me as anything other than a prospective intern or date. Even after I'd managed to get meetings with a few scientists at this or that university, they would take one look at me and have to smother a laugh. I had one guy, a very brilliant economist whom I'd admired for years, offer me a job as his secretary. He liked my 'attention to detail.' I was furious, of course, but as soon as my head cleared, I decided to give these guys what they wanted. And for my next meeting, I went not as myself but as my own assistant. I discovered that a few were willing to take me seriously if they believed I was working for a man. Same applied to all my meetings in DC."

They entered a small break room, outfitted with various appliances, including an espresso machine. "Cappuccino?" she asked.

"No thank you."

"I spent a salt mine on this contraption. You're having cappuccino."

She switched on the machine and rummaged for grounds and milk. "And so Nellie Stone was born—Mr. P. Booth Lyons's indispensable right hand. I assumed that I would shed the deception, of course, as soon as I got a solid foothold or no longer looked like I was nineteen. But as I discovered, once I had created this persona, it was hard to put her back in the box."

"And you could sustain all this for thirty years, on a lie?"

"Oh, it's a harmless lie, isn't it? And few ever questioned my story because I appeared so well informed that I simply *must* have been sent by someone important. As you pointed out, secrecy is part of my business model, so if anyone came at me with too many questions, I would plead confidentiality and trade secrets. Of course, my boss was always far too busy traveling to actually meet anyone in person—though when 'he' was absolutely required, I would send Cavet or some other equally distinguished-looking person in my place. For some reason, I always imagined my fictional Lyons as this patriot, yet vaguely European in bearing and style."

Or pretentious, Philip thought of saying but didn't. He was thinking of that ridiculous condolence letter she'd sent him.

"The day I came up here," he said, "why bother with the whole ruse? What was the point of bringing me here if 'Mr. Lyons' was never going to show?"

She pursed her lips in an effort to contain her own amusement. "I knew that if I got you comfortable enough, I could find out whether you knew where your father's work was hidden. I could find out without Mr. Lyons ever having to arrive."

"I told you I didn't know."

"It was slippery of me. But you see, after a while, my twin identities have become second nature. In fact, I rather enjoy being Ms. Stone." She sighed wistfully as she tamped the espresso grounds. "This was all so much easier pre-internet, of course. These days, everyone demands to know everything instantly."

"Did my father know?"

She nodded. "He was one of the few I told who wasn't working directly for me. It was a risk, but I loved his work, and I trusted him. He, unfortunately, in the end, didn't trust me and backed out of our agreement."

"By dying, you mean."

"By betraying our understanding," she said coldly. "I do have a business to run."

He shouted above the steaming milk. "How can you be sure I'll keep your secret?"

"Doesn't matter. It's time for Ms. Stone to retire. Besides, gone are the days when she could use her feminine charms to get what she wanted. That kind of cheap persuasion doesn't work for me like it once did." She poured the espresso and foam into two cups. "Funny, that may be the last time I tell that story to anyone. I hope it clears everything up."

"Well, not everything."

"We'll get to your father's work soon enough," she said, handing him his cappuccino. "What did you make of Cavet?"

He looked down at his cup, at the Mandelbrot pattern she had fashioned in the foam. "What about him?"

"I recruited him from the London School of Economics in the nineties, where he was doing some startling work on the fractal nature of African villages. Before Cavet, no one had bothered to look at the architecture of these settlements from above. He realized that they are remarkably self-similar, the form of the entire village repeated in the form of the neighborhood, the block, the house—"

"I'm familiar with how fractals work."

She ignored him and continued. "Turns out his research applied not only to villages in Africa but also to settlements all over the world. If one knows what the outside of a town looks like, one can anticipate the interior. The military has been using Cavet's techniques in the Middle East for years, when soldiers enter areas without satellite images."

"But fractals don't get you killed," Philip said. "Guns and bombs do."

"Exactly," she said with emphasis. "Death is unexpected, isn't it, no matter how well we plan for it? Cavet's method is merely a tool. And where his methods end, your father's work begins."

She signaled Philip back into the hallway. Drinks in hand, they clicked down the tile to another set of double doors, where Nellie turned to him with a barely suppressed smile. "I guess I didn't realize how much I was looking forward to showing you this."

"His mathematics, you mean."

She nodded. "Can you think of anything more exhilarating than the realization that the future is, in fact, knowable?"

And with that, she pushed open the doors.

Some time later, Philip sat in a leather bucket chair, picking his way through figures on a wall. He was aware of Nellie breathing in the darkness beside him, her respirations loud enough to make him feel as if his own breathing had stopped.

The equation was of some length—so long, in fact, that its projected image spilled from the wall onto the concrete floor. Was his heart still beating? He couldn't feel it. It was as if his body had gone into a kind of torpor so that his brain alone could barrel ahead. It was a familiar sensation that he'd experienced the few times he had a particularly exhilarating idea in his own work. At such moments, he imagined that his brain was approaching the speed of light, while the variables in front of him slowed to a standstill.

It might have been five minutes since Nellie had flicked on the projector, or it might have been twenty, but he had needed only a few seconds to identify the equation as his father's. It bore all of the signature refinement, the dedication to the graceful, the spare, the clean-swept. But here and there, erupting out of tidy, almost unassuming passages, was a mathematics of such delight and strangeness that it seemed to Philip to be almost a new kind of logic, created elsewhere, extragalactically—as if Isaac Severy had been chosen to introduce this brand of math to Earth. Even if this equation meant nothing, even if it were just delirious ramblings, it was beautiful.

But toward the end of the equation, something happened. The numbers took a sharp turn, as if rebelling, and the accompanying symbols seemed to stick out their Greek tongues. Had he missed something? Was this, in fact, over his head? Bewildered, Philip asked Nellie to scroll back to the beginning.

She didn't seem to register his confusion.

"Lovely, isn't it?" she asked in the same way she had about the lioness trophy in her office. "Of course," she continued, "I'm no mathematician. I had to have one of my guys explain the more arcane pieces. But then it was this feeling of exaltation, like a portal opening—"

"Where did you say you found this?" he asked casually.

"I didn't say."

"He must have hidden it well."

"Not as well as you'd think," she said. "It was, however, password protected. It took nearly a week to crack."

"Let me guess, he left the password hidden in plain sight?"

A pause. "How did you know?"

"Because he can't help himself."

"It was a string of numbers," she explained, "left encoded in a simple game of checkers."

He smiled. "Sounds about right." Turning back to the equation, Philip said, "I would need more time, of course. To fully process this."

"You can sit here as long as you like; memorize the thing if you want. I won't be able to give you a copy, you understand."

"Not until I agree to work for you?"

"You must get tired of my conditions."

Philip started to read the equation again from the beginning but stopped when the symbols began to wag their tongues again. He closed his eyes. Was he really too dim to process this? Is that what it had come to? *"Brain rot,"* he could hear his father hissing. But that's not what was bothering him.

Why had Isaac kept this beautiful math a secret from him?

Philip started to speak, but he knew that if he continued, he would start sobbing. Why not break down right there? Go ahead, curl up in this very expensive chair and cry like a goddamn infant. It seemed like the perfect response to his father's treachery, to his inability to share his work with his son, his favorite child. Why hadn't he trusted him? Hadn't Philip shared everything with his father, told him absolutely everything that was going on in his head? As he asked these questions, his mind conjured up Isaac's cruel response: *"Let's face it, Philip, it's been some time since you've produced good ideas in your own field. You didn't need the distraction. You may have been remarkable once, but . . ."*

Remarkable. There was that word again.

A squeak of impatience from Nellie's chair. "Did you say something?"

"I was thinking," Philip managed dispassionately. "This could be a lot of lovely nothing."

She pulled her chair close. "Let's just assume for a second it is something. And if it *were* something, what might that be?"

"It's not a traffic equation."

"No? How can you tell?"

"From the bits I've seen of my father's traffic project, the math is different. It's difficult to explain."

"Then what is it?"

"You already know. Or you wouldn't be swaggering around like you've won a prize."

"Say it, Philip. Say what it is." The glow from the projection made her eyes almost manic. He had to look away.

"It's a predictive equation."

"Don't be vague. What kind?"

Somehow, Philip had known what kind of equation it was the moment she had switched on the projector. Perhaps for the past week, his subconscious had been working on the problem of his father's obsessive newspaper collection. Isaac had accumulated those clippings for decades, yet the stockpile never found its way into his mathematics—at least, not publicly. But Philip knew his father enough to see that he wouldn't have wasted his time on such a collection had it not held the possibility of a greater purpose. An end point. Isaac Severy had been preoccupied with death to the extreme.

"It's a death oracle, or so you're hoping," he said. "You may as well name it something fancy."

"You're still being vague."

A sharp chill ran up his back. All those clippings had been of fatal accidents, but the ones his father had flagged in Sharpie had been particularly suspicious: a woman whose car brakes failed; an abusive father trapped in a discarded refrigerator while his family was away; a man who accidentally shot his fiancée while cleaning his gun. It hadn't been mundane accidents that had fascinated his father but instead the blurred line between chance and vicious intent, between a genuine accident and a perceived one. This was what Isaac had been attempting to isolate.

"It's more than just death," Philip said at last. "The math indicates intent." He could sense Nellie beaming beside him, willing him to continue. "Homicide prediction in the greater LA area."

"Can you believe you just said that?" She sounded as if she were about to yank him out of his chair and waltz him around the room. "To think what we could have done with this years ago! Can you imagine how it would have been one fateful morning in September to see a map of Manhattan's financial district light up? Or that field in Pennsylvania? Or London? Madrid? What about the Paris attacks two days ago?"

"*If* such an equation were possible."

"If? Open your eyes."

"Whatever it is," he said, "it's clearly about control."

"How do you mean?"

"It's my father's attempt to control the uncontrollable, or at least predict it. As if that could have saved my brother somehow—" He stopped himself, not because he didn't want to discuss his family history with Nellie but because he wasn't sure that Isaac's motivations had anything to do with saving lives. As with most everything in his father's career, hadn't he done it for the thrill of discovery? Isn't that why Philip had chosen theoretical physics? How he wished his father could have shared the math that lay in front of him now—explained to him its wonders and nuances—but Philip had been robbed of that. He fought back against a renewed wave of anger and grief.

"The best inventions are borne out of strife, Philip." Nellie leaned back in her chair. "Why do you think I built this company? Because I'm an innately ambitious person, or because I feel compelled to correct some intolerable imbalance from my past?"

"I wouldn't attempt to understand your motives, Nellie. But I promise to read your memoirs."

"You ready to move on?" she asked.

With a click of a button, the numbers vanished along with their wagging tongues, and in their place appeared a map of Los Angeles County, perforated with colored dots. Each one held a string of numbers: time code.

"You created this from the equation?"

"Oh, no. We're not that far along yet. Your father left this for us. A gift."

"For you to steal."

"For us to find," she corrected him. "The dots are for the month of November. They stop after that. The green ones have been confirmed by us; blue, unconfirmed."

"And you're saying this actually works?" As Philip heard himself pose this question, he could suddenly see a terrible future spinning out before him, one in which control and certainty ruled every aspect of their lives. He shuddered.

"It works exceedingly better than the LAPD's medieval attempts at crime forecasting. We still have work to do, of course."

"And the red?" He silently counted nine red dots.

"Those are happening today."

"How are you verifying these?"

"Police scanners, blotters, internet, newspapers. But often we need to verify them on the scene. That's when I send someone. I believe you know him."

"Someone I know is working on this?"

She smiled. "When you join us, I will happily reveal his identity."

He shifted in his chair, checking his mental Rolodex for a possible traitor.

Nellie flicked a laser pen at points around the city. "The Whittier dot has a time code of early this morning, and Culver City"—she glanced at her phone—"twenty minutes ago. Which, incidentally, my guy has just confirmed. A domestic murder. Very sad."

Philip stared, stunned by her nonchalance. "If these dots are accurate, if people are going to die, why not do something about it?"

"What do you suggest we do? Run around the city playing superhero?"

"Why not?"

"Don't be funny." Nellie clicked off her laser pen. "Our task now is to verify the equation's power and limits. Only then can we begin to decide what to do with the information."

Philip squinted at the map, straining to read the dots. "Tell that to the person who's going to die downtown this evening. Or the one this afternoon in the Angeles National Forest."

"I should add," she said, ignoring his last remark, "that your father distinguished murders from homicides. All murders are homicides, but not necessarily the reverse. Murder requires intent, of course, while homicides can include involuntary manslaughter. Drunk driving, for instance, doesn't figure into Isaac's equation. In the end, it really comes down to intent."

"And suicides?"

"Ah," she said. "In order to create a true murder map, your father tried his best to cancel them out. Not that a suicide map wouldn't be useful on its own, but he wanted the option to filter them. Unfortunately, he never got to it."

"So his equation can't tell the difference?"

Nellie shook her head. "When it comes to a distinction between the two, the equation is blind." She peered at the map. "But then, suicide is murder, isn't it? It's in the etymology of the word, after all."

He frowned. "Then this means that my father's own—"

"Yes," she said. For the first time that day, he detected something in her voice that sounded close to regret: "It means that Isaac's own death was predicted by the equation."

Philip was silent for a moment as he tried to reconcile all he knew of his father—and his apparent suicide—with this new information. Just as an unsettling scenario opened up before him, his phone vibrated in his pocket. He saw that he had somehow missed three calls, one from the house and two from his sister-in-law's cell phone.

"Something the matter?" Nellie asked.

He stood up. "I need to make a call."

A minute later, he was back upstairs in her study. As he headed past the lioness, he couldn't help but glance again at the rifle case. He'd always had a visceral reaction to guns, but at that moment they held a particular dread or a kind of warning: *hurry, hurry, hurry*. Philip pulled his eyes from the weapons and left the room.

In the waiting area, he hunted for a signal. He found a couple of bars near the window, and as he looked out over the water, the sky threatening rain, he dialed Faye.

She picked up immediately. "Is Jane with you?"

"Why would she be with me?" he asked.

"It's just that after dropping the twins off at their lesson, she never came back. We were supposed to go to yoga an hour ago. She's not picking up her phone."

"Did you two fight?"

A sigh. "She said I was smothering her, but it's nothing she hasn't said before."

"Maybe she's at her therapist."

"No, that was yesterday. I didn't want to panic you, but—"

"Start looking."

"I don't have the car."

"Do what you can, Faye. I'm coming home." He hung up.

After trying Jane several times and getting no answer, Philip went to the front door to leave. He was met by Cavet, who stood there like a butler, in shoes this time.

"Leaving without good-bye?"

"Something's come up."

As Cavet opened the door, he simultaneously passed Philip a square envelope, stamped with the brain-spiral. "She was afraid you'd run off before she had a chance to give you the details of the

258

offer. It's all there." Cavet slapped a chummy hand on his back. "I'm looking forward to working with a Severy."

Without a reply, Philip slipped the envelope into his pocket and left.

He knew what he needed to do. He needed to drive quickly toward that red dot on the border of the Angeles National Forest. It seemed an odd place for a murder, at the very edge of the park, south of Mount Wilson. A tiny circle nestled just inside the green expanse . . . Eaton Canyon. Yes, he was sure of it now: that familiar twist of trail that he and Jane knew so well. The time code had read November 15, and then—he closed his eyes, summoning the rest—171126, 5:11 p.m. and 26 seconds. He checked his watch. That was 90 minutes from now.

Starting the car, Philip remembered with growing alarm the discussion he'd last had with his wife in the canyon. He floored the gas and drove as fast as he dared down the hill, casting a swift, paranoid glance in the rearview mirror to make sure Nellie wasn't having him tailed. When he pulled onto the Pacific Coast Highway, his chest was pounding. And soon the pounding beneath his ribs was echoed by a far-off drumbeat in his brain.

23

The Station

Hazel parked the Cadillac in Chinatown and proceeded to Union Station on foot, arriving thirty-five minutes ahead of the time indicated on the map. It wasn't until she neared the station entrance that she realized there was more at stake here than just finding Alex. Someone, presumably, was going to die in a half hour. She wondered if an anonymous tip to the police might be in order, but what would she say? Instead, she called her brother. She was now ready to spill everything to Gregory in one long breath, no longer caring that Isaac had warned her not to. But he didn't pick up. Considering the condition she'd seen him in yesterday, this didn't exactly surprise her. Could he be embarrassed? Hazel left a message asking him to call her, that it was urgent.

She paused to look up at the clock tower: ten minutes to nine. The tower was a familiar sight from childhood trips to the station. Her transportation-obsessed grandfather had considered such visits an essential part of her and Gregory's education. But aside from a few novelty train rides, Hazel had rarely taken the railroad as an adult. A pity, because she had always been a sucker for the majesty of the place. While the building's Mission Revival exterior informed passersby that they were squarely in the Southwest, the interior's Deco typefaces and Streamline Moderne embellishments ushered commuters through the modern age of travel, stylishly directing them to railway platforms, ticket sales, and baggage claim. As she passed beneath the sentinel palms on either side of the arched entrance, she wished for a moment that she had a valise dangling from one hand and a first-class sleeper ticket in the other. The urge to disappear was overpowering.

As this romantic notion subsided, an image of Alex rushed to take its place. Hazel's ears burned with humiliation and anger at the idea of seeing him. Then again, there were dots all over the city. She could see only a fragment of the map on her phone, and he could very well be in Inglewood or Compton or Carson, or wherever else people die. Or, more precisely, where they are murdered. Isn't that what Raspanti had been trying to tell her?

Ordinarily, Union Station would have been deserted that time of night, with only a few desultory travelers among the rows of imitation leather chairs. Or an odd commuter catching a local back to Pasadena or North Hollywood. But the station was remarkably lively. A wedding party had rented out the now-defunct ticketing area, an enormous room off the lobby. The space featured a row of intimidating oak counters designed to imbue the act of buying a train ticket with the gravity of going to a bank. The wedding, which was evidently Old Hollywood–themed, was entering its phase of sloppy abandon. The female guests shrieked and shimmied in their bias-cut dresses, and heavy-lidded men with martini glasses and vape pens leaned on ticket counters.

Hazel hesitated at the information booth, entranced momentarily by the beauty of the celebration. She turned and followed a glamorous couple across the marble floor and past the station's cocktail lounge, which was filled with the moody, antisocial spillover from the wedding. Her breath stopped when she spotted Alex sitting among a clutch of tables just outside the bar. He wore a wrinkled blazer and was nursing a bright-red cocktail. He stared at her, a quizzical expression on his face.

She strode in his direction, trying her best to appear as if she knew what she was doing, as if she had a plan.

He spoke first. "Can I get you a drink?"

She pulled out a chair, but didn't sit. "Whatever you're having is fine," she said coldly, but there was a tremor in her voice.

He glanced around for the waiter. "You shouldn't be here, you know. It's not safe."

"Oh, really. Why's that?"

"After this drink, you should leave. I mean it, Hazel."

There was an arrogance in the way he held up his hand for the waiter's attention. She had gotten Alex all wrong, of course. She had mistaken him for one of her own kind, a geek, all rumpled clothes and bashful witticisms, a romantic at heart who was just waiting for the right person to come along. But now she saw him as a much odder creature: a disheveled playboy who could toy easily with women's hearts because his true love was mathematics. Math may have betrayed him years ago, may have given up her secrets to another man, but he still pined for her, and no one would ever measure up.

"Another Campari and soda, please," he told the passing waiter. "Make that two."

"How international of you," Hazel said. "You pick that up in Europe?"

He turned back to her. His gaze was intense. "From my mother, actually. She's an alcoholic."

Hazel sat down, locking her eyes on his. "I found your wig and mustache."

"Oh, did I leave them somewhere?" He made a show of checking his pockets.

"I assume you also erased the photos on my phone. When did you manage that? When I was answering the door?"

Alex finished what was left in his glass. "All right, I give up. If I erased the photos, how are you here?"

She was furious with him, but she couldn't help return some of his coolness. "I'm here for the party."

He smiled. "Bride's side or groom's?"

Their drinks arrived before she could craft a response. "Do you think the 'event' will happen here?" she asked.

He adjusted himself on his chair. "I know as much about it as you do."

That's when she noticed a camera around his neck, a Leica, half hidden by his jacket.

"What's that for?"

"Documentation."

She glanced at the nearest Deco clock, which read 9:07. "Shouldn't we be calling the police or something?"

"And what do you suggest we tell them? 'You don't understand, Officer, it's *mathematics!*'" Alex laughed into his drink.

"I'm sure we could come up with something smarter than that."

He shook his head. "No police. We need the system to play out without interference."

"So these people—they're just a mathematical system to you? You just observe, snap your picture, and walk away?"

He leaned across the table. "Actually, you're making my job as disinterested observer more difficult. See, in this system here"—he indicated the station with a wave of his hand—"you and I are the contamination."

"But you just interacted with a waiter."

"Hey, I can't remove myself from the system entirely. Plus, this is one of the few 'events,' as you say, where one can get a drink."

"You've witnessed others then."

He nodded. "There were a couple of nasty ones on the east side two days ago. Gang related. I watched from a safe enough distance, with a long lens. I have yet to figure out if Isaac's calculations are total in their omniscience, but I need to be sure that I am not, even as a witness, part of the system somehow. Then again, it's likely someone dies no matter what we do. Even if we try to stop it, we can't cheat the inevitable."

"So the math somehow knows we're here, has already figured that in?"

"Yes. It could be that the equation is, in fact, aware of itself."

Hazel took this in. This idea that the equation knew—that the *universe* knew—what she would do before she did it made her head ache. It was as if someone had just told her that every second of her life had been monitored on surveillance tape. She forced herself to look at the clock again. Fifteen minutes now. She needed to get to the point. "So did you crack the password?"

"With some help." He looked up at her quickly, realizing what he had just said.

Was Alex working for someone? Could Raspanti be right about this *they*? Operating on the assumption that you find out more when you appear to know the answer already, she asked, "Are you at least expensing the drinks to the people you work for?"

"The people I work for. Where'd you dig up that phrase?"

She quickly changed tacks. "Okay. Did you steal the equation for your own benefit? Because some Russian beat you to your precious proof? And now it's your turn to take the credit you so deserve?"

Alex blanched. "You've been speaking to my mother."

"She's pretty chatty when you corner her."

"God, does she love that story. The story of my epic failure." He took a long drink and said, "I don't steal other people's mathematics."

"What do you call breaking into Isaac's hotel room? Or ransacking his office? On the day of the funeral, that was you in his study, wasn't it?"

He smiled tightly. "His work doesn't belong to you, Hazel. You wouldn't have a clue what to do with it. Isn't that why you let me in the room in the first place?"

"It doesn't belong to you, either."

Alex was about to take another drink, but stopped. "It hardly matters. The equation doesn't work."

She sat back in her chair. "I don't understand."

"It doesn't work."

"You wouldn't be here if it didn't."

"The equation is junk, Hazel. The map is a tease. Isaac left behind just enough information to suggest the real thing. Sure, the map's predictions are accurate: Isaac's own death, numerous violent deaths around the city. But the dots stop: Union Station is one of the last . . . Do you know what Isaac left on that computer?"

"How would I know?"

"A phony equation. Trompe l'oeil math—get up close enough, and it completely loses its dimension. Beautiful, sure, and real enough to fool most people, but not me."

She wondered if Alex was making this up to get rid of her. "But if the map works," she reasoned, "the real math behind it must be somewhere."

"Yes, but where? You were obviously the decoy."

She shook her head. "Isaac wouldn't do that to me," she said, trying to swallow back a tightness in her throat. "He wouldn't make me go through all this trouble just to throw somebody off the trail."

"Are you sure about that? The password *was* numerical, by the way, hidden in that silly game of checkers that was staring at us all night. Designed for someone like me to solve."

She looked away, thinking of her grandfather's letter, of the riddles he had crafted just for her. But she would never have decoded a checkers game. So Isaac didn't trust her after all? Was that the ultimate answer to the riddle? "Ha-ha, you thought I meant *you*?"

She laughed sadly. "So I'm just a sucker, is that it? Played not only by you but also by my own grandfather?" It stung to say these things out loud.

"I didn't play you, Hazel."

"No?" She could feel her face getting hot. "You bait me at the Halloween party. You manipulate your way into the hotel room." She cursed her quavering voice, but continued. "You play the adoring Isaac fan—the poor little rich orphan abandoned by his parents—all the while biding your time until you could steal what you wanted."

Alex closed his eyes briefly. "I won't deny that I took what didn't belong to me." He leaned across the table. "But you have to understand: I never hid the fact that I wanted to see the equation. I didn't hide that I've had a less-than-ideal childhood and that I've clung to Isaac and his work as a result. I didn't hide that I was hoping to draw somebody out, somebody who had the information I wanted. I was glad that person was you. But now I'm sorry it was."

Hazel listened, not wanting to believe any of what he said but also knowing that he no longer had any reason to lie to her. Hadn't he gotten what he'd been after? Even if it ended up being a fake? She thought back to the moment she had first seen him at the funeral: the awkward academic at the podium.

"That equation you read out loud," she said. "What was that?"

"It's exactly what I said it was, Hazel, a scrap of his math I found long ago." He leaned back, his voice dropping dramatically but his eyes still fixed on hers. "I thought someone might recognize it. If it turned out to be a piece of the equation I was looking for, I figured I could get a reaction from the person who had the rest."

He was talking so quietly now that Hazel had to lean forward to hear him.

"But the scrap was just that, a scrap of nothing, and all I ended up doing was looking like a fool."

"I can barely hear you. Why are you talking so softly?"

"Because," he said, "I want your face nearer to mine."

Alex leaned across the table and, eyes zeroed in on her mouth, kissed her. Her immediate impulse was to pull away, but when she didn't—when she realized that she'd wanted this since the first time she saw him—a heady current surged through her.

After a few seconds, she sat back in her seat. "What was that for?"

"For the hallway, at the hotel. When I wanted to kiss you but couldn't because I knew I was about to betray you."

"I wish you'd picked the kiss."

"I really wanted to, Hazel."

Her face and neck still burned with the memory of his lips on hers. She wondered if they might do it again, but Alex set his chin in his palm and just looked at her, his eyes taking her in. There was, in fact, a look of regret in his face, mixed with something else: admiration, adoration? It wasn't conspicuous, as if he were trying to convince her of it, but buried, mingled with other emotions and loyalties that were bearing down on him. The arrogance she thought she had detected earlier had disappeared, as had her own anger.

She wondered where this left them, if anywhere. Was the kiss a one-time thing, or might they do a great deal of it in the future?

Alex's expression suggested the latter, but then his brow transformed rapidly into a frown. He appeared to be focusing on something just past her shoulder.

"What is it?" she asked.

"Did you tell anyone you were here?"

"No."

"No one?"

"Why?"

Hazel turned. On the other side of the lobby, a man in sunglasses and a threadbare jacket—who clearly wasn't here for any wedding—was walking unevenly in the direction of the trains. He appeared to have a limp.

Not far behind the man, walking more purposefully, was her brother.

Hazel didn't call out, but just stared. Her hand involuntarily sought Alex's. There was something strange about Gregory, something she had noticed to a lesser degree since Sybil's death but hadn't been able to name. It was as if she were suddenly looking at a person whose body bore the outward shape of a man but had left the sad, wronged child inside, peering out the husk of adulthood.

24

The Canyon

Philip drove as quickly as traffic would permit back to Pasadena, where, just north of the city, two hundred acres of hiking trails and steep gorges carved themselves into the foothills of the San Gabriel Mountains. In the early days of their marriage, when funds had been tight and entertainment options limited, Eaton Canyon had been a frequent destination for him and Jane. Aside from a shared love of science, being out in the open space of the natural world had always united them. But after a wildfire in the 1990s destroyed much of the canyon's beauty, their hiking tapered off, and in recent years, they had enjoyed the park separately—Jane in order to maintain her daily runner's high, and Philip to walk off a particularly stubborn piece of physics. It was only their daughter's death that had brought them there together in recent days.

As Philip slowed near the sign for the Eaton Canyon Nature Center, he saw what he'd been hoping not to see: Jane's green Nissan Pathfinder parked on the road several yards from the park's entrance, its Caltech sticker in the window and crystal necklace dripping from the rearview mirror. It was the necklace Sybil had been wearing that final night when they had all gone out to dinner—the last piece of jewelry their daughter had worn. Philip wondered why Jane tortured herself by placing it in such conspicuous view, but then, everyone had his or her own peculiar way of dealing with the completely undealable.

How he wished that Jane's car were as far from the canyon as possible, far from that little red dot. Assuming the dot meant anything, he reminded himself—assuming it wasn't just some sci-fi fantasy dreamt up by an old man and applauded by a gun-toting heiress. Despite all his father's excellent work in chaos theory and predictive mathematical models, Philip rejected the belief that the world unfolded in deterministic clockwork. He had refused to believe it in his own work, and he refused to believe it now. Yet here he was. Nellie, of course, had found the entire idea thrilling: "Can you think of anything more exhilarating than the realization that the future is, in fact, knowable?" Yes, he could. In fact, he couldn't think of anything *less* thrilling than knowing what's about to happen before it happens. What, then, is the point of anything?

But whether the universe made its decisions by calculation or dice roll, the fact remained: his wife was in the canyon. Find Jane, and everything would be right again. Find her, and everything could be put back the way it was, the way it had been when they'd come here so many years ago.

Philip parked behind the Nissan and opened his glove box, feeling around for his medication. He had already taken a pill earlier, but the last thing he needed was for an oppressive headache to keep him from thinking clearly on the trail. He slid a second pill into his mouth and forced it back with what saliva he could summon.

Behind muddy clouds, a low splotch of sun was dropping rapidly. Realizing he was losing light, Philip rushed to the entrance. The place was deserted. The Nature Center building, a one-story hut with some taxidermic novelties, was closed for renovations. Beside the door, a familiar sign read "No Ranger on Duty—Hike at Your Own Risk." Beneath an illustration of a bad-tempered mountain lion was a list of items hikers were encouraged to carry: water, food, sunblock, flashlight, whistle, walking stick. He had none of these, though he did have a flashlight app on his phone. He took a healthy gulp of water from a drinking fountain before hurrying toward the Eaton Falls trailhead.

It was four thirty. The trail was three miles round-trip, a course that was familiar to him. If he hurried, he could reach the falls in a half hour, eleven minutes ahead of time.

He ran easily for the first ten minutes or so, even in his dress shoes, but as he passed beneath the concrete bridge of an old mountain toll road, which marked the halfway point to the falls, Philip started to slow. It was hotter than he'd realized. Without stopping, he removed his light coat and tossed it onto some boulders near the bridge to retrieve later. He had come upon a shallow stream when someone called to him.

"Hey, man."

He looked up and saw a young couple with backpacks approaching, both clearly puzzled to find this man in shirtsleeves hopping across the water.

"You headed to the falls?" the guy asked, frowning at Philip's oxfords.

Philip nodded, trying to catch his breath. "You see a woman up there?"

The pair looked at each other. The girl spoke first. "Actually, was she like your age? Dark hair?"

"Yeah."

"We saw her a while ago, but I don't think she was up there when we left."

"We did move off the path a couple of times," her boyfriend added, "so she might have passed us."

Philip crossed right into the stream, not caring that his shoes were getting soaked, and hurried past them.

"This place closes soon, you know," the guy called back.

Still feeling overheated, Philip took off his shirt and left it in a thicket of trees skirting the stream. If he ran into anyone else, they would just have to deal with the shock of his undefined midsection. As he followed the stream up the sharp ascent of the canyon, it started to drizzle, and the trail darkened with accreting decimal points. He suddenly remembered an equation that he had created as a child, after his father had challenged him to determine at what point raindrops of 0.04-centimeter diameter, falling at a speed of 9 meters per second and at a frequency density of 15 drops per square meter per second, would saturate 25 square kilometers of space—taking into account raindrop overlap, naturally. Philip had created an equation in ten minutes, knowing, of course, that the bait and switch from meters to kilometers was merely a cheap trick. He wasn't a complete moron, not even at age nine.

Such rapid stunts of calculation had made his father proud, something that young Philip took for granted. As the years went by, though, he learned that engendering pride in his father was a feat harder and harder to come by. The proud tousles to the hair and pats on the shoulder dropped off in their frequency and enthusiasm. But then, that's how it had been with his own children. It had been one thing to praise Sybil's artistic endeavors at age ten, quite another at twenty-five.

The trail was getting steeper—Philip didn't remember the climb being this difficult—and his brain was starting to feel constricted. Why was his medication taking so long to kick in? The sound of rushing water grew steadily louder as he approached the trail's end. Any minute, just around the bend, the falls would appear.

Something in the brush beside the path fluttered and chirped. Probably some quail hiding from the rain. Jane had once been fond of pointing out such wildlife, along with their group names, always with a wink in her delivery. "Oh look, a bevy of quail . . . a kettle of hawks . . . a scold of jays." She could always summon these collective nouns so easily. Perhaps this is where Drew had gotten her talent for recall. "A colony of rabbits . . . a cauldron of bats . . ." But what about a group of one? What would he be called? A struggle. A calamity. An embarrassment of Philip.

Just as he approached the final bend in the trail, something unexpected happened. The rain stopped, and the late-afternoon sun burst from behind the clouds. He was grateful for the extra light, but he hadn't brought his sunglasses—or were they in his discarded coat?—and the sun pierced his eyes. He shielded his face with one hand, trying not to think about the advancing migraine army. Shade. There would be shade at the falls.

When he rounded the bend and stepped into the dark shadow of the surrounding rock face, he looked up and saw her. She stood at the top of the falls, at the very edge, looking down. The sun was behind her, feathering the outline of her body. A phrase of hers came back to him: "I would give you the gift of plausible deniability."

"Jane!" he shouted.

She didn't answer.

Philip blinked. It must have been an extended blink because when he opened his eyes again, she was no longer there. He glanced around in panic, scanning along the top of the ridge and down at the water.

"Jane!"

He kicked off his shoes.

Just as he reached the water's edge, she appeared again, this time standing below the falls on the opposite bank. She was smiling at something just behind him. How had she gotten down there so quickly?

But this second appearance coincided with an urgent stab in his head—a pain more intense than he had ever experienced. That's when Philip knew that Jane wasn't standing there at all. He was alone. The auras were hallucinatory now, as Tom's had been. Oh God, had Jane's car been imagined, too? And those people on the trail?

The sun seemed to be getting brighter, which he didn't understand, not only because of the late hour but also because he was in the shade. Or thought he was. The waterfall seemed to be growing in force, rushing all around and behind his eyes. The rushing was so loud. Why was it so goddamn loud?

Philip cupped his hands over his ears, but he needed to grab his pills. Were they in his pants pocket? Yes, he had slipped them in there as an afterthought. *Good man!*

He sat down at the water's edge to rest. The bottle was almost full. He had all the relief he would need. He tried to dump a couple of pills into his hand, but ended up with five or six. Screw it. "Take as needed"—that's what the bottle said, didn't it, or had he made that up? He dumped them into his mouth, chasing them with a handful of stream water. He seemed to recall that the water from the stream was drinkable, or had been once, but at this point, he didn't really care. Philip wondered if six pills would be enough.

The bottle was soon close to empty. Maybe he should save it for Sybil to put in one of her pieces. But, no, Sybil was dead. He had actually forgotten for a second that his daughter was pulverized and in the ground. A memory of her floated up before him: Sybil standing in front of one of her gallery pieces, an expectant look sent his direction. Then an image of himself, stifling his own disappointment while ladling out spoonfuls of feeble praise. There was nothing more sickening than realizing how much you had hurt your own child. How you hadn't bothered to understand her at all. But then, hadn't this been a Severy family custom? Upholding scholarly achievement to the point of self-erasure? His father had judged him the instant his research had flagged, had dropped hints of "brain rot" and "irrelevance." And suddenly, in a confusion of self-admonition and self-pity, Philip couldn't separate Sybil's heartache from his own.

His head now thrummed in a full orchestra of pain. He sometimes wished it were possible to relocate the pain in all its intensity to another section of his body—stomach, chest, arm, knee, where it might take on less significance—because there was something singularly cruel about an ache in one's head. It assaulted one's very being. How had his brother ever endured it? Tom would have taken the whole bottle. It would have been nothing to him, like popping an aspirin. Philip looked back at his prescription. Maybe a couple more. He scooped more pills and water into his mouth, though he knew this wasn't wise. *You're poisoning yourself, Philip. Killing yourself.*

I know, he answered, *but anything is better than this.*

He blinked out at the water and thought he saw a red dot floating in front of him. It was the dot he had seen on the map, now growing to envelop him. He looked at his watch: 5:04. In seven minutes, someone was going to die in the canyon.

He let his hand drop to his side. He was very tired.

The red dot. What about it had seemed so important? What

had Nellie said? *Murder and suicide—when it comes to a distinction between the two, the equation is blind.*

His head suddenly cleared, the incessant pounding replaced by an overwhelming sense of calm. He looked down at the now-empty bottle as it fell away from his hand.

"Oh, I see . . ." he said aloud. His eyes closed, and he gave in to gravity, his forehead smacking the cool canyon floor.

25

The Event

When Gregory entered the lobby of Union Station, a wedding reception was in full, frowzy swing. Tom was already on the other side of the crowd, past the bar and halfway into the passenger waiting area. It would be impossible for Gregory to lose him now. He could practically feel Isaac's mathematics pushing him (cheering him?) to the predetermined end point. Once it was finished, he would feel the release he needed so badly—the antidote to his fury.

He had been tracking Tom for the past two hours through deserted downtown streets, fantasy-killing him many times over. First, he fed Tom into the rotating steel wires of a street sweeper. Next, he forced him at gunpoint to the observation deck of city hall, folded him over the railing, and watched him scatter on the sidewalk below. Later, he invited Tom to take a ride on the Angels Flight funicular. He tied his feet to a railroad tie, his hands to an axle, and as the funicular ascended, sat back to observe the man's body split open.

When Tom had crossed a bridge overlooking the 101 Freeway, Gregory had briefly considered pushing him into the twinkling red stream of taillights. But the overpass wasn't far enough from the ground to ensure that Tom would die instantly. He might only injure himself, in which case a passing vehicle would need to finish the job. It had worked for Rhoda Burgess, the woman who thought she could willfully ignore her husband's basement hobby of child captivity and get away with it. A similar method had worked for an Echo Park woman who thought she'd convinced police that her six-year-old's third-degree burns were accidental. It was Gregory who decided that the woman's parking brake should fail one day as she was lifting groceries from the back of her car. Her skull, much like Rhoda Burgess's, had succumbed under the weight of a Firestone tire.

Gregory wanted to do something different for Tom, not a repeat performance. He wished he had a few more weeks to think of something on the level of his usual work, but he had run out of time. Besides, if Isaac's universal computer was leading him here, how could it be wrong?

Union Station would be a first for him. They were here only because Tom's usual subway stop had been closed that night for maintenance, and passengers were rerouted to the main hub. Gregory's phone buzzed again. He had a message waiting from his sister, which he was choosing to ignore. There was also a text from E. J.: *You coming in tomorrow morning? People are asking.* Apparently he could no longer be relied on to show up for work. But it didn't matter anymore.

Gregory picked up his pace a bit, only glancing at the festivities around him. He had a brief flash of his own wedding: Goldie standing on the beach in a wispy gown, the most irresistible she had ever been. But however much he had tried that day, he hadn't entirely been able to rid his mind of Sybil. A year before that, his heart had cracked in half at the sight of Sybil dressed in white, binding her fate to that totally average bore of a man just because she was going to have his child. Impossible to believe that in her misery, she would have had a second child with Jack.

Tom veered from the long-distance train tracks to the subway station below. As expected, he chose the Red Line headed for Hollywood. Gregory followed more closely than he had dared previously—so close that when Tom was at the bottom of the escalator, he was at the top. It would have been so easy for Tom to turn around and see the man who had been following him for weeks, even with his poor eyesight. When Gregory reached the platform, he scanned the ceiling and corners for cameras.

He turned back to Tom, who stood behind the yellow line, hands shoved in his pockets. There was one person on the opposite end of the platform, a woman, but she looked infirm and certainly incapable of doing anything about an incident on the other side of the terminal.

Gregory checked the timetable. The train was due in two minutes . . . now one minute. He could just hear a distant rumble moving through the tunnel, very faint. The train was likely at Seventh Street already, or Pershing Square.

He had, of course, considered that he should let Tom go on living his sad life. Incurable, head-fracturing migraines were punishment enough, and by killing him, Gregory would only end his suffering. But then, Tom had lived his entire life like this, and it had led only to his hurting those around him. The world would be a better place with this man removed from it.

"Tom," Gregory said, stepping forward. "Tom Severy." His voice had come out of his throat without hesitation—confident, even— as if it were about to launch into a sales pitch.

Tom turned and looked at him. Nothing. No recognition. He pulled his sunglasses from his red face and squinted in Gregory's direction.

Gregory approached rapidly, causing Tom to take a step back

toward the tracks. Then two steps. Once Tom figured out who was addressing him, once complete confusion had overtaken him, it would be easy. But Gregory needed to make sure Tom knew who he was. This was important.

"Who—?" mumbled Tom. His voice came out in a whimper. The most pathetic sound Gregory had heard from a man. Frail. Fearful. A voice that said, "Don't hurt me."

"Do you know me?" Gregory demanded.

He stepped closer to Tom to let him get a good look at his face. Tom could barely manage a flicker of eye contact, and Gregory wondered how he had ever considered this person a threat to him. To anyone.

"No, I don't—" That awful whimper again. Then Tom knew. A veil of awareness fell over his eyes.

"Do I look familiar, Tom? It's Gregory. You remember Gregory and Hazel Dine. Look at me, Tom."

Tom backed away a couple of steps, ever closer to the tracks. The train was on its way now. They could both hear it.

"Look at me!" Gregory shouted.

Tom tried to speak, but his vocal cords failed him.

For a second, Gregory thought the man was going to collapse right there on the platform, fall to his knees and split his nose open on the concrete. The look on his face was one of such subjugation, a plea for mercy, understanding. It was an expression Gregory had always searched for on the faces of child abusers but had rarely, if ever, found. Yet it was the expression Tom Severy was wearing now, without artifice. A face of complete and wretched openness, a look that said, "I am a pitiful human being. I know that."

Gregory was surprised by the dissipation of his own anger, but the train was coming now. He had no time for second thoughts. *You know how to do this. Don't stop now.*

But as he took a hesitant step toward Tom, Gregory heard a sound behind him that was out of place: the distinct *snick* of a shutter. He turned to find a man about fifteen feet away, pulling a camera from his face. Just as he recognized his cousin Alex, he heard someone call from farther down the platform.

"Eggs?"

Gregory's immediate response to seeing Hazel standing there, besides complete surprise, was bewildered amusement. It was almost funny.

Hazel was no longer looking at him. She was studying the man who stood behind him. "Is that . . .?"

Gregory turned again to face Tom, who by now held a look of strange clarity. Tom looked back and forth between the siblings. The two of them standing there must have felt like the ambush of his nightmares. He held his head in one hand, the way he did just before a migraine hit. He had already crossed far beyond the yellow line, and was standing at the edge of the platform. The train appeared. He turned to face the void and stepped beyond it. Hazel cried out.

And where four people had stood, there now stood three.

26

The Room

Philip awoke in a familiar room. He couldn't figure out why it was familiar, only that he had been there before. The green curtains were drawn, leaving only a small bedside lamp to light the space. He could hardly move. Heavy bedcovers pinned him down. But wait, he was alive. This meant the equation wasn't perfect—there were errors in his father's math. The world wasn't all gears and mechanics and systems. *Uncertainty had won!*

Perhaps his father had known this all along, had known that however well his equation worked, one couldn't entirely escape a certain degree of uncertainty. Is this why he had been hesitant to show Philip the equation? Had he been afraid that his son would find the flaw in his perfect system? Philip would probably never know, but this answer would have to comfort him for now.

How long had he been asleep? He was glad to see a glass of water on the nightstand. With some effort, he propped himself up and reached for it. That's when he heard rustling nearby.

"Feeling better, I hope," said a man with a Slavic accent. "Your migraines are getting worse, then?"

A light went on at a corner desk. There sat Kuchek, of all people, pencil in hand, poised above a notebook. He wore an expression that said he would allow Philip only a cursory moment of his attention.

"Andrei?"

"I hope the bedding is comfortable. I'm not very good with that kind of thing."

"Wait. *You* found me?"

"Someone found you," he said. "You were lucky."

Philip reached for his head.

"You did overdo it," Kuchek continued. "You must be more careful."

Remembering the pills, Philip's hand went to his abdomen. "Did they pump my stomach?"

His colleague's attention had already wandered back to the notations in front of him.

"Was I taken to the hospital?" Philip pressed.

Kuchek held up a finger, frowned, and scribbled something.

Philip glanced around. "I need to call my wife."

Kuchek's pencil kept moving.

"Now is not the time for your mirror symmetry, Andrei. I need to call my family."

"I'm not working on mirror symmetry."

"Then what is so supremely important that you can't get to it later?"

Kuchek didn't answer, but then he never responded to anger or irritation.

Philip fell back onto the pillow. "By all means, Andrei, let me chatter on while you pretend not to hear me. May as well put one of those confessional screens between us."

No response.

"My father used to take me to confession when I was young," he continued. "Not because he was trying to indoctrinate me or anything—he just wanted to give me something to push against, to show me the absurd alternative to science. Though I must admit, I found it strangely comforting."

More scribbling.

"So what shall I confess now? How I tried to kill myself in the canyon because the pounding in my brain became unbearable? That I intentionally OD'd because of a goddamn *headache*?"

Kuchek didn't flinch.

"Or shall I tell you how Jane has been deeply depressed since Sybil's death, and I'm emotionally incapable of helping her through it? Or maybe I should confess how I've been cheating on my wife with one of our doctoral candidates."

Kuchek looked up at last. "Don't flay yourself, Philip. It's natural."

"What is?"

"I fall in love all the time, have quite a lot of sex in my off-hours. Try not to look so surprised."

"You don't have a wife."

"Philip, the passion you have—or had—for your work is the same passion you have now for your lovely doctoral candidate. It's just all mixed up, confused."

This conversation was getting strange. Andrei Kuchek had love affairs? The man didn't even flirt. As far as Philip had observed, Andrei had yet to realize that spouting facts tends to deflate good conversation—like a human web browser always spoiling the fun with the right answer. But perhaps he had misjudged him.

Philip pulled himself to sitting, looked around. "This isn't your apartment, is it?"

"No, but I'll be returning there shortly."

Philip pictured some gangly math kitten waiting on Kuchek's sofa.

"So what is this place?"

"Don't you recognize it?"

Philip glanced around at all the incompatible furniture that somehow seemed to go together. A pine trunk covered with the spillover from an adjacent bookshelf. An antique secretary desk against one wall, a dusty Navajo carpet beneath it. A tacky cupid clock ticking deliberately from a bureau. And then there was a J. M. W. Turner ship-at-sea knockoff that appeared to glow from within.

"I've never seen this room in my life, yet it's familiar."

"You haven't *seen* it, Philip, because the lights have always been off. But it is *your* room."

"My room?"

"I'm not working on my own mathematics, I'm working on yours. I thought you needed some help illuminating the space. So here I am."

"Illuminating the space . . . ? Yes—"

Philip pushed off the covers.

My room! How did I not know it?

As he looked wildly about him, a feeling of rapture grew in his chest. He had spent so much time between these four walls, in the dark, blind, crawling on the floor, grasping, in an attempt to put all the furniture and objects in their place. He had done this so that he might map out one more room in the incomprehensibly expansive mansion of string theory. And here he was now, for real. The light was on, at last! But there were still some dark corners, and he wanted desperately to see everything.

"We have to turn on all the lights, Andrei!" he shouted. "Now! Turn them all on, before I forget—"

"Shh, slow down. One at a time, one at a time."

There was a knock at the door. He looked to Kuchek.

"Who's that?"

"How should I know?"

"Are you going to answer it?"

"Can't. It's not my room."

Philip pulled himself out of bed with newfound energy, but as he approached the door, he hesitated. The knocking continued, except now there seemed to be fists upon the door.

He knew what was on the other side, but he pressed his ear against it to be sure. He could hear their voices: Jane, Sidney, Silas, Faye. And then two more: Jack and Drew. They were all waiting for him.

"Is Grandpa going to wake up?" he heard Drew ask.

"I think so," Jack told her. "Look at his eyelids."

"Philip? Can you hear us?" Jane was pleading. "Someone get the nurse . . ."

"His fingers are wiggling," Silas said.

Then Sidney: "Hey, Dad, wake up . . ."

Philip was struck by the timbre of his sons' voices, how each was distinct and separate from the other. How often he let himself overlook that.

He turned back to the room for one more look. Kuchek gave him a static wave and resumed his work.

I must remember this space precisely as it is so I can re-create it later. I can't forget this moment!

He knew that the finer details of the room would be lost, but he greedily took in what he could. And when he was ready, he put his hand on the knob and opened the door.

PART 3

The unpredictable and the predetermined unfold together to make everything the way it is.

—TOM STOPPARD, *ARCADIA*, 1993

27

The Assassin

Hazel picked up the green telephone as Gregory, on the other side of the glass, did the same. He looked oddly well—relaxed, even—in his standard-issue jumpsuit, and his eyes held unmistakable relief.

"Eggs," she said into the receiver. In that single name, she tried to inject everything she felt about her brother, in all its affection and complexity.

The day after the incident at Union Station, Gregory had turned himself in to the LAPD, but not before officially confessing to E. J., who, after all, had deep down already known. Better to get it over with. The two had then gone together to their superiors with the revelation that Gregory had killed many, many people: fourteen in all. He didn't point out that these were all very bad people; he thought it in poor taste to pat himself on the back. But he did make it clear to the chief of their division that Detective E. J. Kenley had figured out the entire thing and surely deserved a promotion. Maybe, while they were at it, E. J.'s Minority Youth in Peril project could be granted some additional funding. E. J. yelled at Gregory to shut the hell up, but she felt buffeted by so many conflicting emotions that she had to get up and walk out of the room.

Within hours, the story had hit the national news. Hazel felt nauseated by what her brother had done, but she forced herself to listen, read, and watch whatever was available, if only so that it might reveal the part of him she did not know or hadn't wanted to know. She thought she would never hear an end to the phrases cranked out for the occasion—*vigilante justice, renegade cop*—as well as all the predictable allusions to fictional characters who had taken the law into their own hands. A few of the headlines betrayed a certain misty-eyed awe for the detective-gone-bad, with labels like "Abuse Avenger," "Southland Renegade," and "Lone-Wolf Cop." But there had been an immediate backlash against such characterizations, and much online scolding of the media for Gregory's portrayal as some kind of modern-day Zorro or Count of Monte Cristo.

His story elicited plenty of screaming on both sides. One celebrity attorney went on national news and shouted, "If Greg Severy wants to be a Wild West vigilante, let him die like one: at the gallows tree."

Hazel knew that she was supposed to feel some kind of outrage at her brother's actions, something closer to what her sister-in-law was going through: "How could he do this? How could that monster do this to us?" But when Hazel's initial nausea had passed, a curious sense of wonder set in at her brother's hidden motivations, his complete dedication to his crimes, and his ability to conceal his parallel life so effectively. How much mental exertion must it have taken to manufacture these accidents, each one tailored to its unlucky recipient? Her brother may not have been blessed with a mathematical brain, but he had a frighteningly methodical one.

She wondered if Tom would have been his most recent victim had Gregory not been interrupted, and had their former foster father not finished the job for him. Or would the outcome have been the same, regardless of her and Alex's interference? Tom's death had deeply rattled her, not least of all because the instant she had recognized him on the train platform, some ancient anger had risen within her to wish him over the edge. She wanted to punish him for everything he had done and not done, for all the injuries that would never heal, no matter how many years of therapy she and Gregory paid for. And when he had fallen onto those tracks, it was as if she had actually pushed him. A part of her had wanted him to die, yes, but Hazel also knew it was just another of her involuntary mental projections, and when the train screeched to a stop, she felt only horror and pity.

"So here I am," Gregory said flatly. "In the onesie I'll be wearing every day for the rest of my life."

It now occurred to Hazel that the comic violence she had been mentally conjuring for years had been reflected in her brother's mind. But with him, the dark wishes had transformed into action. She smiled sadly.

"E. J. called me before it hit the news. You're like this psycho hero now."

"I wasn't sure you'd come."

Hazel leaned forward, as if they were seated at a café table instead of separated by bulletproof glass.

"I'll visit you as much as I can. I will."

Gregory glanced away. "It's weird," he said. "After so many years of fantasizing about his death, I was actually sorry to see him go over the edge."

"Would you have pushed him?"

He shook his head. "Something happened this time. I couldn't do it. I couldn't do any of it anymore."

Her throat constricted. "I never thought he would look so—"

"Defeated?"

She nodded.

A few seconds passed before either of them spoke.

"Haze? You never said why you were at the station. Don't tell me: the concurrence of events?"

She shook her head. "I only knew that something would happen at that spot. Isaac's math told me."

His eyes flickered with far-off understanding. "So the equation is real."

"Wait, you knew about it?"

Gregory's face twitched, betraying a surfacing memory. "He called me two days before he died, told me he had an equation that revealed the city's murders—including what I was doing. I told him I didn't know what he was talking about, that he'd finally lost it, but somehow I knew it was true. I knew that he saw me."

Hazel was still trying hard to process this. "What do you mean, he *saw* you?"

"He said that his mathematics had led him to me. He wouldn't say how, but all I can think of is that he was testing out his equation and by coincidence saw me at the exact time and place of one of the so-called accidents. Once he'd connected me to that crime, he kept tabs on me. After he died, I found a tracking device on my car."

"If he knew what you were doing," she asked in a low voice, "why didn't he turn you in?"

Her brother leaned close to the glass. "He mailed me a letter just before he died. I left it for you, in our old hiding place. It's quite a read."

This surprised her. But then why should she be surprised that Isaac had written more than one letter? She thought of telling Gregory about her own letter from him but realized they were short on time. She still had so many questions, including one she was afraid to ask.

"What about Sybil?"

He bit down on his lip. "What about her?"

"Isaac predicted her death, too. I found these on a map he left behind." She reached into her coat pocket, where she had kept the two identical dots. She held them up for him to see. "It's the date and time of Sybil's death. Twice."

She detected a disturbance pass over her brother's face, one that for a moment made him look like a boy again. Hazel desperately wanted to embrace him as she had done when they were small, when one of them had been sad and they huddled together on a single mattress—an isle in a sea of hurt. Then the look was gone, and the man was there once again.

"She was pregnant," he said, as if it were a confession.

She frowned. "How do you know? Are you sure?"

"I saw the autopsy."

Hazel pulled the dots from the glass and stared at them in her hand. She saw them now not as redundancies, but twin deaths occurring at the same instant. Is that what Isaac had meant when he wrote *Three will die*?

For one wild moment, she almost asked Gregory where he had been that night. But no. Her brother had adored Sybil. Her next thought was to ask who the father was, but she put this notion out of her mind, too, and said simply, "No wonder Jack was so messed up."

"I don't think he knew."

"How could he not know his wife was pregnant?"

"Autopsy said she was only a couple months along. Maybe she was undecided about telling him."

"Well, he must know now."

He shook his head. "The coroner's office owed me a favor, so I asked them not to disclose it to the family. Least I could do."

"Least you could do?"

"I'm telling *you*, okay? No one else. There's been enough pain."

She nodded in understanding. A door opened behind him, and a guard appeared.

"What's it like in there, anyway?" she asked.

"They keep me busy with dumb work, though I have plenty of time alone to think. I've been writing a lot, just so there's a record of what I've done and why. Maybe someday Lewis can read it, I don't know . . ." He let the rest fall away. "Reflection, I guess that's what my life is now."

He turned to the guard and held up a finger. "Be an aunt to Lewis. He'll love you if you let him."

It wasn't a final good-bye, but tears pooled in her eyes. "Wait," she said, voice breaking. "How's the food?"

He smiled. "Good as any. It's all the same to me."

At the guard's prompt, Gregory hung up the receiver and blew his sister a kiss.

No longer seeing any reason to avoid Beachwood Canyon, Hazel paid her first visit to the house in weeks. She let herself in with a key hidden in a potted palm, stopped off at the kitchen for a butter knife, and climbed the stairs. Outside Isaac's study, she knelt on the floor and pried up the chronically loose plank to reveal a narrow space. Their childhood hiding place was mustier than she'd remembered, with fresh termite trails in the wood. At the bottom sat the letter her brother had promised. After replacing the board, she sat back against the wall to read it. There were two envelopes: a larger one addressed to Gregory at his house and a smaller one folded within, scrawled with the single word *Proof*. She set aside the letter and opened the smaller envelope. In it she found a stack of photocopied clippings, a few of which fell to the floor. She had only to glimpse the headlines to see that these were news briefs detailing unusual deaths throughout LA County: "Family Car Rolls Backward onto Mother," "Man Drowns in Own Bathtub," "Film Producer Dies in Freak Yard Accident." She set these aside and unfolded the handwritten letter, its script shaky.

Dearest Gregory,

As I expressed on the phone when we last spoke, I am conflicted about your actions. On the one hand, you are doing what I and many others can't summon the courage to do: to live out our most violent revenge fantasies against those who hurt the innocent. On the other, I think about the child you once were . . . and my heart splits in half.

I won't go into detail about how I stumbled upon your particular murderous streak among all the homicides of Los Angeles, but I can say that I was hoping it was some grave mistake, some miscalculation on my part. I was devastated to find that my calculations were, in fact, accurate.

Grieved by my own mathematics, imagine!

Why didn't I turn you in? Maybe knowing too much about your unkind upbringing has been my weakness—my own son is the reason for so much of your pain, and for that I feel responsible. Though how your lovely sister was able to rise from the ashes of her youth without vengeance, I do not know.

If you're wondering why I didn't stop you myself—after all, my foreknowledge of these events did allow me to stake out the scenes of your "accidents"—my only defense is this: I dare not tamper with chaotic predestination. We don't yet know the consequences of doing so.

The mathematics must be obeyed, whatever its end.

I will, however, indulge in this mild tampering: I have included newspaper clippings—proof for your records of what you have done. Perhaps seeing them all in one place will convince you to rethink this peculiar habit of yours.

In other news: my own death has no doubt come as a surprise. I'm sorry if I've given you and the family a shock, but it was my time to go. The math has told me so, and I go willingly at the time and place given me.

So after enjoying my favorite breakfast and the pleasures of my morning bath, I will wait patiently for my assassin. If one doesn't arrive as expected—guns blazing—I will proceed to plan B. I call it Christmas in October.

Don't bother looking for my work—you won't find it. The equation itself, I entrust to the one they will least suspect.

I wish you and this murderous city—whose only saving grace, perhaps, is its mathematical grace—my best regards, whatever that's worth.

Much love,

Isaac

Hazel's eyes fogged over. They had been right about her grandfather's death after all. The police—everyone—had been right. The angel of death had appeared to Isaac in the form of an equation, and he had followed it to his own demise.

She felt a strange relief in knowing the truth, however painful it was to see on the page. But this feeling was followed quickly by something else: fear that all her efforts had meant nothing. If she compared the letter Isaac had written her with the one she now held in her hands, his sanity would be difficult to defend. His letter to Gregory was, in fact, a suicide note. There had been no assassin; he had not been killed for his equation. So what about his letter to her? Had it been merely a paranoid entreaty she had been foolish to take seriously? Was the death map some kind of clever mirage?

Had she, Alex, and Raspanti been trying to decipher the raving semaphore of a lunatic?

There was, however, one strange similarity between the letters: a nearly identical phrase that gave her a kind of hope. Hazel reread the letter's final paragraphs, focusing on the sentence: *The equation itself, I entrust to the one they will least suspect.* She had always assumed that she was the one he had been referring to, but then little with Isaac could be taken at face value. As Alex had suggested, the hotel room and its contents had been a devious misdirect to keep those like him occupied. Isaac had intentionally misled her. She had merely been a decoy, and the equation—*the true equation*—was still out there, safely concealed. But if Hazel wasn't the one they would least suspect, who was?

Hazel pulled *Tender Is the Night* from its place on the shelf, where she had returned it on Halloween. She flipped it open, though she didn't know what she could be looking for that she hadn't found already. The Polaroid bookmark was still in place: the playful image of Isaac scribbling a series of prime numbers on a mirror. She wondered idly who had taken the picture, and when. She had been so focused on her grandfather's eyes the first time she looked at the photo that she'd failed to notice the reflection of a camera and tripod at the edge of the mirror, but with no visible cameraman behind it. Perhaps it had been on a timer.

Then she spotted something else. Between the red-inked numbers 59 and 61, in a fragment of reflected silver, was a second pair of eyes staring back. They belonged to a face she knew well, and Hazel now saw that Isaac had been writing the numbers for this face to see—a lesson in primes. The eyes stared at the mirror with the intense interest of someone absorbed in memorization.

28

The Brother

When Philip finally awoke, nearly his entire family was waiting for him, even his sister Paige. He blinked, reached out for Jane, their eyes both filling up.

Whatever the reason for Philip having lived and his brother having not—spooky mathematics, determinism, or just the stupidity of chance—Philip had only very narrowly survived ingesting an entire bottle of migraine medication. His wife, having found him that night at the falls after spotting his discarded clothing along the trail, had tried and failed to get cell phone reception in the canyon. So she sprinted back to the nature center, broke a window, and phoned an ambulance. Jane then recruited two hikers—who, as it happened, had passed Philip on the trail earlier—to help carry his limp body back to the trailhead. When the paramedics arrived, they went to work on him immediately. Jane's speed had saved his life.

"I'm sorry," he managed to croak.

"Don't be. You were coming to find me." Jane insisted it was all her fault for dropping out of communication that day and making everybody panic.

Drew pulled herself away from Jack, who had been released

from the psychiatric hospital a day before, and leapt to Philip's side. "I don't want you to have a headache ever again, Grandpa," she declared. "Did you know dogs can get migraines?" Philip kissed her head. It was the most Drew had said in a long time, and at that moment, Philip nearly prayed to a God he didn't believe in that little Drew be spared the family's cerebral scourge. Either that, he pleaded, or let the future hold a cure for such unreasonable magnitudes of discomfort.

The family waited several days before telling Philip that his brother was dead. The fact that the recently released Tom Severy had not just died, but had intentionally thrown himself in front of a Metrolink train on the same night Philip had been rescued, seemed like information best kept from the still-fragile physicist. When they did finally tell him, he asked numerous questions but remained mostly calm. He looked over at his sister, who, judging from her impassive expression, must have been similarly composed upon hearing the news. "At least he's not in pain anymore," she said softly.

It wasn't so much that Philip and Paige had exhausted all their grief in recent weeks; it was more that Tom's death had always seemed predetermined, or as if it had already happened long ago. For months, both siblings had suspected that their brother was either out of prison or about to be. They had each received the same bright goldenrod envelopes from the Department of Corrections but had let the notices accumulate on their respective desks, unopened. Their father had likely done the same or had tossed them out altogether. For what good had ever come from news of Tom?

Two decades earlier, after a vampiric Tom Severy had been pulled by police from a den of filth and abuse in South Los Angeles—his wife dead, the couple's foster children maltreated—

the Severys had all but pronounced him gone from their lives. Isaac refused to utter his son's name anymore, let alone visit him in prison. "We tried everything. Everything! What else is left?" he said one day, in what would be the last time Philip heard him speak with any real emotion about his younger brother. It was true that Isaac and Lily had overlooked nothing in their desperation to cure their son: they summoned experts, called in favors, and threw money at months-long hospital stays. They'd turned Tom on to antidepressants, acupuncture, marijuana, vitamin B injections, holy basil, St. John's wort, elimination diets, Chinese infusions, plus all manner of quackery and snake oil. But all they had gotten in return was their son's resentment reflected through a prism of fierce physical pain. Isaac and Lily eventually gave up trying to hospitalize him when he began to routinely escape his confinement, preferring instead to seek out powerful anodynes found only on the street.

After his arrest, Philip and his mother had been the only family to visit him in the Los Angeles jail, and later, after Lily could no longer bear it, only Philip made the drive out to the state penitentiary in Lancaster. But Tom hated these meetings, and after one memorable visit, in which he spat out that he despised his brother, resented his superiority and intellectual affectations, and wished nothing more than to see the entire family dead, the trips necessarily tapered off. Tom had been receiving treatment in prison for his migraines, including a controversial shock therapy, but even such extreme measures must have been meager when compared with those sneaky injections Tom had been giving himself for years. Maybe, at last, as Paige had observed, there was some comfort to be had in the fact that Tom Severy was now freed from a life of episodic torture.

Days later, when the Severys let Tom's ashes fall over the Pacific

Ocean from the port side of a rented sailboat, there were only a few tears shed for this strange person who had long ago been one of them. With misty eyes, Philip spoke briefly of the child and young man his little brother had once been—spontaneous, charming, intensely bright, if slightly volatile—before his illness and addictions had turned him mean and unrecognizable. Paige told a story about Tom picking oranges with her when they were both small, an uncharacteristically warm story coming from Philip's sister.

Their mother was there, too. Lily had no idea what was going on, but it had seemed wrong to keep her from her own son's burial at sea. She assumed it was a surprise sailboat excursion organized by Isaac, who, she was convinced, would emerge from the cabin at any moment with champagne and sandwiches. It was on that trip that Philip told his mother she'd be coming to live with them permanently in Pasadena, causing her only to smile absently and pat his arm.

Hazel wiped at her cheeks more than anyone, though her emotions arose more from her own brother's recent incarceration than out of any loyalty to her once foster father. Of course, the news of Gregory's vengeful spree was endlessly more shocking to the family than Tom's death. While Hazel had emerged from her chaotic childhood relatively healthy and undamaged, her brother, despite all appearances, had not. But then, no one knew better than Philip what a difference a couple of years and a fateful twist of DNA can make.

As Tom's dark ashes folded into the sea, Philip thought of the nature and location of his brother's demise: suicide, downtown, on the same day he had nearly died himself. He thought of the fire-red dot on the map Nellie had shown him, placed inside a tangle of downtown freeways—and just fifteen miles northeast of it, at the edge of the mountains, its sibling dot sitting at a canyon riverbed. If the map had gotten its way, both of them should have been dead. The equation was unquestionably powerful. But clearly, as Philip had suspected, there was something off in his father's beautiful calculations.

The Answer

As Tom's ashes dissolved into the Pacific, Hazel made her way toward the boat's cabin. She had to stop and grab hold of the starboard rail for a few breaths. She couldn't let herself fall apart right now. It would only draw unwanted attention. It was true that the memory of her foster father on that train platform had stirred within her a level of compassion that surprised her, but it was Gregory who was making her struggle now. Despite the fact that they had grown apart in recent years, his sudden removal from the real world left her feeling disoriented—the lone survivor on their isle of two.

She paused at the cabin door to make sure she hadn't been seen. Still huddled along the port side were Philip, Jane, Jane's sister, and the twins, looking out at the ocean, where some of the ashes had scattered to the crosswind. Paige sat nearby, scribbling notes to herself and every so often speaking in slow, enunciated tones to her mother. Jack, Goldie, and Fritz Dornbach formed an unlikely trio at the bow. Last, there was the hired skipper, busy managing ropes and canvas.

Alex had not shoved off with them that morning. Hazel hadn't seen him since the night at Union Station, where she had watched him lift his camera to his face for a moment to document Tom's position on the tracks. But he had hesitated, finally letting the camera drop to his chest. Last she remembered, he had walked slowly but deliberately toward the station exit. For all she knew, it would be the last she saw of him.

Hazel closed her eyes and gripped the book she had been carrying around for the past several days.

On the pleasant shore of the French Riviera, about half way between Marseilles and the Italian border, stands a large, proud, rose-colored hotel . . .

She had wasted so much time, but at last she knew what her grandfather had intended for her to do. All along, the equation had been waiting patiently for her to show up, to hold out her hand and ask for it. Hazel wondered how many things in life could be ours if we only knew whom to ask. *Ask.* She took a deep breath, grabbed hold of the door latch, and swung herself inside the cabin.

30

The Recruit

On a gray morning in early December, Nellie Booth Lyons stood at the window of her upper-floor library waiting for the newest member of GSR to arrive. She glanced anxiously from the street to her watch. Late.

Just last week, Nellie had stood at this same spot and watched one of her best people climb into a hired car, likely never to return. "I can't do this anymore," Alex had told her that day. "I need to get back."

"Back to where? Doing what?" she'd demanded.

"There are other things besides mathematics, Nellie."

"Really. Playing at being a photographer? Dating? You need structure. We can give you that here. There are plenty of attractive women in Malibu, Alex, just as beautiful as the women of France." But he didn't appear to be interested in the beautiful women of Malibu. And having replenished his bank account during his time at GSR, he was ready to float across Europe again, sipping cappuccinos and practicing "freelance mathematics," whatever that meant.

The real reason for Alex's departure was more complex, of course. After the thrill of hunting down the ultimate mathematical treasure, there was something wrong with the spoils.

Alex had managed, after snooping through Isaac's study—and absconding with a revelatory bit of typewriter ribbon—to track down the equation to a room 137 and to a certain unmathematical cousin of his. After keeping an eye on her, he had obliquely charmed the poor girl into revealing the hotel room in which the treasure was hidden. On the following night, Alex had circled back to claim the computer and map for GSR, but not before waiting for the cousin to circle back herself and then leave again. He had been briefly troubled by the entire episode—the sneaking around, the betrayal of a family member. "A family member I happen to like," he told Nellie. But at that point, who betrayed whom among the Severys was for her a tiresome detail when she had finally gotten what she wanted: the mathematics of a lifetime.

However, one day, while Nellie and Alex picked through the equation, a fissure appeared, and from that fissure erupted ever-smaller cracks—until a full-blown fractal disaster appeared before them. But she and Alex had disagreed about what these fissures meant:

"The equation is a fake, Nellie, an illusion designed to distract us from the real thing."

"What about the map? It works."

"Of course it works, because Isaac is dangling the results of the true equation in front of your face, to show you what you can't have."

"Fake or not, there is truth in it, Alex. Truth enough to convince Philip Severy, who sat here not long ago and gaped at it. It may take years, but from this illusion, we can reverse engineer the original."

Nellie had hoped Alex would stay and help her untangle the whole mess, but he had come down with a last-minute case of mathematical morality. "For argument's sake, say that I stay, Nellie.

For what? So you can sell the equation to the Pentagon? The Federal Reserve? The banks? Does the future belong to them? I signed on for the thrill of finding the thing—to see it for myself—not so that you could make a slightly taller stack of cash."

She sighed at the memory. How benighted of him to suppose she did this for the money. Nellie would have to manage without him. She had spent too many years trying to wrest mathematics from Isaac Severy, and she'd be damned if she was going to give up now just because the dead man was still pulling pranks. It wasn't fair of Isaac to have shown her what he was capable of, to have given her the suggestion of his brilliance, and then to have backed out on their verbal agreement simply because he objected to the general idea of *winning wars* and *making money*. Isaac had developed a particularly severe case of mathematical morality, and had died for it. More precisely, she had killed him. There was no point in trying to forget, especially on a day like this, with a heavy marine layer lingering, as it had on that morning in October.

Much like herself, Isaac had been an early riser, the type who just couldn't wait to get started on his day, even if it was the day he was to die. Why Nellie had picked the morning of October 17 to drop in on the Beachwood Canyon house unannounced, she couldn't say. She hadn't picked the day for any particular reason. How could she have known there was a dot on Isaac's map corresponding to the date and time of her arrival? She knew only that she was tired of having Isaac followed and was getting exasperated by the chase. She had hoped instead to throw him off balance with an impromptu visit, to further woo the man she had fiercely come to admire—as one admires a distant, brilliant father—and to woo the mathematics that came with him.

There had been no answer at his house. She knew that Isaac

wasn't asleep because she could make out a light inside and hear the Baroque precision of keyboard music. When she tried the knob, she found the door was unlocked, and, well, she just couldn't help herself. What had she been planning to do exactly? Storm his office? Plunder his files? Plead? Threaten? She had no plan, but she pushed open the door and stepped inside. A light from the kitchen fell across the dark floor. A cheerful Bach suite issued from speakers somewhere to her left. The place smelled of toast.

"Mr. Severy?" she called. Then louder, "Mr. Severy!"

She moved in the direction of the light, floorboards cracking beneath her. In the kitchen, she found a pot of cooling water on the stove and a ladle lying on top. She felt cool air on her skin and turned. The patio door was partly open. She walked over to it, peered outside, but it was still too dark to see.

"Mr. Severy?"

A sound came from somewhere at the end of the yard—a stirring, and the lapping of water.

Then he spoke: "Good morning. Join me for breakfast?"

His voice was calm, as if it were the most natural thing in the world for her to break into his house. Now it was Nellie who was thrown off balance.

"I would love some breakfast," she replied as coolly as she could manage. She reached out with her right hand for the patio light switch, but couldn't locate it. "Are we to eat in the dark, then?"

"Whatever you like. It's entirely up to you, Nellie."

A few seconds elapsed. Her fingers moved along the wall until they found the cool metal plate of the switch. It had been placed unusually far from the door, and she had to lean slightly to reach it. It was one of those old push-button switches. She pressed the top button, like a doorbell, and in this simple, nothing movement, something terrible happened. There was a bright flash and a sound, like a burst of lightning and thunder. Then darkness again.

The Bach had stopped, as if on cue. For some reason—instinct, maybe—she looked at her watch. It was five minutes before six, a time that would be imprinted on her mind forever.

"Mr. Severy?" she called. Then, softly, "Isaac?"

She knew there would be no answer. She couldn't see a thing, but she knew what she had done.

Using the flashlight on her phone to light the way, she slid open the patio door and stepped into the crisp morning air. At her feet, an extension cord snaked from the patio outlet, across the grass, and finally to a platform that housed a whirlpool tub. As she made her way across the yard, she could smell it: the odor of burnt flesh and hair. She pointed the light at the still smoking water, where Isaac sat, head bowed to his lap and to a snarl of string lights.

She blinked at his silent gray head, which, unlike her African game—her lioness, her zebra, her antelope—would not be moving again. Not in twenty minutes, not ever. She had pulled the trigger on a taser gun of Isaac's own making.

To anyone happening upon the scene, of course, it would look as if he had done it all himself. But if that was his intention, why hadn't he? With an equation that didn't discriminate between murder and suicide, why involve her at all? But the answer came to her instantly: because he trusted the Reaper to arrive at the appointed time. He needed him to, whatever form he ended up taking. The ultimate affirmation of Isaac's life's work had been his own death.

She turned to the café table. On the side nearest the water, there was a splash of tea left in a cup, a single triangle of toast, and the neat husk of an egg cradled in its holder. On the other side was a second breakfast, untouched. For an insane instant, Nellie considered sampling from the plate he had prepared so carefully for her, though she knew this was unwise. Besides, she felt sick, as she had never felt sick in her life. That smell. After wiping her fingerprints from the patio door, light switch, and front doorknob—just to be safe—Nellie returned to her car. She would drive herself to Malibu and go about her day as if she had never been there at all. She could halt her quest for the equation for twenty-four hours, at least—she certainly respected the man enough not to ransack his house as his corpse lay in the yard—but Isaac's death only made his mathematics more precious to her.

Now Nellie straightened at her library window. Philip's Subaru appeared and stopped in front of the house. He emerged. Perhaps it was best that he had turned down the offer to work for her, however much she might have liked to add another Severy to the company, at least to replace the one she'd lost. In any case, Philip had proven useful as an unwitting talent scout, packaging Anitka Durov as a kind of substitute. Philip needn't ever know, of course, that Nellie had already recruited Ms. Durov months ago for a far less glamorous job: keeping an eye on him and reporting what she found. Anitka had been grateful for the money, but this was before she had fallen in love with Philip, at which point the reports stopped, forcing Nellie to fall back on more commonplace modes of surveillance. Sure, romance was only natural in the course of a young person's life, but Nellie had learned that intimacy was a thing best avoided if one was to get anything done.

The passenger door opened, revealing Anitka. She had refused a driver, presumably because she wanted one final good-bye with her lover. And it was indeed good-bye, because Anitka was not going to be working in California but instead would be flown to GSR's offices in Virginia. Perhaps it was a kind of revenge that Nellie was snatching Philip's mistress from him and spiriting her three thousand miles away—but then again, Philip himself had arranged it.

Nellie glanced at a neat stack of materials on her desk. She wanted them to be visible when Ms. Durov walked through the door. On top was issue 75 of the *European Review of Theoretical Physics*, containing Anitka's bogus article on the early inflationary universe and brane expansion. After reading up on the entire Durov affair, Nellie had come to the conclusion that Ms. Durov, confused PhD candidate though she was, possessed a wild and devious brilliance that could prove useful to GSR. And here Nellie had assumed the girl was merely useful as a spy.

The supplementary materials Philip had provided further convinced her that Anitka was a genuine talent, the most impressive of these materials being the young woman's corrections of one of Isaac's papers. After running the corrections by Alex—who confirmed that his grandfather had indeed made a significant error and that Anitka had quite elegantly righted the mistake in the margins—Nellie was convinced that her search was over. With a natural talent for chaotic mathematics, not to mention a solid background in the mental rigors of string theory, Anitka Durov was the perfect candidate to nurse Isaac Severy's crippled equation back to health. Together, she thought with a smile, they would cast the future into complete transparency. *Imagine!*

Nellie watched Philip lean against his car and pull Anitka to him, their dark coats merging into a single woolly mass. He put his mouth to her ear, and then, as a parting gesture, kissed her forehead, as if seeing a child off to school. Without so much as a glance back at the car, Anitka strode with great intention toward the building. Philip watched until she had gained admittance before driving away.

She could hear Anitka being ushered up the stairs by Cavet, who was trying hard to suppress the pleasure in his voice at the sight of their new hire. Nellie sat on the edge of her desk and picked up a pen, trying to locate a convincingly occupied air. When she found it, there was a knock at the door.

"Yes, come in."

The door opened, and Anitka Durov, now coatless, stepped into the room, wearing a pressed navy suit and heels—a near mirror of Nellie herself. Her new protégée looked outwardly confident, yet her face bore the unmistakable traces of romantic torment. *Oh, you will learn, dear girl. You will learn to divert all of that into a far more useful place.*

Seeing that Anitka was about to apologize for her lateness, Nellie quickly interrupted.

"Ms. Durov!" she said, extending her arms. "Welcome back."

31

The Gift

Philip returned to campus with a conflicted heart. He had just come from ferrying Anitka to Malibu, where in turn Nellie would send her east—the idea being that he was sending her to a place where he would likely never see her again. He desperately needed her gone because where does a person draw the line with betrayal?

But his motives weren't entirely in the interest of morality or even his family; he had also done this for her. Anitka was not suited to the world of academia. She knew this. Yet when they said good-bye that morning, and she looked up at him with doubting eyes, he had nearly pulled her back into the car and asked her to forget the whole thing.

The sting of her absence, both in his chest and in the passage-ways of the physics building, would remain for a while and then fade, to be replaced with a different kind of desire. He thought of his room again, the one he had glimpsed during his coma, and his brain started to ignite with newfound purpose. There was much to do. His room was waiting.

But before Philip could get back to work, there was something he couldn't put off any longer. He unlocked his office. Hidden away in a desk drawer sat a flat package covered in brown paper. It had been given to him on his last birthday, but he had neglected to unwrap it, and there it had sat for almost a year. It was only when Jane recently asked about it that he remembered where it was. "I'll hang it in my office," he assured her. "Try not to hide it behind the door," she replied.

Philip set down the hammer and nails he'd borrowed from a custodian and opened the drawer. He tossed aside the forgotten envelopes from the Department of Corrections and pulled out the package. He tore off its wrapping and, setting the artwork in the chalk tray of his blackboard, stepped back to view it properly. It was a small black frame, exactly a square foot in area, and two inches deep. In the center, caught delicately between two pins like a rare butterfly, hung one of Sybil's found objects. He knew the artifact immediately: a scrap of paper, slightly yellowed and ripped along one edge. It was very old—twenty years, at least. Penciled on its surface was a series of squiggly arrows and small circles. He recognized it as one of his re-creations of a Feynman diagram: an illustration of the strange behavior of quantum particles, as described by Richard Feynman. The circles represented virtual particles, and the arrows, a particle of light's possible trajectories. It had been Philip's attempt to illustrate the behavior of light to his then-young daughter, of how photons "choose" their paths when bouncing off a mirror. He never thought that Sybil had cared for these things or had even retained these small lessons, yet she had kept this relic all these years.

It was a striking object on its own, and not just because of its content but because of its presentation. Sybil had suspended the drawing carefully between two layers of glass in such a way that ambient light reflected off the surface and made the diagram seem to glow. She had deftly manipulated the very light particles he had been illustrating for her. He saw at once that the entire thing was beautiful. Had all Sybil's pieces been similarly beautiful? Had he simply failed to realize as much?

Philip fell back in his chair, dropped his head into his hands, and wept. He wished Jane could be there with him now, because he'd tell her what he had realized too late: that their dear daughter, after all, had been remarkable.

32

The Sphinx

Arrangements were made. In turning away from her life of the past ten years—her store, her boyfriend, the tug of her brother and Los Angeles—Hazel was shedding the old, the nostalgic, the past. She was now sprinting toward the uncertain, the shining, the present tense. At least, this is what she told herself one day in mid-December, as an Alitalia Airbus carried her into another hemisphere.

In a day's time, she would meet Giancarlo Raspanti in Milan. Once they were in a secure location, she would complete Isaac's final request in handing over his most treasured work to a trusted colleague—work that now lay close to her skin, tucked inside a money belt. Every so often, she would slip her hand over her belly and feel the paper crinkle, just to make sure it was still there. She had asked for it eight days ago, and it had been given to her by a sphinx. Just like that. Sphinxes, of course, have their riddles.

After stealing into the boat's cabin that day, she had found the children sitting on the pine-planked floor: Lewis smacking at a noisy, bright-buttoned game, and Drew cross-legged, an artist's pad open in front of her. Hazel had poured herself a glass of fizzy water to subdue her growing seasickness before turning to the children.

She sat down on the bench directly above the little girl and watched her rip a drawing of a beach scene out of her notepad. Beneath it was a second drawing, of a woman with a giant head, long, flowing hair, and what appeared to be wings sprouting out of her neck. Drew may have been a bright child, but her artistic skills sat squarely within her age group.

"Is that your mommy?" Hazel asked.

"Yeah. Daddy says she's an angel now. But I don't know."

Drew set aside the drawing and began sorting a giant box of crayons by color.

Knowing there would be few opportunities to be left alone with her, Hazel acted quickly. She pulled the Polaroid from *Tender Is the Night* and set it on the floor next to the crayon box. Drew stopped sorting and frowned at the image of her great-grandfather writing on a mirror.

"Do you remember when that picture was taken?"

"Yeah."

"What do you remember about it?"

Turning away from the photo, Drew began reciting, "Two, three, five, seven, eleven, thirteen, seventeen, nineteen, twenty-three, twenty-nine, thirty-one—"

She would have kept going had Hazel not gently stopped her. "Wow, how many prime numbers do you know?"

"A hundred. Up to five hundred and forty-one."

"That's impressive. Did Pa-Pop teach you that?"

Drew nodded.

"What else did he teach you?"

Drew turned and looked Hazel hard in the face. She said quietly, "I don't know." After a moment, she added, "Unless you know the magic word."

"Magic word?" Hazel laughed. "*Please?*"

Drew snorted. "No."

Hazel's gaze fell on the girl's other drawing: a flock of *M*-shaped birds floated in a white sky above a shallow carpet of sea. In one corner, a mangled stick person was suntanning on a sliver of beach, soaking up rays from a tremendous sun.

A definition that had been scrawled in the book came back to Hazel, "of or pertaining to the seashore."

"Littoral," she said aloud, but Drew kept drawing, as if she had heard nothing.

Hazel opened the novel again to the string of numbers written on the inside cover: 137.13.9.

"Is it a magic word or magic number?" Hazel asked.

"A magic word is a magic word," Drew answered.

Hazel looked back at the numbers, running a finger over them. Wouldn't it be strange if the key to this thing that everyone wanted—the code that could unlock the most coveted mathematical technology—was scribbled in graphite in the corner of a paper book? And for the first time, she saw the digits as something other than an obscure mathematical series: she saw them as a game, not unlike her book oracle. She turned to page 137 and ran her finger down the text until she hit line 13: *and she was absorbed in playing around with chaos; as if her destiny were a picture puzzle . . .* She counted out the ninth word. Of course.

"Chaos," she said. It was a simple word, one she might even have guessed. But then it wasn't the key that had been the trick all along; it was the lock.

Drew looked up. "What?"

"Chaos."

Drew nodded at her with shy approval. The little girl then

carefully withdrew a brick-red crayon from its box and pulled the pad of paper close. She located a fresh page, and after positioning herself on her stomach, worked at the pad for the next fifteen minutes. She scribbled numbers and symbols with rounded proportions, some of which Hazel recognized, and many—Greek in origin—that she didn't. When Drew finished the first page, she turned it over to write on the back. When she had exhausted the first sheet, she started on a second. Halfway down the back of the second sheet, she sat up and casually handed the pages to Hazel, as if she were merely a court reporter who had taken dictation.

Drew blinked up at her. "It was really hard to remember. Can I forget it now?"

"Yes," Hazel said. "You can."

On the back of the last page, she noticed something that wasn't mathematics at all. Set apart from the equation was a message:

My Dear,

   You solved my little puzzle, as I knew you would. I am forever in your debt for safeguarding this. Do you believe me now that you have a logician's mind? In knowing your own power, your possibilities become infinite. Don't ever doubt it.

Love,

Isaac

Tears spilled from Hazel's eyes. After taking in the message one last time, she folded the sheets in half, and just as she was opening her purse, she heard the door click. She looked up, quickly wiping at her eyes, and saw her uncle Philip standing there.

He shut the door behind him and, without a word, stepped over to the counter. He poured himself a glass of water. After a long drink, he turned to her and extended his hand.

She hesitated.

"Let's see it, Hazel."

She handed over the pages. He unfolded them and for several minutes took in the deep-red scrawl, his eyes moving back and forth down each page.

"No wagging tongues," he muttered.

"Sorry?"

"Nothing."

After ten minutes, he turned back to her. His look was one of strange acknowledgment, as if he were finally seeing her.

"So, you," he said. "He left it to you."

She nodded. "Well, to Drew, really. But yes."

Philip looked down at his granddaughter and then back to Hazel.

Suddenly she felt ashamed that it was she and not Philip who had been given Isaac's most prized composition. She wanted to apologize—to explain that Isaac had needed to leave it with someone outside mathematics. Perhaps, in his way, Philip's father had been protecting him. She wondered how to say all this without making the situation any more uncomfortable.

As she opened her mouth to speak, he stopped her.

"Just tell me this. Are you doing what he would have wanted?"

"Yes."

"Well, then," her uncle said, "that's all I need to know."

He handed back the pages and paused at the door, giving Hazel a final smile before leaving the cabin.

She slipped the paper into her purse and stood up. On the counter, someone had placed a group portrait of the family—an old photo that had been taken on a trip to Disneyland. Hazel singled out Isaac's proud, paternal head, and smiled at him. "I found it," she said, tears returning to her eyes.

Now, as she looked out the triple-paned window, past condensed water droplets and onto clouds blanketing the ocean, she wondered what would become of the equation. When she had asked Raspanti this, he would speak only of *genieschultern*: the shoulders of genius. He hinted at brilliant jewels that were lodged inside the equation, from which additional mathematics could be mined—the less predictive and potentially less dangerous kind. As for her grandfather's other request, that the contents of his hotel room be destroyed, this was, of course, impossible. But then, if Alex was right, and Isaac had been dangling a red herring in front of everyone while keeping his true gem artfully hidden, well, it hardly mattered.

At first, Raspanti had been skeptical that Hazel had the equation in her possession. In fact, he hung up on her twice. But after she repeatedly insisted in a series of cryptic emails and phone messages, he said finally, "If what you are implying is true, Hazel, you must come to Italy at once." He bought her a first-class ticket and called her to say, "My wife and I, we will take you to Rome by way of Florence and Pisa, where the great mathematician Leonardo Fibonacci worked. I'll teach you the beauty of your grandfather's mathematics while you gaze at the beauty of our country. I insist."

An Italian vacation! She would wander up and down the Mediterranean while she figured out what the hell she was going to do with the rest of her life. Could anything be better?

She'd flown back to Seattle to oversee the shuttering of her store and to say good-bye to the old-world fantasy she had wrapped herself in these past seven years. At an in-store auction, she sold off her banker's lamps, pedestalled reference books, Christopher Wren architectural prints, cracked leather chairs, frayed kilim rugs, and probably a city block's stretch of warped shelving. She got a decent price for these, given that most of the buyers were rich techie types hoping to infuse their bland apartments with a vibe Hazel dubbed "destitute intellectual clinging to the past."

She stacked nearly all of her library into boxes—saving only the most precious volumes for herself, including the Fitzgerald hardcovers—and sold her collection to Books Now!, an across-town competitor specializing in politically engaged fiction and nonfiction. The owners, an older couple with no children, had been looking to draw a more general readership to their store and were thrilled when Hazel was willing to part with her inventory at such a fire-sale price. She wished them luck and promised to send all her customers their way.

One rainy afternoon, Hazel broke the news to Chet over lunch, apologizing for the hit to his already modest writer's income. Over lobster bisques, she slid across the table a hardcover copy of George Gissing's *New Grub Street*, which Chet had been steadily working through for the past year but had never finished.

He smiled, pushed up his oversized glasses, and let the Victorian novel fall open to its Guttersnipe bookmark.

"I'm sad to see the store go, Hazel, but then, I got what I came for." He produced a small cardboard box from his messenger bag.

"What's this?"

"Open it."

She pulled off the top to find a manuscript: *Amazon Warriors*. By Chet Hu.

"Is this real?"

"I told you I had big plans for that article." He laughed. "What did you think I was doing that whole time?"

In the back of her store that night, she read Chet's manuscript, a dystopian tale—half truth, half fiction—about a near future that no longer valued ink and paper. At its center, a doomed shopkeeper waged battle against bad plumbing and other natural disasters in order to preserve the world's last cache of hardcover books. At least the spirit of her store, Hazel told herself, would live on in the pages of a book.

As she set down the last page and looked around the tiny back room, she was suddenly gripped by sadness. She imagined her brother sitting in his cell at that very moment, scribbling in his diary. She wondered if he would get along with his bunkmate or have the temperament to weather prison life. How odd that Gregory's basement confinement so many years ago had eventually led him to another kind of confinement. Lying back on her mattress, she looked up at the ceiling and recalled the imperfect constellations they had so cheerfully created together in their bedrooms. She hoped that as he lay on his prison bunk, her brother might glance up one night and remember that amid the disorder of their childhoods, there had been glimpses of real happiness.

It was early morning when Hazel stepped off the plane at Milan's Malpensa Airport. She made her way down a shiny white hall toward the arrivals gate, anticipating that the car Raspanti hired would be waiting. As she pushed through a revolving door and into a crush of drivers, she hunted for her name among the signage. After a minute, she spotted a familiar word: *Herringbone.*

She held up a hand.

"You are Miss Herringbone, yes?" he asked.

"That must be me."

She turned, and that's when she saw him, standing a few yards away in a slightly ill-fitting suit, looking directly at her. His hair was wild, but his face recently shaven, and he held a to-go coffee cup in each hand. He grinned at her, though a trace of fear passed over his features.

For several long seconds she didn't move, wanting to be absolutely sure she was seeing this right. She turned to the driver: "Hold on."

She walked toward Alex, who met her halfway.

"Cappuccino?" he offered. "They really know how to make them."

"I can't begin to imagine what you're doing here."

"What *I'm* doing here?" he said. "I live here."

"Italy or the airport?"

"Well, neither, but I do live in Paris, a mere train's distance away. I have a photo gig at the CERN particle accelerator later today, which happens to be down the road."

"So you really *are* a photographer."

Alex smiled somewhat self-consciously. "It should be fun— you know, lots of wide-angle shots of nerds puffing themselves up in front of billion-dollar machinery, arms crossed, that kind of thing. Anyway, thought I'd swing by, welcome you to the Continent."

She took one of the cappuccinos, still marveling at his being there in front of her. "What about your other job? You *were* working for someone, weren't you?"

He nodded gravely. "I quit."

She couldn't be sure if this was true, though she desperately wanted it to be. "How did you find me?"

He scratched his chin. "Well, not to seem too pleased with myself, but many years ago, as you may recall, I solved one of Hilbert's twenty-three problems. Someone else crossed the finish line first, but I solved it nonetheless. In comparison to that, do you think locating one woman is all that difficult?" When Hazel didn't appear impressed, he added, "I found an article about your bookstore online and called the guy who wrote it. Chet? Nice guy, though I really had to charm him for your whereabouts."

She nodded, inhaling the aroma from her cup. "You're good at that."

"The far more interesting question," he continued, "is why you're in Milan."

"I'm taking a trip."

"Not for math-related reasons, I hope."

"I'm visiting a friend."

"Good," he said, with a wink in his voice that reminded her of Isaac. "Because there are other things in life besides mathematics—" He suddenly looked in the direction of the baggage carousel, then held up a finger, and disappeared.

He reappeared a moment later with her luggage, the bag that had been stamped with an oversized H. S.

"I put two and two together," he said. "Unless this belongs to the German physicist Horst Störmer. That guy would monogram his Nobel if he could."

Suppressing a laugh, she said, "It was a gift."

Alex set down her bag and frowned. "I lied to you just now. I mean, before."

"About there being more to life than mathematics?"

"No, about having a photo shoot at CERN. That's next week. I came all the way here just to see you."

She looked down briefly, trying to hide the extent of her delight. "So, tell me," she said, looking up. "What are these other things besides mathematics?"

"Oh, I have an entire list. If you have some time, I'm happy to go into detail."

Hazel felt her entire body thaw, as if for years she had been lying out in open tundra, and only now was the climate shifting.

She turned to the driver and signaled him to follow. Then she and Alex walked out the doors of the airport and into the low, wintry light that was rising to meet the continent.

Acknowledgments

First, to agent-of-my-dreams Lisa Bankoff, I can't thank you enough for taking a chance on me and my story. Heaps of appreciation to Kaitlin Olson at Touchstone for her enthusiasm, spot-on instincts, and for making the editing process such a happy one. And to the entire Touchstone team for their outsized talents and care with this book.

My research would have been unthinkable without enormous help from Mordechai Feingold at Caltech, whose reading lists and professor lunches brought me into the lives of mathematicians. I owe additional thanks to John Schwarz and Shuki Bruck at Caltech, Ed Witten at the Institute for Advanced Study, and Robert Sacker and Scott MacDonald at the University of Southern California. I'm in awe of what you do and forever grateful for your guidance. On the law enforcement front, much gratitude to Vincent Neglia, who gave me an insightful peek into the LAPD.

My smart, eagle-eyed readers, I love you: Holland Christie, J. C. Conklin, Coralie Hunter, Kate Kennedy, Julianne Ortale, Lorna Owen, John Douglas Sinclair, and Peter Spiegler. Thank you to Geoff Nicholson for your Luna Park counsel. And to the bighearted Gabrielle Burton, who insisted on helping me at the worst possible time in her life. I'll never understand it or forget it.

Rebecca Agbe-Davies: you kept me off the streets. May all writers have such fun survival jobs and supportive friends. Thanks to Jennifer Lange for her friendship and confidence that I would make something of this thing. Jenna Turner and the crew at Susina Bakery: you fixed me gallons of tea and let me sit at that corner table for hours. It didn't go unnoticed.

Greg Beal and Joan Wai, you run the best writers' club around.

Heartfelt appreciation to the Rabb family—Theodore, Tamar, Susannah, and Jonathan—for your keen eyes and unflagging support. To my talented sisters, Moksha, Starlet, and Ananda, for cheering me on and tolerating the refrain *I have to write*. And to my parents, Peter and Linnah, thank you for your unwavering belief in me and for always charting the unconventional course.

And finally, to my husband, whose belief in this book rivaled my own. Somewhere, in a sad parallel universe where there is no Jeremy, there is no book.

About the Author

Nova Jacobs holds an MFA from the University of Southern California School of Cinematic Arts and is a recipient of the Nicholl Fellowship from the Academy of Motion Picture Arts and Sciences. She lives in Los Angeles with her husband, Jeremy. This is her first novel.

The Last Equation *of* Isaac Severy

Nova Jacobs

This reading group guide for The Last Equation of Isaac Severy includes an introduction, discussion questions, ideas for enhancing your book club, and a Q&A with author Nova Jacobs. The suggested questions are intended to help your reading group find new and interesting angles and topics for your discussion. We hope that these ideas will enrich your conversation and increase your enjoyment of the book.

Introduction

Just days after mathematician and family patriarch Isaac Severy dies of an apparent suicide, his adopted granddaughter, Hazel, receives a letter from him. In it, Isaac alludes to a secretive organization that seeks his final equation—the culmination of his life's work—and charges Hazel with safely delivering it to a trusted colleague. But first she must find where the equation is hidden—and why it's so vitally important.When Hazel realizes that she's not the only one seeking the equation, she learns that its implications have potentially deadly consequences for the extended Severy family, a group of dysfunctional geniuses unmoored by the sudden death of their patriarch. Now, Hazel must unravel a series of confounding clues hidden by Isaac, drawing her ever closer to his mathematical bombshell—and forcing her to rely on those who may be less than trustworthy.

Topics & Questions for Discussion

1. This novel is equal parts family drama, literary mystery, and suspense thriller. Which element of this genre mash-up did you most enjoy, and why?

2. Contemplate the Pierre-Simon Laplace quotation that opens the novel, especially in the context of the exploration of predetermination at the center of the story. How would "such an intelligence" (in other words, a predictive power that eradicates uncertainty) be a blessing, and in what ways would it be a curse? Was this "intelligence" a burden or a gift for Isaac Severy himself?

3. Familial expectations and pressures are the lens through which we meet most of the main characters in the opening funeral scene of the novel, especially in Philip's introductory chapter. How did this inform your initial impression of the family dynamics of the Severy clan?

4. Isaac's passing leaves a different void in the life of each character. Whom do you think feels this loss most keenly? Who plays a similar role as patriarch (or matriarch) in your own family?

5. Raspanti, the ultimate inheritor of Isaac's equation at the novel's end, introduces the idea of *genieschultern* ("on the shoulders of genius") when discussing the value inherent in Isaac's equation. This concept—an allusion to Sir Isaac Newton's quote, "If I have seen further, it is by standing upon the shoulders of giants"—suggests that if the equation is not used for its predictive abilities, it can serve as the seed for other types of equations. Do you think that the equation should have been destroyed? What are the risks of the "shoulders of genius" concept, and what are the potential benefits?

6. In a rare conversation between Paige and Hazel, the estranged Severy aunt says to Hazel, "Your generation could stand to live in the pursuit a bit more. You're all rushed to get to the end. To *succeed*. [. . .] It's an empty way to live, in constant pursuit of the trophy." Dissect this philosophy; do you agree or disagree?

7. Describing Isaac's equation, Nellie asks: "Can you think of anything more exhilarating than the realization that the future is, in fact, knowable?" Would you find clairvoyance "exhilarating"? If you could use a predictive equation akin to Isaac's formula to foresee only one type of phenomenon, what would it be, and why?

8. The dynamics at play in the Severy clan are complicated to say the least. How do you reconcile Isaac's cruelty to Philip (or perhaps, Philip's *perception* of intense judgment and derision from Isaac) with the kindness that Isaac shows to Hazel and Gregory?

9. How did you react to the revelation of Gregory's murderous double life? Was there a moment in the novel (prior to the big

reveal) when you sensed that Gregory could be capable of this level of duplicity and brutality? Do you understand, or sympathize with, the motivations behind his vigilante killings?

10. Throughout the novel, secrets of every variety are revealed about each character—affairs, betrayals, shocking backstories. Which character's secret surprised you the most, and why?

11. What was your reaction to the revelation of five-year-old Drew's role in Isaac's sprawling mathematical mystery? Did you ever sense that Drew would play a greater role in the novel?

12. In your opinion, who is ultimately the most tragic character in the novel, and why? Which character(s) do you believe emerge redeemed, and which do not?

13. The author has a background in screenwriting; what scene (or scenes) in particular could you see playing out on screen, or felt especially cinematic?

14. Throughout the novel, the author explores the concept of predetermination. Ultimately, Isaac's equation proves fallible when Philip survives his suicide attempt. What do you think of this outcome?

15. Consider the Tom Stoppard quotation that opens Part Three: "The unpredictable and the predetermined unfold together to make everything the way it is." This perspective merges these two divergent concepts to explain the way of the world. What are your thoughts on this world view? What moments in the novel (or, to take the question a step further, what moments *in your own life*) represent "the unpredictable and the predetermined unfold[ing] together"?

Enhance Your Book Club

1. Ask each member of your book club to bring (or create) a family tree, tracing their lineages as far back as they can. Can anyone trace a specific intellectual gift, or even a vocation, back through his or her family tree, the way mathematics is a defining element of the Severy clan? If so, what are those genetic gifts? Launch a deeper discussion by posing the following question to each member of your book club: *Do you embody any defining intellectual or professional "family traits"? (Or, do your siblings and/or cousins exemplify a trait that you do not possess, making you an outlier like Sybil?)*

2. One of the main clues that Isaac Severy leaves behind is found hidden in a copy of F. Scott Fitzgerald's *Tender Is the Night*. Read this classic story in tandem with *The Last Equation of Isaac Severy* to deepen your discussion of the literary mystery at the heart of Nova Jacobs's novel.

3. In many ways, the peculiar Severy clan recalls the dysfunctional Tenenbaums, the family at the center of the beloved Wes Anderson film from 2001. Precede your book club meeting with a screening of *The Royal Tenenbaums*, and

have fun identifying the parallels between the two families, as well as what distinguishes them from one another.

4. Cast the movie version! Ask each member of your book club to pick known actors to take on the roles of the novel's main characters. Bring images to share, and cast the cinematic adaptation as a group!

5. Hide the time and location of your book club meeting to discuss *The Last Equation of Isaac Severy* in an anagram, equation, or puzzle—see how many book club members can crack the code!

A Conversation with Nova Jacobs

Given your background as an LA–based screenwriter, what made you decide to tackle this particular story as a novel rather than a screenplay? What about this story and these characters felt better suited to a novel than a film or television series?

I'd love to say that my thought process on novel versus screenplay was as considered as the phrasing of this question, but in truth my path to writing a novel was messy and confusing. At the time, I'd just had a script development project fall through and—coupled with the financial crash and my getting laid off from a copywriting position—I was feeling a general lack of control over my life. Besides wondering how long I could continue to call myself a screenwriter, I craved a project over which I had total creative command. The beauty of a novel is that it doesn't need producers or exorbitant financial backing to exist; when the writing is done, the thing is complete, not just as a story, but also as an object you can hold in your hands. The desire to write a book came first, followed by the story, and I was pleasantly surprised to learn what an immensely freeing process it was. Screenwriting, by comparison, is much more hemmed in by structure, brevity, and formatting. I don't know that the Severys would have sprung to life were I working in any other medium.

Isaac Severy's predictive equation could have been applied to any phenomenon. In fact, we are initially led to believe that his work was centered on predicting traffic patterns. What drew you to the idea of using mathematics to predict the dark subject matter of murders and suicides—intentional deaths?

I love how *The New York Times Book Review*'s crime critic, Marilyn Stasio, talks about what she calls "normal" novels: "I keep saying 'Where's the body? Kill someone . . . Let's move this along.'" I wouldn't go that far myself—my tastes are more varied—but I've always been drawn to mysteries and thrillers, which usually require a dead body somewhere to be of any interest. Apart from my natural tendency toward the morbid, I was intrigued by the LAPD's crime forecasting algorithm, which I'd just begun to read about around the time I was planning my novel. Besides finding impersonal, computerized law enforcement pretty terrifying (mathematician Cathy O'Neil is terrific on this topic), it got me thinking: what if this kind of forecasting were unerringly accurate? And what if one were able to narrow this type of prediction to murder? Once I had underpinned this idea with chaos theory, I just ran with it.

The way some families revere athleticism or perhaps artistic endeavors, this family holds left-brained intellectualism in the highest regard. How did this idea of the "hereditary monarchy [of] true brilliance" first originate in your mind?

The phrase originated entirely as a way for P. Booth Lyons to get under Philip's skin, though it is intended as flattery. There was an early passage that I've since removed for the sake of pacing, in which Philip considers his academically anemic children, and how the Severy's intellectual lineage could be wiped out in a single generation, like the Romanov dynasty: *If brilliance was a hereditary monarchy, then Philip supposed there was always the danger of a coup, in which an entire bloodline could be hauled down to the basement in the middle of the night, Red Army style, lined up and shot.*

What drew you to mathematics as the subject matter to explore in your debut novel?

I found my way to mathematics through the back door of theoretical physics, which has long been a fascination of mine. I credit my dad for instilling this interest in me at a young age; he went through a phase of reading physics books, and then imparting lessons to me on Schrödinger's cat, the collapse of the wave function, or whatever he happened to be studying at the time. My dad was also my third-grade teacher at a private school in Flagstaff, Arizona, where one day he taught a lesson on Einstein's theories of special and general relativity. You'd think this would be over the heads of a bunch of eight- and nine-year-olds, but the delightful thing about Einstein's theories is that they are so visual—his thought experiments in particular involve no mathematical talent to understand them, just a willingness to accept the counterintuitive and bizarre. Aside from my being dazzled by the properties of light, gravity, and space-time, I couldn't get over the fact that there was a man called Albert Einstein who had done all this stuff for a living, *as his actual job.* My fascination with theoretical physicists (and later mathematicians) as characters has stuck around.

As much as I love a good thought experiment, I have a brain stuck squarely in the humanities. Like Hazel, I never got past pre-Calculus in high school, and to be frank, naked data and numbers on a page bore me. I actually had these bizarre fantasies while writing my novel that I would one day be unmasked as a fraud—as if someone at a future book signing was going to leap out at me and demand I solve a differential equation on the spot. This was, of course, the unhelpful part of my brain telling me that I had no qualifications in the subject and what the hell was I doing? I didn't always know what I was doing, but I'm glad I kept at it.

During all this, I kept returning to the question of who mathematicians and physicists (particularly string theorists) are at heart: men and women sitting alone in a room, puzzling through how the universe outside the room works. I was so entranced by this idea, but it took longer than I care to admit to understand *why* it probably captivated me: Isn't this the perfect analog for what writers do? Do we not spend most of our time inside a room, putting symbols to a page, trying to make sense of the world outside?

The mathematical concepts and puzzles presented in this novel are extremely complex. How did you research the math and science components of the story?

We're fortunate to live in a time of such stellar science writing. My own reading included Brian Greene, John Gribbin, Michio Kaku, Lisa Randall, Sean Carroll, Graham Farmelo, Richard Feynman; and on the mathematics front, James Gleick, John Derbyshire, Ian Stewart, and a wonderful little book by G. H. Hardy called *A Mathematician's Apology*. I'm also lucky to have a historian father-in-law who put me in touch with one of his former students, Mordechai Feingold, who teaches History of Science at Caltech. Feingold steered me in the direction of more arcane reading than what I was likely to find on the science shelf at the bookstore. After I felt sufficiently armed, I convinced a handful of mathematicians and physicists whom I admired to sit down with me for informal chats, which included a couple of lunches at Caltech's Athenaeum club. Taking my ideas out for a spin with scientists I'd only read about up to that point was some of the most fun I've had. A few were entertainingly blunt about certain facets of my story. "That would never happen" is something I heard more than once, usually delivered with a laugh or amused shrug. In the interest of grounding the more fantastic aspects of my story in reality, some were kind enough to let me pester them with follow-up questions during the writing process.

The foster siblings at the novel's center—Hazel and Gregory—suffered unspeakable cruelty at the hands of their foster parents, especially Tom, which has serious consequences on Gregory's behavior in the present-day narrative. How did you develop this shocking and tragic backstory? What type of research did you have to conduct to understand this level of trauma?

It's not always easy to pinpoint where story lines come from, beyond some mysterious region of the subconscious. That said, I researched the history of child welfare in Los Angeles County, including the history of MacLaren Hall—where Hazel and Gregory would have spent their early years—and the abuses that went on there before it was finally shut down in 2003. I was fortunate to have now-retired LAPD detective Vincent Neglia from the Juvenile Protection Unit walk me through his general day-to-day, which gave me a sense for the sorts of cases that would come across his desk and the psychological stress this type of profession would bring with it. As Neglia pointed out, the mistreatment of children knows no particular neighborhood or economic class. This was never far from my mind as I tried to work through how certain members of a privileged, educated family such as the Severys could be capable of cruelty to children—both the overt, illegal kind (as in the case of Tom) and the subtler, deceptive variety (as is on display among other members of the family).

In the early pages of Chapter 1, Hazel reflects that, "In a mostly unstable life, books had been the only reliable refuge she had known." What role do books play in your life?

I was one of those kids who had a flashlight under the covers far past bedtime so that I could finish just one more chapter of Nancy Drew or C. S. Lewis, and later, Agatha Christie or Stephen King. Apart from the classics assigned in school and the odd Margaret Atwood, my choices were not particularly literary—I tore through a lot of mystery and suspense. My parents actually forbade me from reading Stephen King, so I had to borrow those books from the library on the sly and hide them in creative places around my room. The fact that they thought these novels might be a threat to my development strikes me as quaint now (and if my parents are reading this, they are just now discovering my treachery!). I guess that's my roundabout way of addressing the question. Books were something for which I was willing to be sneaky and risk reprimand—and still would if it ever came to it.

Your novel encompasses three distinct story lines. How did you decide to tell your story in this way as opposed to from one point of view?

I chose the structure on instinct, taking the risk that if it failed, I'd have to try another approach. But mysteries with either shifting points of view or multiple narrators carry a certain exhilaration that I knew I wanted to replicate. The Victorian novelist Wilkie Collins is a genius with this kind of plotting. *The Woman in White* and *The Moonstone* are not concise by any means, yet I find them as page-turning as anything modern. There's a certain charge the reader gets from shifting voices and perspectives—turning reader into detective, gathering evidence from each character—that I felt I couldn't generate from having a single protagonist.

You grapple with big ideas in this novel: coincidence versus predetermination, chaos theory, and free will. Were you ever intimidated by the prospect of delving into such dense topics? What was your greatest challenge in doing so?

If I wasn't intimidated at the outset, it was only because I had no idea what I was getting into. The nice thing about writing a novel is that the longer you spend with it, and the more years you live inside your characters' heads, the deeper your story becomes. I had no lofty ideas of tackling important philosophical questions, but because my characters are scientists—and would by extension entertain questions of determinism, free will, and coincidence—I discovered connections I wouldn't have originally made. For instance, it was a happy accident to find Isaac's and Philip's disciplines diametrically opposed in a way that worked for that relationship. I guess the trick for my next book is to locate that kind of richness without spending six years in the writing of it.

You illustrate deeply complex family dynamics with grace and authenticity in this novel. Who is the patriarch (or matriarch) of your own family? Are any of the characters or family dynamics portrayed in this novel inspired by members of your own family or friend circle, even in small part?

Though I've no doubt scrambled some of my own family dynamics into my novel, as writers will do (past the point of recognition, one would hope), the senior members of my family would probably balk at the matriarch/patriarch label. More likely, I've taken the idea of the brilliant paternal figure—one who playfully, even cruelly, manipulates the unwitting main characters—from the literature of my childhood. Willy Wonka of *Charlie and the Chocolate Factory* comes to mind, but even more so, Sam Westing from Ellen Raskin's *The Westing Game*. When I had the latter read to me in grade school during our daily story time, I am pretty sure my little head exploded. How ingenious to have a puzzle built in that young readers could solve! I reread that book enough times that I've probably internalized it. I didn't realize until I was deep into my own novel how much Sam Westing there is in Isaac Severy—that is, the puzzle-mad genius who continues to control his legacy from beyond the grave.

You are the recipient of an Alfred P. Sloan Foundation grant for promoting science in film. Why is this an important mission for you?

I think of it less as a mission than my natural attraction to the intersection of science and art. The merging of left-brain/right-brain worlds has long felt like a creatively fertile area for me; or, to put it another way, it's a lot of fun to write intensely brainy characters who act in fanciful, illogical—and frankly dumb—ways.

The right-brain/left-brain duality is a simplification, of course. During my research, the theme of scientific creativity came up quite a bit. Many mathematicians and physicists will tell you that their discipline requires not just the gift of logic, but also a great deal of imagination. The grand scientific leaps of Albert Einstein and the first quantum physicists—and later the string theorists—required an enormous amount of creative vision. This certainly felt like an underexplored area to me.

I'm also drawn to a subset of science fiction that is not exactly "sci-fi," but rather fiction about scientists, with its feet planted more in reality than, say, *Dune* or *Blade Runner*. It just happens that my interest aligned with the Alfred P. Sloan Foundation, whose film grants promote enriching depictions of science and scientists. They have generous grant programs for film students and film-makers, and I was thrilled to receive one in grad school. Besides that, we live in an age where scientific fact is, sadly, cast in a sub-jective, political light. I don't pretend that my stories will change this, but I hope that I can contribute in my own way to science and scientists being considered not somewhere outside mainstream culture, but as a part of art, literature, and generally being alive.

Though you're a writer by vocation, this is your debut novel. What's your next writing project? And if the next project in the queue isn't a novel, do you have ideas for your next work of narrative fiction?

I was intensely secretive about my first novel from the start, not telling anyone outside my family and a few close friends that I was writing the first draft. Even then, I was vague about the story for fear it would fall like a soufflé. I'm in the research phase for my next novel—one that may require some fieldwork away from my desk—so my instinct is to protect the poor thing while it's still defenseless and vulnerable to attack. Sorry to be coy.